ANOTH

Hope grabbed her purse and stepped out of the with Jane and Claire following. They all gathered at the back of the vehicle and set off together toward the main entrance. But a familiar-looking Jaguar parked in the rear lot caught Hope's attention.

Why was it parked all the way back there when there were plenty of spaces in the main lot? The driver's side door was open. Before she realized it, she'd broken away from her group and was heading toward the lone car.

"Hope! Come on!" Drew broke into a jog toward her. "The napkin, remember? Meg's team will get inside first. Norrie can't win!"

"Just a minute." She reached the car, and the vanity license plate, "Lionel #1," confirmed the car belonged to Lionel Whitcomb. What was it doing there with the driver's door open? Where was Lionel? Why had he parked all the way up there? Hope continued around the front of the car and came to a hard stop.

She gasped, and one hand flew up to cover her mouth, while the other stretched out and planted itself on the hood of the car to steady her body.

She'd discovered why she hadn't seen Lionel.

He was lying on the asphalt with a large red stain spread out on his white shirt . . .

Books by Debra Sennefelder

Food Blogger Mysteries

THE UNINVITED CORPSE

THE HIDDEN CORPSE

THREE WIDOWS AND A CORPSE

Resale Boutique Mysteries

MURDER WEARS A LITTLE BLACK DRESS

Published by Kensington Publishing Corporation

Three Widows
and a Corpse

Debra
Sennefelder

KENSINGTON BOOKS
KENSINGTON PUBLISHING CORP.

www.kensingtonbooks.com

To my friend Jennifer.
Thank you for your friendship, your encouragement,
and the lemons.

ACKNOWLEDGMENTS

Thank you to my readers and the Cozy Mystery Crew for your support, kind words, and for buying my books. Thank you to my critique partner, Ellie Ashe, for helping shape this book into what it is today. Thank you to fellow authors and friends Jenny Kale, Linda Reilly, Shari Randall, and Lena Gregory for your inspiration, support and knowing just the right thing to say when the writing gets hard. I'd be remiss if I didn't give a big shout-out to an amazing group of authors, many who've become my friends that joined me in the path to publication, Authors '18. We met online thanks to Dianne Freeman, and together we navigated the world of publishing. Thank you to my editor, John Scognamiglio, Arthur Maisel, Lauren Jernigan, Larissa Ackerman, Ross Plotkin, and the whole team at Kensington for bringing *Three Widows and a Corpse* to publication. Thank you to my agent, Dawn Dowdle. And thank you for choosing to read this book.

Chapter One

Hope Early caught her reflection in the side window of the main entrance and leaned in for a closer look. With a critical eye, she inspected herself from top to bottom. *Again.* Did she look like the professional food blogger she was? Did she look too eager? Did she look as nervous as she felt?

I've got this.

She looked successful and efficient and ready to take on anything the staff of *Cooking Now* magazine could throw at her.

So why was she a bundle of frazzled nerves?

Because it was like the first day of school.

She pressed the door buzzer and tamped down her nerves. For goodness' sake, before turning her food blog into a full-time career, she'd spent years as a magazine editor. She released the button and chided herself for being ridiculous.

A glimpse of someone walking toward the door caught her attention. She pulled back from the window and inhaled a deep breath.

The temperature had to have soared at least another ten degrees from the time Hope left her house. For her first day, she'd chosen a white, button-down shirt, navy pants, and her most comfortable pair of shoes. When she headed out her front door, she was confident she'd selected a perfect balance of professionalism and comfort, but standing out in the late-August heat, she doubted her choice because the shirt now clung to her back.

The door opened and a blue-haired, multipierced twentysomething appeared. An intern, Hope guessed.

"You're Hope Early?" She opened the door wider. "We've been expecting you. I'm Kylie. Follow me."

Hope stepped into the vestibule and welcomed the chill of the air conditioner. She followed the young woman, who'd found a balance in her own appearance by marrying the edginess of unusual hair coloring and multiple piercings with test-kitchen-appropriate clothing—black pants, a white shirt, and an apron with the magazine's logo on it.

At the door to the kitchen, Kylie punched in her code. "You'll get your own code sometime today." She held the door open for Hope and gestured for her to enter.

It'd been a long time since Hope had been in a test kitchen. When she was the editor of *Meals in Minutes*, she'd visited their kitchen at least once a week for recipe tastings. The nervousness she'd experienced moments before had disappeared, and in its place was a twinge of nostalgia. She hadn't realized how much she missed being part of a magazine.

Beyond the well-appointed test kitchen of stainless-steel appliances, bright lights, and thousands of dollars' worth of photography equipment was the familiar buzz creating a magazine generated. The ideas, the disasters, the deadlines, the creative differences. It was what had fed Hope for years and, in one sweeping glance, what she yearned for again.

She shook off the thought. Her decision to leave publishing after her loss on the reality baking competition show *The Sweet Taste of Success* was the right one. As a food blogger, she was her own boss and in control of every aspect of her business. Like the collaboration with *Cooking Now*, which had been a year in the making.

Hope had worked on a sponsorship with a spice company, which led to a few articles written for *Cooking Now*'s website over the span of several months. That handful of articles led to this assignment to develop healthy, easy-to-make recipes. A mixture of giddiness and butterflies swirled in her belly and she smiled. But while it felt like home, she needed to remember this was only a visit.

The test kitchen was a combination food prep area, photo studio, and office for the main staff of the magazine, all of whom were busy starting their day. Hope walked farther into the kitchen and passed a wall of stainless-steel shelves loaded with a variety of bowls, plates, pots, and glassware. One by one, the heads of the magazine staff looked up and appraised Hope.

Yeah, it felt like the first day of school.

"Hope's here!" After her announcement, Kylie broke away and went to one of the smaller kitchens, leaving Hope standing alone in the middle of the open space.

"Thank you for the announcement, Kylie." A woman about Hope's age pushed back her chair from her desk and stood. Hope recognized her as May Henshaw, senior editor, from her photograph in the magazine, though an irritated twist to her lips replaced the broad smile she'd flashed for her readers. Hope guessed the editor didn't approve of Kylie's very informal introduction.

"Good morning, May. I'm happy to meet you in person. I'm very excited to be here." Hope extended her hand to the editor.

While they'd worked together previously on articles for the website, they'd never met in person. May stood a couple of inches taller than Hope, and her blond hair was pulled back into a severe bun and her crisp white chef's jacket was buttoned up over a pair of black pants.

"Of course you are." After the firm handshake, May shifted her body so she had a full view of the test kitchen. "We've never collaborated with a food blogger before. Let me introduce you, and then you can start work. I hope you'll be able to adjust to our schedule." May led Hope over to the cluster of desks. "It's imperative we stay on schedule."

"I understand. I was a magazine editor." Hope wasn't sure why she said that. May knew her credentials.

"*Meals in Minutes.* I recall. Cute magazine."

Cute magazine? Now, if that wasn't a backhanded compliment, Hope didn't know what was. Yes, *Meals in Minutes* focused on shortcuts in the kitchen for the harried masses, but the recipes were solid, practical, and delicious. Hope remembered she was only here for a short time and it was best not to rock the boat.

"Hope, this is Kitty Ellis. She's our test kitchen manager and we'd be lost without her." May led Hope to a row of desks pressed up against a whitewashed exterior wall and bordered by a long section of more stainless-steel shelving filled with bins of linens, utensils, and flatware.

"Hi, Hope. I love your blog." Kitty extended her hand.

"It's nice to meet you," Hope said.

"You'll work here." May pointed to the desk beside Kitty. "You'll find you're all set up for emails and you'll also find one with all the information you need about working here. Get yourself settled and then Kitty will get you situated in one of the kitchens so you can start working. Remember, this isn't your home kitchen. We're not here to socialize. We all have assignments and deadlines."

With a firm nod, May turned and returned to her desk, clicking on her keyboard and then sipping her coffee.

Kitty smiled and leaned forward. "She's really not too bad."

"You sure?"

Hope slipped her tote bag off her shoulder and spent the next twenty minutes reviewing her emails and confirming her new passcode for the building.

Cooking Now magazine was located on the campus of Great Living Publications, just thirty minutes from Jefferson, making the commute easy, but not as easy as her current one. She went from her bedroom to her kitchen to her home office, definitely a sweet commute.

Though the opportunity to work with *Cooking Now* was too good to pass up and commuting for a few days wasn't the worst thing. However, leaving her dog, Bigelow, home alone with the newest addition to the family, a fluffy white cat named Princess, was a little nerve-racking. Both of them had done some damage in the house as they worked through their personal boundaries. She hoped they called a cease-fire and slept all day.

"I stocked your refrigerator with all the ingredients

you requested. You're all set to start whenever you'd like. In the back room, across from the studio kitchen, you'll find coffee and tea." Kitty had approached Hope's desk, ready to show her to her workstation.

Hope gathered her papers together. The butterflies in her belly returned. She'd been working on the recipes for the magazine for weeks to get them perfect for the six-page spread in the January issue. Her name would be prominently displayed, giving her a further reach to attract new readers to her blog. The recipes needed to be better than perfect.

Yeah, no pressure there.

"You run a very efficient kitchen." Hope stood and followed Kitty to the middle kitchenette. The cooking area was fully equipped with everything she needed, including top-of-the-line appliances.

"Thank you. I love my job." Kitty grabbed an apron from a shelf and handed it to Hope. "Let me know if you need anything." She walked back to her desk.

Hope glanced at the logo on the apron. Two large C and N letters with the magazine's name in smaller print and the tagline, *cook with confidence & flavor*. The magazine had gone through a major facelift five years earlier and shifted the original mission from talking to a narrow group of advanced cooks to reaching a broader group of beginner-to-intermediate cooks. Coinciding with an editorial shift, a staffing change had happened. New editors came on board with fresh ideas. From what Hope had seen so far, it looked like the publisher made the right decision.

After tying on the apron, she looked around her kitchenette. She took in a deep inhale.

Time to get to work.

She fell into her rhythm of cooking and blocked out the sounds of the test kitchen. She didn't hear the chatter or the beeping of appliances or the hurried footsteps from one end of the room to the other. She was fully in her zone, focused on the recipes, and tuned out all the distractions around her. The result was two whole-grain noodle bowls and a smoothie.

The focus of the January issue was a healthy restart, and Hope wanted to make sure each recipe she contributed wasn't only healthy and delicious but easy to make so any level cook could be successful, yet a little challenging so a more experienced cook could feel accomplished. It was a fine line to walk, but a necessary one if she wanted to continue working with the magazine in the future.

She finished chopping a bunch of chives and then moved over to the pot and ladled out a cup of vegetable broth over a bowl of noodles. She gingerly sprinkled the chives over the nutritious soup. She smiled with satisfaction.

"Looks delicious." Kitty had come up behind Hope. "I think your feature is going to be a hit with our readers. It's *fresh.*"

"Thank you. After a month of holiday baking and eating, by the time January rolls around, I'm looking for light-and-easy meals."

"The annual sugar cookie coma. I'm very familiar with it." Kitty laughed. "I can't even think of the holidays. It's too freakin' hot. The humidity is a killer. Still hard to get used to. I came over to see if you'd like to join me for lunch. I can show you where the cafeteria is."

"Sounds good. Let me clean up quick." Hope popped

the bowl of soup into the refrigerator and wiped the countertop after setting her pots and utensils in the dishwasher. After untying her apron, she grabbed her tote bag from her desk and joined Kitty on the walk to the main building.

To get to the two-story building where the editorial offices were located, they crossed the narrow road that stretched from one end of the campus to the other and traveled along a paved path bordered with well-maintained gardens. They chatted all the way to the entrance of the building. It looked like Hope had made a work friend already. The dread that had settled in her as she drove to the magazine about not fitting in had vanished.

The lunch menu in the Great Living cafeteria was impressive. Three prepared hot dishes, along with an endless combination of sandwiches and a salad bar. Staring at the chalkboard menu, Hope had a hard time deciding what to order. She chose a grilled chicken salad with dressing on the side.

"Do you always eat so healthy?" Kitty glanced at her grilled cheese and ham panini with a side of chips.

Hope wished. "No. I'm in the middle of baking pies for my blog, which means I need to watch what I eat."

Hope followed Kitty to a table for two in the sunroom, which looked out onto the patio and a small pond filled with koi. The grounds of the publishing company were idyllic. It definitely wasn't home, but she could see herself working here.

"How long have you worked here?" Hope drizzled the vinaigrette dressing on her salad.

After swallowing her bite of panini, Kitty reached for her soda. "About a year. I was a little hesitant to move out of the city, but once I did, I fell in love with the area."

"It's very different from working in the city. I mean, look at the pond." Hope gestured out the window as a bird flew by.

"You're originally from around here, right?"

Hope returned her attention to the younger woman seated across from her. Kitty's strawberry blond hair was pulled back into a ponytail and her full face had only a hint of makeup, mascara, and eyeliner.

"I was born and raised in Jefferson and moved back a couple of years ago."

"After the reality show?"

"I'd quit my job to appear on *The Sweet Taste of Success*. After the show, I had to decide whether to stay and get a new job or pursue my blog full-time."

"Any regrets?" Kitty asked before taking another bite of her sandwich.

"Sure. But I don't dwell on them. What's done is done. What about you? Where did you study?"

"The Culinary Institute of America."

"Impressive."

A redness tinged Kitty's cheeks. "It was tough. But worth every minute. I learned a lot and made good friends. Did you go to cooking school?"

"No, I'm self taught. I learned most of what I know from my mom."

"My mom isn't a big cook. She makes the best reservations." Kitty laughed. She plucked a chip out of the snack-size bag and crunched.

"Sounds like my sister."

"Well, I think people like my mom and your sister serve a very important role. Without them, who would eat what we cook?"

"A very positive outlook."

"Isn't that what we need? Positivity? I mean, look at what's going on in your town. The scandal with the former mayor and the developer. From what I've seen on the news, it looks really ugly."

Hope took a bite of her salad to delay answering. Discussing the events that had played out at the beginning of the summer wasn't on her top ten list of things to talk about. A murder had led to a corruption scandal, and Hope had managed to get herself involved in both investigations.

Not many people were happy with Hope's snooping. Her sister, Claire Dixon, had tried to stop her from tracking down a killer. And Hope's new boyfriend, Ethan Cahill, the chief of police, wasn't happy with how close Hope almost came to getting herself killed.

Hope shook off the negative thoughts and focused on the here and now and didn't want to talk about the current scandal rocking her hometown.

"Do you know either man?" Kitty pushed away her tray after draining the last of her soda.

Hope nodded. "I do. And because the case is about to go to trial soon, I don't think I should discuss it."

She hoped she wouldn't have to testify. Each time she thought about it, she had an overwhelming feeling of the willies. The last thing she wanted to do was come face-to-face with the murderer again.

Kitty broke eye contact for a moment. "I understand. You do know it can be really boring up here. A little juicy gossip would be welcome."

"I'm sure there'll be a lot more to come out as the court date gets closer," Hope said.

She finished her salad in silence while Kitty checked her phone for messages.

"All set?" Kitty slipped her phone into the back pocket of her pants.

Hope nodded again as she lifted her tray. "Thanks for asking me to lunch."

"Hey, I know what it's like being the new kid in school." She smiled and then led Hope to the trash and recycling station on their way out of the cafeteria.

Hope pushed open the door of the main building and stepped out into the hazy, humid afternoon. For the past couple of weeks, she'd been obsessed with her first day at the magazine and the recipes, so she hadn't given much thought to the recent events in Jefferson until Kitty mentioned them. Now they were front and center in her mind.

Kitty followed Hope out to the sidewalk, and they fell into a companionable silence, though Kitty did greet a few coworkers as they passed by.

Hope pushed away thoughts of the upcoming trial and enjoyed the walk across the campus on the return to the test kitchen. She had so much going right in her life for a change, she was just going to focus on the positives—a new opportunity and a chance to expand her business.

Chapter Two

Hope opened the door of the Merrifield Inn and stepped into the foyer of the grand Victorian house on Main Street. Soft, classical music drifted from the living room. Hope peeked in, looking for Jane, but found several guests had gathered for what she expected was afternoon tea. Sunlight from the large windows overlooking Main Street and French doors leading to the patio bathed the room. Antique furnishings, handed down from one generation of Merrifields to another, filled the spacious room. Not seeing Jane, Hope continued to the reception desk.

There was a little brass bell on the desk and, just like when she was a little girl, Hope was tempted to ring it. She hovered her hand over the bell, ready to tap it, when Jane appeared from the kitchen, carrying a plate of scones.

"No need to ring the bell, dear. I've been expecting you." Jane Merrifield's face was bright and her signature pink lips curved into a smile.

Hope giggled as the older woman bustled by her.

"I'll be right with you, once I deliver this plate to our

guests." Jane continued into the living room and a loud round of appreciation for the treats greeted her.

"They're all set for now." Jane returned to the lobby. She grabbed a folder from the desk on her way to the dining room.

Hope followed. The dining room, a mirror image of the living room minus the French doors, reminded Hope of when dining was more than a quick meal consumed between running here and there. A gleaming hardwood floor, intricately carved trim work, and well-curated art hanging on the walls harkened back to a time when meals were enjoyed over several courses and good conversation.

White cloths draped all the tables, and each was set for tomorrow's breakfast service.

"Let's sit in here and review the list for the scavenger hunt. Everything seems in order." Jane chose the table closest to the entrance and sat.

"Good to hear. I hate to jinx it, but the hunt always goes off without a hitch." Hope pulled out a chair. She'd been on her feet all day, except for the thirty-minute lunch break with Kitty. She was used to being on her feet because she tested and photographed recipes all the time in her home kitchen, but working on the hard floor of the commercial test kitchen had irked her lower back. She eased down onto the chair and set her tote bag on the floor.

The Annual Scavenger Hunt was started in Jefferson twenty years before to raise money to renovate the community center. The event continued to provide ongoing funding for the center. Hope's mom was one of the first organizers, along with Jane's sister-in-law, Sally.

The event was near and dear to Hope's heart, and

when she lived in the city, she'd made a point to come home for the weekend of the scavenger hunt. She joined dozens of town residents and together they all embraced the silliness of searching for so-called treasures throughout the town.

"No need to worry about jinxing the event, dear. I doubt anything can go wrong. We have everything all buttoned up, and the weather is going to be nice. No rain. It's going to be a night of good fun for everyone." Jane opened her folder.

Hope pulled out her own folder from her tote bag. "All the teams have been assigned?"

Jane looked up from her papers. "Two teams had been short one person, but luckily, we had two last-minute sign-ups. Our team is all set. It's you, Claire, Drew, and me. By the way, how is she doing?"

Good question. Claire had lost the special election for mayor of Jefferson over the summer. Never known for not giving 100 percent, Claire had campaigned hard for the office. It was understandable to be disappointed about losing, but Hope wasn't sure it was the defeat itself or the person who won the election that upset Claire so much.

"She's doing okay."

Jane slid Hope a doubting look. "Your sister isn't used to losing. And the loss was a high-profile loss to boot. But I suspect it'll make her stronger in the long run."

"I hadn't looked at it that way."

"Make sure Claire does." Jane's head turned at the sound of the front door opening and then closing.

A guest hurried by them on the way to the staircase.

"I can't believe I almost forgot to tell you." Jane leaned forward and her blue eyes twinkled. "We've had two new guests check in. Both women have the same last name."

"Relatives?"

Jane shook her head. "No. Both women said they didn't have any family here and neither asked about the other woman."

"Do they have a common last name? Like Smith?"

Jane tilted her head. "No. Their last name is Whitcomb."

"As in Lionel?"

Jane nodded. "Sally says it's a coincidence."

"Are you telling her about our new guests?" Sally Merrifield ambled into the room carrying a glass of iced tea. The retired head librarian of the Jefferson Library was a spinster who preferred the company of her plants to most people. Her weathered face was thanks to her years of gardening from the first sign of spring until the beginning of winter. When her hands weren't in freshly tilled dirt, she had her nose in a gardening book. "I have to keep my eye on her or else she'll search their rooms." Sally pulled out a chair at the table and joined Hope and Jane.

Jane feigned a look of hurt. "I'd do no such thing. It would be an invasion of their privacy. But I might follow them." She flashed a mischievous grin.

Hope pressed her lips together. She attributed Jane's overactive imagination to the fact that she'd written five mystery novels earlier in life. The now seventysomething widow was retired from writing, but her mind was still a fertile plotting ground.

"She's always looking for intrigue." Sally sipped her iced tea. "How's the Scavenger Hunt going?"

"It looks like we have everything under control. All the teams are assigned, we have desserts coming, and the hunt list is all printed up." Hope was impressed by how the event coordinator, Angela Green, managed the volunteers and organized all the tasks right down to the smallest detail without missing a beat. It meant Hope didn't have to worry about anything other than her own part—baking.

Sally leaned forward and lifted a paper from the pile in front of Jane.

"Magazine subscription card. A restaurant napkin. Photo with the mayor." Sally's thinned eyebrows arched. "Does Maretta know about this?"

Hope tilted her head sideways. "She should. It's been on the Scavenger Hunt list every year since the first hunt. The photo with the mayor is a town favorite."

Silence descended upon them for a moment, and then the three of them chuckled at the thought of Maretta Kingston being besieged by town residents with their cell phones for selfies.

"I wish I could be at Town Hall Friday night," Jane said between laughs.

"Me too. It's all in good fun, so I can't imagine Maretta's nose getting too out of joint." Hope returned to reviewing her list. She had a few dozen cupcakes and cookies to bake by Friday night. Normally, it wouldn't be a problem, but with the assignment at *Cooking Now*, she was on a tight schedule.

"Tell us, how did your first day at the magazine go?" Sally asked.

"Good. I got through some recipes. The test kitchen manager, Kitty, is really nice. May, the senior editor, is . . . well . . . I don't think she likes food bloggers much. All in all, it's a nice change of pace to get out." Hope closed her folder and shoved it back into her tote bag. "I think we're good for Friday night. I'd better get going. Bigelow and Princess have been left alone all day. I'm scared of what my house looks like."

"Cats and dogs. They have a long history of discourse, but they are also known to become the best of friends. Give them time. They'll sort it all out." Jane smiled.

"I appreciate the words of encouragement. I'll share them with Bigelow and Princess." Hope stood and hitched the shoulder straps of her tote over her shoulder.

"And I'll keep you apprised of the two Miss Whitcombs." Jane closed her folder.

"Please do." Hope walked away.

"Don't encourage her," Sally called out.

Hope laughed, waving her hand as she exited the inn. Stepping out into the air was like stepping into a furnace. The temperature hovered around ninety, with a hideous amount of humidity blended into the air. She couldn't wait to peel off her shirt and slacks for a tank and shorts and flip-flops. As she was about to round the corner to the parking lot, she made the impulsive decision to endure the unbearable heat and trek over to her favorite coffee shop, The Coffee Clique.

Inside, she ordered a tall iced hazelnut coffee and a cinnamon roll. She should've remained strong. She had eaten a healthy salad for lunch, but when she saw her most favorite pastry in the whole wide world in the case, she had to have it. She considered it a little celebration of her first day at the magazine.

With her iced coffee and pastry, Hope stepped out of The Coffee Clique to head back to her vehicle. She took a sip of her drink. It was a welcome relief from the heat of the day. Her pace was quick. The sooner she got home, the sooner she could indulge in the cinnamon roll. The layers of light, buttery pastry swirled with cinnamon and sugar and a gooey icing.

Her daydream was cut short when a woman bumped her and jostled her iced coffee.

"I'm so sorry. I wasn't looking where I was going." The woman stepped back, putting a little space between herself and Hope. She lifted her cell phone and frowned.

"No harm done. I wasn't exactly looking either."

"What did we ever do before these things?" The woman shook her head as she lowered the phone. Her brows furrowed. She didn't look happy, and Hope guessed it had to do with the person who had been on the other end of the text or call she'd just finished.

"Tell me about it."

The woman eyed the bag in Hope's hand. "I discovered this place the other day, and let me tell you, it may be worth moving east for their pastries."

"You're not from around here?"

"I'm from Arizona. I'm here for a visit. Forgive me. I'm being so rude. I'm Miranda Whitcomb." She extended her free hand.

Hope shook Miranda's hand. The woman stood the same height as Hope, with shoulder-length auburn hair and tastefully applied makeup. The deep berry shade applied on her lips shone and drew attention away from the deep creases around her dark eyes. Then it struck Hope. Miranda must be one of the two Whitcomb women who registered at the inn.

"Nice to meet you. I'm Hope Early. Are you staying at the Merrifield Inn?"

"Yes. It's a lovely place."

"Indeed it is. What brings you to Jefferson?"

"Family business." Miranda's phone buzzed and she made an apologetic face and turned to step away to answer the call. "Hi . . . No, that won't do. We have to meet . . . No, you're not putting this off any longer. You've had what, thirty years? Friday . . . Don't play with me. I'm dead serious." Miranda glanced over her shoulder.

Hope gave a weak smile before she took a sip of her iced coffee and turned away. *Awkward.* She couldn't help but overhear the one-sided conversation. When she looked back, Miranda was walking toward the inn. Was Miranda related to Lionel Whitcomb? Was it him who was on the other end of the phone?

Hope stopped at the curb and waited for a break in traffic before crossing the street. When she caught one, she dashed across, her beverage sloshing in the cup, and stepped up on the curb as the front door of the Jefferson Town Realty office opened. Lionel Whitcomb and another man came barreling out. Their movements were large and their voices loud as they came face-to-face on the sidewalk.

"I thought you wanted to make a deal. What do you really want, Lionel?" the man demanded.

"One friggin' call. You storm out of our meeting because of one friggin' call? You know, I have other matters to attend to. I had to end something. What am I doing? You were looking for an out. You had no intention of coming into this deal." Lionel's sagging cheeks puffed out as he spat his words.

"Of course not. You know what? This isn't working anymore." The man turned and stormed away.

"Damn it! You owe me! Remember, you owe me!" Lionel threw a fist in the air before he noticed Hope

standing there, frozen by the scene that had just
played out in front of her. "What are you looking at?"

"I . . . I . . ." she stammered. She looked in the direction the other man went off to and didn't see him, but
a dark Mercedes sedan pulled out of a parking space.

"Lionel, do you want to continue our meeting?"
Alfred Kingston had appeared at the door. He was the
owner of Jefferson Town Realty and the husband of
the town's new mayor. Middle-aged, with thinning hair
and a protruding belly, he was a docile man by nature
with a keen eye for real estate. "Where's Rupert?"

Rupert? Hope searched her memory and recalled
Lionel had a business partner named Rupert Donnelly. If what she'd witnessed was any indication of
how the men communicated on a regular basis, they
must've had a very rocky partnership.

"He left." Lionel shifted his attention from Hope to
Alfred. "He's not in. He's wasted my time." Lionel
marched off in the opposite direction of the other
man and then disappeared inside a sleek silver Jaguar.

Hope approached Alfred, who still held open the
door to his office and looked pale. He probably hadn't
expected his meeting to end in a loud argument.
Then again, when Lionel Whitcomb was involved, one
should expect a temper tantrum.

"What was that all about?"

"Good to see you, Hope." Alfred let the door close
behind him and stepped farther out onto the sidewalk. "Not every meeting goes well."

"Talk about an understatement. They were loud
and angry. From what I heard, it was because of a tele-
phone call?" Hope wondered if the call Lionel made

was the one she'd partially overheard just a moment ago. The timing seemed to suggest so.

"Lionel's phone kept buzzing, and then he stepped out to make a call. Rupert got all hot about it and stormed out of my office." Alfred glided his hand over his head. "Now it looks like the deal is sunk."

"I thought the medical office project was dead," Hope said.

Lionel had begun clearing a lot by the Village Shopping Center for a medical office complex. But it got tangled up in Lionel's legal battle, and the site was now fenced up with no prospect of being developed.

"It's probably not a good idea for me to discuss the meeting." Alfred frowned.

Hope didn't need for him to expand any more on the topic. She knew enough from Claire's long career as a real estate agent to know Alfred was looking for the exclusive listing of the development. He was probably betting on the town eventually giving the green light to construction and Lionel raising more capital. Now, with the meeting having gone kaput, he was probably looking at kissing his exclusive listing goodbye.

"I understand. I'm sorry your meeting ended in such a bad way." Hope took another drink of her iced coffee.

Alfred pivoted and reached for the door handle. "How's Claire doing? I miss her around here." He was a kind person and her sister had liked working for him. If only he wasn't married to Maretta.

"She's doing okay. I know she misses you and all her coworkers."

"Then I hope she'll be coming back soon. We've gotten some new listings I know she could sell in a heartbeat. Tell her, please." Alfred opened the door and entered the office.

Hope lingered for a moment longer and then pulled herself away from the real estate agency. Whatever was going on with Miranda Whitcomb was none of her business, and neither was the situation between Alfred and the two real estate developers. The last time she poked her nose into where it didn't belong, it almost got her killed.

An old saying popped into her head—once bitten, twice shy. A good reminder to her of how she should tread when it came to other people's business. Walking along Main Street, heading in the direction of her car back at the inn, she sipped her iced coffee. Yep. She was definitely twice shy.

Her iced hazelnut coffee was almost gone by the time Hope pulled into her driveway and shut off the ignition. She grinned at the welcome sight of Ethan and Bigelow up ahead by the patio. From her vantage point, they seemed to be playing fetch. Too bad her adopted dog wasn't much of a team player. She dropped her car key into her tote bag and then glanced at the pastry bag. She wasn't expecting Ethan to be there until later. *Shoot.* She'd have to share the pastry.

She pushed open the car door and walked toward Ethan. He'd thrown a ball and Bigelow chased after it.

"Thought you'd be home earlier." He met Hope halfway. Dressed in jeans and a polo shirt, Hope couldn't remember if he was on duty or not. As the chief of police, he didn't always wear a uniform and his hours were unpredictable.

"Sorry to keep you waiting. I stopped by the inn to go over last-minute details for the Scavenger Hunt."

"It gave us guys some more bonding time." Ethan broke into a grin as he closed the small space between them.

She caught a whiff of his musky aftershave as he wrapped an arm around her and pulled her in for an I-missed-you-all-day kind of kiss. The gentle pressure on her lower back and the kiss sent a spark through Hope. Oh, yeah, she definitely could get used to those kinds of welcome-home greetings. The shift in their relationship over the past couple of months had taken them from the friend zone to romantically involved. Before she took the plunge, she'd worried about ruining their friendship, but it got stronger as they became closer.

Bigelow raced back without the ball in his mouth. The medium-size brown-and-white dog wagged his tail and jumped on Hope to welcome her home. She'd been trying to train him since she took him in, but he had a lot of energy and a lot of charm, which made training a challenge because she kept spoiling him. Maybe the training issue lay with her and not Bigelow.

Gently, she pushed him down and then lavished him with kisses. All the training books she'd purchased did say to remain firm with the dog. With his head tilted sideways and his big brown eyes staring at her, staying firm was no easy feat.

"And you stopped at The Coffee Clique?" Ethan eyed the pastry bag.

"I did. Got me a little treat. I'm happy to share," she fibbed.

"No, you're not." Ethan dipped his head for another kiss.

"Maybe . . . maybe we should go inside." Hope eased back from Ethan and pressed a palm to his chest.

Her neighbors' homes weren't close on Fieldstone Road, each house set on at least two acres, but her neighbors liked to walk, and she didn't want to give them a show.

"Good idea. Come on, Bigelow." Ethan turned and walked, along with Hope and the dog, into the house.

They entered through the mudroom and went into the kitchen, which opened to the family room. The large space had been gutted and remodeled when Hope purchased the home, giving her a dream kitchen, complete with a six-burner stove and two wall ovens, and a generous-size living space anchored by an original fireplace.

She dropped her tote and the bag from The Coffee Clique onto the center island. It was a mindless act, something she'd taken for granted since moving into the house, but almost losing her beloved home reminded her how important even the smallest things were. A few months earlier, her home had been intentionally set on fire with her trapped inside. She'd escaped with bruises and a concussion, while her home faired about the same—there was damage, but it wasn't a total loss.

"Where's Princess?" Hope scanned the family room and didn't see the white cat she'd recently adopted after the owner passed away. With no place other than a shelter to go to, Hope took the cat into her home.

Life was hectic already, but a cat was an easy pet. Or so she thought.

Ethan shrugged. "Not sure. She's probably curled up on top of something, sleeping." He walked to the refrigerator and pulled out a pitcher of iced tea and poured a glass. "How was your first day at the magazine?"

Hope plated the cinnamon roll and cut it in half. She broke off a piece of her half and popped it into her mouth and chewed.

"It went okay. The test kitchen manager, Kitty, is really nice. We had lunch together. May, the senior editor, doesn't seem to appreciate food bloggers."

"Sounds like high school." Ethan pulled off a piece of the cinnamon roll and chewed.

"In some ways, yes. I got through a few recipes and everyone liked them. I think it'll be a good feature."

"Good exposure for you."

Hope ate another piece of the pastry. "Who knows? Maybe I can become a contributing editor. That would be a nice gig to have. A little steady work, but not a big commitment. Actually, it would be ideal."

"Just be careful not to take on too much. You don't want to be working twenty-four seven."

Hope sipped her iced coffee. "I already work twenty-four seven. The hazards of being self-employed and renovating an old house and raising chickens. Anyway, when I stopped at the inn, Jane told me two new guests had checked in and both women have the same last name."

Ethan took one more piece of the cinnamon roll before he walked to the family room and collapsed into an armchair. Bigelow followed and settled by Ethan's feet.

"Aren't you curious?" Hope asked.

"No. I'm actually hungry. Do you want to go out?"

Hope shook her head. "I'm going to take a shower and then I'll grill." She walked out from behind the island. "Their last name is Whitcomb. Isn't that odd?"

"A lot of people have the last name of Whitcomb."

Hope rolled her eyes. "Two women with the same last name come to Jefferson, of all places, and Lionel Whitcomb just happens to live here and is going to trial. You think it's a coincidence?"

Ethan's gaze trained on her. "Jane has a very active imagination and you have a way of getting yourself into trouble."

"I know. I'm just curious. I met one of the women on my way out of The Coffee Clique. She was texting and walked right into me. Her name is Miranda Whitcomb."

"She introduced herself?"

Hope laughed. "Yes, she did. I didn't pry it out of her, I swear. Anyway, she got a call and I overheard it. Well, at least her end of it. She was trying to force someone to meet her on Friday. I think she was talking to Lionel Whitcomb. It doesn't sound like it's going to be a happy reunion if they meet."

Ethan leaned back and scrubbed his face. "Hope . . ."

"I know. It's none of my business why Miranda Whitcomb or the other Whitcomb lady is here in Jefferson." Hope sat on the sofa, across from Ethan. "What's going on with Lionel's case?"

"Not sure. It's in the hands of the DA now."

"I wonder what Elaine will do if Lionel is convicted. I don't exactly see her as one of those wives who'll visit Lionel in prison."

"There'll probably be a quick divorce and she'll be off looking for her next husband."

"You're probably right. She'll be on the prowl for husband number five."

"Number five?"

Hope nodded. "She was married three times before Lionel. I wonder what happened to them."

"What are you going to grill?"

"Is that all you can think about, food?"

He chuckled. "I'm a guy."

"Fine. I'll go shower. How do steaks sound?" Hope stood.

Ethan grinned. "Perfect. I'm going to go back to the office. There's some paperwork I should finish up and then I'll come back."

"Okay. Don't forget about the Scavenger Hunt. Friday night you'll have to fend for yourself for dinner."

Ethan groaned.

"What? The hunt is fun."

"Fun? Half the town running around in groups doing stupid things. It's a recipe for disaster."

"Nonsense. We've been doing the hunt for twenty years. Nothing ever happens, but it's a good time for everyone." Hope stood and headed out of the room. "Nothing is going to go wrong. Trust me."

Chapter Three

"Good morning, girls." Hope carried a bucket from the feed storage area she'd carved out of her barn to the coop. She'd repurposed an empty stall to give her chickens a home with an extra layer of protection against the weather and predators.

A round of happy clucks returned her greeting and grew louder as she approached the feeder. Her girls were hungry. Wasting no time, she hoisted the bucket over the aluminum container and let the grain-based feed rain down until the feeder was full.

A loud cluck drew Hope's attention downward. Helga, her four-pound Hamburg hen, stood beside her foot. She'd slipped into her muddied, scuffed barn boots as she dashed out of her house with Bigelow. If her food blog ever tanked, she could rock a fashion blog.

She laughed at the ridiculous thought. "I better stick to developing recipes. Right, Helga?"

Feathered bodies brushed by her bare legs. Pandemonium had ensued, and she scooted out of the way. When the hens finished eating, they headed outside for a day of free-ranging.

She returned the bucket to the table and pulled off her work gloves. She'd wanted chickens from the moment she made an offer on the house. There were numerous benefits of raising the birds besides having fresh eggs. The chickens were great hunters of insects, resulting in natural pest control, and they were happy to eat scraps, so Hope would have less food waste.

Bigelow's playful, friendly bark drew Hope's attention outside. Hope suspected a neighbor was taking a morning stroll.

Peering out of the barn, she spotted Bigelow trotting to the road and followed him. She came to the end of her property and saw someone. But she wasn't a neighbor.

Fieldstone Road had recently become a place of curiosity. Morbid curiosity, thanks to a tragedy a few homes away from Hope's.

Hope stepped off the sidewalk and approached the stranger. Maybe the "For Sale" sign drew the woman's interest and Hope would have a new neighbor.

"Good morning!"

The woman looked over her shoulder and her gaze immediately drifted to the dog. "He's adorable. What's his name?"

Bigelow sauntered over to the stranger and sniffed her legs, then lifted his head for a pat.

"Bigelow." Hope joined her dog.

"What a very proper name for a handsome boy." The woman gave him one last pat on the head and then shifted her attention to Hope.

"Are you interested in purchasing the lot?" Hope gestured to the open space behind the woman.

It was only a matter of time before someone purchased the property and built a new home. Every milestone for the new owner would be a sad reminder for Hope of what had happened at Thirty-Three Fieldstone Road just months earlier.

"Why is there an empty lot on this road? What happened?"

"A house fire."

Hope crossed her arms over her chest. A heaviness plopped in her stomach. The memories of the fire were as menacing as the flames Hope saw that night. She could still smell the smoke, feel the heat, and hear the wailing sirens. She shuddered.

"How terrible. Was anybody hurt?"

Hope hated talking about the incident, especially when just days later the arsonist struck again. "Are you interested in purchasing the lot? It's a nice street."

"I'm sure it is. But I'm only visiting." The woman extended her hand. "I'm Rona Whitcomb."

Hope shook Rona's hand. "Welcome to Jefferson. Are you staying at the Merrifield Inn?"

"I am. The ladies who own the inn are very interesting. Is it true one of them was a mystery writer?"

"It is. Jane wrote five mystery novels years ago."

"She's very inquisitive. But I guess when you own an inn, that's in your DNA. In fact, it's something I would love to do. I'm a people person. I can talk to anyone, anywhere. My mom called it a gift. My sister calls it nosy." Rona chuckled.

"I think it is a gift. I'm Hope Early."

"You live on this street?"

Hope nodded and pointed. "Over there."

"And you're a blogger?"

"Yes. Do you read my blog?"

"No. It was a lucky guess. Your shirt." Rona pointed to Hope's tank top.

Hope looked at her outfit of the day. She'd paired her cutoff jean shorts with a top her niece, Hannah, had given her as a birthday present. The message T-shirt read *I ♥ Blogging*.

"Right. I have a food blog. *Hope at Home.*" It had become an automatic reflex to include the name of her blog whenever she told anyone what she did for a living.

Rona shrugged. "I'm not much of a cook."

Fifty percent of the time, when Hope told people what she did, she received that response. She'd learned to move on with the conversation. She wouldn't convert a noncook into a cook or a reader of her blog in one short meeting.

"Are you out for a morning walk?"

Rona nodded. "I love to get out before breakfast, but I have a bad sense of direction. I got turned around somehow and now I think I'm lost. How do I get back to Main Street?"

"You're not far. Just continue that way." Hope pointed to the direction ahead.

"Great! I'm starving. They feed you like a queen at the inn. I think I may need to take a couple of walks a day." Rona started walking and Hope fell in step with Bigelow by her side.

"Well, Jefferson is beautiful. You'll have pleasant walks. Are you here for business or pleasure?"

"Neither, I'm afraid. It's family stuff. You know, it's time to settle some things. Thanks for the directions. It was nice meeting you." Rona's pace picked up as she continued along the road and eventually disappeared around the curve.

Hope looked at Bigelow.

His big eyes stared at her and blinked.

"Who are those women? Are they related to Lionel?" Bigelow barked.

"I know. I know. Mind my own business and make breakfast. Come on. Let's go inside."

She patted her leg and Bigelow sprang into a trot back to the house. She couldn't help but glance over her shoulder to where Rona Whitcomb had stood moments ago. "It has to be more than just a coincidence those women have come to Jefferson."

"The house is right on the beach. Floor-to-ceiling windows. It's like the waves are crashing right into your bedroom. It's amazing." Drew Adams stepped out of Hope's SUV.

From the moment Drew hopped into the passenger seat, he'd been jabbering on about his upcoming vacation out on Long Island. More precisely, the Hamptons, where the wealthy spent weekends recharging and being seen.

"How much money does Fritz have?" Hope came around the vehicle with her purse in hand. She'd returned home from the magazine and changed into a denim shirtdress and a pair of low-wedge sandals for the Scavenger Hunt. She wanted to be comfortable and cool. Well, as cool as you could get on a hot August day.

On the way out the door, she'd tamed her shoulder-length dark hair into a ponytail and pleaded with Bigelow and Princess to behave while she was out. Neither animal offered any assurance.

"Gobs. His inheritance is off the charts. You can't begin to count the money. Or, how many houses he owns." Drew had chosen a navy-blue polo shirt paired with khaki chino shorts, his summer go-to for looking pulled together and cool. He'd slipped into a pair of pristine vanilla-white canvas sneakers.

Hope approved his choice in footwear, comfy and he'd be fast on his feet to snatch up the treasures they needed to collect. Speed was the secret to winning.

"Sounds like you'll have a good time in the Hamptons." A slight twinge of jealousy pricked at Hope. She'd love a week away in the playground of the Manhattan elite. Lying on a sandy beach with a summer read and no chores or recipes to create or posts to publish or photographs to edit; it sounded like heaven. It also sounded like she'd spread herself too thin.

"You bet I am! One whole week of sand, drinks with little umbrellas, and no Norrie Jennings. It can't get much better."

Hope nodded in agreement. Her best friend had been dealing with a new staff reporter on the *Gazette*. To describe Norrie as ambitious would be an understatement. She'd proven during the last murder investigation in town she wasn't above borderline dishonest tactics to get her byline on the front page.

"I hope you enjoy the week. You've earned the vacation." Hope set the strap of her purse on her shoulder.

Drew nodded. "You got that right, sistah. When was the last time Claire went out in public?"

Hope waved away Drew's exaggeration and proceeded to the front door of Claire's four-thousand-square-foot house. "She's not a hermit."

Drew lifted an eyebrow. "If you say so."

"I do." Hope led the way to the double front doors of the oversize house. Hope had thought her sister was crazy when she purchased the huge home, but she saw the appeal. A classic facade of brick and tan siding, the solid house stood on a hill with expansive views of neighboring horse farms and the gentle, rolling hills their section of the state was known for. So what if you needed a map to find your way through the massive structure?

She dug into her purse for the spare key Claire had given her years before and let herself and Drew inside. They stepped into a two-story foyer, gutted by Claire, that boasted a striking black-and-white tile floor and a chandelier that reflected fragments of light from the late-afternoon sun streaming in the tall casement window above the entry. If you stood at the right angle at the right time, it was like staring at a kaleidoscope.

"Claire!" Hope called out and stepped farther into the house, with Drew behind her.

She dropped her purse on the stone-veneered table positioned in the center of the room. The sweetness of the lily arrangement on the table brought a smile to Hope's face. She loved flowers. Too bad there wasn't enough time in the day to devote to her garden.

"Coming!" Claire's voice didn't drift from the other room. Rather, she full-on shouted at Hope.

Drew grimaced. "What's with the tone?"

Hope shrugged. "I have no idea."

Claire appeared from the living room, and Hope's mouth gaped open. The woman standing in front of her wasn't *her* sister.

Couldn't be.

The imposter wore elastic-waist, bubblegum-pink shorts with a sloppy, half-tucked graphic T-shirt. Her normally coiffed hair was pulled into a messy topknot and on her feet were orange clogs.

"Clogs?" Drew whispered over Hope's shoulder.

"Clogs." Hope stared at the unusual footwear choice.

What happened to Claire's designer sandals that showed off her pedicure?

"What on earth are you wearing?" Hope closed the gap between them. She'd never seen her sister look so unkempt. Even after the birth of her two children, Claire had on a full face of makeup for photographs and refused to wear anything hospital issue. Yeah, she was one of those patients. To see Claire messy and discombobulated sent Hope into protective sister mode. She had to do something.

Now.

Claire looked at herself and shrugged. "I was outside in the garden."

"You hate gardening," Drew said.

Claire looked up and cocked her head sideways. "What else is there for me to do now?"

Hope and Drew exchanged a worried look.

"Intervention," Drew mouthed silently.

Hope pressed her lips together and shook her head. "Honey, we need to get you ready. Tonight's the Scavenger Hunt, remember?"

Claire's shoulders sagged. "I'm really not in the mood to go out today." She swiveled and walked back into the living room.

Drew scooted up to Hope. "What are you going to do?"

"I'm not sure. I've never seen her like this before."

"Clogs. She's wearing clogs and shorts with an elastic waistband. We have to stage an intervention or who knows what'll be next? Tank tops with *I heart* something written on it."

Hope glared at Drew. "Hey, I have tops like that."

Drew gave her a need-I-say-more look.

"Never mind." Hope broke away and followed her

sister into the living room. With its coffered ceiling, custom wallpaper, and marble fireplace, the room was a showpiece. Claire had spent over a year decorating the house and continued to tweak the décor on a regular basis to keep it from becoming stale.

Claire slumped into a plush armchair. "You two go on without me."

"We're not going without you. Right, Drew?" Hope glanced over her shoulder.

He hadn't followed her. He remained in the foyer.

"Drew!"

He plodded into the living room. "What she says. But you can't go dressed like that." He extended his forefinger and waved it up and down at Claire.

"Not helping." Hope looked back at her sister. "We need four people on a team. Without you, we only have three."

"Find someone else." Claire's voice was monotone and barely audible.

"No, we can't. You signed up for this hunt and you always keep your word. You're not going to let us down, are you?" Hope appealed to Claire's sense of responsibility. She always kept her promises. *Always.*

Claire stared at Hope for a long moment. "What difference does it make? It's a stupid scavenger hunt."

"You love the hunt," Drew exclaimed. "You love beating the pants off the other teams, just like your sister. But you? I'm not gonna lie; sometimes you scare me with how into it you get."

Claire leveled an empty gaze on Drew. "I'm not beating the pants off anybody these days."

"All right. This has to stop." Hope marched to her sister and squatted to be at eye level with her. "You lost the election, but that doesn't mean you're a loser."

"Do you need a dictionary? Losing the election makes me a loser."

Hope counted to ten mentally. Her sister was trying her patience. "You worked hard and you gave it your best, but—"

"But I lost! To Maretta Kingston, of all people. Why did she have to run for mayor? Why? Tell me why?"

Hope channeled her inner cheerleader one more time. "We don't know why she ran for mayor and now it doesn't matter. You can't let this loss define who you are. You need to get back to living your life and to your career."

"My career? I can't go back to the real estate office. I can't work for the Kingstons anymore. Not with Maretta popping into the office all the time. She's right down the street in Town Hall." A deep sigh escaped Claire's bare lips. She hadn't even put on gloss for an added pop of shine.

"You plan to avoid Maretta for the next two years? It'll be hard to do, because Jefferson isn't a big town." Drew drifted over to the sofa opposite Claire and dropped onto a cushion.

"It's an option." Claire gave a half shrug.

Hope glanced upward, looking for some divine inspiration. She was running out of patience. She'd listened, given Claire a shoulder to cry on, and served up homemade strawberry ice cream with sprinkles, and yet her sister remained in a funk.

Maybe it was time to try a new tactic.

"No, it's not! You need to stop this pity party." Hope straightened up and propped her hands on her hips.

The one tactic she hadn't tried was going old-school mom on Claire. As kids, they'd called their mom's reality checks "going nuclear." Their mother empathized, coddled, and soothed only up to a point, and then she went "nuclear" when her daughters seemed to wallow too long.

"You think I'm having a pity party?" Claire's voice raised as her face reddened.

"I know you're having a pity party." As the words came out of Hope's mouth, she could hear her mother. After she'd received the divorce papers, Hope had fallen into her own funk, and it was her mother who'd snapped her out of it with those exact words.

"Pity party for one." Drew raised his forefinger in the air, earning him a stern look from Hope.

Hope turned back to her sister. "You can't spend the next two years feeling sorry for yourself. You lost the election. Suck it up."

"That's your advice?" Claire folded her arms over her chest and frowned.

"Yes. Yes, it is. Come on, Claire. What kind of example are you setting for Logan and Hannah? They're watching how you handle this defeat. Do you want them to see you're too weak to pull yourself back up after a loss?"

Claire's mouth gaped open at her sister's harsh words. "I'm not weak."

Hope gave a quick tilt of her head and lifted an eyebrow, questioning her sister's statement.

"I'm not." Claire unfolded her arms and dipped her head. She was silent for a moment.

Hope suspected she was having some private inner reflection.

Drew popped up off the sofa and scooted up behind Hope. "Genius."

Hope nodded in agreement. Using the kids against her sister was a last resort, and she prayed it worked.

"No, it's not how I want my children to see me."
Claire lifted her gaze. "I want them to be resilient and
be able to rise above defeat. You're right. I need to show
them how." A hesitant smile settled on Claire's lips.

Hope reached for her sister and brought her up to
her feet. She wrapped her arms around Claire and
squeezed tight. "That's my girl. Let's start now with
you coming to the hunt with us."

Drew wrapped his arms around Hope and Claire
for a group hug.

"But first, you need to shower and change into
some decent clothes and, for heaven's sake, burn
those shoes." Drew pulled back and gave one more disapproving glance at Claire's footwear.

Hope released her sister. "While you get ready, I'll
make us something quick to eat and then we'll pick
up Jane."

"Sounds good." Claire's smile settled, and she
looked genuinely happy at the moment. "How about
some chicken salad?"

"You got it." Hope ushered her sister out of the
living room and to the staircase. "It'll be ready by
the time you come back downstairs."

Halfway up the stairs, Claire halted and looked over
her shoulder. "Remember, not too much mayo. Oh,
and go light on the onion." With her last instruction,
she picked up her pace and dashed up the rest of
the stairs.

"She's back." Drew slung his arm around Hope's
shoulder. "I don't think there's any turning back now.
You sure this is what you want?"

Hope inhaled a breath. "I think so. I should, right?
Come on. Let's make dinner." She patted Drew's chest

and headed for the kitchen. "Give Jane a call and let her know we'll be there soon with Claire."

The Jefferson Community Center was home to a variety of events and activities throughout the year. In late August it was HQ for the Annual Scavenger Hunt. All the volunteers had arrived hours earlier to set up the refreshments and snacks, along with the registration table.

Hope glanced around the hall, which was filled with chatter, laughter, and good-hearted competition. The energy level in the room was contagious and, with Claire beside her, she couldn't have asked for a better evening.

Teams huddled together to review the hunt list of twenty-five items they needed to collect. The rules were simple. The teams couldn't collect more than one item at any one location, and they needed to stay together. The first team to collect all the "treasures" in the shortest period of time won.

The first-place and second-place teams won a bevy of prizes donated by local businesses, but what was most prized were the bragging rights of winning. For three years in a row, Hope and Drew's team had won the hunt. If they won this year, they'd beat Meg Griffin's record of consecutive wins.

A twinge of pettiness pricked Hope. Her childhood rivalry with Meg continued to play out into adulthood because Meg couldn't seem to let go of the past. Since she moved back to Jefferson, there had been glimmers of hope for a truce between them, of burying the past for once and for good, but each time they got close, something thwarted the reconciliation. Another proverbial shoe always seemed to drop, propelling them back to their frenemy state.

Drew approached with the hunt list and Jane beside him. The four of them huddled to review the items they needed to collect. A chocolate chip cookie recipe. Hope had those, so Jane made a note on the sheet of paper that they'd stop at Hope's house. Next was a movie ticket stub. Drew had one from the latest Nicholas Sparks movie. Jane made another note. A magazine subscription card. Claire had dozens of magazines at her house and Jane jotted down the stop at Claire's house. They decided they had enough to start and would work through the list once they got into Hope's vehicle. All four of them headed toward the door, passing Meg's team.

Hope noticed the team was short one. Sally Merrifield and Norrie Jennings were reviewing the hunt list, but Elaine Whitcomb was missing. The rules of the Scavenger Hunt stated a team couldn't take part without four members. It looked like Meg's team might have to forfeit. Hope fought hard not to smile.

"Trouble with her team?" Drew nodded in Meg's direction as he walked with Hope. He'd turned up the volume on his voice just loud enough for Norrie to hear. Her head swung up and she gave him the hairy eyeball, and he grinned.

"Looks like it. Wonder where Elaine is." Hope led her team out of the Community Center and toward her vehicle. "Actually, we don't have time to worry about Meg and her team. We have a hunt to win." Her rallying cry received a round of "yes, we do."

With all her passengers buckled in, Hope set off to their first stop, her house. Their last stop before arriving at the Avery Bistro was the Merrifield Inn to collect a bank deposit slip, and back into the SUV they went for the drive over to the restaurant.

Hope navigated her vehicle along Main Street and then made a turn on Copper Hill Road and followed along the curvy road until she came to Cobblestone Court, and three more quick turns landed her on the road where the Avery Bistro was located behind a tall, solid, green fence.

Once a farm, the old house was now a contemporary dining establishment offering a seasonal, locally sourced menu. The two-story building, painted green with crisp, white trim, had two additions that created a courtyard complete with a fountain, flagstone paths, and seating for casual gatherings or cocktail parties. Three arched French doors looked out over the courtyard and, from the main drive onto the property, you could see glimpses of the diners.

"Leila and Dorie's team are already here? Looks like their adding Matt to their team is paying off," Jane said from the front passenger seat.

Hope saw Leila Manchester's team posing for a selfie in front of the restaurant's plaque on the fence. A pump of adrenaline shot through her. They needed to pick up their pace. A newbie like Matt Roydon couldn't take the win from Hope and her team.

"How'd they get here so fast?" Drew pointed to Leila and Dorie's team.

"I wonder how much more they need to get." Claire leaned forward and rested her hand on the back of Hope's seat. "Do you think they're ahead of us in collecting items?"

"Don't know. We have to stay focused. We can't worry about the other teams. Let's get the napkin and then pose for a selfie." Hope pulled into the parking lot.

She parked her vehicle in a space in the front section of the lot. The back section was used for overflow parking. Hope shut off the ignition as Meg's minivan pulled up alongside Hope's vehicle. She got a look at the front-seat passenger. Elaine Whitcomb. Darn. She'd shown up.

"Come on! Meg's team is here now. They can't beat us!" Drew pushed open his door and jumped out.

Hope grabbed her purse and stepped out of the car, with Jane and Claire following. They all gathered at the back of the vehicle and set off together toward the main entrance. But a familiar-looking Jaguar parked in the rear lot caught Hope's attention.

Why was it parked all the way back there when there were plenty of spaces in the main lot? The driver's side door was open. Before she realized it, she'd broken away from her group and was heading toward the lone car.

Voices drifted through the warm night air, and she looked over her shoulder. Meg and Norrie had gotten out of the minivan and were talking loudly. She wondered if there was a leadership coup about to happen on the team. Both women had a hard time playing nice with other people. Meg was headstrong, while Norrie was devious.

She turned her attention back to the Jaguar up ahead and continued forward.

"Hope! Come on!" Drew broke into a jog toward her. "The napkin, remember? Meg's team will get inside first. Norrie can't win!"

Hope nodded. She understood Drew's concern, but her curiosity was in control now. She navigated around some potholes and deep cracks to reach the rear section of the lot, climbing uphill until she passed the closed kitchen entrance.

"Just a minute." She reached the car, and the vanity license plate, "Lionel #1," confirmed the car belonged to Lionel Whitcomb. What was it doing there with the driver's door open? Where was Lionel? Why had he parked all the way up there? Hope continued around the front of the car and came to a hard stop.

She gasped, and one hand flew up to cover her mouth, while the other stretched out and planted itself on the hood of the car to steady her body.

She'd discovered why she hadn't seen Lionel.

He was lying on the asphalt with a large red stain spread out on his white shirt, and his beady eyes were wide open but lifeless.

Her stomach clenched and a wave of dizziness threatened to knock her to the ground. She pressed her hand down firmer on the hood of the car and willed herself not to pass out.

"What are you looking at? We're going to lose." Drew came up behind Hope. He grabbed her shoulder. "Oh. My. God!"

"What's going on with you two?" Claire reached Drew and tugged on his arm. "Come on. I thought you wanted to win this year?"

Hope's mind raced with competing thoughts—she was going to be sick, the police had to be called, and Claire needed to be moved away from the body. The body. A roll of nausea nearly sent Hope heaving.

A bloodcurdling scream, which all of Jefferson had to have heard, jolted Hope. She swung around. It was Claire screaming. She'd discovered what Hope and Drew were looking at. She'd finally seen the body.

Jane came up to the three of them and gasped, grabbing hold of Hope's arm. "You've done it again. You've found another body."

Chapter Four

"Lionel's dead." Hope wasn't sure what made her state the obvious, but she did. Maybe it was because those two words kept repeating in her head as she tried to come to terms with finding his body. Her stomach clenched as she stared in disbelief at the body.

A man with a long list of enemies had had his life snuffed out right there in the parking lot. *Wait.* Her breath caught. Was the bloodstain on his shirt spreading wider? She elongated her neck to get a closer look. Was there a chance he was still alive?

She looked at Drew. He'd shifted into journalist mode without missing a beat. The shock of discovering Lionel was replaced with confidence and professionalism. He'd lowered next to Lionel and checked his carotid pulse.

"He's dead all right." Drew stood.

With her trembling hand, Hope pulled her purse forward on her body and reached inside for her cell phone. She needed to call the police. Report a murder. *Again.*

She was becoming a frequent caller to 9-1-1.

Before she could punch in the three numbers to

get help, voices approached, and she looked over her shoulder. No doubt Claire's scream and the small crowd at the Jaguar had alerted everyone outside the restaurant to something being wrong.

Something terribly wrong.

Meg rushed toward them. Her chin-length, dark blond hair bobbed, and a flash of annoyance crossed her face. Hope guessed Meg thought they were pulling some stunt to distract other teams from the hunt.

"We need to keep back. We can't contaminate the crime scene." Hope stepped away from Lionel's body to create a barrier between him and everyone else.

"Crime scene? What on earth has happened?" Meg tried to peer around Hope and see what the problem was.

"Yep, we need to keep back." Drew echoed Hope.

Hope glanced over at Drew. Now standing, he tapped on the keyboard on his phone.

"What are you doing?" Hope asked.

He didn't look up. He just kept typing. "My job."

"Hope's right. We need to keep this area cleared for the police to do their job." Jane moved away from the Jaguar.

"He's been shot! Look at all the blood! And the hole! I'm going to be sick." Claire clamped a hand over her mouth, spun around, and ran toward the restaurant.

"What's going on? Hope, what are you . . ." Meg stopped talking once she noticed Lionel's body.

Another scream pierced the shocked silence, and all heads turned to Elaine, who'd approached. No one had seen her until her scream. Standing a few feet away from her now-dead husband, she froze in place in her studded sandals as her face crumpled into despair and disbelief.

"Elaine, you shouldn't be here." Hope's heart broke for the woman. The sight of Lionel's lifeless, bloodied body was unsettling to her, so she couldn't imagine the impact it was having on his wife.

"Lionel! Oh my God! Lionel!" Elaine lunged forward, but Meg grabbed her arm.

"No. You can't go to him right now." Meg's hold tightened as Elaine struggled. "I could use help here!"

Hope rushed to Meg and helped keep Elaine from charging toward her husband. "Someone needs to call the police and we should go into the restaurant. There's nothing we can do for him now."

"What did you do?" Meg's voice was tight with accusation as she shifted her hold from Elaine to an embrace to comfort the crying woman.

"What? Me? Nothing. I found him." Now wasn't the time for their stupid feud to flare up again. Hope wanted to get Elaine away from her husband's body.

But Meg wasn't budging. "You just had to find another body, didn't you?"

"This isn't my fault."

Elaine yanked herself free from Meg. She huffed. Her grief-stricken face morphed into anger, and her voice raised to a level Hope had never heard before. "My husband is dead. Someone murdered him and you two are bickering? Seriously?" She huffed again as she tucked a lock of her bleached-blond hair behind an ear. To trek around town looking for treasures, she'd chosen a sleeveless, body-hugging, denim jumpsuit with a V-neckline that looked like it was stretched to its brink, thanks to Elaine's ample chest.

Elaine's momentary break from grieving shocked

Hope and, by the look of surprise on Meg's face, she was shocked too.

"When was the last time you saw your husband?" Drew approached with his cell phone.

Hope had seen him in action before. He'd have his handy-dandy recording app queued up for the exclusive interview.

Both Hope and Meg glared at Drew for his insensitivity, while Elaine dissolved into deep sobs.

"Drew, now's not the time," Hope scolded.

Drew ignored Hope. "Has your husband been threatened recently?"

Elaine shook her head; her tassel earrings dangled. She blinked several times and, within a moment, she'd composed herself enough to answer Drew's questions.

"Rupert. They had a huge fight." Elaine's voice hardened. "He threatened to kill my husband."

Drew inched closer to the widow. "Rupert Donnelly, his business partner?"

"Drew, Elaine's had a traumatic shock." Hope was certain her suggestion was falling on deaf ears because Drew didn't reply.

He didn't even look at her. She couldn't blame him for doing his job. He was the first reporter on the scene. But could he rely on the outbursts of a woman who was staring at her husband's dead body?

"Do you know why your husband was here tonight?" Norrie Jennings wormed her way into the fray, perched and ready to steal Drew's exclusive.

"This is my story." Drew tossed a quick, sharp look at his rival.

"We'll see." Norrie thrust her phone toward Elaine to record the interview. "Mrs. Whitcomb, were you planning to meet your husband here tonight?"

"Oh. My. God! Lionel! My husband is dead!"

The new outburst had all heads turning toward Miranda Whitcomb. Her fast walk turned into a full-on sprint toward the group. Matt Roydon, who was right behind, intercepted her.

"Let go of me! He's my husband! What happened?" Miranda cried out while struggling to break free of Matt's hold.

Hope felt for the woman, but it was best to keep her from the body. Matt worked out. He was strong, and keeping Miranda away from the scene didn't appear to be a challenge for him.

"Your husband? What's she talking about?" Elaine looked confused, despite her Botox injections.

"She's Miranda Whitcomb," Hope said.

"And you know how?" Meg raised a questioning brow as she rested a hand on her hip, waiting for an answer.

"She's a guest at the inn," Jane added.

"Hope, has anyone called the police yet?" Matt still restrained Miranda from rushing forward. A former police officer and now a practicing criminal defense attorney, he understood the importance of keeping a crime scene from becoming contaminating.

Though, Hope was certain, some contamination had already occurred.

She shook her head. She hadn't had the chance to complete the call. Lionel's murder was turning into a three-ring circus. "Could you?"

"What in the world is going on out here?" Rona Whitcomb came up to the group as a curious bystander, but when her gaze shifted from everyone around her to Lionel's body, she heaved a deep sob. "Lionel? Is he . . . dead?"

"Who are you?" Meg cast a suspicious look at Rona.

"His wife, Rona Whitcomb." She wiped away the flood of tears streaming down her face.

Hope and Drew and Jane shared a glance.

Three widows?

"This is insane. He's *my* husband. *My* husband is dead. You two are trying to pull some kind of scam. Well, it ain't going to work." Elaine wagged a manicured finger at the two interlopers.

Miranda squared her shoulders and stared daggers at Elaine. "I'm his legal wife. Our divorce wasn't finalized. I came here to settle things with him."

"Settle things? Like, murder him?" Elaine challenged.

"I did no such thing." Miranda lifted her hand and pointed a finger at Elaine. "You probably killed him because he lied to you."

Jane sidled up to Hope and whispered, "This should prove very interesting."

"Have a seat, Miss Early." Detective Sam Reid gestured to the chairs in front of the restaurant manager's desk and then closed the office door.

Within minutes of Matt calling 9-1-1, the first of the police vehicles arrived on the scene, and then Reid pulled up in his unmarked car. A uniformed officer situated the witnesses in one of the private dining rooms and stood with them to make sure they didn't discuss the incident.

Incident.

So clinical. So antiseptic. So much more pleasant than the word *murder.*

One by one, the witnesses entered the restaurant manager's office for an interview with Reid.

"Routine," one officer said.

"Standard procedure," another officer said.

"Déjà vu," Hope said.

She eased onto a chair in front of the desk, which was disheveled. Probably because the detective had commandeered it. A wire tray held papers and files haphazardly arranged, as if they'd been tossed in there in a hurry.

Beside the tray was a triple photograph frame, and it looked askew. The frame probably had been shifted from its original position when Reid settled at the desk. She leaned forward and adjusted the frame, angling it to where it made the most sense—in full view of the person seated at the desk.

That was when she noticed the small black notepad opened to a clean sheet of paper on the desk.

Hope was familiar with that notepad.

Reid had taken a few statements from her over the past several months. She wondered how many notepads he'd gone through since the first interview she'd had with him. Did he use one per case?

She gave herself a mental shake. What difference did it make? None. No difference. It was her mind trying to think about anything other than Lionel's dead body with a bullet wound and all the blood.

With her self-realization complete, she leaned into the chair. Reid walked to the desk and sat. She caught a gleam of amusement in his eyes. She had no idea her slight OCD tendencies amused him.

"I gave my statement to the first responding officer."

Reid pulled out a pen from the breast pocket of his

navy blazer. He had an extreme runner's body, the type
that bordered the fine line between healthy and obsessed. The structure of his blazer gave him some extra
bulk and also concealed the Glock that could level the
playing field against anyone bigger and stronger.

After he clicked his pen, he jotted down a note and
then looked at Hope.

The gleam of amusement she'd seen in his eyes
moments before had vanished and been replaced with
empathy. Without saying a word, he made it clear he
understood how difficult the evening had been for her.

Tension released from her neck and she felt like
she could breathe again. This time sitting across from
Reid was a different feeling than the others. He appeared to be more compassionate—in his own way.
And she wanted to help the detective catch the killer
any way she could. If repeating the horrific experience
of finding Lionel's body could help him, she'd gladly
tell the story over again. And again, if necessary.

"You and your team had gotten out of your vehicle
and all four of you headed toward the restaurant, correct?" he asked, getting back to business.

"Yes. We came here to get a napkin."

"The restaurant was okay with you taking a napkin?"

Hope nodded. "We'd return it tomorrow. The restaurant supports community events. They even donated a
prize for the winning team."

Reid jotted down more notes. About the napkin?
How was that pertinent to Lionel's murder investigation? Curious about what he was writing, she was
tempted to lean forward and sneak a peek, but she
didn't have the energy to attempt reading his scrib-
bled notes upside down. If he wanted to write about
napkins, who was she to question him?

Reid looked up. His expression was blank. Not blank in a clueless kind of way. Blank as in not giving any hint about what he was thinking kind of way. Though Hope had an idea of what the detective was thinking.

This wasn't the first time she had been questioned by him in a murder investigation. In fact, it was becoming a habit. One she needed to break.

"I see. Your team heads toward the entrance while you head toward Mr. Whitcomb's car. Why did you approach the car?"

Hope shrugged. "At first, I didn't know it was Lionel's car, though it looked familiar. Something seemed off. The car was parked up in the rear lot when there were plenty of spaces in the main parking lot. The driver's door was open, too. I guess I was curious."

Reid jotted down more notes. "You approached the vehicle and found Mr. Whitcomb on the ground, shot once and deceased."

Hope winced at the memory. Hearing Reid recap the events so efficiently unsettled her. And also made her want to add how her heart had slammed so hard against her chest, she considered it a miracle it still was inside her after she discovered Lionel's body. But all she could manage to say was, "Yes."

"Your team then joined you, and then the other teams, followed by Miranda Whitcomb and Rona Whitcomb?"

"Don't forget Elaine," Hope added.

"No, I haven't." He nodded and then jotted down more notes.

"Do you know why Miranda Whitcomb and Rona Whitcomb were at the restaurant?"

"No. Now that I think about it, it seems very convenient." What were the odds all three of Lionel's wives just happened to be at the restaurant when he was killed?

"I'm looking into the matter as a part of this investigation, Miss Early."

Hope shifted in her seat. She was getting antsy. She wanted to leave the restaurant and go home. There, she'd slip into her pajamas, grab the carton of chocolate chip ice cream out of the freezer, and snuggle with Bigelow. She wasn't sure if Princess would be willing to offer any comfort, and, not having owned a cat before, Hope wasn't sure if she could rely on the feline for sympathy. But she had things to wrap up at the Community Center. When she'd committed to helping, she hadn't expected the night to end with murder.

"Yesterday I ran into Miranda when I came out of The Coffee Clique. She was texting, not paying attention to where she was going, and walked right into me. After she apologized, we chatted a little. She said she was here on family business. Then she took a call. She stepped away, but I heard what she said."

"What did you hear?"

"She told the person they had to meet, and she wouldn't be put off any longer. Something about waiting thirty years. Then she said 'Friday,' and that she was dead serious."

Reid dipped his head and made more notes. "Did Ms. Whitcomb say anything else?"

Hope shook her head. "No. She walked away. Then, this morning, I met Rona Whitcomb."

"You meet a lot of people," Reid said.

"I do. Rona was out for a morning walk and ended up at the Olsen property. She said she was lost, so I directed her back to Main Street."

"Did she say why she's here in Jefferson?"

"Family business. We didn't talk for long. I had to leave for the magazine and she headed back to the inn."

Reid closed his notepad. "Did you see anyone in the rear parking lot as you approached the car? Around the building perhaps?"

Hope thought for a moment, replaying the events to just before finding Lionel's body. Her walk from her car, negotiating the potholes, the glow of the light by the closed kitchen door, and Lionel's car. Nothing seemed out of the ordinary.

"No. The door to the kitchen was closed. It was only Lionel. Do you think his death has something to do with the charges he was facing?"

"Thank you for your statement, Miss Early. Please don't forget this is an official police matter and your help isn't needed with the investigation."

Reid was chastising her, and she'd done nothing wrong. Except, she'd allowed her curiosity to lead her to a dead body. Reid might have had a point. Not too long ago, on two separate occasions, her inquisitiveness had led her into the crosshairs of two killers. Perhaps Reid's preemptive lecture was a good thing. Maybe she'd listen this time.

"I understand. Hopefully, you'll find the person responsible soon. Oh, sorry, I did forget to mention one thing."

Reid nodded for her to continue.

"Elaine said Rupert Donnelly threatened to kill Lionel."

"When did she say that?"

"Right after we found Lionel."

Reid jotted down the nugget of information. "Did she say anything else?"

"No. She was very upset, as you can imagine." Hope shimmied to the edge of her chair. "Can I go now?"

"Yes. If I have any further questions, I'll be in touch."

"I'm always happy to help." Hope stood and walked to the closed door. "One more thing." Hope looked over her shoulder. "The key was still in the ignition."

"So?"

Hope lifted her shoulders. "Nothing, I guess. Wasn't Lionel planning on coming into the restaurant? Why else would he have come here? But he drove to the far section of the parking lot, left the keys in the ignition, got out of his car, and then was shot. Sounds like he had a meeting set up with the killer."

"Remember what I said, Miss Early, about interfering in my investigation. Good night." With a firm nod, he lowered his head and checked his cell phone.

Hope pulled open the door and stepped out into the narrow hallway. It held several closed doors and the opening to the restrooms. A man's voice drew her attention and she stopped, glancing down the short hallway between the two bathrooms.

All Hope could see was his back. His face was turned away. Though his stature, tall and beefy, and his salt-and-pepper hair looked familiar. He held a cell phone close to his ear.

"Shot. How the frig did this happen? No. Listen. We can't let anyone find out. Understand?" His voice was familiar too.

Rupert Donnelly!

"Is there a problem, Miss Early?" Detective Reid called out from the office doorway.

Hope snapped around toward the detective and then glanced back to Rupert Donnelly, who'd looked over his shoulder at Hope.

"I have to go," Rupert said into the phone and gave Hope a dark look.

"No, nothing, Detective Reid." Hope turned and proceeded along the hallway and walked to the restaurant's main entrance, where the hostess stood with a group of scavenger hunters.

The topic of their conversation was Lionel's murder. No surprise there. Hope ducked around them to avoid being dragged into the discussion. On her way to the exit, she spotted her neighbors Leila Manchester and Dorie Baxter seated at a table in the dining room. The jovial mood they'd exuded earlier about the hunt had diminished, replaced by a somberness. The evening had taken a morbid turn.

A dead body wasn't on the Scavenger Hunt list.

Hope worried the murder would forever mar the event. Then she chided herself for thinking about the event while a life had been snuffed out. Though many would argue the victim wasn't the most liked person in Jefferson.

Lost in her thoughts of the deadly turn of events, she wasn't watching where she was walking and slammed right into Matt Roydon's chest.

"Hey. You okay?" He looked down on her with concern as he steadied her with his hands. Now a weekender, he split his time between his law practice in the city and his new home in town. This was his first Scavenger Hunt in Jefferson. Finding a dead body during the hunt wasn't the best first impression.

She drew back and offered a weak smile that only made him look more concerned. She sighed. She hated having people worry about her.

"I'm fine . . . I think." She extricated herself from Matt's hold.

"Sorry to have to tell you this, but you don't look fine. Let me drive you home and we can pick up your car tomorrow." Matt reached out his hand and stroked Hope's arm. "Come on. Let's go."

She worked her lower lip between her teeth, wishing Ethan were there. She'd glimpsed him on her way to talk with Reid. Where was he now?

"I can't believe this happened tonight. Of all nights. The Scavenger Hunt has been a tradition for years, and now it will be remembered for Lionel Whitcomb's murder."

"Sad to say, but you may be right. I can't believe you stumbled upon another dead body. A murder, no less." Matt gave a wry smile, softening his strong, angular face.

Hope rolled her eyes and regretted it. The stress of the evening, compounded with exhaustion, made her irritable. "It's not like I went looking for a murder victim."

"Really? I heard you broke away from your team to go to the car."

"Everyone's making a bigger deal of this than it actually is. I saw something I thought was odd, and I went to check it out. And there he was. Dead."

"You're making light of the situation."

"I guess I am. I just found a man shot to death and had to deal with those three hysterical women. You saw, there was almost another crime scene between them." She exhaled a breath. "I need a drink."

"Wine?"

"I thought you knew me. A latte with an extra shot."

"The Coffee Clique?"

"Yes, please."

Matt extended his hand and guided Hope to the

exit. Outside, the night was heavy with humidity and lit up by strobe lights. For sure, not an average night in Jefferson. Hope took in the whole messy scene. Then she caught sight of two technicians wheeling a gurney toward the Jaguar.

They'd come for Lionel's body.

Hope shuddered. She'd barely had time to mentally regroup when Norrie Jennings blindsided her and Matt. Norrie came out of nowhere with her cell phone poised, ready to record Hope's official comment.

Weren't the police keeping the press back?

"Hope, what was it like finding Lionel Whitcomb's body?" Norrie fell into pace alongside Hope and Matt.

"Miss Early has no comment," Matt said.

"Are you her legal counsel?" Norrie asked.

"No comment," Matt said again.

Drew bustled over, putting up a protective hand. "It's been a traumatic night for her. Leave her alone."

Norrie dropped her hands to her side. "You can't tell me what to do. I'm a reporter. I'll talk to whoever I want to."

"Not my friend you won't."

"Let's break this up. Hope has nothing to say. This is an ongoing investigation, and she's not at liberty to discuss what happened with the press." Ethan had swooped in and put himself between Hope and Norrie.

Hope exhaled a whoosh of air. Ethan's presence was a lifeline she hadn't realized she needed. Her head was jumbled with thoughts of the event, the screams, Reid's questions, and her answers. Did she say the right things? Did she tell him everything she knew? Why was she second-guessing herself? Why did she have to check out Lionel's car? She wanted to reach out and grab Ethan to steady herself. But she couldn't.

He was on duty. She forced herself to maintain her composure and not crack.

At least not yet.

"Do you have any viable leads?" Norrie shifted from Hope to Ethan in a blink of an eye, making Hope feel like yesterday's news and relieved at the same time.

"Please be respectful to the witnesses. Discovering a dead body is upsetting, and no one needs your hounding," Ethan said. Norrie opened her mouth to say something, but he cut her off. "I'm serious, Miss Jennings. Leave the witnesses alone."

"Fine. For now." Norrie relented, after flashing a dark look at Ethan.

Ethan nodded. "We'll have a statement ready in an hour."

"I hope you'll have something to say other than 'no comment.'" Norrie huffed, then turned. "It's not like it's the first body she's ever found." She tramped away.

Drew smiled. "She's so pushy."

Ethan shifted his attention to Drew. "I'm going to have to ask you to do the same."

Drew's face dropped and his mouth gaped open, while his gaze shot back and forth between Hope and Ethan. "What? Hope and I are friends."

"Drew, I'm tired and I want to go home." Hope looked at Matt. "Can I have a rain check for the latte? And I can drive myself home. I'm okay. Really."

"Text me if you change your mind. Good night, Ethan." Matt gave Hope a quick hug and then walked back to the restaurant. She suspected he was going to check on the rest of his team.

"I'll write up what I have so far. See you in an hour, Ethan." Drew shoved his hands into his pants pockets and followed Matt. To his credit, he seemed to take the news Hope was off-limits in stride. But she had a feeling he'd be showing up at her house later for a little visit.

"You holding up okay?" Ethan reached out for Hope's arm.

She shrugged. "I guess."

"I seem to remember you saying nothing ever happens at the Scavenger Hunt."

"Looks like I was wrong. You gonna arrest me?"

"Only if you interfere with the investigation."

Hope half-smiled. "Reid has made it clear I'm to stay out of it completely. I assured him I would. After all, it's not like Elaine and I are friends. But I am curious about Miranda and Rona. I told Reid everything I know about them and about the conversations I had with them."

"Conversations? When did you talk to them?"

"Miranda, yesterday. You don't remember me telling you when I got home with the cinnamon bun and before I told you I'd grill a steak?"

Ethan nodded, and a flicker in his eyes told Hope he recalled their conversation. Or he only remembered the food. She wasn't sure.

"Anyway, this morning I had the chance to talk to Rona. I wonder why they both came to Jefferson now. And I just saw Rupert Donnelly in the restaurant. Elaine said he'd threatened to kill Lionel. Do you think it's a coincidence he's here tonight?"

"It's none of your business."

"I know, I know. As curious as I am, I'm happy to leave this whole mess to Reid and your department.

Because it's going to be ugly with those women claiming to be Lionel's wives."

"Thanks." Ethan's lips set in a grim line.

Hope didn't envy him. He'd not only be investigating the murder, but he'd have to sort out the status of those three women's relationship to Lionel and handle the new mayor. Maretta Kingston had zero experience dealing with a serious crime like murder. "Reid interviewed Claire and Jane, so you can take them home."

"We first have to go to the Community Center. Not every team is involved in this mess. We still have to award the winning team."

Ethan pulled Hope in for a hug. "It's not your team this year."

"Nope. I guess our winning streak had to end at some point." She molded into his embrace.

His arms wrapped her in safety and security. Her face pressed against his broad chest, his heartbeat calming.

"Chief!" an officer called out from the main entrance of the restaurant.

Hope silently cursed as Ethan's embrace lightened and he gave her a kiss on the cheek. "Sorry. I have to go. I'll call you later." With the promise made, he jogged off to join the other officer and they headed back to Lionel's car.

Hope adjusted the strap of her purse on her shoulder and walked toward her vehicle. She paused and looked back at the crime scene. She wasn't a fan of Lionel Whitcomb, but he didn't deserve to die the way he had. Shot down in an empty parking lot and left to bleed out. Someone hated him enough to lure him there and take his life. Hope guessed that was what happened when you built a life on deceit and bribery.

Chapter Five

Hope yawned again, interrupting the cracking of the second egg for her Double Chocolate and Walnut Muffin recipe. Her sleep had been disturbed every hour on the hour. Okay, maybe it wasn't every hour, but, standing there in the middle of her kitchen with heavy eyelids, it sure felt like it'd been every hour. Each time she closed her eyes and drifted off to sleep, the sound of Claire's screams and flashes of Lionel's body popped into her head.

With the egg cracked into a small glass prep bowl, she was ready to add both eggs into her muffin batter. Baking helped clear her head, and she desperately needed that.

She added one egg at a time, mixing after each one to incorporate, but being careful not to overmix because she didn't want tough muffins.

With her spoon, she beat in the eggs. To make muffin batter, she preferred to mix by hand rather than using one of her three high-end electric mixers. For most people, having three mixers would be overkill, but because she worked on multiple recipes a day to keep up with her blog schedule, she needed more than one. Besides, she'd received one from the manufacturer when they sponsored her fall baking guide last year, complete with a giveaway. One of her readers won a limited-edition mixer in time for the holiday baking season.

Hope focused on the pretty design of the mixer to keep her mind from drifting back to last night and what had caused her to toss and turn.

She yawned again. When she'd checked her alarm clock at half past four, she realized it was a losing battle to try to fall back to sleep. She slipped out of bed, leaving Bigelow curled up at the foot of the bed, and went downstairs. She brewed an extra-strong pot of coffee. With a filled cup, she searched the internet for stories on Lionel.

Not exactly an ideal way to start the day.

The stories about his untimely death recapped the criminal charges he'd been facing and his long history of developing controversial properties. Those projects were mostly residential, and most of the opposition came from local organizations charged with protecting open space in their communities. Though Lionel always got the okay to develop. Just like he had in Jefferson.

Maybe his death hadn't been connected to his legal problems. Maybe somebody had enacted revenge for a past deed. Whatever the reason for his death, Hope promised she wouldn't become involved, but there was no reason she couldn't be curious about the murder just like everybody else in town.

She opened the container the chocolate chips were in and reached for a cup measure. After she scooped out the chips, she tossed them into the mixing bowl. She considered for a moment: was that really enough chocolate chips? She shook her head. No, it wasn't. She reached her hand into the container and sprinkled in a handful of the morsels. The spontaneous addition was because she believed deep in her heart chocolate made everything better.

Next, she added a heaping amount of chopped walnuts. She combined the new additions into the batter with her spatula. The thick, rich, packed-full-of-chocolaty-goodness came together, and her mind let go of the horrible event of the night before.

After dividing the batter into muffin tins with an ice cream scoop, Hope set them in the top oven to bake for twenty-three minutes and busied herself with cleaning up. Within a matter of minutes, the soothing smell of chocolate filled the kitchen and her mood started to brighten.

See, chocolate made everything better.

The clock on the oven's control panel showed Hope the muffins would be ready just as her neighbors Leila Manchester and Dorie Baxter would be passing by her house on their three-mile walk.

Every morning, the senior ladies headed out for their walk, come rain or shine or nor'easter. Whether bundled up in layers or stripped down to shorts and sleeveless performance tops, they got in their steps. Hope didn't doubt the events of last night would deter them from their walk, but it probably would be a somber outing because both ladies were present when Lionel's body was found.

Another image Hope couldn't shake was the look on their faces while they sat in the restaurant's dining room. Horrified and grief-stricken, like everyone else last night. While they enjoyed gossip a little too much, they were sweet women who shouldn't have had to come so close to murder.

With the muffins baking, Hope started a fresh pot of coffee.

By the time the coffee was brewed, the muffins were out of the oven and on a cooling rack. Another glance at the oven's clock showed she had just minutes to spare. In a blur of activity, thanks to an unexpected burst of energy, Hope filled a carafe with the coffee and set it, along with cups and a pitcher of milk, on a tray. Next, she filled a cloth-lined basket with the muffins. When she reached the French doors to the patio, Bigelow was awake and sniffing around for a treat.

His nose pointed up to the tray and his brown eyes were laser-focused on the basket of muffins, but, considering their main ingredient was chocolate, he wouldn't be getting any. She dashed out to the patio and set the tray down on the table, then hurried back inside to grab two peanut butter biscuits for Bigelow. She used them to lure him outside so she could keep a lookout for her neighbors.

Right on time. Hope spotted the women approaching her house. Bigelow was busy devouring a biscuit and not interested in visitors, leaving Hope to walk alone to her front yard and wave the women down.

"Good morning, ladies." She shielded her eyes from the bright sun. "How was your walk?"

"It's good to get out and get some fresh air." Leila came to a stop. She looked bright and crisp in a pair of aqua-colored Bermuda shorts and a coordinating striped top. A white visor topped her head of silver hair and shielded her eyes from the sun.

"I've just taken a batch of Double Chocolate and

Walnut Muffins out of the oven. And I have a fresh pot of coffee. Would you like to join me?"

"Absolutely." Dorie came to a halt beside Leila and checked her fitness tracker. Dressed in a similar outfit, she'd chosen a headband to keep her silver hair off her face. She was the model for senior fitness. When she wasn't walking the neighborhood, she swam at the gym and took yoga classes at the Community Center.

"Good thing we did our walk." Leila followed Hope, along with Dorie, around the side of the house to the patio.

Finished with his biscuit, Bigelow looked up and, when he saw Leila and Dorie, popped up and trotted over with his tail wagging to greet the ladies. Both women obliged before they took their seats at the table, and Hope filled the three coffee cups.

"This is a nice treat." Leila plucked a muffin from the basket and pulled back its wrapper.

"I think after what happened last night, we need a little pick-me-up." Hope stirred a dash of milk into her coffee. She wasn't sure what cup number it was, but she was certain the caffeine hadn't kicked in yet.

"It was a horrible way to end the Scavenger Hunt for all of us, but I can't imagine what it was like for you, Hope. After all, you found Lionel's body." Dorie took a drink of her coffee and then helped herself to a muffin. She glanced at Bigelow, who sat between her and Leila, and gave her sad, puppy dog eyes as if he hadn't eaten in days. "Chocolate isn't good for pups."

"Bigelow, come." Hope patted her thigh, and Bigelow gave her a concerned look, as if he was worried he'd miss out on a falling piece of muffin. He had a bad case of FOMO: fear of missing out. But she guessed most dogs did, while Princess couldn't have cared less.

She made an appearance briefly for breakfast and then took off to one of her hiding spaces for her morning nap. Hope patted her thigh again, and Bigelow snuffled as he stood and walked toward her. Clearly, he would have the last word. When he reached Hope, he sat next to her chair and slid down to relax on the stone patio, but he didn't take his eyes off the table. Just in case.

"I heard Maretta lost it when she was informed about the murder." Leila took another bite of her muffin. She set it on a napkin and chewed as she leaned in to her chair.

Dorie nodded as she wiped her hands free of crumbs. "I heard she whined about the selfies with the mayor. Apparently, she was overwhelmed by the volume of people."

"Milo never complained," Leila said.

Dorie shaded her eyes against the sun with her hand and gave her friend an irritated glance. Hope had seen the look before between the two women. Friends for decades, they bickered like an old married couple.

Leila straightened, lifted her cup, and propped both elbows on the table. "Don't look at me like that. Milo was a good mayor."

Dorie shook her head. "It doesn't matter now, does it?"

Leila shrugged after finishing her drink. "Poor Elaine. The shock of seeing her husband and those two women claiming to be married to Lionel. How on earth is it possible? You can't be married to more than one person at a time."

"They're called bigamists, Leila. Apparently, Lionel was one." Dorie refilled her cup.

"When I was at the Community Center, I noticed Elaine missing from her team. Did either of you see her arrive?" Hope bit into her muffin and her eyes fluttered with happiness. The deep, rich flavor layered from the cocoa powder and melted chocolate chips, combined with the crunch of the walnuts, was heavenly.

Dorie and Leila looked at each other and nodded. "We noticed also," Dorie said.

"I saw Meg's team leave the Community Center. Elaine wasn't with them. But they were all together when we arrived at the gas station to pump gas for a stranger. You should have seen the strange looks Matt got. He's such a gentleman and pumped for us while Meg had Amy pumping gas. Elaine sat in Meg's mini-van with her arms crossed over her chest. She didn't seem to be having fun."

Hope took another bite of her muffin. She chewed slowly and wondered how late Elaine had been to join up with her assigned team.

"Do you think Elaine killed her husband and that's why she was late Friday night?" Dorie leaned forward and rested her elbows on the table.

"I don't know, Dorie. The spouse usually is a person of interest. I'm sure the police will figure it out soon enough," Hope said.

"I hope it's figured out before anyone else gets killed." An edge crept into Leila's voice. "If Elaine is the killer, at least we know there won't be another murder. But if it wasn't her, will the killer strike again?"

The three women went silent, and Hope could practically hear an ominous and dramatic soundtrack playing over Leila's question. She cleared her throat.

"Elaine is hardly a killer. Maybe it was a robbery

gone bad and Lionel was just in the wrong place at the wrong time." Hope hoped she was right. Their cozy little town had had enough drama for a lifetime recently. What were the odds of that happening again?

Hope arrived at the Merrifield Inn as promised. After dropping Jane off at the inn following the Scavenger Hunt last night, Jane had told Hope to stop by first thing in the morning. Hope didn't need to ask what for because she knew her friend too well. Over tea, they'd review what had happened at the restaurant.

She opened the front door and stepped inside. Voices drifted from the dining room, and the aroma of bacon made her mouth water.

She turned into the dining room and her appetite waned at the sight of Maretta Kingston. Dressed in a gingham shift dress with a pleated ruffle neckline, the dress bordered between feminine and preppy, not typically Maretta's style. She was more the buttoned-up, drab kind of gal. The abrupt change in fashion style for the sixtysomething woman gave Hope pause.

Jefferson's new mayor ate her breakfast while reading a newspaper. It was easy to blame Maretta for Claire's bout with melancholy. But Hope reminded herself the majority of the town voted for Maretta. They were the ones to blame. She gave herself a mental shake. She didn't want to blame anyone. She only wanted her sister to be happy again.

With the reminder front and center in her mind, Hope pushed off and walked toward Jefferson's mayor. Her focus was on an article she was reading and she didn't seem to hear Hope approach. Or, if she did, she chose not to acknowledge Hope's presence beside the table.

"Good morning, Maretta." For a fleeting second, Hope considered calling her Madam Mayor. But that seemed over the top.

Maretta's gaze shifted from the newspaper to Hope. She peered at Hope over her bifocals. "Do you really think it's a good morning?"

"It's a figure of speech."

Maretta gave Hope a flat stare and Hope sighed. Maretta made nothing easy.

"It's been nonstop since I woke up this morning. Phone calls. Emails. Text messages. The media is all over Lionel's murder. You have no idea how much time this will take up. I suspect Detective Reid will understand and be willing to work extra-hard to wrap up this case quickly." Maretta lifted the linen napkin from her lap and dabbed the corners of her mouth and then reached for her coffee cup.

Hope replayed Maretta's sentence just to confirm she had heard her correctly. Maretta believed being besieged by phone calls from the media was comparable to having to investigate a murder. The woman was clueless about how hard it was to investigate, but Hope had firsthand experience, and tracking down a killer was no easy feat.

"Murder is simply unseemly." Maretta set the delicate, floral-pattern cup back down in its saucer.

"I agree. The police have been working around the clock since . . . I discovered his body." Hope gulped.

Maretta tilted up her head. "Since you've moved back to Jefferson, there have been several murders. Whatever was unleashed when you came back here, I really wish it would be contained, because I have no desire to continue dealing with murders in *my* town."

"I'm confident, as a reasonable adult, you can't possibly blame me for the murders." It was a stretch to refer to Maretta as reasonable, but Hope didn't want to make the situation worse.

Maretta scoffed.

"I'm certain Ethan and his department are doing the best they can to find the killer and bring him or her to justice."

"As they should be. Chief Cahill had better find the murderer soon. It's bad publicity for the town." Maretta stood and dropped her napkin on the table. "I have work to do, in addition to dealing with the press." She snatched her plain black purse from the back of the chair and swept by Hope and stomped out of the dining room.

A moment later, Hope heard the front door open and close.

"Wow! She's something."

Hope's head turned at the sound of Rona's voice. She hadn't noticed her when she entered the dining room. If she had, maybe she would've bypassed Maretta and saved herself from being accused of unleashing some kind of evil in town.

"Sorry. I didn't mean to eavesdrop, but she wasn't exactly quiet. Who is she? How come she's blaming you for the murder?"

"She's Maretta Kingston, the town mayor, and it's a long story." Hope approached the table for two in the corner. Rona's swollen, red eyes were far more welcoming than Maretta's had been to Hope.

"She's the mayor? Interesting choice. Forgive me. Would you like to join me?" Rona gestured to the chair across from her. She looked like her night hadn't been any more peaceful than Hope's. Her blond hair, with pink highlights, was flat and messy. Gone were the sculpted spikes from yesterday, and a veil of exhaustion covered her makeup-free face.

"Thank you." Hope pulled out the chair and sat. "How are you doing?"

Rona glanced down at her plate of scrambled eggs and bacon, which looked untouched. "I feel numb. I can't wrap my head around what happened." She looked up. Sadness radiated off of her.

"I'm sorry for your loss."

"That's kind of you to say." Rona gave a weak smile. "I think you're the only person, other than sweet Jane and Sally, who have acknowledged my loss. I guess most people don't think it's much of a loss. Miranda has refused to speak with me, and Elaine treated me like I was invisible last night."

"I think everyone is in shock. Between the murder and you and Miranda showing up and claiming to still be married to Lionel."

"I know how it looks. But I'm not lying. Our divorce wasn't completed."

"If you don't mind me asking, why did you come to Jefferson after all these years?" Figuring she would be staying for a while, Hope rested her purse on her lap.

When Rona reached for the teapot and filled the empty cup in front of Hope, she was certain she was staying and about to hear how Rona became wife number two.

After setting down the pot, Rona lifted her cup and took a sip. "I've been looking for him for years, and a few weeks ago, I was online and a friend shared a Facebook post from, of all people, Elaine Whitcomb."

Hope took a drink of the tea. Earl Grey. One of her favorite blends. "What kind of post?"

"A beauty video. Elaine was showing how to contour cheekbones. I know, silly, right? But I was bored and it was interesting. I looked at her profile. She has absolutely no security settings, and then I saw a photo of her and Lionel. *My* Lionel. I read through her posts. She bragged about her house, her car, her husband. *My* husband. It didn't take me long to find out where Lionel was living, and here I am. And he turns up dead. Just my luck."

Social media was a huge part of Hope's career. It was a way for people to find the information they needed, like a recipe or a DIY project. There was also the dark side of social media, stalkers and the like. If Elaine had taken a few precautions with her security online, Rona might not have been seated across from Hope.

"You've been looking for him since he left you?" Hope asked.

Rona leaned back. "You ask a lot of questions."

Hope dipped her head. Rona was politely saying she was nosy.

"I'm curious by nature, but I understand if you prefer not to talk about it." Hope took another drink of her tea and waited for Rona to decide.

"I don't mind talking about it. It's not a secret. I was young and a hopeless romantic. I never thought my marriage would end. Until it did. Out of nowhere, Lionel packed his bags. After he left, I hired a private investigator. The PI was very handsome. And I was young and vulnerable. One thing led to another. I guess I stopped looking for Lionel because I was having a good time with Jake. Then I met this amazing artist."

"You fell in love?"

Rona's cheeks flushed. "I did."

Hope smiled. Rona had found happiness after her disastrous marriage. The two of them had something in common. Both were living testaments that there was life after a divorce. A wonderful life.

"I fell hard. So hard, I moved to Italy with Edward. We lived there in pure bliss until he died."

"I'm sorry."

"We had a good life. After his death, I came back to the States. His death reminded me of how short life was. I needed to get my affairs in order, and top on the list was finding my no-good husband, completing our divorce, and moving on with my life."

"But you didn't know where he was until you found Elaine on Facebook?"

"Correct. Once I located him, I decided to come here and confront him. Now, I don't know what will happen. Miranda claims her divorce wasn't complete either, so she was still legally married to him at the time of our wedding. I don't think I'll get anything."

"Why not hire an attorney to contact Lionel?"

Rona shrugged. "I wanted to face him. To find out why he left and then collect what was owed to me. I make no bones about that. But I didn't kill Lionel. Why would I? It would just make the situation more complicated. And make me a suspect, which Detective Reid insinuated."

Hope finished her tea. Rona was right. Killing Lionel wouldn't get her what she wanted. She stood a better chance of settling with Lionel if he were alive. Now she'd have to deal with the estate and complicated would be an understatement of how things could turn through litigation.

"One more question, if you don't mind. Why were you at the Avery Bistro last night?"

"A gal has to eat." Rona flashed a smile.

Hope's cell phone pinged, and she murmured an apology, then pulled it out. It was a text from Claire.

Ready to go in ten minutes.

Earlier, Hope had suggested retail therapy for both of them. Claire had sounded excited about the outing, but she had to get the kids off to school before she could go.

"I'm sorry. I have somewhere to be right now." She'd have to find Jane and arrange to catch up later. Hope slipped her phone back into her purse and then pulled out her business card and handed it to Rona. "If you need anything or want to talk, call me."

Rona smiled. "*Hope at Home*? You appeared on some reality baking show on the Culinary Channel. I didn't know you lived here. Small world."

"It most certainly is." Hope stood.

"You do believe me?"

Hope wasn't sure what to believe. She could imagine a confrontation between Rona and Lionel getting heated, and Rona lashing out at her bigamist of a husband. Lionel had a way of bringing the worst out in people with his obnoxious personality.

"I believe you've told me the truth." Hope walked out of the dining room a little regretful she couldn't say what Rona wanted her to say. She hated to admit it, but her sister had been right about her. She was a people pleaser.

Chapter Six

"Whew! I think I not only got in my daily step goal but then some." Claire flashed a victorious smile when she claimed a table in the mall's crowded food court. She dropped to a chair and set down her bevy of shopping bags next to her.

"I wouldn't be surprised if you did. I think you went into every store." Hope followed her sister and set the tray on the table. She'd ordered them coffee and grilled chicken salads for lunch. They needed to take a break and refuel before continuing with their impromptu shopping spree. She slid off the handles of her shopping bags, which hung off her wrists. They landed on the floor and she landed on a chair.

"Like you didn't also?" Claire gestured to the bags beside Hope's chair.

"Point taken. Here, eat your lunch." Hope handed one bowl to her sister, along with a small container of dressing. She opened her utensil packet and the lid of her salad bowl. "Are you feeling better?"

Claire nodded. "I am. Thanks. This is what I needed."

"Running up your credit card bill?"

Claire shook her head, and her shoulder-length

blond hair swung. For their outing, she wore a pair of navy ankle pants paired with a polka-dot blouse and flats. Claire was an experienced shopper and knew comfortable footwear was a must when shopping in the mall. Hope was glad to see her sister out of those heinous shorts and unflattering clogs.

"No. Getting out."

"Out of your house? Yes. Good idea." Hope tossed her salad to combine the peppercorn ranch dressing she chose. Unlike her sister, she didn't opt for her dressing on the side.

Claire drizzled half the vinaigrette dressing over her salad. "I'm talking about getting out of my head. Last night was a good start, but then it ended with Lionel's murder. The bright side is, I wasn't thinking about losing the election. Rather, the whole mess is now Maretta's responsibility. I truly dodged a bullet."

Hope grimaced.

"Oops. Sorry. Poor choice of words." Claire pierced a tomato chunk with her fork and chewed.

"I think you're the only one who came out of last night with a bright side. But I'm glad you have."

Claire reached for her coffee and took a drink. "To be honest, I don't believe the funk I've been in has been all about losing the election."

"What do you mean?" Hope asked after she swallowed a piece of chicken.

"Running for mayor took me way out of my comfort zone. Real estate has been my career since I graduated college."

"I get it. When I appeared on *The Sweet Taste of Success*, I was out of my comfort zone. I didn't know what was in store for me or how my life would change."

"Exactly! Galvanizing a political campaign challenged my organizational skills and my resolve, and also challenged me to look beyond selling houses for the rest of my life."

Her sister's reflection of her past and contemplation of what the future held for her resonated with Hope because she'd gone through the same experience.

The difference between the sisters was that after Hope's appearance on the reality show, her marriage had imploded, while Claire's marriage strengthened. Claire's husband stood by her, worked as hard as she did during the campaign, and consoled her on election night. A twinge of envy pricked at Hope. The night the national TV audience saw Hope lose the grand prize on the reality show, her husband was nowhere to be found. He was off with his new mistress, and Hope sat alone in their Upper West Side condo.

Hope rested her elbows on the table, her chin on her clasped hands. "May I offer you some advice?"

"You mean I could stop you?"

"Ha ha. Hilarious."

Claire tossed her head back and laughed. "What is your sisterly advice?"

"Follow your heart."

Claire's face grew serious. "You know what Mom and Dad would say about your advice."

"Yes, I know. I got the lecture." Hope dropped her fork and channeled her mother's *tone.* The one that accompanied all her lectures. "'We didn't raise you to throw away all the education you received or toss away your goals on a whim.'"

"'Play it safe,'" Claire added.

Hope nodded. "Safe would've been going back to magazine publishing, not choosing to blog full-time."

"It's been worth it, though, right? Would you make the same decision again?"

"Absolutely. It's been worth all the sacrifice, hard

work, long hours, and juggling to stay afloat. And today, I'm in a position where brands come to me, like *Cooking Now*, and my eProducts are selling well enough for me to afford this little shopping spree without too much guilt." She glanced at her bags. She'd have to hustle to pay off her credit card bill, but she loved each purchase she'd made. And it'd been a while since she'd splurged on herself.

"I have to figure out what to do next."

"Whatever you decide, you'll succeed. Just go for it."

"I'm not sure right now what *it* is."

Hope reached for her coffee and took a sip.

She had confidence her sister would figure out what to do next with her life. And she was confident their mother would chime in with her opinion.

Hope pushed open her back door and stepped inside. She negotiated her way through the mudroom with too many shopping bags and a hyper Bigelow welcoming her home. His toenails tapped on the wide pumpkin pine floorboards she'd salvaged from Vermont after she purchased the house. Prior to installation of the antique flooring, the kitchen and family room had been a hodgepodge of bland hardwood. It lacked the contemporary country vibe she wanted.

She reached the island and set down the bags and dropped her purse on the countertop. Bigelow wasn't patient. He wanted affection ASAP. She obliged by swooping down and lavishing her pup with kisses and pats. His eyes warmed with contentment.

With a final scratch on his head, Hope stood up and walked over to the coffee maker. Bigelow busied himself inspecting the bags by sticking his head in each one and sniffing.

"Hey, you're being rude." She darted back and shooed him from her purchases. The dog backed away, then slid down, resting his head on his front legs and giving Hope sad-dog eyes. She melted, as usual. "You're curious. I know the feeling." She returned to the coffee maker and prepared a pot of hazelnut coffee.

With the coffee brewing, she opened the refrigerator. She was starving, despite having lunch at the mall. Shopping for most of the day worked up an appetite and, lucky for her, being a food blogger meant there was always something to eat. At eye level was an apple pie.

She grabbed hold of the pie plate and pulled it out.

She'd been working on apple recipes, and her trip to a local orchard a few days earlier had yielded her dozens of apples to make into all kinds of recipes—sweet and savory.

She set the pie on the island. She moved to an upper cabinet to pull out a mug and then retrieved a knife to cut into the pie. When the coffee maker beeped, she filled her cup and savored a drink. She was now fortified for what the rest of the day brought.

There were emails to read, ads to create for her blog, and recipes to proofread for *The Sweet Taste of Success* cookbook.

The reality show had announced it would publish a cookbook featuring recipes from its season one competitors. She'd hesitated in rekindling her relationship with the show because she was all about moving forward and not looking back, but she was contractually obligated to take part. A bonus was that the book's release could help promote her blog.

Before she could take another sip, the doorbell rang, sending Bigelow into excitable-greeter mode and tearing out of the family room. Hope's mug landed on the island with a thump, coffee sloshing over the brim, and she raced after her dog. She nabbed him by the collar a nanosecond before he jumped and scratched the front door.

"Sit!" she commanded, but Bigelow barked and tugged forward. "Sit!" Her second command got his attention, and the doorbell rang again. She looked over her shoulder at the door. "Just a moment!" She turned back to Bigelow. "Sit!"

Bigelow finally settled into a proper sit.

"Good boy," she praised.

The doorbell rang again.

"Just a moment!" With Bigelow situated, she pulled open the door, curious to see who the impatient person on her porch was.

It had better not be another window salesman.

Once the warm weather came, an army of door-to-door salesmen headed out to sell new windows to homeowners in her area. Every week brought a new one. What irked her the most was, not one of them noticed she'd already replaced all the old windows with new, energy-efficient ones.

"What took you so long? I've been standing out here forever." Elaine propped on her hip and pursed her lips.

Hope would've preferred the window salesman. "What are you doing here?"

"You won't believe what's going on. Lionel's death. It's a nightmare." Elaine entered the house without an invitation and continued straight through to the family room. Having been in the house only one time before, Hope was surprised she remembered the layout.

Hope closed the door and then released Bigelow from his sit position. It impressed her that he hadn't jumped all over Elaine, though she wouldn't have been too harsh on him if he had.

She caught up with her unexpected guest in the family room.

"Do I smell hazelnut coffee? I'd love a cup. It's been one of those days."

Hope offered an obliging smile. "Coming right up." Before she prepared the coffee for Elaine, she wiped up the spill she'd made moments before on the island. "Would you like something to eat? I have an apple pie and scones."

Hope was obsessed with feeding people, even guests who showed up unexpectedly. It was the way she was wired, like Claire calculating square footage when she entered a home. When she was a little girl, her dolls had the best tea parties, and when she got older and was able to help her mother in the kitchen, she'd gladly prepared a plate of cookies or brownies to serve to visitors.

Elaine raised a hand. "Too much sugar. I have to watch what I eat."

"You have amazing willpower." Hope's willpower was pretty much nonexistent and the reason for her daily runs. She glanced at the apple pie on the counter and sighed. No pie for her. At least not until Elaine left. She lifted both mugs and carried them to the pedestal table, then gestured for Elaine to join her.

Elaine took a step forward and stopped short when a whirling ball of fur came barreling into the room at full speed. *Princess.* Her long, silky white hair blew in the breeze she created. She took a sharp turn around Elaine's feet, which had Elaine teetering on her four-inch stilettos. Princess leaped onto the narrow table behind the sofa, just grazing a decorative orb with her fluffy body. She jumped onto the sofa while Elaine regained her balance.

Hope lowered her gaze and suppressed a laugh.

"You let your animals on the furniture?" Elaine gave a disapproving look at Princess, who wasn't the least bit interested in company or the visitor's opinion.

"They're family." Hope sipped her coffee.

Bigelow joined her and sat pressed against her leg.

Elaine shook her head. "If you say so. I've heard you also own chickens. Why?" Elaine walked to the table, her off-the-shoulder red dress flouncing with every step. She sat across from Hope and laid her nude patent clutch on the table.

"For the eggs. But I don't think you came here to talk about my animals or where they sleep. What's going on, Elaine?"

Hope had learned to be direct with Elaine. The woman's over-the-top tendencies and skilled, back-handed compliments made it difficult, if not impossible, to have a friendship with her. The woman had trust issues.

Elaine's bare shoulders sagged, and she exhaled a sad breath. "I need someone to talk to. Hope, you're my only friend. I'm not sure what happened, but I realized I don't have any friends except you."

Hope remained silent for a moment, not sure what to say to her guest. In Elaine's mind, she considered them friends. Hope wasn't sure how Elaine came to that conclusion. A few months ago, she'd unfriended, unfollowed, and unliked Hope on all social media and had even threatened to hashtag Hope as a busybody.

Maybe their visit to The Coffee Clique at the start of the summer had forged the friendship, though Elaine had stuck Hope with the bill.

"What about friends from college?"

Elaine shook her head. "No. I wasn't a part of any sororities."

"Neighbors?"

Elaine shook her head again. "No. I don't know them. Hope, it's all a mess." She laced her fingers around the mug and lifted it to her lips. She took a long drink.

Hearing Elaine had no friends wasn't a shock. She'd seen other women just like her who woke up one day with no one they could call a friend, a confidant, or an ally. When a person put ambition and greed and selfishness above all other things, life could become lonely.

"Miranda and Rona are claiming to still be married to Lionel. How could it be possible? He married me. I have the license." Elaine looked at Hope with wide eyes full of worry.

"I don't pretend to understand all the legal stuff, but it sounds like the divorces weren't completed. I have the legal documents from my divorce, so I'm certain my marriage is dissolved."

Elaine nodded. "I have mine too."

"Did you ever see Lionel's divorce paperwork?"

"No. He never showed me. He kept all those types of papers locked up in his safe."

"Do you have the combination?"

"No. He said I had no reason to go in there. Do you think he knew all along he wasn't legally divorced?"

Hope shrugged. "It's possible." She sipped her coffee.

Being seated across from Elaine wasn't the most comfortable feeling, considering their history, but there was a sadness reverberating off her, and it tugged at Hope's heart. Less than twenty-four hours earlier, Hope had found Elaine's husband shot to death. Hope couldn't imagine what it must have been like for her. One moment you're taking part in a silly activity and the next, you see your husband with a fatal gunshot wound. Hope blinked hard to erase the image she had of Lionel's body.

"From the questions Detective Reid asked, I think he suspects me of killing Lionel." Elaine's hands shook as she lifted her mug to take another sip of coffee. "I could never do such a thing."

"He's doing his job. He has to ask a lot of hard questions to find the truth and the killer. You were late last night to join your team."

"I was . . . wait, do *you* think I murdered Lionel?"

"I didn't say that. But I'm sure Reid asked you why you were late." Hope would bet money someone had let slip that Elaine hadn't been on time to join her team.

"He did. Someone told him I was late."

Cha-ching. If only she'd actually bet money. "What did you tell him?" Hope pushed. She wanted to hear Elaine's explanation.

Elaine huffed. "I don't have to explain myself to you."

"No, you don't. But friends talk to each other, and sometimes they ask hard questions." Was it right to appeal to Elaine's vulnerabilities to get information out of her? Hope wasn't sure, but she reasoned any information Elaine shared she'd turn over to the police to aid in finding the killer.

"Fine. I was late to meet up with my team because I lost track of time. It happens every now and again when I'm getting ready. My lashes gave me a hard time."

"Your lashes?"

"You have no idea how long it takes to look this good. It's a lot of work." Elaine batted her lashes to drive home the point. "The police are wasting their time looking at me as a suspect. I loved Lionel and would never hurt him. But he had a lot of enemies. The former mayor and his wife are two. Also, Miranda and Rona. If it's true Lionel abandoned them, they'd have a motive for murder." Elaine leaned back and crossed her arms over her chest, seemingly satisfied with casting aspersions on other people.

Before Hope could respond, the doorbell rang, and she excused herself. Bigelow followed her to the front door, but for this next visitor, he played it cool.

Hope still made him sit before she opened the door. "Good boy." With Bigelow situated, Hope pulled the door open.

Good grief.

"I'm sorry to show up without calling, but I had the most horrible experience, and I needed someone to talk to. You said I could talk to you." Rona wrung her hands.

"What happened?" Hope looked over her shoulder. The last thing she needed was for Elaine to find Rona on the porch.

"Miranda and I had an awful fight at the inn. She's being unreasonable. I'm all alone there with no friends or family, and my husband is dead." Rona's eyes misted and she sniffled.

"*My* husband is dead!" Elaine thundered toward the door and yanked it open wider, giving Bigelow enough space to dart out.

Smart dog.

Hope wanted to follow him but was caught between the angry widows, and leaving them alone didn't seem like a good idea.

"Please, calm down. There's no reason to raise our voices." Hope directed her comment to Elaine.

"There are plenty of reasons to raise my voice," Elaine countered.

"I'm not looking for trouble," Rona said.

"Well, too late! I don't know what kind of scam you're running, but if you're looking to get money from *my* late husband's estate, you're out of luck." Elaine stepped in front of Hope and positioned herself right in front of Rona. "Maybe you killed Lionel because he wouldn't give you any money."

"You're crazy. I hadn't seen Lionel, well, not until last night after someone killed him. Maybe you found out he was still married to me and, in a rage like the one you're in right now, you killed him." Rona wasn't backing down. She'd lifted her chin and leveled a death glare worthy of Hope's mother.

Setting aside her admiration, Hope needed to rein in both women or else . . . well, she didn't want to think about what could transpire between them.

"Elaine, Rona, you both need to calm down. This is my house and I can't have you two arguing like this." Hope stepped out from behind Elaine.

"I'm not the one who started this," Rona said.

"Well, I will be the one who ends it." Elaine jabbed

her finger in the air, her eyes narrowed and her nostrils flared. But she had nothing on Rona's glare.

An approaching vehicle prompted Hope to turn her attention to the road. A Jefferson PD vehicle pulled into her driveway. Ethan was behind the steering wheel.

She let out a relieved breath. Reinforcement.

Rona looked over her shoulder. "The police? Who called the police?"

Elaine smirked. "Looks like you'll be booted from Hope's property because you're trespassing."

Bigelow greeted Ethan after he climbed out of the SUV. Ethan gave the pup a quick pat and then pivoted to assess the situation on the porch. He grinned.

He grinned. Seriously?

Hope's mouth gaped open in disbelief.

"What's going on?" Ethan climbed the porch steps, and his grin deepened.

"She's trespassing," Elaine answered.

Ethan's gaze traveled from Elaine to Rona to Hope. "Hope? Are either of these women trespassing?"

"No. They both came over to talk." She'd become the sounding board for grieving widows in Jefferson.

Rona backed away from the front door. Her eyes watered again. "I've caused a problem here and I'm sorry. I didn't mean to upset Elaine. I didn't know she'd be here. Detective Reid informed me that I can't leave town right now, so I'll just go back to the inn." Rona turned and rushed down the steps.

"Wait," Hope called out. She jogged after Rona. "You're welcome here. Though now isn't a good time, with Elaine here. Please, do call me."

Rona dug into her purse for a tissue and dabbed her eyes. "You're very kind." She offered a quivery smile before following along the path to the street and then heading in the direction of Main Street.

Hope returned to the porch. "You can stop grinning now," she said to Ethan.

"Elaine's the last person I thought I'd find in your house." Ethan tossed a look to the front door.

Elaine had disappeared from the doorway. With any luck, she was inside, grabbing her clutch and getting ready to leave.

"Tell me about it."

"This is what you get for sticking your nose into our investigation."

"Hold on, Chief Cahill. I'm doing no such thing. Elaine came because she wanted to talk to a friend. And Rona showed up because Miranda was mean to her."

"Wait, you and Elaine are friends? Since when?"

"I'm not sure." Hope walked to her front door. "Why did you come over?"

"I was patrolling and saw the scene on your front porch."

"Hope!" Elaine bellowed from inside.

"Sounds like your friend needs you." Ethan wiggled an eyebrow.

"Guess I can't convince you to come in and join us?"

"Absolutely not." Ethan leaned forward and was a breath away from Hope's lips. His dark eyes turned devilish. "But, you know, I kinda like it when you call me Chief Cahill. Maybe I can frisk you later and you can call me Chief again." He flashed a wicked smile before he gave Hope a quick kiss and then jogged down the porch steps. He climbed back into his SUV and pulled out of the driveway.

The man was incorrigible.

A scream from inside her house startled Hope. She spun around and dashed inside.

What on earth had happened now?

She came to an abrupt halt when she reached the family room and took a breath. Nothing was wrong.

Elaine stood by the French door that opened to the patio and pointed at the chicken on the other side of the glass door.

"Why is it peeping in the house?"

"Her name is Poppy."

Hope walked past Elaine to open the patio door. Poppy liked hanging out on the patio and often perched on a chair during the day while the other chickens foraged on the property. Hope scooped up the Rhode Island Red hen. The rust-colored bird had the trademark red-orange eyes and reddish-brown beak, with yellow feet and legs of the breed. She also had the sweet disposition and hardiness that made Reds a favorite with chicken owners.

Elaine approached Hope and the bird with hesitant steps.

"She doesn't bite."

"What about salmonella? Should you be handling her without gloves? Never mind. I have to go. I need to soak in a tub. I need to relax. Destress." Elaine strutted back to the table and picked up her clutch.

"A bath sounds like a lovely idea." Hope set Poppy down on the patio and closed the door behind her and walked to the table. She swiped up Elaine's mug and placed it in the dishwasher.

"I have to make funeral arrangements for Lionel. I should've asked Chief Cahill when my husband's body will be released." Elaine walked out of the family room, toward the front door, and Hope followed, happy to show her guest out. "Be a dear and ask him for me the next time you see him. Thanks so much for your help."

Elaine wiggled her fingers in a wave and opened the front door. She descended the porch steps. Her hips swayed as she walked to her luxury sedan.

Be a dear? Hope closed the door and locked it. She returned to the kitchen and refilled her mug and then sliced the apple pie. She slipped a generous wedge onto a plate and carried the plate to the table. After she settled, she pulled her tablet toward her and searched the internet. She came across another story about Lionel's death and the three women claiming to be his wives, yadda, yadda, yadda. Hope skipped that section. She scrolled down to a paragraph about Jefferson's former mayor and the charges he faced because of his connection to Lionel.

Elaine wasn't wrong in suggesting the police should look at the former mayor and his wife as suspects. Both had lost their reputations and their businesses and could lose their freedom if they were convicted of taking bribes from Lionel. Hope would never have considered mild-mannered Milo Hutchinson as a murder suspect had she not had an unpleasant encounter with him and then learned about his criminal dealings. His wife, Pamela, was a cool, calculating woman, and Hope wouldn't rule her out as a murder suspect. That was if Hope was investigating Lionel's murder, which she wasn't.

Chapter Seven

*Sunday mornings are the best! Over the years,
how I spend my Sunday mornings has changed.
Throughout school, I squeezed in every extra minute
of sleeping late on a Sunday I could get away with.
While working my way up the magazine editorial
ladder, I got up early to enjoy the one day of the week
that was truly mine. I read the newspaper leisurely in
my pjs, made a big, beautiful breakfast, and spent the
day either reading or visiting museums and exploring
the city. Now, back in Jefferson, I still wake up early,
mostly because of the chickens, and I make a big,
beautiful breakfast, but my Sundays aren't as
leisurely as they used to be. Not when I have a
century-old home to finish renovating.*

Hope loved weaving in bits and pieces of her life
with her recipe posts. Connecting with her readers was
a must to growing her blog. The word "authentic" was a
buzzword in the blogging world. From Hope's experience, buzzwords got overused and diluted and exploited
to where they became jokes. Nonetheless, she strove to

be authentic and relatable to her readers. They were smart. They could identify a blogger being fake from reading just one paragraph of a blog post.

She clicked off the post and navigated to the analytics, where she scanned her page views and page interactions. She smiled. All looked good.

"Good morning!" Drew bounded into the kitchen from the mudroom. He'd texted her after his workout and wangled an invitation for brunch out of her. "Am I late?"

Hope looked up from her tablet. Showered and freshened up after his spinning class, Drew wore a white polo shirt he'd tucked into a pair of paisley print shorts, and his denim-blue canvas sneakers completed the outfit.

"Just in time." Hope set down the tablet and went to her double wall ovens. She grabbed two pot holders and pulled a frittata out of the top oven.

She loved frittatas for their simplicity and for the wow factor all in one dish. Because frittatas were delicious and versatile, she believed every cook should have a basic frittata recipe in her recipe box. The variations of the dish were limitless. Leftover ham or extra asparagus could easily be tossed into the egg mixture for a hearty meal.

"I love Sunday brunch." Drew helped himself to a cup of coffee and took it to the table. "Frittata. Yum. Is Ethan coming over?"

Back at the oven, Hope closed the door. "I'm not sure. He's going to try. I have toast." Four slices of whole-wheat bread popped out of the toaster. Talk about perfect timing. She plated them and carried the plate to the table. Drew wasted no time. He'd already helped himself to a wedge of the frittata.

"This looks delicious. Good thing I went to spin class." Drew took a drink of coffee and, after setting the cup down, leveled a serious look on Hope. "We need to have a talk."

Hope returned to the table with a filled cup of coffee. She served herself a wedge of the egg dish and then buttered a slice of bread. "What about?"

"A few months back, I asked you if I could investigate the next murder on my own."

"You did? When?"

Drew pouted. "I knew you'd forget. It was the day we picked up all the stuff for Princess after you adopted her. You agreed to stay out of the next murder investigation."

Hope searched her memory and came up with nothing. The time around adopting Princess was hectic. She'd barely escaped an attempt on her life. Trying to pinpoint a conversation about something she thought wouldn't happen again was futile. She'd take Drew's word she promised. "I am staying out of this investigation." Hope scooped up a forkful of frittata and chewed.

Drew rested his elbow on the table and his chin on his hand. "Really? How do you explain Elaine and Rona being here yesterday?"

"You heard?"

"Everybody has." Drew pulled back; his arms flailed out for emphasis. "One of your nosy neighbors must've caught sight of their knock-down, drag-out fight."

Hope cringed. With neighbors, she expected to have a little invasion of her privacy, but it seemed her neighborhood had a high level of nosiness and gossiping. Moving to a more remote property sounded appealing.

Drew ate some of his frittata and chewed, making a yummy face. "Delish. Seriously." He took another mouthful.

"Thank you. What you've described happening is an exaggeration. Yes, voices got loud, but it was nothing like you're saying."

"If you're not investigating, why were they here?"

"To talk."

"Who are you, their therapist?"

"No. I guess I'm a friendly ear to unload on. They're both going through a rough time."

"What did they say?"

"I'm not discussing what they said with you. Butter your toast before it gets cold." She shifted the conversation from Elaine and Rona.

Drew slathered his slice of toast with butter and took a bite. "I'm still confirming Lionel's marital status to Miranda and Rona. It's a big mess. Who would've thought Lionel Whitcomb was a bigamist?"

"Only if his previous marriages weren't dissolved. You don't know for sure yet if Miranda and Rona are telling the truth. Have you been able to find out if Lionel was arriving or leaving the restaurant Friday night?"

Drew swallowed his bite of toast. "Arriving. He was meeting with his business partner, Rupert Donnelly."

"They've been partners for years, haven't they?"

"Yes. What I'm hearing is, their partnership has been rocky lately because Rupert has been concerned about getting caught up in Lionel's legal problems. Who knows what the DA's office could uncover as they dig further into Lionel's business dealings."

Hope took a bite of toast and considered Rupert's current predicament. He'd found himself partnered with a man who got himself arrested and charged with felonies. She wondered if Rupert had suspected his partner was committing crimes all along. Or had he been a part of the bribery scheme? Had he been looking for a way to make the criminal investigation go away, possibly by getting rid of Lionel?

"Rupert could've had a motive for murder. If you kill the prime target of an investigation, it's reasonable to assume the investigation will stop." Hope leaned back.

"Ah . . . you're on to something. Rupert could've met Lionel outside and shot him and then made his way back around to the front of the restaurant and entered, all while his business partner lay bleeding out in the parking lot."

"It's a theory I'm sure the police are looking in to."

Drew set down his fork and wiped his mouth with a napkin. "You're really not going to investigate?"

"No. Why would I? Do you want another slice of frittata?"

"Yes, please."

Hope happily scooped out some more of the egg dish for Drew. "I should text Ethan to see if he'll make it over."

"He's not here by now, so he probably won't. Maretta has been all over him and Reid. I even heard she reminded Ethan he works for her."

Hope grimaced. "That doesn't sound good."

"I can't believe the town elected her mayor. She has no clue what she's doing. Claire would have been the better choice. How is she doing, by the way?"

"Good. We went shopping yesterday, and she's definitely getting back to herself. She needs to figure out what to do next."

"Well, I know what I'm going to do next after I finish brunch. I have an interview with Miranda. I got it before Norrie could land it." Drew's chest puffed out as satisfaction glimmered in his eyes.

"Congratulations on the exclusive."

Hope wasn't surprised Miranda was giving an interview. It was an opportunity for her to tell her side of the story. She might be able to provide documentation proving she was still legally Lionel's wife and proclaim her innocence in the murder. It also was smart to get out ahead of Elaine or Rona.

Though doing an interview was risky. Miranda would have no control over the final product. Lucky for her, Drew had ethics and wouldn't inflate or interject a narrative whose sole purpose was to sell more papers. Yeah, she was lucky Norrie wasn't doing the article. Otherwise, it could be filled with innuendo and pseudofacts. How the reporter remained employed baffled Hope.

"She says she wants to get out her side of the story. My guess is, she's going for the wronged woman angle. You know, swept off her feet, dumped for another woman, yadda, yadda, yadda."

"The other woman being Rona?"

Drew shrugged. "Not sure yet. Who knows? There could be another Mrs. Whitcomb we don't know about yet. I'd love to get an interview with Rona. Because you and she are best buds, how about asking her if she'd like to be interviewed?"

Hope didn't take long to answer. "No. We're not best buds and I'm not getting involved, remember?"

"She showed up at your house yesterday. Sounds like you're involved, at least a little." Drew held up his hands with his thumb and index fingers really close together. "A little."

Hope shook her head. She would remain steadfast. She wasn't involved.

Twenty minutes later, Drew had finished his second helping of frittata and headed out for his interview with Miranda.

Hope wasted no time in cleaning up and then grabbed Bigelow's leash to take him on a walk before the day got too hot. Back inside with the air conditioner blasting, she settled down for a quiet day of catching up on her blog.

After a quick session of outlining some new posts, she opened her photography software. It was time to edit the photographs she'd taken of recipes. Aside from publishing them on her blog, she'd post them on her social media and on websites devoted to sharing food photos. Most of those sites weren't easy to get published on. They had high standards for what was referred to as "food porn," photographs that left you drooling and famished. To get to that level of photographic skill, she'd spent hours taking photographs and editing. All the hard work paid off, because now she was a regular contributor and got a lot of views on her blog from those sites.

Selecting the perfect photo was a tedious process. Halfway through the hundreds of photographs she'd taken, Ethan called to let her know he'd be working straight through into the evening, so he'd miss dinner. The lure to running a small department for him was the lack of bureaucracy that burdened bigger ones, but it also meant he worked with a lean staff, and when major crimes hit, like murder, it meant longer hours and no days off until the crime was solved.

A little bummed she'd be eating alone, she was grateful for the now longer stretch of uninterrupted time for editing.

Bigelow must have sensed her disappointment because he padded over to her from his comfortable bed in the corner of the family room. He settled beside her leg and she smiled. His unconditional love never failed to melt her heart.

She placed her hand back on the mouse to finish editing the photograph of the triple decadent brownies she made last week when a crashing noise from the dining room made her jump.

Princess.

On her way to the magazine, Hope grabbed her travel mug from her vehicle's console and rallied the enthusiasm she'd had last week, when she started at *Cooking Now.*

It wasn't the going to work part that had her in a glum mood. Rather, it was the inevitable questions about Jefferson's latest murder.

When the previous murders occurred, she'd been able to cocoon in her house after finding a dead body and not have to deal with the outside world. But not today. Today she was reporting for work, and she'd be facing coworkers who she expected would have questions.

Braced for an onslaught of questions, Hope entered the test kitchen with some prepared responses like *I'm sorry, I can't discuss the case,* and *yes, it was awful finding a dead body.*

The second option made her flinch. For a civilian, she'd definitely discovered too many dead bodies.

Maybe her ex-producer, Corey Lucas, was right when he suggested months ago that she combine her food blog with a crime blog. True crimes investigated with recipes. Now she had to admit the idea didn't sound so silly. It sounded like it could be successful.

When she entered the kitchen, it surprised her to find a hushed tone and solemn-looking faces greeting her as the door closed behind her.

She said good morning to her coworkers and received only a few murmured greetings back. She made her way to her desk. Hope set down her travel mug and tote bag. The stillness in the room was unsettling.

What on earth was going on?

"It seems you've had a busy weekend." May Henshaw approached Hope with her hands clasped together and her thin lips firmly set in a grim line. Her judgmental gaze had narrowed in on Hope. "A man was murdered in Jefferson Friday night."

May's tone rankled Hope, and she didn't understand why she was upset. But now she understood the weird vibe in the kitchen.

"It's a shame." Hope pulled out her chair and sat. She dug through her tote bag for her recipe notebook. She used a spiral notebook for recipe development. In there, she kept her notes on ingredients, cooking times, and details about each recipe test. "I'm going to bake a flourless chocolate cake today."

May moved closer to the corner of Hope's desk. "I've heard it wasn't the first time you've found a dead body and somehow gotten yourself involved with those murders. They even arrested your sister for a murder."

The hairs on the back of Hope's neck pricked up. May was crossing a line. "My sister didn't murder anyone. I'm sure when you searched online you also found that piece of information."

May crossed her arms over her chest. "*Cooking Now* doesn't need sordid publicity. Even though your presence here is temporary, you're still a part of this magazine."

Temporary. The magic word.

There were only a few more days at the magazine before her assignment ended and she'd be done with May's disapproving looks.

While she wasn't looking to appease the editor, Hope understood her concern for the magazine. She also didn't want negative publicity directed toward *Cooking Now.*

"I'm only a witness in the investigation, nothing more, I assure you."

"Fine." May lowered her arms and then spun around. She walked away, toward the studio kitchen, and disappeared. They were shooting a video series on holiday cookie baking. Hands down, her favorite type of baking. The thought of sugar cookies made her smile. Last week, she got a peek at the recipes, and now she was looking forward to a little taste testing later in the day.

At least she had something to look forward to.

She scanned the short list of emails and clicked onto each one to read. The more focus she put into the emails, the less she was thinking of May. And a few deep breaths helped too. When May emerged from the studio kitchen and marched to her desk, Hope barely gave the editor a thought.

Kitty came rushing into the test kitchen with apologies for being late. She shuffled by May's desk, who looked up from her planner with a scowl. Kitty gave a weak smile and continued to her desk next to Hope's. She dropped her overstuffed, canvas shopping bag, her purse, and a plastic bag bursting with groceries on the desk's surface. She wiped a bead of sweat from her brow.

"It's been one of those mornings. My car wouldn't start and then I had to stop for groceries." Kitty leaned toward Hope. "May looks especially perturbed. What did I miss?"

"A lecture on how finding dead bodies is bad for the magazine."

"Oh." Kitty pulled back. "I can't believe there was a murder in Jefferson and you found the body. How awful!" Kitty wheeled out her chair from under the desk and sat.

"It was. The whole scene was crazy and surreal." Hope turned her attention back to her emails. There was an appointment request from the editor-in-chief, along with May and the managing editor. Hope wasn't sure if it was business as usual. Perhaps there was another assignment they wanted to discuss with her. Or it could be about the recent event in Jefferson. With a little uneasiness in her belly, Hope accepted the meeting.

"I heard three women claim to be his wife." Kitty unpacked her canvas bag, laying out the boxed teas on her desk.

"You heard correctly. It appears Lionel Whitcomb's ex-wives believe their divorces weren't completed."

"How can that happen these days?"

"Well, the first wife married him about thirty years ago. So I guess it's possible."

Kitty shook her head vigorously. "Sounds like Lionel Whitcomb was running some kind of scam duping innocent women. Men like him think they can get away with whatever they want and consequences be damned. They leave broken families and children in the wake of their greed and lust."

"Kitty! We're waiting." May stood and gestured for Kitty to join her in the kitchen they used for photographing recipes.

"Sorry." Kitty jumped up and gathered the boxes of tea and scooted across the room. Hope wasn't sure what feature they were working on for the tea, but given the trials of the past few days, she'd love a cup of tea. Before she could stand and head to the back room to brew one, she received a text message from Elaine.

Need to talk to you about Lionel's funeral.

Chapter Eight

Hope snipped a handful of flat-leaf parsley from her plant. She inhaled the fragrance and, for a moment, was transported back to her mom's kitchen garden. Elizabeth Early maintained a small garden off her kitchen, where she planted a variety of herbs. Parsley, basil, and thyme were the stars of the garden because, as she would say, they were the workhorses in the kitchen. From the time Hope was allowed to use scissors, she loved nothing more than to grab the large enamelware bowl her mom used and putter in the garden to collect herbs. Sometimes she took the risk and selected a new herb for her mom's recipe. Her mother would always smile and happily toss in the new addition to her recipe.

A chorus of chicken chatter brought Hope out of her thoughts and she glanced at Poppy, who was perched on a chair. She dropped the clump of parsley into her bowl. While she had her mom's set of three nesting bowls, she didn't have her kitchen garden just yet. What she had were two metal stands on her patio covered with an abundance of potted herbs.

Not exactly what she'd envisioned when she bought her house. Thanks to unexpected repairs to the house after the fire, the vegetable and herb gardens had to be postponed to next year. While the setup wasn't ideal, it was far better than the skimpy herb garden on her windowsill back in the city.

Poppy was still chattering as Hope added another heap of parsley into the bowl. The sound of her favorite hen soothed her after a hectic day.

While she was at the magazine, the test kitchen had been busy with a cover photo shoot, recipe testing for the January issue and a special bread issue, and then a tasting in midafternoon. Hope made three recipes, including her Flourless Chocolate Cake recipe. The cake was the only one of the three recipes included in the tasting, and it received positive feedback and the approval to be included in the article. Though the mood in the test kitchen had changed little over the course of the day, thanks to May's sour mood.

If that weren't bad enough, the text message she'd received from Elaine led to a lengthy phone call about the reception following Lionel's burial. Somehow, at the end of the conversation, Hope had found herself the caterer for the reception.

During the drive home from the magazine, she replayed the conversation in her mind a few times, trying to pinpoint the moment the job of providing food for thirty guests became hers.

Between the sobs and the sniffles and the why-me cries, Hope offered to help in any way she could and then, bam, Elaine composed herself and thanked Hope for offering to provide the food. Of course, Elaine would reimburse her for the cost.

THREE WIDOWS AND A CORPSE

"Can you believe it? By the end of the call, I was the caterer," Hope said to Poppy.

Poppy clucked.

"Thirty people. In two days. Talk about short notice."

Poppy stretched her body, wings spreading out, and then she settled back down.

"Give the woman an inch and she . . ." It was no use complaining. Hope had offered to help. She snipped off another bunch of parsley. "I realize she's going through a rough time."

"Do you always talk to your chickens?"

Hope stopped in midsnip of the oregano plant and laughed. Lost in her venting, she hadn't heard Amy's car pull up in the driveway.

"She's a great listener." Hope set down her scissors on the plant stand and lifted the bowl.

She carried it over to the table, where she'd set out a pitcher of lemonade and two glasses in anticipation of Amy's visit.

Before she'd left *Cooking Now* to head home, Amy Phelan had called to let her know Town Hall had approved the Labor Day Parade schedule and she'd drop it off on her way home from work. Hope had told her to come around back because she'd be outside working.

Amy walked to the table and set down a folder. Her wavy blond hair framed her oval-shaped face. She pushed her gold-toned sunglasses onto her head, revealing tired brown eyes.

"Long day?" Hope filled both glasses with lemonade and handed one to Amy.

"That obvious? It's been exhausting lately at the office, and Alfred has been uncharacteristically grumpy."

Hope sat and gestured to a chair opposite her. She

wanted to hear more about Alfred's bad mood and, apparently, so did Poppy because she hadn't moved.

Amy had been the secretary at Alfred Kingston's real estate office for years. She was probably the only other person in Jefferson who rivaled Claire for information about who was selling, who was buying, how much they paid or how much they lost.

"He looked frazzled last week when I ran into him outside the office. It was the day Lionel and Rupert Donnelly had a meeting there."

Amy rolled her eyes. "Talk about a meeting from hell. From the moment they arrived, I knew it would end poorly."

"How so?" Hope sipped her lemonade and waited for Amy to continue.

Amy's forehead wrinkled and her shoulders rounded. "Their vibe. The looks they gave each other. Mr. Donnelly barely said a word. Then he started yelling at Lionel and stormed out. Alfred was wasting his time. Mr. Donnelly wouldn't invest in the horse farm."

"What horse farm? I thought the meeting was about the medical office development." Hope inched forward, setting down her drink.

Amy raised her hand to push her hair out of her face. "No, it's been stalled since it got caught up in Lionel's legal problems. No way was he going to get permission to move forward on it. Alfred called him in to discuss the old Parson horse farm."

Hope leaned back. Alfred had led her to believe the meeting was about the medical office project. Why hadn't he mentioned the horse farm? Probably because he was a smart businessman and wanted to keep the project quiet until he had a deal with the Parsons. If he was so smart, why would he want to go into business with someone who was facing possible jail time?

"Alfred wants to develop the thirty-six acres into a condo development and, somehow, Lionel got involved, but he was having a problem with cash flow, so he tried to bring in Rupert."

Hope had taken riding lessons at Parson's when she was a kid. She remembered the three Parsons— Dorinda, Hildy, and Bart. Dorinda, the eldest of the three siblings, taught the classes, while Hildy managed the business and Bart maintained the barns and property. Hope recalled Dorinda had passed away a few years ago. Since then, the farm had continued its descent into disrepair and closed down.

"Wait, why would Alfred go into business with Lionel when he was waiting to go to trial?"

Amy shrugged. "My best guess is money. Lionel was a lot of things, including a good salesman. I'm sure he convinced Alfred he would beat the charges."

"By chance, did you overhear any of their discussion during the meeting?"

"Like did I eavesdrop?" Amy took a drink of her lemonade.

Hope winced. She had pretty much asked Amy if she snooped on her boss. Not cool.

Amy giggled. "I tried. But I didn't hear much."

Hope reached for her glass and took a sip, feeling a little better knowing she hadn't insulted Amy.

"All I know is Hildy and Bart Parson are divided on selling the property. And Rupert wanted no part. It disappointed Alfred, but he's determined. In fact, Hildy and Bart came into the office to meet with Alfred this morning."

Hope's eyes widened. Based on what Amy said, Bart

Parson had a motive to kill Lionel if he believed his death would stop the development.

"What's going on, Hope? What are you thinking?" Amy's voice deepened with concern.

Hope didn't want to alarm Amy with the possibility Bart Parson could've killed Lionel and that Alfred could be in danger if he proceeded with the development. She had no proof, only a theory based on a hunch.

"It's nothing." Hope leaned forward. "Do you think Alfred will be able to get financing for the development?"

"I don't know. I kind of hope he doesn't. I'd hate to lose all that land to condos, you know?" Amy finished her lemonade and Hope changed the conversation to the parade. They were weeks away from the big day and there was a ton of work to do.

For the next thirty minutes, they covered a lot of ground regarding the parade. They both had their checklists updated and a date set for the next committee meeting. Amy left, and Hope gathered up the pitcher and glasses and went inside, leaving Poppy to fly off the chair and catch up with the other hens. Hope's plans for the evening included cooking for the reception in two days. After her call with Elaine, she had brainstormed a simple menu and had enough ingredients in her pantry to start preparing food. She also wanted to think through what she'd learned about Alfred and the Parsons.

Closing the French doors behind her, Hope's thoughts wandered back to Bart Parson. A tall, brooding man who preferred the company of horses to people. How far would he go to protect his family's legacy from being bulldozed and turned into condos?

* * *

Two days later, with no breaking news on the murder, Hope hurried through the hallway in Town Hall to catch the press conference. Would any new facts be revealed? A quick check of her watch told her the briefing had already started. Shoot. Thanks to road repair, she was caught in traffic on the drive back from the magazine.

She arrived at the open doorway of the first-floor meeting room and stepped inside. Reporters from newspapers and other media outlets crammed into the room to get an update on Lionel's murder investigation. Positioned in front of an oil painting of a long-deceased mayor of Jefferson, Ethan stood at the podium with Detective Reid beside him.

"Yes, Karina, we have leads, but at this time in the investigation, I'm not at liberty to expand any further." Moving his gaze across the row, he pointed to another reporter for the next question.

Dressed in his uniform, Ethan stood solid and unshakable. His professional manner instilled confidence that the Jefferson Police Department had everything under control.

Detective Reid, dressed in a gray suit, stood stoic and alert. His gaze scanned the room like a hawk looking for his next meal.

She inched farther into the room and wondered what she'd missed. Had there been a break in the case? If so, Drew would be a very unhappy camper.

He'd called as she was leaving *Cooking Now* to attend the press conference and complained his editor assigned him to interview the owner of Bark Boutique, Jefferson's new pet supply shop.

"When do you think you'll make an arrest, Chief?" a reporter asked.

A tap on her shoulder had Hope looking behind her and missing Ethan's answer. She was surprised to see Maretta. Why wasn't she up at the podium with Ethan and Reid?

"I hope you're happy."

"Are you still trying to blame me for the murder?"

Maretta reached into the pocket of her cardigan and her bony hand pulled out a cell phone. After she swiped it on, she held it up to Hope.

Hope craned her neck to read the screen.

> Hope Early, the food blogger behind *Hope at Home*, finds another body. It seems the quaint town of Jefferson, Connecticut, is becoming more known for its murders than for its antique shops. Perhaps Ms. Early should blog about how to solve a murder rather than about how to bake cookies.

Hope groaned. Her eyes squinted to read the website's address, hoping it was a small one with little traffic. No such luck. The post was on one of the biggest websites on the internet. It was where people went for news, entertainment, sports, and now about Hope's proclivity for finding murdered people.

"You just had to find another body, didn't you?" Maretta lowered the phone and shoved it back into her pocket. "And your beau has made no headway in the case."

Hope opened her mouth to defend herself as Ethan appeared at her side. "I didn't expect to see you here."

"Oh, hi. Is the press conference over?" Hope looked around the room and saw reporters busy on their phones while the town employees filed out of the room. Yes, it was over.

"We were just talking about you, Chief." Maretta stiffened, though Hope didn't understand how she could become any stiffer. "I'm not happy with the lack of progress so far."

"Neither am I. Short of the murderer coming in and confessing, we have to work the leads and evidence. That takes time," Ethan said.

"I expect to be briefed every day on your progress, or lack of it." She gave a curt nod before walking away to join a cluster of reporters to answer questions.

Ethan leaned toward Hope and whispered, "I wish Claire would've won the election."

Hope held back a smile. The sentiment seemed to be a common one. "Can you sneak away for coffee?"

"Sorry. I have to get back to the PD. I'll call you later about dinner, okay? I'll make it up to you. Promise." He squeezed her arm before breaking away to catch up with one of his officers, who was heading out of the meeting room.

The reporters were packing up and Maretta slipped out a side door. A part of Hope felt sorry for the older woman. She'd been on the job only a few weeks and there was a murder in town to deal with. Then again, it wasn't a secret the mayor had to deal with unpleasant things from time to time. Maretta was unlucky in the fact that the first unpleasant thing she had to deal with was murder.

"Hope!" Norrie Jennings called out from a few feet away and hurried over to her. "I need to talk to you."

"About what?" Hope's spine straightened as she braced herself for another unpleasant conversation.

Norrie smiled and, to Hope's surprise, it wasn't a conniving smile. Actually, her smile was pretty. A polka-dot headband that coordinated with her ballet flats held her auburn hair off her face. If Hope didn't know better, she could easily make the mistake of trusting the reporter.

"I'd like to ask you a favor."

"A favor?" Hope eyed the twentysomething reporter suspiciously.

"You don't owe me anything. It's me who owes you an apology, and I should've given you one sooner. During the Lily Barnhart investigation, I got over-zealous. I promise it won't happen again."

An apology from Norrie? Hope never saw that coming.

"Thank you." Hope couldn't help the hesitation in her voice. After all, she was talking to Norrie Jennings, a cutthroat reporter who displayed no shame in how she got front-page bylines. "What's the favor?"

"I want to interview Elaine. Get her side of the story about her late husband's other two wives."

Hope raised a hand to stop Norrie from continuing. "I can't help you."

"I'm not looking to do a hatchet job. I'm looking to tell her side of the story."

Hope figured Norrie wanted to get Elaine's side of the story because Drew got Miranda's yesterday. Norrie sounded sincere, but Hope doubted her sincerity ran very deep.

"Goodbye." Hope walked away, but she didn't get very far.

"Isn't it interesting that suddenly Elaine is at your house asking you for favors, like helping with her husband's funeral reception this afternoon? I bet she's even asked you for help in clearing her as a suspect. After all, you're dating the chief of police."

Hope stopped. How did Norrie know about the reception? She turned around, all the while chiding herself. She should've known better and kept up her guard. Norrie was singing a new tune, but she was the same competitive reporter she was when she invaded Hope's privacy during the last murder in Jefferson. "What does my relationship with Ethan have to do with the murder investigation?"

Norrie shrugged and stepped forward. "Tell me, do those sweet nothings you whisper into the chief's ear at night include your belief Elaine couldn't have possibly killed her husband? Is that what you and Elaine are doing? Manipulating the police?"

"What's wrong with you? How dare you ask me those questions?"

"I'm not the only one who's asking those questions. It's hard to believe it's a coincidence you and Elaine have become best friends just when she needs an ally to keep her out of jail."

"You have a lot of nerve."

"I'm trying to help you."

Hope barked a laugh. "You have a funny way of doing so."

"Elaine is using you." Norrie gave Hope a concerned look. Her deep-set amber eyes softened, and she sighed. "She's using you just like she used her husbands. Lionel isn't her first dead husband. And you're not her first *friend* involved with a local cop."

"Norrie, stop. I'm not being used, because I have
no influence over what the police do. None." Hope
turned and hurried out of the meeting room. Her feet
moved as fast as they could, heading for the exit.
Outside, the humid air seized her, and her breath
caught.

Could what Norrie said be true?

Was Elaine using her because of her relationship
with Ethan? Could she be lending a shoulder to lean
on to a murderer?

"Hey, Hope!" Drew's voice grabbed Hope's attention, and she turned.

Her gaze fixed on the tray of iced coffees he carried.
Bless him. She needed a drink of something after her
two unpleasant encounters. Why on earth had she decided to go to the press conference?

"I missed it, didn't I?" Without waiting for a reply,
Drew handed Hope her coffee. "Stupid business
profile."

His messenger bag was slung crossbody, and he'd
donned his favorite aviator sunglasses. He lifted his
cup from the tray and took a drink. "What's wrong?
You have a funny look on your face. Well, not ha ha
funny. Weird. OMG. I missed something big, didn't I?
They announced who the killer was while I was interviewing the Bark Boutique's owner."

"No. They don't know who the killer is."

"Then what's wrong?" Drew took another drink of
his iced coffee and looked at Hope in confusion.

"I talked to Norrie." Hope gulped her iced coffee.
Between the August heat and the run-in with Norrie,
she was hot. Very hot.

"Ahh . . . explains the weird look on your face. I'd

love to commiserate with you about Norrie, but I have to file this story. My editor is in a full-on, take-no-prisoners mode these days. Something's up at the paper."

There was always something going on at the *Gazette*. Staff shake-ups, budget cuts, shrinking circulation. "No . . . no. We have to talk now."

"What's going on?"

"Well, if you stopped talking about yourself, I could tell you."

"Whoa! Food blogger gone cray cray?"

"This is serious, Drew." She tugged at his arm, pulling him away from the front of Town Hall. She wanted no one overhearing their conversation. "Norrie intimated that Elaine is using me because I'm involved with Ethan."

"No?" His eyes bulged. "Tell me everything. Leave nothing out." He extended a hand and guided Hope to a bench that flanked Town Hall's front entry. It was a nice spot to sit and take a breather. Or, in their case, a nice spot for Hope to describe her encounter with Norrie.

Hope sat and set down her drink beside her. "She said Lionel wasn't Elaine's first dead husband, and she'd befriended a wife or girlfriend of a cop at some point."

"That's all?"

"She was vague. I know Elaine was married three times before Lionel. But I don't know what happened to those ex-husbands. What have you come across?"

Drew sat at the other end of the bench. "I haven't dug deep into her past marriages. The story is about Lionel's marital history."

"Why didn't you? She could be a black widow."

"Wait, are you freaking out about this?"

"No! Yes. Maybe." Hope inhaled a deep breath and regained her composure. She was on the verge of a public meltdown. She'd had one before in front of Matt, and it wasn't pretty. "If she's using me, it's for one reason only."

"Because she's the killer."

"And believes I can persuade Ethan to shift the investigation away from her. I never thought my relationship with Ethan would become so complicated." Hope lifted her cup and took a sip of her iced coffee.

"It always is, sweetie." Drew reached out and rubbed her arm. "I'll write up this business profile. I promise it'll be my fastest article ever. And then I'll dig into Elaine's past and find out what Norrie is talking about. You know, she could just be messing with you. Maybe she's trying to get you to trust her so you'll give her information she suspects you've learned from Ethan. If that's the case, she's wasting her time because I can't get anything out of you."

Hope blinked. Drew made a good point. Norrie could think Hope had an inside track to the police investigation. She didn't doubt Norrie would exploit anything or anyone to get her next lead.

If someone was using people, her money was on Norrie.

"You're probably right. I almost forgot. Amy came by last night to drop off the schedule for the parade. She told me Alfred is trying to buy the Parson horse farm, and that's what Lionel and Rupert were doing at the real estate office last week. He was trying to make a deal with them."

"I thought you were staying out of the investigation." Drew leaned back and crossed his legs.

"I am. I told you I wasn't going to get involved. We were talking and she mentioned it." Hope was pretty certain it had happened like that. She stared at her drink. Thinking back to the visit, Hope did lead Amy into a conversation about Alfred and Lionel. She pressed her lips together. It was official. She couldn't mind her own business.

"What else did she tell you?"

"Bart Parson didn't want to sell. He has a motive for killing Lionel if what Amy said is true. She also said Alfred is determined to develop the property into condos, which means Alfred could be in danger if Bart is the killer."

"That's an awful lot of theories for someone who's not investigating a murder."

"Fine. I'm investigating. I can't help myself. Besides, I'm the one who found Lionel's body."

"I knew it!" A smile twitched his lips. "I also know there's nothing I can say to discourage you."

"You're not angry?"

He stood and looked at Hope. "Just in case Norrie isn't yanking your chain, be careful when you're at Elaine's house. If she's a black widow, I don't think she'd hesitate to kill a food blogger who's catering her husband's funeral reception. You know?"

"Got it."

Drew's parting words weren't at all comforting to Hope. In fact, they chilled her right down to the bone.

Chapter Nine

Hope surveyed the buffet one last time on her way back to Elaine's kitchen. She rearranged the container of coffee stirrers, snatched up a handful of emptied sugar packets, and straightened the stack of napkins. She gave a satisfied nod. The table looked good.

Hope had arrived at the Whitcomb house after the press conference and found Elaine's housekeeper, Iva, had set out all the plates, glassware, and utensils. Elaine had good taste. Hope recognized the china pattern. She'd spotted the set on a recent visit to a high-end department store. There were no thrift store or tag sale finds for Elaine.

With the buffet table all set, Hope reheated her Artichoke and Spinach Pasta Bake, warmed the Parker House rolls, and tossed the salad with her balsamic vinaigrette. She also had a prepared tray of chocolate cookies and shortbread bars ready to be set out with the coffee.

She wove through the mourners, who chatted in hushed tones in the cavernous room set off from the dining room. She wasn't sure what the room was used for. She'd seen the living room, the den, and the dining room, but this room only containing the buffet table and a substantial fireplace surrounded with white marble was a mystery to her.

A ballroom maybe?

Who had a ballroom these days?

Because she wasn't buying the house, it didn't matter what the intended purpose of the room was. She continued to the kitchen and pushed open the swinging door. She had some serious kitchen envy going on.

Upgrades everywhere, from the appliances to the countertops. And not just any upgrades. After she'd signed the papers for her house, the first room she'd tackled was the kitchen. She was determined to take it from its vintage 1980s—yes, that's what the seller's agent had used to describe the white-with-wood-trim cabinets, tiled countertops, and white appliances—to contemporary with warmth and functionality. She believed the two concepts could go hand in hand with painted cabinets, granite countertops that were durable yet neutral in tone, and high-end, stainless-steel appliances for years of reliable service. The remodel of her kitchen took a huge chunk out of her budget, but nowhere near what it cost the Whitcombs to outfit their kitchen.

Dark walnut cabinets, which Hope was certain were all custom, lined the walls and were also the base for the massive island that was covered by a slab of gold-flecked white marble. She'd priced out a similar stone and had nearly choked on the salesperson's estimate. Clearly, the Whitcombs swallowed the price easily, probably with the aid of a beverage from their dedicated beverage center. She wondered how often the built-in coffee maker was used. It still looked brand new. She sighed.

Hope discarded her envy. Her kitchen might not have all the bells and whistles, but there wasn't one inch of her kitchen that wasn't appreciated, or used, for that matter. She checked the countertop coffee maker, which was brewing a second pot of coffee for the guests. It'd been set out when Hope arrived, and she figured Elaine didn't want her using the expensive built-in one for the guests.

The coffee was almost finished brewing, giving her a few minutes to continue her research. She grabbed her purse and pulled out her cell phone and resumed her research into Elaine's previous marriages.

She'd been in such a hurry to get from Town Hall to her house to pack her vehicle with the food for the reception, she hadn't had time to finish her search into Elaine's past.

Norrie's comments about the widow using Hope because of her relationship with Ethan gnawed at her.

On the internet, she searched Elaine's name and then clicked on links. One link was to a newspaper article about her second husband's murder. Clive Bass had been killed during a break-in at his office. The cause of death was blunt force trauma to the head.

What were the odds Elaine would have two husbands who were murdered?

The article mentioned a police detective, and Hope wondered if it was his wife or girlfriend whom Elaine had befriended, like Norrie had said.

The kitchen door swung open, and Hope jumped as her head turned from her phone, nearly dropping it. She caught it before it landed on the travertine-tiled floor. Clearly, Drew's cautionary warning from earlier still rattled her.

"There you are." Jocelyn Donnelly entered the kitchen. The thickset, middle-aged woman, the wife of Lionel's business partner, Rupert, looked more composed now than when she'd first arrived at the Whitcomb house. She had had an emotional breakdown after paying her condolences to Elaine and run off to a bathroom.

"I'm making a fresh pot of coffee." Hope shoved back her phone into her purse and zipped it up securely.

"Good. I could use a cup." Jocelyn stopped at the megasize island and rested her hands on the beveled-edged granite surface. She was at least ten years older than Elaine. Dressed in a muted tweed suit, her dark hair was pulled back into a sleek chignon, and tiny lines creased the corners of her teary blue eyes.

"It must be a very draining day for you. You and your husband knew Lionel for several years." The coffee maker beeped, signaling the brewing was complete, but Hope ignored the alert. She closed the space between her and Jocelyn. "If you don't mind me asking, did you or your husband know about Miranda and Rona?"

"Quite a spectacle, isn't it?" Jocelyn lowered her eyelids.

Hope suspected she wanted to roll her eyes but was too classy to do so.

Jocelyn stepped back from Hope and walked along the ten-foot island, gliding along her manicured fingertips as she walked. "We knew Lionel had been married before, but we didn't know the details of the marriages or divorces."

The door swung open, and Claire popped her head in. "Hope! You have to get out here now! Miranda has shown up."

"Oh, boy," Hope muttered.

"Why on earth would she show up here today?" Jocelyn followed Hope out of the kitchen.

All three of them reached the foyer, their heels clicking on the marble tile, and at the door stood Miranda and Iva Johnson.

"I want to see Elaine. I want to know why I wasn't invited to my husband's funeral or reception. Why is everyone paying their respects to his glorified mistress?" Miranda's nostrils flared and her lips flattened into a serious expression.

"You have no business being here," Iva spat back. The housekeeper's hands balled into fists she propped on her hips.

No good would come from a confrontation between Miranda and Iva. Hope had gone to high school with the housekeeper, who'd grown up from an angry teenager to a bitter woman. She'd wasted a good part of her life by mixing pills and alcohol and taking dead-end jobs one after another. Not a loyal person by nature, Iva was only protecting Elaine at the moment because she was being paid. If she didn't get a check, Hope had no doubt Iva would escort Miranda to Elaine in a heartbeat.

Seeing a stalemate, Hope lunged forward. "This isn't the time or place to be doing this. Everyone's emotions are running high."

Miranda raised a palm to Hope to silence her. "I appreciate what you're doing, trying to help, but this is none of your business."

"She's right, you know," Iva said with a smirk.

A flurry of clicking drew their attention to the front step.

Good grief. Hope wasn't surprised to see Norrie. The reporter had a way of turning up like a bad penny.

"Looks like I arrived just in time." Norrie lowered her camera and stepped forward.

"No, you haven't." Hope marched to the door and slammed it shut.

"What are you doing here?" Elaine had pushed her way through the guests in the foyer. Wearing a snug, black, cold-shoulder dress with a plunging neckline and leopard stiletto heels, she didn't look like the typical grieving widow. In fact, the lace handkerchief in her hand seemed nothing more than a prop. "You murdered my husband!"

Here we go again.

"Elaine, you can't go around making such accusations." Hope walked away from the door toward Elaine.

"I did nothing of the sort." Miranda pointed her finger at Elaine. "You found out he was still legally married to me and you killed him."

"What is going on here?" Rupert Donnelly had made his way through the cluster of guests. His hefty, solid frame easily parted the curious onlookers. "This isn't your house, you weren't invited, and you've upset Elaine. I must insist you leave" He guided Miranda to the door, which he opened and shooed her out.

"We'll see about this being my house." Miranda huffed and turned. She descended the front steps and Rupert closed the door.

Hope, like everyone else, was stunned into silence by the heated argument. A loud, wailing sound broke the tentative silence. Elaine covered her face with her hands and sobbed. She turned around and rushed up the stairs.

With the show over, the guests began to disperse. Most of them headed to the buffet.

The coffee.

She needed to set out the fresh coffee, but Rupert was walking toward her from the closed front door.

The coffee could wait.

"Thank you for handling Miranda. This whole situation isn't good for anyone. I guess the claims on Lionel's estate from Miranda and Rona are an added complication for you, on top of Lionel's legal issues." Hope kept her voice conversational. She wasn't sure if Rupert would brush her off or confide in her. While she braced for the big brush-off, she hoped for the latter.

Rupert nodded slowly, as if he was carefully selecting what to say next. "The legal issues Lionel was dealing with didn't affect me. The developments in question were separate from Whitcomb and Donnelly. Lionel was working on those projects on his own. I had no exposure to any legal actions. Now, as far as the ex-wives are concerned, I suspect it will get nasty because each believes she's entitled to Lionel's half of our business."

"I'm sure the lawyers will sort everything out."

"At a very high cost, I expect."

Hope was all too familiar with lawyer fees. Between her divorce, incorporating her business, and buying her home, she'd had a slew of attorney bills in a short period of time.

"It's good to hear you're not at risk because of Lionel's bad business decisions. It was smart to protect yourself. Given everything that has happened, I was surprised to hear you considered going in on the Parson farm development. But I guess you didn't see any risk. At least, from a legal standpoint."

"What do you know about the Parson farm deal?" His posture perked up, as if he'd been alerted to a threat.

"Not much. I know you weren't interested in it, but Lionel was."

"Miss Early, I don't know what your game is, but I suggest you stay out of my business."

His voice was frosty, but it was his stare that left Hope frozen in place. She didn't blink, she didn't twitch, and she didn't breathe.

"And I also suggest you forget what you overheard at the restaurant the night Lionel was killed. That call was not for your ears."

"Rupert, we should be going before there's any more drama." Jocelyn approached her husband and slipped an arm around his. Her focus was on the front door.

Rupert flashed a wide smile at Hope, as if he hadn't just conveyed a veiled threat. "It was nice to have finally been able to speak with you, though I wish it was under different circumstances." He turned and, with Jocelyn, who murmured a goodbye, left the house with arms linked.

Hope exhaled the breath she'd held while being threatened by Rupert. She reminded herself she'd been face-to-face with killers before, and Rupert had a long way to go before becoming as intimidating as they had been.

She returned to the buffet table and checked on

the food. Someone had set out the coffeepot and tray of cookies. Hope suspected Iva had done the unexpected and actually helped. She immediately regretted the thought. Iva had her share of troubles and Hope shouldn't judge the woman. What was the old saying about walking a mile in someone else's shoes? Heavens knew, Hope never wanted to walk in her former class-mate's shoes. Ever.

Hope picked up two discarded napkins. The chafing dish was nearly empty, only a few spoonfuls left. Once again, her tried-and-true pasta bake was a hit. The salad was gone, and the bread basket was empty. There'd be little to pack up. She lifted the empty salad bowl.

A woman dressed in a striped linen blazer and sand-colored ankle pants joined Hope at the buffet and reached for a cookie.

"Elaine mentioned you catered all of this. Do you do weddings?" the woman asked.

"No, I'm afraid I don't. I'm just helping this time. I'm Hope Early. I'm a food blogger, not a caterer." Hope juggled the dish and napkins to extend a hand.

The woman shook Hope's hand. "Nice to meet you. I'm Billie Tomlinson. Well, I guess it would be nicer to meet under better circumstances."

Billie's grip was firm. She looked to be in her fifties but in superb shape. Her honey-colored skin glowed. Her cropped, reddish-brown hair was glossy, with a sweep of bangs covering her forehead. Gold-tone, hammered disc earrings dangled from her earlobes.

"How did you know Lionel?" Hope reached for the empty water pitcher.

"Here, let me help you. Doesn't Mrs. Whitcomb have a housekeeper? I thought I saw her."

"Iva. She's here somewhere." Hope let Billie take the water pitcher. She headed to the kitchen with Billie beside her.

"I'm the executive assistant at Whitcomb and Donnelly."

"Have you worked for them long?" When Hope reached the kitchen, she pushed the swinging door. She set the bowl in the sink and took the pitcher from Billie.

"About five years now." Billie nibbled on a cookie.

"Being their executive assistant must be a challenging job; they're both very driven businessmen." Hope tossed the crumpled napkins into the trash.

"More like pains in the patootie. I spent most days refereeing and cleaning up their messes. Believe me, five years is a long time. But it was shocking to find out someone murdered Mr. Whitcomb."

Hope rinsed the salad bowl, then pulled open one of the two dishwashers and set the bowl and pitcher inside. "I'm sure the shock of Lionel's death hit your whole company hard."

Billie arched a brow. "Not exactly. Mr. Donnelly came in Monday morning and acted like nothing had happened. Let me tell you, between us, I kinda enjoyed the day."

"How so?"

"It was finally peaceful. For the past few months, he and Mr. Whitcomb had been fighting like cats and dogs. Now, they've always had a rocky partnership, but it had gotten so bad, I thought they'd come to blows any day."

"Do you know what had caused the dissension between them?"

"No." Billie glanced at her watch. "I should get going."

"One more question, if you don't mind. Did Lionel ever mention the Parson horse farm?"

"No. But he got an angry call from a Bart Parson last week. Why?"

"It's nothing. Someone mentioned the farm. Thank you for your help." Hope was also thankful for the information Billie had given her.

"No problem. If you know anyone who needs an assistant, please let me know. I've been thinking about making a change and now seems like a good time. Mr. Whitcomb's death proves life is short." Billie reached into her purse and pulled out a business card. "My cell number is on it." She turned and walked out of the kitchen.

Hope tapped the card in her palm. She grabbed her purse and slipped the card into a side pocket. While office drama was always intriguing, what really had caught her interest was the angry call Bart made to Lionel before his death. She couldn't help but wonder if Bart had been desperate enough to keep his family's land that he'd resorted to murder.

Bart Parson's home sat just a few feet from the heavily traveled Greenwood Road. When Hope and Claire took riding lessons as teenagers, the road was quiet enough to ride their leased horses along. Now Hope wouldn't dare do such a thing. A speeding car whizzed by, and she shook her head. The price of development. She turned her attention back to the house. The two-story, red farmhouse was shabby, and not in a chic sort of way. Peeling paint, missing roof shingles, and a crumbling chimney left Hope frowning.

Years ago, the home had been charming. In the summer months, flower pots nestled on the porch spilled over with blooms, and at Christmas, twinkle lights lit up the house. Now it was sad-looking.

She walked along the battered brick path to the porch carrying a container of chocolate cookies and shortbread bars. They were extras she had from the reception. She climbed the two weathered steps and knocked on the front door. After a few seconds, she heard footsteps advancing, and then the door creaked open.

A tall woman with long, gray hair to her waist and sallow skin squinted at Hope through the partially open door.

"Hi, Hildy. I'm Hope Early. Do you remember me?" Hope searched the woman's dull eyes for any recognition. None was forthcoming.

"Hope Early?" Hildy stared at Hope, and then she smiled. "Elizabeth's daughter? Yes, yes, I do." She opened the door wider, and a cat slinked by and darted down the porch steps.

"Elizabeth's my mother. I was thinking of my riding lessons and thought I should stop by for a visit. I baked." Hope handed Hildy the container. Her baked goods were always a welcome gift, and she'd hoped they would gain her entry into the Parson house so she could ask some questions about Lionel's offer on their property and find out how firm Bart was against selling the farm. Aware of what she'd promised Ethan and Drew, she would take any information gleaned from Hildy straight to them.

"Your mother was a fine baker. Are you?" Hildy stepped back and gestured for Hope to enter. Dressed in a pair of baggy, cropped white pants and a lime-green T-shirt, Hildy was bordering on the frail. She towered over Hope by a few inches, but her shoulders slumped forward, and when she turned to lead Hope inside the house, the hump on her back was visible through the thin shirt.

"Thank you. She taught me everything I know."

Hope stepped into the house and entered the living room, which was tiny and in desperate need of an airing out. Nicotine odor hung in the air. Hope suspected the walls weren't a muted shade of beige but rather white layered with years of smoke.

She spotted another cat seated on the arm of a chair, licking its paw.

"We'll see." Hildy's smile widened and revealed cigarette-stained teeth. She then led Hope into the kitchen.

The pint-size room was laid out to be functional, but Hope wasn't sure if the old appliances were. The dark wood cabinets had seen better days too. Some of their doors were loose and the hardware was missing.

"Sit." Hildy dropped to a chair at the table and opened the container. She reached in for a shortbread bar and took a bite.

Hope peered out the window over the sink for Bart. There was no sign of him. A ball of fur startled her. The dark gray feline had jumped up onto the table and rubbed its head against the container.

How many cats did the Parsons own?

Hildy swatted at the cat and it jumped down. "That's

Edgar. He thinks he's the king around here." She laughed, and it turned into a hacking cough.

"Would you like a glass of water?"

Hildy waved away the offer and her cough lingered for another moment. "Nah, I'm good." She finished eating her cookie.

"Is Bart home?"

"He's around somewhere. We may live in the same house, but I don't keep tabs on him. I appreciate the visit and the cookies, but I'm curious as to why you've shown up suddenly after all these years. And don't bother with the nonsense about reminiscing." Hildy helped herself to a chocolate cookie.

Hope wriggled in her seat. She'd forgotten Hildy's tendency to being direct and her ability to hold a grudge for an indeterminate amount of time. Maybe visiting the Parsons hadn't been the best idea. Their property was located on the edge of town, far away from any other houses, and if Bart was the killer, she'd just put herself into a very sticky situation.

"Have you heard about Lionel Whitcomb's murder?"

"Who hasn't? It's a shame. He was going to make us rich."

"How so?"

Hildy waved her half-eaten cookie. "Turns out we're land rich. Which doesn't help pay the bills. Look at this place. It needs a hell of a lot of work and we can't afford it. Mr. Whitcomb said he would buy all this and turn it into condos." Hildy finished chomping on her cookie and leaned forward. "I was dreaming about buying one myself."

She broke out into a deep laugh that turned into another hacking cough.

"Your brother wasn't on board with selling to Lionel?"

"That old stick-in-the-mud? He has some idea he should die here in this house. He almost did last week, but they saved him." She sounded disappointed.

"He called Lionel last week. Do you know why?"

Hildy licked her lips and considered Hope for a long moment. "Did you come here to find out if my brother killed Mr. Whitcomb?" She reached for the lid and covered the container and shoved it across the table to Hope. "You should give your mother a call. You need some more baking lessons. They aren't as good as her cookies."

Hildy stood and breezed past Hope.

Stunned, Hope grabbed the container and stood to follow Hildy to the front door. It was clear her visit was over.

"I didn't mean to offend you." Hope reached the now-open door.

"And all along I thought your sister was the bratty one. Two peas in a pod." Hildy closed the door, shuffling Hope over the threshold.

With the door slammed in her face, Hope stood on the porch feeling exposed and frustrated. It wasn't the first time she'd been tossed out of someone's house, but it was becoming more common now, since she'd begun channeling her inner amateur sleuth.

And, honestly, she wasn't sure which irritated her more, being shown the door or having her cookies critiqued.

"I guess your visit didn't go as expected."

Drew.

Hope looked over her shoulder and there he was,

standing on the crumbling walkway with his arms crossed over his chest with a caught-ya look on his artificially tanned face. Not a sun worshipper, he got his tan thanks to a pump bottle and a sponge. And when he shared his self-tanning sessions, they always fell into the TMI category.

"What are you doing here?" Hope turned around to face Drew. She wished he'd wipe the smirk off his face.

"I came to talk to Hildy and Bart, but I'm thinking now may not be the best time because you've annoyed them."

"Only Hildy. I don't know where Bart is." Hope descended the porch steps.

"Why are you here?" Drew planted a hand on his hip while the other hand gripped the strap of his messenger bag.

"I spoke with Rupert at the reception and when I mentioned the condo deal, he got very tense and warned me to stay out of his business. He also said the call I overheard the night Lionel was killed wasn't meant for my ears." Hope started walking to her car. Her fishing expedition had been a bust.

Drew grabbed her arm and stopped her from walking any farther. "Whoa. What call?"

"I didn't tell you?"

"No."

"After my interview with Reid finished, I was on my way out of the restaurant and I passed the hallway that led to the restrooms. Rupert was down the hall on his cell phone talking to someone. He said Lionel had been shot and wanted to know how it happened. And then he said they can't let anyone find out."

"Find out what?"

Hope shook her head. "I don't know. He finally saw me, and I walked away."

"I can't believe you didn't tell me."

"I'm sorry. I forgot." Hope continued to her vehicle with Drew beside her.

"Want to hear what I know?"

Hope stopped again and cocked her head sideways. "What do you know?"

"Three things." Drew held up a finger. "One, Bart isn't the killer because he was in the hospital Friday afternoon until the next morning." He held up a second finger. "Two, Milo and Pamela Hutchinson were in a group therapy session—marriage counseling of all things—at the time of the murder. So the ex-mayor and his wife have an alibi."

"Rats." Three prime suspects—well, at least in Hope's mind—had airtight alibis. "What's number three?"

Drew grinned as he lowered his hand and opened his messenger bag. He pulled out a composition notebook and handed it to Hope.

"Three, you're involved and now you have a notebook to jot down your ideas and theories. No need to thank me. Just keep me in the loop." Drew walked past Hope toward his car.

Hope juggled the notebook and the container of cookies. "You're not going to get all upset and remind me how I've broken my promise?"

"I thought about it. But I figure if you help, I'll have a better chance at scooping Norrie. So, it's a win-win for me."

"You're really good with this?"

"Well, there's one more thing."

Of course there is. "What?"

"Are those cookies? I'm famished. Running down all those alibis left me with no time for lunch." He eyed the container and looked hopeful.

Hope handed him the container. "Enjoy."

"What's the plan? Who are you going to talk to next?" Drew lifted the lid from the container and took out a chocolate cookie.

"I don't know. I need to think."

"What recipe are you going to make? You always bake when you need to think."

"I do, don't I?" With Bart and the Hutchinsons ruled out as suspects, Hope needed to think about who else wanted Lionel dead and why. Good thing she'd purchased a twenty-pound bag of flour the other day and collected a bounty of eggs from her hens, because she had a lot of baking to do.

Chapter Ten

Hope stepped around her camera and gingerly moved one of the morning glory cookies on the backdrop paper. She'd returned home from the Parson farm and, as Drew predicted, baked. Motives, suspects, ex-spouses alive and dead, all jumbled together in her head, and she needed clarity before she could begin to process the information.

What better way than to bake a batch of morning glory cookies? The recipe wasn't difficult, but it was time-consuming and the perfect vehicle to help her collect her thoughts. She'd developed the recipe for her *Cooking Now* feature. The cookie was perfect for a grab-and-go, healthy breakfast. Muffinlike in texture, it was dense and satisfying.

She'd set to baking after letting Bigelow out to do his business and a quick check on Princess, who elongated her furry body into an oh-you're-home-already kind of stretch. Not deterred by the aloofness, Hope bent down and scratched the cat's head, right between her eyes, and the feline purred gently. Hope smiled. While Princess had an independent streak, she was still lovable. Most gals were.

In the kitchen, she shifted her focus to the cookies in hopes of letting her subconscious wade through all the information she'd learned so far, which admittedly wasn't much. By the time she'd set out all her bowls and pulled out the spoons and whisks and ingredients, she was in the zone of baking.

The slow weep of the locally sourced honey into the measuring spoon, the hard sound of chopping walnuts on her mother's cutting board, and the whizzing of her megablender turning almonds into butter took her so far away from murder and lies and hysterical widows that, by the time the oven's timer beeped, she was clearheaded and ready to jot down notes in her new composition notebook.

But first, she had to photograph her cookies. As she mixed the dough, she'd decided to write a series for her blog about the behind the scenes of the collaboration, giving her readers a rare glimpse into the magazine's test kitchen and her recipe development process. She wouldn't be able to share the recipes just yet, but she could tease her readers with photos of the recipes they could get in the January issue.

With the cookie in the far-left corner of the photograph frame moved ever so slightly, she snapped another photo, and another one, before glancing at the camera's screen and reviewing the photographs. Almost there. She'd been using the flat lay as she went along. Shooting from directly above, the layout gave her blog readers or social media followers a bird's-eye view of the recipe. That had become her latest photographic obsession.

She viewed the last few photographs with a critical eye. The sprinkling of chopped walnuts to the layout was a good call. Unlike the decision she'd made to visit the Parsons' earlier.

In hindsight, she realized going out to the isolated horse farm was a bad decision. It would have been unlikely for Bart to confess to killing Lionel if he were the killer. And if he were, she'd put herself in danger. Then there was the harsh critique of her baking skills.

She shook off Hildy's angry words. They weren't personal. Rather, they resulted from her lashing out at the easiest target. Hope reached into the container on the side and snatched a cookie. Taste testing was an ongoing process, and the reason why she ran several days a week. When she finished eating the cookie, she continued with the photo shoot. She fussed with the composition of the shot and snapped away, hoping to get the hero shot, the one all her readers would salivate over.

During the session, her mind kept drifting back to Lionel. How could Miranda not know she wasn't divorced? How could Rona not pursue a divorce after Lionel left her? Why didn't Lionel legally end those marriages? What really went down between him and Rupert? Had one of the heated arguments they had at the office Billie had told her about led to murder?

All of those unanswered questions gave Hope a headache. She paused to stack three cookies and add a glass of milk on the edge of the frame. She reviewed the photo in the screen. Satisfied, she continued photographing.

After a food photography course a few months earlier, she'd invested in a C-stand to mount her camera on for overhead photographs, rather than continuing to climb a ladder to get those shots. Now she couldn't imagine ever going back to contorting herself into a pretzel.

Another unanswered question that fell into the none-of-her-business category was why neither Miranda nor Rona had remarried. Then again, if they'd tied the knot again, their new marriages would have been invalid.

She shuddered. How horrible it would've been to learn your new marriage was bogus because your first one never ended. That would've been a horrible thing to happen if she and Ethan married.

Whoa.

A couple of months of dating didn't mean they were going to a chapel and exchanging vows anytime soon. No, this time around, she planned on taking it slow. Real slow.

She'd been down the road of falling head over heels in love and saying "I do" sooner than she should have.

Six months after meeting Tim, they got engaged. Way too fast.

Then again, Ethan wasn't Tim, and her relationship with him was different. They'd known each other since high school. He was the cool football player with the cool car who dated the cool cheerleader. Yeah, Ethan's cool meter was through the roof. She was his sister's cookie-baking, bookworm friend. He barely noticed her back then. After graduation, they'd all gone their separate ways.

She went to New York City to attend college and Ethan went to a state university and got on to the Hartford Police Department. They'd remained friends, running into each other at town events when they both came home for visits.

When Hope moved back to Jefferson, their friendship strengthened and flourished into something unexpected. Never in a million years did she ever think she'd be dating Ethan Cahill.

She noticed the shift from friend to something more and worried it would ruin their friendship if they made the leap. But their first date kicked Hope's worries to the curb. Their first kiss sent off fireworks and a tingling of warmth right down to her toes, leaving no doubt there was chemistry between them. She'd also never forget the look on his face when she opened her eyes after the kiss. Her heart swelled with joy, contentment, and love.

She was in love.

Too bad love was a fickle emotion, and one that came with the highest of highs and the lowest of lows. She'd learned a big life lesson thanks to her divorce. The word "love" shouldn't be tossed around recklessly or prematurely. Which was why she hadn't shared the feeling out loud with Ethan.

She backed away from the table in her office she used for most of her photography. Nothing fancy. Just a wide, flat surface tucked under a large window. One wall in the room was lined with floor-to-ceiling bookcases, while the other wall had shelves of props and supplies. She set her hands on her hips. She was confident she'd gotten a few good photos to work with. Time to wrap up the shoot. She flicked off her camera and cleared the table. Packing up the cookies into a plastic container, she tried to envision what it was like for Miranda or Rona to wake up one day and learn they were still married to their husband.

Talk about a terrible day.

A crashing sound startled Hope, and she spun around. Princess sat on the desk, licking her paw. The paw she'd just used to knock the cordless phone off the surface.

Hope groaned. When she took Princess in, she'd

expected the cat would be docile. After all, an elderly woman had owned her and also because she looked angelic. Well, apparently, looks were deceiving. Princess was proving to be anything but angelic.

She'd walked to the desk to replace the phone and shoo the cat off when she was stopped by a loud, rapid knocking at the mudroom door. Princess lifted her head and gave Hope a cool look with her deep blue eyes.

"I'll be right back," she told the feline.

Hope crossed the small hall between the office and the mudroom, where the laundry room was tucked in, and hurried to the door. The rapid knocking got louder, and her curiosity was piqued. Who was the impatient person on the other side?

She pulled open the door and found Elaine standing there in midknock. At the reception, she'd avoided being alone with Elaine. It felt a little hypocritical, being there to support the widow while snooping into her past.

"What are you doing here?"

"My life is a nightmare. Haven't I suffered enough with the loss of my husband?" Elaine breezed by Hope and strutted into the kitchen. Her alligator-embossed satchel dangled from her manicured fingertips and her heavy-handed application of a floral perfume left a trail in her wake.

"Please, come in." Hope shut the door and followed Elaine into the kitchen. When she reached the island, she noticed Princess had made her way into the family room and up onto the sofa table. The cat was like a ninja.

"Detective Reid showed up after everyone left. He's trying to make a case against me. You should have heard his questions. You know, he asked me the same questions he asked me the night of Lionel's murder. I think he's trying to trip me up because he thinks I killed Lionel."

"He's doing his job."

Elaine shook her head and raised a finger. "No, he's trying to railroad me. I can't let him. I couldn't survive prison." Her eyes watered and she dug into her satchel for a tissue. She patted her eyes and blew her nose.

Elaine's burst of emotion tugged at Hope. She was struggling with her husband's death and Reid's scrutiny. Definitely not an easy spot to be in.

"Aren't you going to say something?"

"You really don't have a girlfriend you could talk to about this?"

"Hope, you're the only person in a long time to show any kindness to me." Elaine sniffled.

"What about Jocelyn? Her husband and Lionel had been partners for years." Hope moved to the refrigerator. She needed a drink. Too bad there wasn't any liquor, not even an open bottle of wine, in the refrigerator. She grabbed the lemonade pitcher's handle and made do.

"We never clicked. She's older than me and tends to be a little judgmental. I get that a lot." Elaine tucked a lock of her bleached-blond hair behind her ear.

No surprise there.

Hope took out two glasses from an upper cupboard and filled them with lemonade. She slid one toward Elaine and then took a gulp from her glass. She felt sorry for Elaine. She couldn't imagine not having her sister or Drew or Jane to turn to during her crash-and-burn period before settling back in to Jefferson. Hope took another gulp of lemonade.

More tears had Elaine plucking out another tissue.

"I'm sorry you're going through this, but I don't know how I can help you."

Elaine blew her nose. Her flawless makeup was now spotty and, thanks to her emotions, she'd need a lot of skin-tone corrector to hide the redness blotching her face from crying.

"You've solved murders before. You can do it again. For me."

"Elaine, I'm not an investigator. I'm a food blogger."

The waterworks paused. Elaine cocked her head sideways and gave Hope a pointed stare. "I know what you are. Someone who can't mind her own business. You stuck your nose into a murder investigation months ago and you took your theories to the police and look where it got Lionel."

"You're blaming me for his murder?"

"Well, partially it's your fault. You set off a domino effect when you morphed into . . . who's that detective in those books? Nancy Drew! Yes, her. You went all Nancy Drew on the investigation and my poor Lionel got caught up in your zealous behavior."

Hope refilled her glass. Despite not wanting to, she could see how her last venture into amateur sleuthing had resulted in Lionel's arrest and white-collar-crime charges. Though she could argue that eventually, it all would've come out anyway. A person could only hide the truth for so long. With all those rational arguments for why she wasn't responsible for Lionel's legal problems or death, why did she feel guilty?

Hope glanced over the rim of her glass at Elaine. She wore a dress and carried a bag that cost more than Hope's mortgage payment. One would think with all her money and a huge house she didn't have a care in the world. Yet she looked scared and vulnerable.

Hope set the glass on the island. "I have two questions I need you to answer honestly. I want the truth."

Elaine nodded her compliance.

"The reason you were late to the Scavenger Hunt was because you had problems applying your false eyelashes, correct?"

"Yes. I got glue in my eye. I was running late and rushing. I had to flush out my eye with saline solution. Then I chipped a nail, so I had to do a quick touch-up. You don't know how lucky you are. Taking care of this," Elaine did a Vanna White gesture to her body, "takes an enormous amount of work."

Hope opened her mouth to say something but closed it. She was pretty sure she had just been insulted.

"What's the next question?" Elaine looked eager, as if she was answering questions on a game show.

Hope's cell phone rang, interrupting the conversation, much to her dismay. She wanted to get to the next question while Elaine was willing to answer. She retrieved her phone from the back pocket of her jean shorts. It was Drew. She excused herself from Elaine and walked over to the sofa.

"What's up?" she asked after swiping the phone on.

"I talked to Elaine's stepdaughter, Julia Bass. She still lives up in Rye Mill, and she'll see me tomorrow."

"Tomorrow? That's great. Rye Mill—it's about a two-hour drive up north, isn't it?" She lowered her eyelids and silently cursed. She shouldn't have said the town's name out loud. Discreetly, she looked over her shoulder at Elaine. Had she heard Hope's question?

"It is. I just got to the office. Gotta go."

The line went silent and Hope swiped her phone off.

"Something wrong?" Elaine asked after she finished sipping her lemonade.

"No. Nothing's wrong." Hope slipped her phone back into her pocket and joined Elaine at the island. "Let's get back to what we were talking about. My second question is, did you kill Lionel?"

Elaine gasped. "I didn't kill him." She reached out and took Hope's hand in hers. "I'm scared. I'm scared the police won't look any further than me. I understand the detective suspecting me. I had reasons to do what he thinks I did, but I swear, I'm innocent."

"I can't make any promises other than that I will stand by you during the investigation."

Elaine squealed with delight, wrapping her arms around Hope in a tight hug. "Thank you! Knowing you believe me and you'll have my back means the world to me. Thank you! Thank you!"

Hope winced. Elaine's tight hold hurt and her flowery fragrance assaulted her nose. She extracted herself from the hug and put some space between them. Elaine grabbed her satchel from the island and waved goodbye as she exited through the mudroom. Hope followed and closed the door behind her unexpected visitor. Clicking the lock, she hoped when Drew finished talking to Julia Bass he'd have answers and they'd know more about the circumstances around the murder of Elaine's second husband.

Chapter Eleven

"I'm surprised you wanted to have lunch here," Claire said to her sister when they reached a table for two by the window overlooking the Avery Bistro's herb and vegetable garden.

"It's important we show our support for the restaurant after what happened here Friday night. Besides, it's still my favorite restaurant." Seated, Hope accepted a menu from the hostess.

"Your waitress will be over in a few minutes." The hostess smiled before returning to her station.

"You're telling me it's only because of community support we're here today? Because I overheard what you said to the hostess. You asked her about the murder." Claire opened her menu and browsed the lunch selections.

Hope looked over her menu at Claire. "Just making conversation."

"Ah-ha. So you're not trying to solve the murder?"

"I might have the balsamic chicken with rice."

"I'm thinking you're at it again, and for the life of

me, I can't figure out why. It was Lionel Whitcomb who was murdered. He wasn't exactly a pillar of society. The police have a lengthy list of suspects, starting with his three widows. Why you would want to try to solve that slob's murder is beyond me." Claire snapped her menu closed. She had an intense dislike for the late developer. At the end of last winter, he'd chosen another listing agent for his last residential development in town.

"Regardless of his standing in the community, he was a victim."

"What about the people who suffered because of his illegal criminal activity?"

"What are you going to order?" Hope didn't want to argue with her sister.

"The Caesar salad."

Hope closed her menu. "I know the type of man he was. Elaine asked me to help."

Claire rolled her eyes. "Stop right there. She made you feel guilty, didn't she? Sure, you were sticking your nose into an investigation like you're doing now, but you had the best intentions and what her husband did was wrong. He broke the law."

Their waitress approached and took their order. She dashed back a moment later with a bread basket, which Claire pushed away. Hope was happy to see her sister turn up her nose at carbs. Another sign Claire was returning to her old self.

Before the waitress dashed away again, Hope took the opportunity to ask her a question. "Were you working Friday night when the *incident* happened?" The question prompted a glare from her sister.

"Sure. Talk about a crazy night." The waitress leaned

forward and lowered her voice. "You know, about the time the *incident* happened, I heard a car backfire. Now, looking back, I'm thinking I heard the shot. Creepy, huh?"

"All the way in the dining room?" Hope asked.

"No. I was back by the kitchen, refilling a water pitcher. Your lunches will be up soon." The waitress scooted away to another table.

"Rupert told me he was meeting Lionel here Friday night. He also said he wasn't involved with any of the Jefferson developments, that they all belonged to Lionel."

Claire shrugged her shoulders. "Where are you going with this?"

"What if Lionel didn't limit his illegal activities to his Jefferson projects? What if he was doing the same thing on projects owned by Whitcomb and Donnelly and Rupert found out?"

"Your theory is Rupert lured Lionel here, met him outside, shot him, and came in here to wait for his dinner companion to show up?"

"It's plausible." Hope reached for a roll.

Her sister might be anticarbs, but Hope wasn't. Nor was she antibutter, and she slathered the roll with a pat and took a bite. The more she thought about her new theory, the more it made sense because Lionel could've easily bribed other town officials without Rupert knowing.

"I guess it's possible. Partnerships are always dicey." Claire unfolded her napkin and placed it over her lap.

"I've heard Maretta is giving Ethan a hard time about the investigation. She must bombard him every morning for an update."

"He's said little about Maretta." Finishing her last

bite of the roll, Hope realized he had said little about the case. She understood he couldn't share information directly affecting the case, but he barely talked about it, and when he did, he was vague. Very vague.

"I don't doubt Maretta is hounding him. Neither one of us has any experience running a town, but at least I had experience running my business. Well, hopefully two years from now everyone will come to their senses and elect someone more suited for the job."

"Do you think you'll run again?"

"Doubtful. I'm thinking I got lucky by losing. This whole mess of Lionel's murder and the fallout on the town is Maretta's problem." Claire reached for her water glass and took a drink.

Hope leaned back, and that was when she caught sight of a waiter emerging from a hallway carrying two plates out of the kitchen. Beyond the kitchen was the rear parking lot, where Lionel had parked Friday night. If the waitress heard what she thought was a car backfiring, maybe someone in the kitchen heard the shot. Maybe someone saw something.

Maurice Pomeroy. He was the chef, and a former high-school classmate of Hope's. With any luck, he'd be working that day.

"I'll be right back. I'm going to the restroom." Hope slipped off her chair and walked toward the back of the dining room. Instead of veering right, toward the restrooms, she went left, pushed open the kitchen door, and entered into the controlled-chaos environment known as the lunch rush.

Maurice barked orders from his station in the middle of the efficient and bright kitchen. He stopped in midsentence when he noticed Hope. Smiling, he tossed the white towel he held over the shoulder of his chef's jacket.

"Good to see you, Hope."

"Same here. It's been a long time." Hope walked around the center workstation toward Maurice. He stood several inches taller than her and, over the years, his lean physique had filled out to a softer, rounder version and his chestnut-colored brown hair had receded, but his trademark smile was still there.

"Certainly has. Glad you stopped in to see me. I try to get out to the dining room, but sometimes it's too crazy in here."

Now it was Hope's turn to smile. Maurice was making it easy for her.

"Like Friday night?"

He nodded, blowing out a breath. "We've never had so much excitement or bad press. I'm sorry the guy's dead, but why did it have to happen here? We've lost a lot of reservations. But it's picking up." He walked to the grill and checked on two chicken cutlets. A sous chef busied herself with whisking a cream sauce and another kitchen worker zipped by Hope, carrying a stack of plates.

"Glad to hear."

"I heard you also had your own bit of excitement yesterday at the Whitcomb house with one of the so-called widows and Iva. How is she mixed up in this?"

Gossip traveled fast in Jefferson. "She's the housekeeper."

"Glad to hear she's doing something productive. Though someone said she'd stolen jewelry while cleaning a house. I guess people really don't change."

Hope was familiar with the rumor. Claire had hired Iva to clean her house not too long ago, mostly out of pity for a former classmate. The old saying of no good deed going unpunished held true for Claire. Shortly after Iva cleaned, Claire discovered several bracelets went missing. Claire fired Iva, and then Iva turned around and bad-mouthed Claire for not paying her in full for services rendered.

"Maybe you're right. Look at Lionel Whitcomb. He had a lot of enemies."

"Yeah, three of which are those women who claim to be married to him. Man, what a mess." Maurice moved away from the grill and back to the center workstation.

"Were you here Friday night?"

"Right until closing. I never thought in a million years there'd be a murder here."

"A waitress said she heard what she thought was a car backfiring outside the kitchen. Did you hear anything?"

Maurice was silent for a moment. "Come to think of it, I did. It sounded like a car backfiring. I mean, what else could it have been?" His face blanched. "Was it really a gunshot I heard?"

"Probably."

"Wow, I didn't put it together. You know, Friday night we had everyone from the Scavenger Hunt streaming in searching for their treasures and we had a birthday party in one of the private dining rooms. People everywhere, orders, yeah, really busy." Maurice shifted over to the commercial stove and lifted the lid off a twenty-quart pot while lifting a spoon. He stirred the soup. "Wait."

"What is it?"

Maurice pulled back from the stove and returned the lid to the pot, setting down the spoon. "There was something else. Man, I can't believe I blanked on this. Before I heard what I thought was a car, I caught sight of someone out in the parking lot."

"The rear parking lot?" Hope pointed.

"I was passing the door." Maurice gestured to the exit. "And I saw a car. I thought nothing of it. But now, thinking about it, I remember seeing the back of a man, and it looked like he was talking to someone."

"Did you see who he was talking to?"

"Maurice!" a male voice shouted.

"No. I only saw the back of the man. Sorry. Look, I have to get back to work."

"Sure. No problem. But you have to tell Detective Reid, even though you didn't get a look at the person Lionel was talking to."

"I guess you're right. I will, when I finish work tonight. Good seeing you." Maurice darted away to the other end of the kitchen.

Hope savored the moment. She'd just uncovered a new witness for Reid's investigation. Maybe she was good at this sleuthing thing after all.

"'Scuse me, ma'am." A busboy shuffled past Hope with a tub of dirty dishes, pulling her from her thoughts, and she realized she needed to get back to Claire.

Satisfied she'd helped Reid a smidge, Hope exited the kitchen. She wasn't hopeful he would thank her if Maurice's statement led to a break in the case, which it could if Maurice remembered more than he thought he saw.

She arrived back at her table and found lunch had been served and Claire was eating her salad.

"Have a nice chat with Maurice? Don't try to deny it. I know he works here, and you were gone longer than you should have been," Claire said in between bites.

Seated, Hope lifted her knife and fork and sliced into her chicken glazed with a balsamic dressing with a side of fluffy white rice. "Yes, and because I talked to him, he remembered something he will tell Reid about."

"See you're at it again." Meg Griffin approached the table with a dour look that rivaled Maretta's default facial expression of bitterness. Despite their age difference, the two women had a lot in common.

"Hello, Meg," Claire said after she sipped her water.

"We're just enjoying our lunch." Hope bit into the chunk of chicken.

"I don't think so. You weren't so stealth when you entered the kitchen. What does your boyfriend think of you poking around the murder case? I'm not sure why you'd waste your time. Everyone knows Elaine killed her husband."

Meg was a jealous person by nature and had proven it again and again since grade school, especially with Hope. When Hope got a role in a school play Meg wanted, Meg did her best to undermine Hope. And it seemed Meg hadn't outgrown the behavior. Elaine was a flirt and had been friendly with Meg's husband, Jerry, one day. Hope couldn't condone Elaine's flirting, but no one would seriously think Elaine would leave megabucks Lionel for Jerry, who had to turn in his luxury sedan and downgrade to a less pricey model. No one except Meg.

"She was late joining our team, and the reason she was late was because she was murdering her husband."

"When did she meet up with your team?" Hope set down her utensils and considered what Meg was saying.

"We waited twenty minutes for her to show up after your team left. We thought we'd have to forfeit, but then she came rushing into the Community Center all out of breath and in those ridiculous shoes. How on earth she expected to traipse around town in those was beyond me. Then again, she knew we'd find her husband dead and she wouldn't have to continue with the Scavenger Hunt."

Hope did a quick calculation. The Avery Bistro wasn't far from the Whitcomb house. Elaine could've driven to the restaurant, killed Lionel, and then driven to the Community Center.

"Was this your team's first stop?" Hope asked.

Meg crossed her arms over her chest. "Yes. Elaine said we should get the easiest items first, like a napkin, and then the next stop would be a few minutes away at my house to get a recipe card. I thought it would help us make up time."

"You're thinking Elaine set this whole thing up, aren't you?" Claire asked her sister and then glanced at Meg. "Did you tell Detective Reid what you just told us?"

"I think you have me confused with your sister. I've told the police everything I know. I'm not trying to play Nancy Drew, or whatever the name of Jane's amateur detective was." Meg swung around and tramped off to a table across the dining room.

"What are you thinking, Hope?" Claire lifted her fork and returned to eating her lunch.

"Did you know Elaine's second husband was murdered and they never caught the murderer?"

"No! Are you serious? Hope, you need to stay away from her. She could be dangerous."

"I'm not so sure. I don't see her as a killer."

"I'm sure her two dead husbands didn't either." Claire crunched on a cucumber.

Hope reached for her water glass. "You may have a point."

Their conversation shifted from murder to plans for a Labor Day cookout at Hope's house. They lingered a little while longer over coffee, allowing Hope to relax and enjoy her moment as a lady who lunched. Then it was back to reality.

She dropped Claire off at her house and then headed to *Cooking Now* for a few hours.

The full-time staff had to attend a company meeting, which meant she didn't have to go in until after two. She parked in one of the handful of empty spots for visitors to the test kitchen building. Inside, Hope settled at her desk and turned on her computer. She then opened the company's website and clicked on the Careers tab. She searched the employment opportunities and came across an open position for an administrative assistant for the craft magazine.

"Looking to stay on?" Kitty peered over Hope's shoulder.

Hope's fingers paused on her keyboard. She hadn't heard Kitty approach.

"I know someone who might be interested in this position." Hope clicked on the detail list of the position requirements and then clicked on the printer icon.

"A close friend?" Kitty shuffled back when Hope pushed her chair away from her desk and stood.

"Not really. Someone I met the other day. She was Lionel Whitcomb's assistant." Hope walked to the printer and took off the printout. Back at her desk, she slipped the paper into her tote bag.

"Nice of you to help someone you don't know. It's always good to have connections." Kitty walked to her desk and sat.

"I guess so." Hope returned to her seat and closed out of the company's website. "How do you think the Flourless Chocolate Cake recipe went over?"

Kitty lifted her chin and smiled. "It was delicious. Everyone loved it. Including May."

"Good to hear." Hope's walk to her assigned cooking area had a little spring in it. Impressing May wasn't easy. Maybe she was winning the woman over. Hope had a feeling by the end of the assignment, May would see food bloggers in a whole new light. She tied on an apron. Her plan for the afternoon was to work on her morning glory cookie recipe.

Working in the test kitchen was a nice reprieve from the past few days. She didn't have to worry about Elaine barging in and there'd be no talk about murders, and she wouldn't be thinking about her list of suspects. Even Kitty's curiosity had tempered down.

Hope was looking forward to losing herself in her recipe and then biting into a cookie. Because she packed the cookies full of healthy stuff, she wouldn't feel the least bit guilty.

By the time Hope finished drying the mixing bowls, the timer went off and she slid out the two baking sheets from the oven. She set them on a cooling rack, where they'd stay for at least five minutes.

Her phone buzzed. An incoming call from Drew. She snatched up her phone from the counter and walked out of the kitchen to the hallway. To her left was the building exit, straight ahead was the entry to the photo studio, and around the corner to her right were the restrooms.

"Got your message. So, what's up?" Drew asked.

The test kitchen door closed, and Hope walked a few feet, stopped, and leaned against the wall.

"Claire and I went to the Avery Bistro for lunch. I wanted to give you a heads-up for your story."

"I'm listening."

"Just promise me you'll confirm before you write anything."

"Seriously? Do you think I'm a hack like Norrie?"

"No, no, I don't. I didn't mean to insult you."

"Just tell me what you got. I'm almost to Rye Mill."

"A waitress said she heard what sounded like a car backfiring around the time Lionel was killed."

"Meh."

Hope sighed. She thought Drew would've shown more enthusiasm about her newly uncovered information.

"Maurice Pomeroy said he remembered hearing the backfiring also."

"Meh."

"He caught a glimpse out the kitchen's back door around the time he heard a car backfiring and saw a man talking to someone. He was in shock Friday night and forgot to mention that to the police. But he's going to when he gets off tonight."

"Are. You. Freakin'. Serious? You know what you have? You know what I have now? A witness. Thank you, Hope!"

"Well . . . Listen, there's one more thing . . . Drew?" The line went silent, and Hope pulled the phone from her ear. No bars. She'd lost her connection. Darn. She quickly sent a text message letting Drew know Maurice didn't get a good look at the man, nor did he actually see the person the man was talking to.

After sending the text, Hope lowered the phone and sprinted to the test kitchen door. She needed to get the cookies off the cooling rack. Over the threshold, she heard her name from behind.

"Thanks." Kitty rushed to the door, her hand extended to grab the knob. "Are those cookies done yet?"

"Yes, they are." Hope transferred the cookies to a third cooling rack and lifted one. She broke it in half to check its density and beamed. She took a bite. Perfect.

Chapter Twelve

The first thing Hope did when she arrived home was to let Bigelow outside. Next was to find Princess. The cat was curled up in a tight ball on Bigelow's bed in the family room. A quick check of the downstairs revealed the domestic furball terrorist hadn't broken anything while Hope was away. With Bigelow back inside, Hope went upstairs to change into her painting clothes—cutoffs and an oversize shirt. Spattered with paint and wood stain, the shirt was a fabric journal of how far she'd come since fleeing the city. After a quick dinner, she set to work in the living room.

Hope lowered her roller to the paint tray on her ladder's pail shelf. She wiped her sleeve across her forehead. Happy to be done with the first coat of paint, she climbed down the rungs. It was time for a water break. She walked across the drop cloth and picked up her tumbler off the gallon of primer. Sipping, she gave the fireplace wall an appraising look. Not bad. Actually, the medium shade of gray freshened up the room.

For the three other walls, she'd chosen a crisp white. Those gallons were stacked in a corner of the room. More than she probably needed, but they were gifted to her by Frye-Lily paints as part of her role as their brand ambassador. An old door with chipped and weathered paint was propped up against the wall with a new lease on life. It was her latest DIY project. On the window portion of the door she'd sprayed a product that transformed the window into a vintage-looking mirror. To date, the project was one of the most popular blog posts, and it didn't hurt that she'd included a recipe for blondies, a bonus treat for herself and her readers. Upcycling and baking, always a win-win on her blog. The mirrored door would be hung over the sofa when the room was finished.

She set the tumbler back down. Ready to climb back up the ladder, she paused when her phone rang. "Boys of Summer." Ethan's ringtone.

A cool song for a cool dude.

She crossed the room to the sofa table, where she'd tossed her phone when she entered the room. The few pieces of furniture she brought back to Jefferson were clustered together in front of the windows. The other pieces she'd purchased since buying the house were stored in the garage.

"Hey, change your mind about dinner? I have leftovers I could reheat." She turned to face the fireplace, then leaned against the arm of the sofa.

"I ate something quick. But I was thinking about coming over. You still up?"

"Yes, I am. In fact, I just painted the fireplace wall in the living room."

"Ambitious."

Hope chuckled. "Or crazy. I'm exhausted, but I needed to do it before I chickened out on the color and selected something else."

"It's not like you to be indecisive. Why were you having such a hard time with the living room paint color?"

"I'm not sure. To be honest, I don't know if I like it. It needs one more coat and then I'll decide. Anyway, come on over. I have some apple pie left and a whole batch of morning glory cookies."

"Sounds good. Be there in a few."

She disconnected the call and set down the phone. A bark and a glimpse of fur caught her attention. Princess sped into the room and headed right for the ladder. Hope's heart sank with dread. Bigelow followed the cat's path. More dread. Princess careened under the ladder, taking a hard turn to avoid the corner of the room. Bigelow didn't run under the ladder. Rather, he skimmed the ladder, knocking it hard with his side. So hard, the ladder rocked.

Hope watched frozen in horror as the ladder tipped sideways. Her eyes bulged as Bigelow darted away a nanosecond before the ladder crashed onto the floor and the paint in the roller tray splattered all over the drop cloth. In the blink of an eye, both animals were out of the room.

Hope snapped out of her I-can't-believe-my-beloved-pets just did that fog and dashed to the drop cloth to inspect the hardwood floor beneath. She held her breath. Was her antique floor damaged? Would she need to refinish it again? She lifted a corner of the cloth, careful not to let any excess paint spread, and exhaled her breath.

The floor was safe. Not a drop of paint.

But she had a mess to clean up.

She picked up the ladder and stood it upright. By

the time Ethan arrived, she'd discarded the disposable roller tray, and then he helped her gather up the cloth.

"You have your hands full with those two." Ethan followed Hope into the family room. "Where are they?"

"No idea." She loved them, but at the moment, she didn't want to see either one of them. If she could, she'd give them a stern lecture and punishment. But they were animals and all she could do was forgive them for being rambunctious. She continued to the kitchen and plated two slices of Dutch apple pie and filled two glasses with milk.

Thanks to hours of recipe testing squeezed into her tight schedule, she had pies, applesauce, and a basketful of apple-walnut muffins.

Ethan didn't waste any time breaking off a piece of his pie slice. After he swallowed his bite, he grinned. "Delicious as always."

"Long day?" Hope claimed the seat across from Ethan and took a sip of milk.

"Very." He ate another bite of the pie.

"Any progress on the case?"

Ethan gave her a cautious look. "I'm not at liberty to discuss it."

"You are looking at Rupert Donnelly, right?" Hope ate a bite of pie. She enjoyed eating pies as much as she enjoyed baking them. The rolling of the dough, the crimping of the pie crust, and, for the Dutch apple pie, she loved the crumb and streusel topping. The flavors of the sweet apples, cinnamon, and brown sugar mingled together made her very happy. For a fleeting moment, she'd forgotten about the paint-splattered mess that occurred in her living room.

"Why are you asking about Rupert?"

"Drew and I were talking . . ."

"I already don't like the sound of that."

"Ha. Ha. Anyway, isn't a partnership like a marriage? Aren't the spouse and business partner usually the first to be looked at?"

Ethan reached out and covered Hope's hand with his. "Babe, what part of I-can't-discuss-the-case didn't you understand?" He squeezed her hand.

His touch was warm and reassuring, but his words felt like cold water splashed on her. Not because he was shutting her down about discussing the case, but because he was shutting her out.

"How about we discuss hypotheticals?"

"No. This pie is superb. Definitely a keeper." He pulled back his hand and finished his slice.

"Thank you," she muttered as she moved her hand and her lips twisted. He may not want to discuss the case, but she had something more to say about it. "Do you know if Maurice Pomeroy showed up at the police department yet to see Detective Reid?"

"No idea. Besides, Reid left after his shift. Why?"

"Claire and I went to the Avery Bistro for lunch and I talked to Maurice. He said he heard a noise outside around the time Lionel was killed and saw a man standing by a parked car talking to someone. He wasn't sure if it was Lionel because the man had his back to the kitchen door."

Ethan set down his fork and wiped his mouth with a napkin. "You're doing it again."

"No. I'm not. I was simply talking to Maurice and I'm telling you what he said. He also said he would tell Reid everything." Hope leaned back, putting a little more space between her and Ethan.

His dark eyes narrowed on Hope and his lips twitched.

"He said he was in shock and forgot what he'd seen. He's not even sure it was Lionel."

"I warned you. Reid warned you."

"I didn't interrogate him." She didn't think she interrogated him. Though she had asked the questions that led to Maurice recalling what he'd seen. If she'd just popped in to say hi and left, would he have remembered?

"Okay, okay. I appreciate you telling me this and not trying to find out who Lionel, if it was him, was talking to." Ethan's phone rang, and he swiped it on after he pulled it out of its pouch. "Cahill." He listened for a moment. "How bad?" He frowned. "Damn it. I'll be right over."

He disconnected the call.

"What happened?" She wanted to add "If you're at liberty to tell me," but she didn't.

"Maurice Pomeroy was run down in the parking lot of the Avery Bistro. He's dead."

Hope gasped and leaned forward. "He was murdered!"

"We know little right now," he cautioned.

"We know he was a witness in a murder. He planned to tell the police what he saw. Lionel's murder is connected to Maurice's death. I'm certain."

Ethan was quiet, as if he was processing all the information and trying to figure out what was happening in Jefferson. "I've gotta go. I'll call you later." He stood and headed for the mudroom, then stopped. "Hope, do you know if Maurice told anyone else?"

"No, I don't."

"Did you tell anyone else?"

"Claire and Drew."

He shook his head. "I want you to be careful."

"I will. I promise."

"Lock up." Ethan disappeared into the mudroom.

A moment later, Hope heard the door open and close. Bigelow scampered into the kitchen from the hall and arrived at her side. His brown eyes looked remorseful and her heart softened. She reached out her hand and patted him on the head. "All's forgiven. I can't stay mad at you. Come on, we have to lock up."

With Bigelow following her, Hope walked into the mudroom and locked the door. She stared out through the door's glass panels at the darkness. Every fiber of her body screamed it wasn't a coincidence. There was one killer cleaning up, making sure there were no witnesses.

Hope couldn't stay home. After tidying up the kitchen and putting away the painting supplies, she'd texted Drew. He'd just returned from Rye Mill and was on his way to the restaurant. They agreed to meet.

Up ahead, police lights flashed, lighting up the night sky. It was déjà vu all over again. Same location, same scenario.

Avery Bistro and a dead man.

Hope glimpsed a figure emerge from the darkness in her side mirror and the passenger door of her vehicle opened, letting in the sounds of radios squawking.

Drew climbed in and closed the door after he settled into the passenger seat. "Does Ethan know you're here?"

She shook her head. She hadn't heard from him since he'd left her house earlier. He'd told her to lock up, but he hadn't told her to stay put.

"What happened?" Hope asked.

"Maurice was walking out of the kitchen toward his pickup truck when a dark vehicle came speeding from the rear parking lot and hit him. There was a sous chef in the kitchen. She heard the speeding vehicle. She looked out the door in time to see Maurice get hit. The car never stopped."

"Did the sous chef see the driver?"

"No."

"So the car was lying in wait for Maurice?"

"Seems like it. There's an entrance to that section of the parking lot from Orchard Road." Drew pointed out the front window of the car.

Hope remembered the small turnoff from the dead-end road into the parking lot. There were a few houses scattered on the road, but it was mostly wooded. "The car must've come from there."

"The police are questioning everyone who was in the restaurant, but most of the staff had already left. I'd better get back."

"Right." Hope's gaze drifted back to the windshield and to the scene unfolding in front of her. "I pushed Maurice to go to the police, to tell them what he saw."

"You're not responsible for his death. At some point, he would've remembered and gone to the police. Besides, we're not sure if his death is connected to Lionel's murder."

Hope leveled a look on Drew. "This isn't a coincidence. Did you tell anyone else what I told you about Maurice going to the police?"

Drew shook his head. "And give away an exclusive? No way. How about you?"

"Only Claire, when I got back to our table."

"Were there other people around?"

"Sure. It was lunchtime."

"Gotta go. I'll keep you updated. And fill you in on my visit with Julia Bass later. Can't do it now."

"I understand. Call me."

Drew opened the passenger door and climbed out of the vehicle. When he closed the door, Hope started the ignition and pulled out of her parking space. She drove slowly by the restaurant and spotted Ethan exiting it with Detective Reid behind him. She pressed on the accelerator so as not to be seen by either one.

It'd been almost a week since someone killed Lionel and, so far, there didn't seem to be any viable leads. And now another man was dead. Murdered, if tonight's witness was accurate.

Hope flicked on her blinker and made a right turn. The temptation to drive down Orchard Road was overwhelming, but she reasoned the police would look there for evidence. And it would be difficult to explain her presence there if she was spotted by an officer.

Her drive home revealed Jefferson was tucked in for the night. The homes she passed had front lights glowing and curtains drawn. In the morning, they would all learn about another death.

Sadness stabbed at Hope's heart.

When she lived in the city, it wasn't unusual to read in the paper about a murder somewhere in the five boroughs, but when it happened in Jefferson, it was particularly sad because she knew the victims. They weren't anonymous people. Maurice had a dream of opening his own restaurant and now he'd never have the opportunity.

She flicked on her blinker and made a left turn onto Beaver Ridge, a long stretch of road lined with a deep forest on either side. She'd be back home in just a few minutes. Beaver Ridge was curvy and twisty, like most of the roads in the northwest section of the state.

In the daylight, it was a beautiful drive with full, lush trees and thick patches of wildflowers growing along the roadside. At night, it was desolate, and shadows cast from trees, thanks to a full moon, were a little scary.

She reached an intersection and made a right turn and then another right onto her street. She passed by Dorie's house, Gilbert's house, and the empty lot. She'd never get used to it and hoped someone would make an offer on the lot and build a new house soon.

She reached her driveway. At the start of the summer, construction on her garage was completed. Her bank account took a big hit because of the new building, but it was worth it. Winter was a few months off, and now she wouldn't have to deal with de-icing her car every morning, and the two-bay garage provided organized storage space, always a bonus. She'd also splurged on a garage door. She wanted one with modern efficiency but looked like an authentic carriage door to complement her farmhouse. Yes, it was another large expense, but after the job was completed, she was happy with her decision. From the door to the sconces to the trim, all the details gave Hope the look and feel she was going for.

She drove into her gravel driveway. Her headlights shone on the white garage door and her mouth gaped open at the large block letters scrawled across the door.

Stay out of it.

Hope shifted her vehicle into Park and leaned forward onto her steering wheel.

Stay out of it.

She canvassed the area surrounding her garage. No one. She opened the car door and climbed out.

Her steps toward the door were slow and deliberate.

Stay out of it.

She shuddered. Four little words meant to intimidate her. To warn her. To scare her.

Why?

Who?

Stay out of it.

Like hell she would. Not now.

Chapter Thirteen

Hope placed her order for a large hazelnut coffee sans the cinnamon roll. Maurice's death and the cryptic message scrawled on her garage door had made for a restless night's sleep and a major loss of appetite. Waiting, she checked her phone and found several messages. The editor of *The Sweet Taste of Success* cookbook, a representative from a spice brand she'd been trying to connect with, and one from May at *Cooking Now* were among the emails.

She slipped her phone back into her purse and reached for her coffee. While she wasn't hungry, she was desperate for caffeine and expected to be consuming a large amount to get through the day. As she turned to join Jane at a table, Hope bumped into Norrie Jennings.

"Just the person I want to talk to. My sources tell me you spoke with Maurice early yesterday. What did you two talk about?"

Not much of a greeting. A good morning would've been nice.

"No comment." Hope sidestepped around the pestering journalist.

"Any idea who vandalized your house last night? The message seems to show you've become involved with something. Is it the murder investigation of Lionel Whitcomb? What has Elaine said about the other two Mrs. Whitcombs?" Norrie followed Hope.

The rapid-fire questions dizzied Hope. After all, she was running on only a few hours' sleep. She halted and turned to face Norrie.

The sometimes-innocent-girl-next-door look Norrie flashed for the world when it was convenient for her vanished. In its place was the cold, hard stare of a determined reporter.

"Again, no comment." Hope continued to the table but heard Norrie grumble before she exited The Coffee Clique. "Good morning." Hope set down her coffee and sat across from Jane.

"She's persistent." Jane directed her attention back to Hope. "You've been holding out on me." Her bright pink lips pursed and her hooded eyes, swept over with pale blue eyeshadow, narrowed on Hope.

Hope lowered her gaze to avoid the disapproving look. She took a long drink of her coffee. Her third so far. She'd consumed the first two between feeding her chickens and giving a report to a police officer about the vandalism. Because of Maurice's death, she'd waited until the morning to call to report the incident. The police had more important things to deal with than graffiti last night. She also wanted to delay the lecture she was sure Ethan would give her. She took another drink of her coffee.

Jane called in the middle of the officer's visit and Hope filled her in on the cryptic message. She also gave her a quick recap of her conversation with Maurice.

"Yesterday I was so busy. I intended to tell you all

about what Maurice said. Which wasn't much. He never saw the person Lionel was talking to. And he wasn't certain it was Lionel he saw, but the timing suggested it was."

"It appears the killer didn't know that. Otherwise, why kill Maurice?" Jane broke apart the chocolate chip scone in front her. Her mint-green tunic brightened her face, and she wore her favorite pearl-stud earrings. She looked less put out than she had when Hope first joined her.

"You believe Maurice's death is connected to Lionel's?"

"You don't?" Hope's shoulders sagged. In her gut, she knew the two deaths were connected.

"You feel responsible?" Jane popped a piece of scone in her mouth and chewed.

Hope nodded. "Drew says it's not my fault."

"It isn't. It's the fault of the killer. You know, Barbara Neal faced a similar situation in *Dead by Senior Year*."

Hope groaned silently. Once again, she was about to be compared to Jane's fictional creation, and she wasn't sure if that was a healthy thing.

"Her classmate was murdered after Barbara convinced her to go to the college administration to report an inappropriate exchange between her and a professor. Back then, those things weren't discussed like they are now. The victim was often the maligned person and blamed for the situation. Well, after the girl made the report, she was murdered. And Barbara felt guilty. Maybe if she hadn't encouraged her friend to go to the administration, she'd be alive."

Hope hated to admit it, but there was a case for the

comparison. "There's no guarantee the classmate wouldn't have been murdered anyway."

"Exactly! What was known for certain was, the girl would have lived with the shame of the incident and the burden of never speaking out for herself. She'd have been a victim for her entire life. What Barbara did wasn't wrong. And she decided to seek justice for her friend."

"You're saying I should do that?"

"It's the only thing you can do. Now, because someone vandalized your home with a message we believe is connected to the murders, I'm fairly certain you've raised your profile with the killer."

"Great." Hope's goal since she went full-time with her blog was to raise her professional profile with brands and readers, not with killers.

"Don't forget, you helped to solve two previous murders. I've told you before, you have a mind for murder."

"I think I got lucky, in more ways than one. Besides, I don't think I'd know where to start. Three women are claiming to be his wife, and I'm guessing the number of people who had a grudge against Lionel is extensive."

"True. You'd want to start close to home."

"Elaine?"

"What about Elaine?" Drew asked as he pulled out a chair at the table and sat. He dropped his messenger bag on the floor and took a drink of his cappuccino.

"We're discussing where Hope should begin to investigate." Jane popped another piece of scone into her mouth and chewed. She wiped her hands on a napkin and reached for her tea.

"Do we know where Elaine was last night?" Drew

reached out and broke off a piece of Jane's scone, which earned him a slap on the back of his hand and a stern look from the older woman. He grinned before devouring the bite of pastry.

"No, we don't." Hope leaned back. "We also don't know for certain if Maurice was murdered."

"He was. The police are now investigating the hit-and-run as a murder. They didn't find skid marks at the scene. It was intentional." Drew stared at Jane's scone. "I'm famished. I should've gotten a pastry. Be right back." He stood and dashed to the counter.

Jane leaned forward. "You have to find out where Elaine was last night."

"I'll try to see her today."

"See who?" Drew returned to the table with a mega-size blueberry muffin.

"Elaine," Jane said.

"Speaking of Elaine, I need to fill you in on what happened yesterday up in Rye Mill when I visited Julia Bass." He pulled back the wrapper from his muffin and took a bite before continuing with his update.

"We don't have all day," Hope snapped.

"Somebody is cranky pants." Drew wiped his mouth with a napkin.

"Somebody's garage door was vandalized last night," Hope pointed out.

"Right. Sorry about that." Drew lifted his cappuccino and leaned back and crossed his legs. "She's the daughter of Clive Banks and he was Elaine's second husband."

"We know who she is and who her father was," Hope said.

Drew shot her a you-need-to-calm-down look. "She

didn't say much about Elaine we don't already know. According to Julia, her stepmother didn't have close friends until Clive was murdered. Suddenly, Elaine made a new friend, Willa Hayes. They met for coffee and had lunch together. It seemed to Julia the new friend was helping Elaine get through her grieving, the shock of Clive's murder. It wasn't until months later that Julia learned Willa was the wife of a police officer, one of the responding officers the night they found Clive dead."

"Seems a little convenient." Jane crossed her arms over her chest.

"Doesn't it?" Drew took another bite of his muffin and swallowed. "Now, the police officer wasn't investigating the case. However, the optics of this raises the question of whether Elaine was trying to gain information about the ongoing investigation."

"What are you thinking, Hope? You're very quiet." Jane uncrossed her arms and finished the last bite of her scone.

Hope traced the rim of her coffee cup with her forefinger. "It seems convenient. How did Elaine meet Willa? Clive was a prominent member of the town. Willa had to have known Elaine was his widow."

Drew shrugged. "The stepdaughter didn't know."

"If I'm correct, Rye Mill isn't much bigger than Jefferson. They could have known each other before Clive's murder. Like you and Elaine," Jane said.

"It's possible. Drew, did Julia say anything about her father's will?" Hope asked.

"Elaine got half the estate, with the rest split between Julia and her brother. Believe me, Julia is still furious. She considered taking Elaine to court but didn't want to continue dealing with her."

"I'm guessing Lionel's estate goes to his wife because he doesn't have any children," Hope said.

"Which wife?" Jane asked as she swiped up the crumbs around her plate.

"Yes. Which wife?"

The question had all three of their heads swiveling toward Detective Reid, who'd approached the table covertly.

Hope sighed. First Norrie and now Reid. She needed more caffeine.

"Good morning, Detective. It's always nice to see you." Jane grabbed her to-go teacup.

"I hope I'm not interrupting." Reid made his way around the side of the table, giving him eye-to-eye contact with Hope.

"No, never." Drew gathered up his cappuccino and half-eaten muffin and slung his messenger bag over his shoulder.

Hope watched them, puzzled by their quick movements and clipped words. Maybe it was the lack of a good night's sleep that caused her to be slow on the uptake—they were leaving. Hightailing it out of the coffee shop. Abandoning her with Reid.

In unison, Drew and Jane said, "We should go now." And, in a blink of an eye, they were out the door, leaving Hope alone with the detective.

She looked back to Reid. "You sure know how to clear a room."

Reid laughed, flashing a rare smile. "It happens more than you'd think."

Hope didn't doubt it. "Please join me." She gestured to Jane's now-vacant seat. Having him seated across from her was preferable than having him standing over her.

He accepted Hope's offer. "I've been briefed on the vandalism at your house last night. The message painted on your garage door seems to be specific. What are you being cautioned about staying out of?"

Cautioned? Interesting take on the glaring threat.

"I don't know." She lifted her cup and took a drink.

"I think you do. I think you've inserted yourself into another police investigation. I think you're making someone nervous."

"The killer?"

"Ms. Early, this isn't one of Mrs. Merrifield's novels. Recently, you've found yourself in harm's way and, by some miracle or just plain luck, you've survived. It's a known fact, luck has a way of running out."

"I know." She laced her fingers around her cup. "Honestly, I haven't inserted myself in your investigation." Though technically, asking Hildy Parson and Maurice questions could be considered interfering.

"How do you explain your conversation with Maurice Pomeroy yesterday?"

"It was part catch up and part . . . to ask if he'd heard what the waitress had described as a car backfiring. I admit I'm curious."

Reid leaned forward and rested his forearms on the table. His somber, close-set eyes focused on hers. Yep, there was a lecture coming, and she deserved it. Braced for a polite yet firm warning, Hope shifted in her seat, straightening her shoulders and preparing to tell the detective she understood.

"I appreciate your honesty. And now I'll admit something."

Her ears perked up, and she leaned forward too.

"I'm impressed by your ability to notice and recall the innocuous, to piece together the solutions to the previous murders we've had in Jefferson." He quickly raised his forefinger to stave off her reply. "However, you're a civilian and have no business tracking down a killer. While a part of me is impressed by you, let me be clear. I won't hesitate to arrest you for interfering in my investigation. And the chief won't be able to help you. Am I clear?"

I impressed him.

An interesting turn of events, and it left her at a loss for words.

"Ms. Early?"

"Sorry. Yes. You are crystal clear. But I have one question."

"Of course you do."

Hope ignored his wry tone. "Lionel wanted to develop the old Parson horse farm into condos, but Bart Parson was opposed to selling the property and had an alibi for the night of Lionel's murder. But maybe there's someone else who didn't want Lionel to make the deal. Maybe another developer?"

Reid stood, pushing back the chair. "I can't comment on an investigation. However, I'm not ruling out the theory you laid out. One more thing. You should consider installing a security system." Not waiting for a reply, he walked out of the coffee shop.

A ping from her cell phone alerted Hope of a new text message. She grabbed the phone out of her purse. The text was from Jane.

Please, be careful, dear. Someone has you in his or her sights.

Hope lowered the phone and slumped back in her chair. Not exactly comforting words.

Outside The Coffee Clique, Hope's mind turned over Jane's grim text message, which she knew was intended to be helpful. A honking horn caught her attention, and she recognized the sleek sedan. The passenger-door window lowered as she approached Matt Roydon's Lexus and leaned in. She peered inside the luxurious interior. The lawyer did well for himself.

"Good morning."

"Coming or going?" he asked.

"Going home, then I'm off to the magazine."

"Get in. I'll give you a lift."

Hope welcomed the offer. The thought of walking back home in the humidity, even though she wore shorts and a cotton T-shirt, didn't appeal to her. Her favorite season, autumn, was a few weeks away, and she felt like a kid on Christmas Eve waiting for the big day.

"How's it going at the magazine?"

"Good so far. I'm there for a few more days. It's been nice to get out and work somewhere other than my kitchen. It's a different energy, you know?" Hope adjusted the seat belt and snapped it secure.

"I get it. After I got my law degree, I worked for a large firm before going out on my own. It's a different experience."

Hope had met Matt months ago when a local real estate agent was murdered. He'd been the police detective on a cold case she believed was instrumental in the woman's murder.

"You never said why you left the police force to become a lawyer." Hope looked over at Matt. His mussed, sandy-blond hair matched his casual dress of a button-down shirt and khaki shorts. Looked like his weekend was extending into weekdays.

"Not much to tell. I'd thought about law school when I was in college, but being from a cop family, my future was, as they say, sealed."

"I didn't know you came from a line of cops. How many?"

"My dad, his dad, my uncles, and my brothers. There's a strong line of blue in the Roydon clan. It's great for them, but I wanted something else. After ten years on the job, I decided to go to law school."

"How'd your family take it?"

"Not well at first, especially because I became a criminal defense attorney. My family's motto is 'lock 'em up.'" He turned and grinned at Hope.

She laughed. "I guess family can be challenging."

"Speaking of family, how's Claire doing? I left her two messages. I was hoping she could help me finish decorating the house. When she showed the place, she rattled off a long list of ideas. I've done what I can, but now I'm stuck."

Claire had made it her mission to find Matt the perfect weekend house in Jefferson because she believed he was a good catch for Hope. Though they both came to the realization they weren't each other's type. They'd settled into building a solid platonic friendship.

"Give her a little more time. She's coming around. I'm seeing the old Claire come back. In fact, I got a lecture from her recently."

"Let me guess. It had something to do with Whitcomb's murder." Matt turned onto Fieldstone Road and into Hope's driveway.

"Good guess. While I was a little annoyed at the lecture, it was nice to see my sister coming back."

Matt opened his mouth to say something but closed it as he shifted his car into Park. Hope guessed he was trying to figure out what was going on with the blue tarp cover on her garage door.

"Someone spray-painted a message on the door. It said, 'stay out of it.'" Hope didn't want to drag out the conversation. And because there was a tarp, it wasn't like she could hide what had happened.

Matt looked over at Hope. Deep furrows lined his brow. "Do you think they randomly selected your house for vandalism?"

"No, I don't."

"Then what do you believe caused the vandalism?"

"I'm not on the witness stand and you're not cross-examining me."

"Too bad, because if you were you'd be under oath to tell the truth."

"I am telling you the truth."

"Hope, have you put yourself in the crosshairs of a killer again?"

Hope didn't reply. Instead, she unbuckled her seat belt.

"I know cops who go their entire careers without confronting as many killers as you have."

A tapping on the passenger window interrupted their conversation or interrogation, depending on how you looked at it. Hope pressed the power button and lowered the window.

Her contractor, Liam Ferguson, stood there shaking his head.

"How bad is it, Liam?" Hope braced for the worst-case scenario—replacing the door.

"Bad. Needs to be replaced. Have you checked with your insurance? I think they will cover the replacement."

"I'll contact my agent, and in the meantime, order a replacement. I can't leave it up there." She pointed to the big, ugly tarp.

"Sorry I couldn't give you better news." Liam looked over his shoulder and muttered something Hope couldn't hear. He turned back to her. "What's wrong with people these days?" He didn't wait for a reply. He marched to his truck and pulled out a clipboard and began writing something. Hope guessed he was calculating his labor charge. Great. More money she didn't have.

"Did you file a police report?" Matt asked.

"This morning. The police had their hands full last night. Want to come in for a glass of lemonade?"

"Can I have a rain check? I'm meeting someone for coffee."

"Someone? A date?" Hope welcomed a change of topic. Matt, like her, had gone through a rough breakup and indicated he wasn't ready to dip his toe back into the dating pool. Looked like things had changed. And by the hint of color on his cheeks, she was right. "What's his name?"

"Mitchell. He's also a lawyer. Personal injury."

Hope reached out and patted him on the arm. "Good for you."

"It's only coffee."

"It's a start." Hope stepped out of the car. Before she closed the door, she asked, "One quick question. If Miranda and Lionel's marriage was never dissolved, what happens to Elaine?"

"I can only speak in hypothetical terms. If the first marriage wasn't dissolved, the estate goes to the legal wife, which would be the wife from the first marriage."

"The two other spouses would receive nothing?"

"Legally, they wouldn't be entitled to anything from the estate. I'd expect all the parties could come to an arrangement, but it's unlikely, given the high emotions of the parties involved."

Hope chuckled. "High emotion is an understatement when it comes to those three women. Thanks for the lift." Hope closed the door and made her way around to her mudroom as Matt backed his car out of the driveway. She dug her keys out of her purse. She almost felt sorry for the lawyers who would be retained by the three widows. They'd definitely be earning their billable hours.

"I'll call you when I get a delivery date," Liam called out as he climbed into his truck.

Hope waved goodbye before stepping into the mudroom. After the damage to her house at the start of the summer, the last thing she needed was another insurance claim. She tossed her purse onto the bench. How much would her premiums go up? Maybe installing a security system would help offset the looming increase.

Stay out of it.

If only she could.

Chapter Fourteen

Hope's fingers flew over the keyboard in a race to complete her article for *Cooking Now*. She had one paragraph to finish. When she typed the last word, she reached for her cup and took a drink of lukewarm coffee. Talk about disappointing. She'd need a refill of hot, strong coffee to get her through the proofread of the article before sending it to the editor.

The test kitchen was quiet. Most of the staff had returned to the main building. Kitty had left earlier with a long list of supplies and ingredients to purchase. She was responsible for ensuring every recipe produced met the magazine's highest standards. She also made sure everything was done on schedule and spent hours shopping each week for supplies.

The food photographer wasn't around either. Hope guessed he was in the photo studio editing the images for the January issue he'd shot all week. The two interns had their heads together, reviewing tomorrow's schedule before May dismissed them for the day.

Hope had done her best to stay out of May's path during her time at the magazine. May had a clear dislike for Hope's day job. She also got the feeling appearing on a reality baking show was right down there with being a food blogger where the editor was concerned. It was amazing how far down May's slender nose she could look upon people.

Regardless of May's feelings for her, Hope couldn't let them affect the work she'd agreed to do for the magazine. They'd hired her to produce a feature article on quick, healthy meals for the January issue. So far, mission accomplished.

Five recipes for the magazine and three more for the website were done. Now she needed to put the final touch on the article. Polish it up so it shone.

Before diving into the proofread, she wanted to scan through the photographs of the noodle and grain bowls she'd created. A few clicks on her keyboard and the file was open. She leaned closer to her screen to examine each photo, enlarging some to get a better look. Her lips curved upward. The photographs were stunning. During the photo shoot, she'd observed the staff food stylist at work and taken notes. She was always looking to improve her photographs because they captured her readers' attention. A great photo could stop a person from scrolling on in an instant and bring them to the post and recipe.

"Hope."

Hope lifted her head and looked over her shoulder. May was approaching her desk. "What's up?"

"My son isn't feeling well, so I have to head home. Are you almost done?"

"Almost. I have a little more work."

"I prefer not to leave you alone in the kitchen."

"I'll be fine."

May jutted out her chin. "I'm sure you will be; you're an adult. It's company policy."

"I understand. I won't be long." Hope still doubted May's primary concern was the company policy.

"Very well. Make sure you turn off the lights and lock the door to the kitchen." May walked to her desk and gathered up her purse and tote bag and then left the kitchen.

"I hope your son feels better," Hope called out. When the door closed, she returned to the computer.

She continued going through the photographs, getting lost in the subtle nuances of the lighting and angle of each shot.

A deep yawn reminded Hope how late it was getting. She'd fallen down the rabbit hole of viewing hundreds of photographs. Another yawn.

Her cell phone pinged, alerting her to a text message from Claire.

Meet for dinner?

What time was it? Hope looked out the window. It was dark. A quick glance at the computer told her it was after eight. Shoot. She should have left by now. So much for not being long.

She typed a quick reply to Claire, letting her know she was leaving the office now. She rushed to pack up her tote bag. She had leftovers she could reheat, so they'd have a quick meal.

With her stuff packed, Hope headed to the exit. She flicked off the light switches, and the kitchen went dark. She made sure the door locked. May would have nothing to complain about.

Stepping outside, she saw the night air wasn't as thick as it had been earlier in the day. But humidity still clung to Hope as she walked toward her vehicle.

She hated rushing the seasons, but autumn couldn't come soon enough for her.

With the test kitchen being so far away from the main building on the campus, an eerie sense of isolation enveloped her. The dark overhead lamps didn't ease her feelings. She wondered if their timer was off schedule or if they didn't work at all. It was a safety issue, even if the magazine was located in a safe town. It was odd she also considered Jefferson a safe town, yet there'd been two murders here in one week.

Thinking about the two murders wasn't the best idea when she was walking alone in an empty parking lot in the dark. When she arrived, the parking lot was full, except for one spot in an area that edged an embankment with no barrier.

Another safety issue.

She shouldn't spend too much time worrying about such concerns. She was only there for a few more days. There were safety issues to worry about at home. Top on her list was purchasing a home security system, cameras, and floodlights with smart technology.

Her contractor had suggested such a system when her home renovation began, but she didn't like being a prisoner in her own home—having to punch in a code when she left and punch in a code when she got home. Now, looking back at not just the garage vandalism but other incidents that had happened in her home, she was rethinking her original decision. If she'd already had the system installed, she and the police would have gotten a clear image of the vandal.

She decided to call Ethan. Maybe he'd come over for a late dinner like Claire was. She dug into her tote bag for her phone as her car came into view. She walked around the front of her vehicle. Her fingers searched the side pocket where she thought she'd put the phone. It wasn't there. She rummaged through the tote, pushing aside her wallet and about a million other things stashed in there.

Success! She'd found her phone. Just as her fingers grasped the phone, she heard a sound from behind her.

She stopped. The hairs on the back of her neck rose and her skin prickled. Someone was behind her. She felt it in her core. Before she could look over her shoulder, a hard shove pushed her. She yelped as she tumbled forward, tripping over her feet and landing on the pavement, leaving her close to the edge of the embankment.

She'd lost her grip on her phone and her bag fell off her arm.

I need my phone!

She tried to look up, to see who had pushed her, and that was when the sole of a shoe pressed against her back.

She struggled to get away, but being on the ground and stunned from the attack left her at a disadvantage.

Get it together.

The shoe against her back pressed harder and, with a final thrust, her body began its descent down the embankment.

She screamed as she tumbled down the slope. Fear pulsated through her as she bumped over branches, rocks, and dusty dirt. She grasped for anything that could stop her body from falling. Her fingers always missed.

How far would she fall?

Her stomach hit a rock in midturn, and then she rolled along a patch of dry, crunchy leaves.

How deep was the embankment?

Her eyes squeezed shut to keep out the dirt, but she slit one open in time to see a clump of broken branches and tree limbs below where she was heading.

She braced herself for the impact with the debris. Her body landed hard, but she'd stopped. She exhaled a relieved breath and opened her eyes. One wayward branch was too close to her face, and she swatted it away.

She lay there bewildered. The only sounds were her heavy breathing and nature's playlist of frogs and crickets. The latter would soothe her, but lying there battered and bruised, she found no comfort, only anger.

Someone had pushed her. Risked her life. Why?

Stay out of it.

Was it that person? The vandal who'd scrawled the cryptic message on her garage? The person who'd murdered two people?

She'd find no answers lying there under the dark sky. She looked up to the top of the embankment where she'd been pushed from.

No one.

Whoever shoved her and then sent her careening down the embankment was gone. Probably long gone, unless he or she had stood to watch their handiwork.

Before she made another move, Hope did a quick inventory of her body.

Her arms seemed fine. No pain. No protruding bones. Though there were a few scratches. Same with her wrists. She wiggled her toes, and there didn't appear to be any obvious injuries. Well, only to her pants, which were ripped in several places.

She stood, keeping her moves slow and steady. Upright, she did another quick inventory of her body.

All felt good until she put weight on her left ankle. A shot of pain traveled through her.

Her plan to make it up to the parking lot was in jeopardy if she couldn't walk. She'd been right about the embankment being a safety hazard. But being right was of little comfort at the moment.

She looked for her tote bag. Maybe her phone was nearby too.

Could she be so lucky?

She spotted her bag caught on a nub of a log up ahead.

She sucked in a fortifying breath and hiked up, wincing and cursing each time her left foot hit the ground. Just a few more steps. She tried to focus on the bright side. If her ankle was broken, climbing would be impossible.

Focus on the good news.

She reached the log and grabbed her tote bag. She disengaged the handles from the nub while balancing on her right leg. Not so easy when her whole body was shaking. She searched inside for her phone, but it wasn't in there. Damn! It must've fallen out during the scuffle.

She'd have to call for help from the test kitchen. With her tote bag slung over her shoulder, she pushed onward to reach the parking lot. She tried not to cry, but tears streamed down her face with every step closer to the parking lot.

Not too much farther.

She arrived at the top of the slope and paused for a moment to compose herself. Wiping away the tears, she took in a grateful breath. She was safe.

Hope hobbled to her vehicle and noticed two things right away. First, two of her tires were slashed. Outrage bubbled up in her, but the second thing she noticed trumped the outrage—her cell phone on the ground. She bent over, balancing precariously on her right leg. It was cracked, but when she pressed the Home button, the screen lit up and she got a signal.

Yes! It worked.

She tapped on the Contacts app on her phone.

She pressed Ethan's contact.

Only minutes earlier, she was calling him to invite him to dinner.

Now she was calling to report an assault.

Chapter Fifteen

"Is it my imagination or has Helga become more aggressive?" Ethan set the basket of fresh eggs on the kitchen island and then inspected the peck marks on the back of his hand.

After he'd driven Hope home last night, he'd offered to come over first thing in the morning to do the chores. She'd gratefully accepted. Her ankle injury hadn't required a visit to the emergency room, but it made for an uncomfortable night's sleep and a slow go in starting her day.

Too bad Helga didn't appreciate Ethan's helpfulness. The four-pound Hamburg hen was a silver-spangled variety, and she flaunted her good looks. She also wasn't shy about expressing her displeasure. She'd pecked at Hope, too, but over time, the bird had taken it down a notch; now, looking at Ethan's hand, Hope guessed the bird hadn't completely turned a new leaf.

"She's feisty. It's part of her charm."

Ethan snorted.

While he washed his hands, Hope poured a cup of coffee. She handed him the cup after he dried his hands. He flashed a grateful smile and then went to the table.

When she had called him last night after climbing up from the ravine, he'd immediately contacted the local police department and, within minutes, police cars sped into the parking lot. He'd arrived with lights and sirens not long after the first responding officers. She was confident he'd broken every speeding limit to get to her, even though she assured him she was okay. She'd been in the middle of giving a statement to the first responding officer and insisting she didn't need an ambulance when Ethan rushed to her. He pulled her into his embrace and whispered thanks that she wasn't seriously hurt. Being wrapped in his arms comforted her, and she felt safe.

"How are you feeling? Should you be standing?"

"Probably not. But I can't just sit around all day. I'll go crazy." Hope filled her mug and added milk. "Have you heard anything about the incident?"

"Nothing yet. There's not much to go on. The magazine's security cameras didn't capture any usable footage. It looks like what happened was out of range. Honestly, the magazine needs to upgrade their security. Something you need to consider."

"I have security." Hope nodded in Bigelow's direction.

He was sleeping on his bed in the corner of the family room. He'd gotten up bright and early with Hope, gone outside to do his business, and returned for breakfast, which Ethan prepared for him, and then curled up for his first nap of the day.

"Actually, I think Princess may be fiercer."

"Where is the little terror?"

Hope shrugged. "Haven't seen her since you fed

her breakfast. Thank you for helping. Even though I'm able to walk, I couldn't have done the chores out in the barn."

"You need to take it easy. Stay in, bake something, write a blog post, read a book. Do something besides snooping around for the killer." Ethan took a long drink of his coffee. He'd made his point. He suspected the assault on Hope was connected to the murders and she couldn't disagree. But if the killer knew how little she actually knew, he or she wouldn't have wasted time trying to scare her off.

There was a knock at the back door.

"You locked it?" Hope asked.

"As you should all the time." Ethan stood and walked out to the mudroom and returned with Drew behind him.

While Drew flung open his arms as he approached Hope, Ethan sat back down at the table.

Drew pulled her into a big hug. "So glad you're okay. I was scared to death when Claire called me last night and told me what happened."

She could imagine the state Claire was in when she called Drew last night. After Hope's call to Ethan, she'd called Claire, who hadn't taken the news well. In fact, she took it so badly, Hope had to pull her phone from her ear because her sister was yelling. Luckily, the police had arrived, and Hope had to end the call. The cops might not have been able to save her from the assailant, but they saved her from her sister . . . well, at least for a little while.

Hope would have to face her sister at some point.

"I'm okay. I'm going to live."

Drew's hold on Hope was tight, but when she tried to break free, he tightened the hug.

"Drew, I'm serious. I'm okay. You can let go of me."

"Oh, okay." Drew released Hope and stepped backward, giving her a once-over from head to toes. "I hate the thought of someone attacking you from behind. Talk about cowardly."

"Tell me about it." Hope took another cup from the cabinet and filled it with coffee for Drew. She gestured to the carton of milk on the island before she lifted her mug and limped to the table, hiding the stabs of pain shooting up her leg. If either Ethan or Drew saw her as much as wince, they'd force her to stay put, and she hated being confined.

"Any leads on who did this?" Drew topped off his coffee with milk and joined Ethan at the table.

"Not so far." Ethan checked his cell phone as he drank his coffee.

"You didn't catch a glimpse of who did this?" Drew asked Hope.

"No. It happened so fast. By the time I realized someone was behind me, it was too late. I was pushed. I'm sure the police will find out who attacked me." Hope took a drink of her coffee and leaned back.

"From what I've learned so far, there's little for them to go on. Too bad you didn't get a look at the person." Drew's gaze drifted to the island and onto the egg basket. "Did you make breakfast yet?"

"No. Would you like something to eat?"

Drew's shoulders lifted, and he smiled. "An omelet would be great."

"Drew, she hurt her ankle," Ethan said.

"It's okay. It'll only take a few minutes to whip up an omelet and then I'll rest." Hope eased up and, with her cup, limped back to the island to start cooking.

"I scooped Norrie. Again. I just filed my story with my editor." Drew gave a little smug shoulder shimmy.

"Is that so? What do you have?" Ethan's voice had taken on a serious tone.

Drew tilted his head. "I believe the police haven't even stumbled upon this information." His lips slid into a priggish smile that matched his shoulder action.

"Drew." Ethan's voice deepened and he lowered his phone.

Ethan's intensity should've made Drew squirm, but, to his credit, he didn't. Instead, he crossed his arms over his chest and returned Ethan's glare.

Oh, no. A showdown.

Ethan waited, not saying a word or breaking eye contact.

Hope held her breath.

Drew rolled his eyes and leaned forward, uncrossing his arms. "Fine. But you can't share this publicly until my article is published."

"You don't get to set restrictions on my department." Ethan's posture stiffened, and Hope looked at the bowl of cracked eggs. She hated when Drew and Ethan got into disagreements about the public's right to know.

She heated a pan on the stovetop and resumed whisking the eggs with water. The steam from the water made for a nice, fluffy omelet.

"I really need the exclusive, so try to help a guy out."

"No promises." Ethan shoved his cup aside and leaned back.

"I tracked down a birth certificate for a baby named Katherine. Miranda was listed as the mother and Ken Ellis was listed as the father."

Hope's head swung up as she poured half the egg mixture into the pan.

A baby?

"Based on my research, Miranda gave birth a few months after Lionel left her. I can do simple math. I suspect Ken Ellis isn't the biological father." Drew took a drink of his coffee and eyed Hope. "Have you any of your honey wheat bread left?"

Hope nodded. Once a week she made a loaf, and there was still some left. Perhaps she'd bake another loaf, seeing as she was limited in what she could do until her ankle healed. Returning her attention to the omelet, she added leftover diced tomatoes and a handful of shredded cheddar cheese to the egg mixture.

"She's not a short-order cook," Ethan admonished.

"I'll make the toast myself." Drew stood and walked to the island. He pulled open the bread drawer and grabbed the loaf of bread.

"How'd you get the birth certificate?" Ethan asked.

"I have my sources and methods." At the island, Drew opened the bread bag and pulled a serrated knife from the walnut knife block.

Hope folded over one side of the omelet and then slid out the egg dish, allowing it to fold over itself on the plate. It was a perfect cocoon of fluffy eggs and melted cheese with a brightness from the tomatoes.

"Isn't Kitty a nickname for Katherine?" Hope handed Drew the plate and gestured she'd take care of the toast. What were a few more minutes on her aching ankle? She could make both men fend for themselves, but she couldn't help herself. She enjoyed cooking for others. With four slices of bread in the toaster, she returned to the stovetop, took out another pan from the lower cupboard, and began making a second omelet.

"It could be." Drew sat at the table and broke into his omelet. He made yummy noises as he chewed.

Ethan stood and helped himself to a coffee refill. "Why are you asking, Hope?"

She recalled Kitty's words after Lionel was murdered. She was talking about herself.

"Men like him think they can get away with whatever they want and consequences be damned. They leave broken families, children, in the wake of their greed and lust."

"I've been working with a woman named Kitty Ellis at *Cooking Now* who is young enough to be Miranda's daughter. I think she's Miranda and Lionel's daughter." Hope sprinkled tomatoes and cheese into the second omelet. Ethan hadn't asked for one and he wouldn't, because she was injured. But he'd had a late night and was up before dawn. He needed to eat something and not just grab a bagel on the way to the police department. While the omelet cooked, she buttered the toast and replaced the bread into the bag and then put it back into the drawer.

"No!" Drew flipped open his messenger bag and pulled out his notepad and quickly jotted notes. "This is huge!"

"I'll have Reid look into it." Ethan joined Hope at the island. "Maybe it's a good idea to stay away from the magazine until we know who pushed you and slashed your tires."

There was that look again. The one she saw on Ethan's face in the few seconds between him arriving on the scene and pulling her into his arms. Worry, fear, relief all rolled together and making her feel guilty.

Wait. Why was she feeling guilty? The person who'd pushed her down the embankment should bear the full weight of remorsefulness. Not her.

"I don't want to overreact or change my life because of what happened last night." Hope leaned her arms on the island, shifting some body weight off her ankle.

"It's not just one incident. There was the message spray-painted on your garage door," Ethan reminded her.

She plated the omelet.

"Thanks." He carried the plate and coffee cup back to the table.

"I have a little more to do on my feature and the editor in chief wants to meet with me." Hope set the pan on a trivet.

"Why?" Ethan broke off a piece of the omelet and chewed.

"Not sure. I'll be careful, and I'll leave when it's still light out." Hope pushed off the island. "I think I need to sit."

Ethan jumped up from his chair and rushed over to her. He wrapped an arm around her waist, taking the weight off her ankle, and guided her to the table. His cell phone dinged, and he read the new text message.

"Sorry. I've gotta go. Drew, can you stay and clean up the dishes?"

Drew had a mouthful of toast, so he nodded his reply.

"Thanks." Ethan kissed Hope on the head. "Don't overdo it today. And be careful." He grabbed a slice of toast to take on his way out the back door.

"I think I'll pay Miss Ellis a visit." Drew drained the last of his coffee.

"When?" Hope pulled Ethan's plate toward her. He'd left half the omelet. She picked up his fork and finished what remained.

"You heard what Ethan said. He wants you to take it easy and stay out of trouble." Drew finished eating his toast.

"There are a lot of things he wants." She smiled. She hated going against his wishes, but she was a big girl and could take care of herself. After all, she'd managed to get herself out of the embankment the night before.

"You think Kitty pushed you?"

Hope shrugged. "No idea. But I'm curious if she's Miranda's daughter."

"Let me do my job." Drew wiped his mouth with a napkin, then stood. He walked to Hope's side and held out his hand. "You're staying put."

"But . . ."

"No buts. I'll go talk to Kitty. You'll stay and rest your ankle." He tugged her up and assisted her to the family room. They made their way to the sofa and she sat. Next, he retrieved her laptop from the coffee table and handed it to her. "I'll clean up and you can do some work."

She opened her mouth to protest, but Drew raised a finger.

He grinned. He seemed to be enjoying bossing her around. "This isn't up for negotiation."

Her lips twisted with frustration. When did he start listening to Ethan?

Hope pushed open the front door and immediately regretted calling her sister for a ride to the Merrifield Inn for two reasons.

The first reason was having to listen to Claire once again read her the riot act about putting herself in danger. Hope tried to tell her sister she was simply walking to her car, but, because Claire was on a roll, she couldn't get in a word. She'd resigned herself to listening and nodding. That way her sister could get the lecture out of her system.

The second reason was the scene she'd just come upon. She considered retracing her steps back out to the sidewalk and waiting for Claire to come back for her.

But it was too late. Sally had spotted her.

"Thank goodness you're here. Maybe you can talk some sense into them." Sally gestured to Miranda and Rona, who were nose to nose in a heated discussion in the lobby of the inn. "We can't break up this catfight." For Sally to admit she'd failed to shush someone meant the situation had gone totally awry.

"I will fight for what's mine. You don't intimidate me." Rona seemed to be all fired up. She poked a finger at Miranda, just shy of touching her.

"You can fight all you want, but it'll do you no good. Everything goes to me. I've already consulted with my lawyer." Miranda rested her hands on her hips. Dressed in a black-and-white, polka-dot chiffon dress, she appeared poised and confident. She'd finished the outfit off with simple, low-heeled black wedge pumps and a round white purse.

"I've got a lawyer too." Rona lowered her hand and took an equally defiant stance. Her short hair had sculpted spikes again, and she wore a cap-sleeved, bleached-denim dress and gold-tone sandals. She'd added a long, beaded necklace with a cross pendant and a scarf fringed with pom-poms for a bit of boho flair.

Elaine had been an outlier in the group but now jumped into the fray after pulling her phone from her designer purse and holding it up for the two other women to see. "Hold on one second. I'm his wife. We were married in a lovely service in front of hundreds of people. See. Our wedding photos."

Those photographs started a new round of legal threats in high-pitched voices all at once. The three of them jabbered away, but none of them was being heard.

It gave Hope a headache, and she'd only been inside the inn for a few minutes. Then it struck her how all three of Lionel's wives were very different. He didn't seem to have had a type. There was the conservative Miranda, the free spirit Rona, and the over-the-top, showy Elaine.

She wondered which type he had preferred.

"There you are, dear." Jane ambled toward Hope from the living room. She must've been out on the patio with their other guests because Hope caught a glimpse of the patio door closing behind her. "So glad you were able to get out. How are you feeling?"

"Not too bad. I promised Ethan I'd take it easy today." Though Hope doubted he would consider her going to the inn as taking it easy.

"Good to see you're listening." Sally didn't bother to hide the sarcasm.

"You know, dear, I wouldn't have called and asked you to come over if it wasn't important. You can see things are getting out of hand." Jane's thin eyebrows drew together and she wrung her hands.

"Because you two are so interested in Whitcomb's widows, you both can clean up this mess. And I expect you'll do it quickly. We have other guests." Sally marched away after making her expectations clear.

Hope and Jane looked at each other. Hope considered rock, paper, scissors but didn't think Jane would go for it. So, she sucked in a breath and limped toward the three widows. "Good morning," she said in her perkiest tone and received three glares in return.

So much for perky.

"This is a waste of time. You two can battle it out for whatever may be available after the estate is settled. Though I can't imagine me not inheriting everything." Miranda tilted her head back and smirked. Her confidence was high.

"We'll see about that!" Elaine spun around and marched out of the inn without so much as a goodbye to Hope.

"I'm not leaving empty-handed. Not this time." Rona stalked up the staircase and disappeared down the hallway.

"Quite a scene, wasn't it? To be honest, I'm exhausted from all this nonsense." Miranda dug into her purse for her compact and checked her makeup.

"This is a serious matter. Lionel was a bigamist, and he's left a big mess." Hope tried to understand Miranda's perspective, but it was hard. She was still legally married to the man, but they'd been living as a divorced couple all these years, so did she really deserve the entire estate?

"I'm aware of how serious this is and how much it's costing me. Lawyers aren't cheap." Miranda snapped shut the compact.

"There's no chance the three of you can work out a compromise? Maybe mediation?" Hope asked.

Miranda scoffed. "And give those two bimbos money? Not a chance."

"If you did, then there'd be less money for you and your daughter, Katherine."

Miranda's face shifted from triumphant to stunned

in a matter of moments. Her eyes clouded with worry and she chewed on her lower lip.

"How do you know about Katherine?" she asked in a hushed tone.

"Is she Lionel's daughter?"

"How dare you stick your nose into my private business?" Miranda breezed by Hope and headed to the living room. Her stride was quick and purposeful. She wanted distance from Hope.

Hope followed. Limping, she took longer than she normally would to catch up with Miranda. "I'm trying to help. Is Katherine, or Kitty, his daughter?"

Miranda wobbled and stretched out her hand to the wingback chair to steady herself. "Kitty. How do you know that's what we call her?"

"I've been working with her at *Cooking Now* magazine."

Miranda dropped onto the chair. Her bravado vanished. In its place was panic. She set her purse on her lap and fussed with its strap.

"I'm guessing I'm right. Kitty is Lionel's daughter."

"You have to understand. Kitty grew up believing Ken was her father. She only learned the truth last year, when he died. She'd gone through some papers and came to me with questions." Miranda lowered her eyelids. "I told her about my marriage and divorce from Lionel and she figured out the truth."

"How did she take it?"

Miranda chewed on her lower lip. Hope suspected she was trying to decide how much to share.

"Not well. She was angry at Ken, and at me. I couldn't blame her." Miranda paused. "This isn't easy for me. Lionel had left. There was no explanation, and then I found out I was pregnant. Ken came along, and he was the type of man who wouldn't walk out on us. I wanted her to have the stability of parents who would be there, no matter what."

Hope's ankle throbbed. She'd been on it too long. She eased down on the ottoman in front of Miranda. Perhaps being at eye level might make their conversation less adversarial. "You did what you needed to do for Kitty's best interest."

"She didn't see it that way. We both lied to her. But we had no idea where Lionel was, and Kitty didn't want to see him either. She was angry with him."

"Angry enough to confront him?"

Miranda sucked in a breath at the insinuation.

"Do you think Kitty could've confronted him?" Hope asked.

"She's not a killer."

"A witness saw Lionel talking to someone before he was murdered. Was it you?"

"No. And I assure you it wasn't Kitty either." Miranda jutted out her chin. "I think I've said too much to you about this. I expect what I've shared with you will remain between us."

"'There have been two murders. The police need to know everything."

"I forbid you to repeat what I've just said." Miranda rose to her feet, her purse tumbling, but she caught it before it landed on the floor.

"What we talked about isn't privileged information."

"If you're acting as an agent of the police, nothing I said can be used against me."

"Acting as what?"

"It's not true you're dating the chief of police?" Miranda challenged.

Hope gasped. "What?"

"You have my word. I'll make your life a living hell." Miranda stormed out of the room.

Hope's gaze followed the woman as she disappeared up the staircase.

Jane shuffled into the room with a pensive look on her face. "She doesn't look happy. What did she say?"

Hope stood and adjusted her purse strap on her shoulder. "Lionel was Kitty's father and she threatened me."

Chapter Sixteen

Claire arrived back at the inn to pick up her sister and Hope requested a stop at The Coffee Clique before heading home. Claire obliged and, with a short drive along Main Street, they were in line to place their orders.

"Any luck finding out what's going on with all those new followers?" Claire asked before taking a drink of her iced vanilla latte and scoping out the coffee shop for a table, which was busy for late morning.

Hope shook her head. While checking her social media accounts after Drew deposited her on the sofa, she had discovered dozens of angry comments. They all accused her of buying followers and likes.

"Not yet. So far, it doesn't look like anyone tagged me, so I don't understand where they all came from."

While it could raise a blogger's profile among brands to have hundreds of thousands of followers, when they'd been bought, they were pretty much useless. The best way, and, admittedly, the hardest way, to gain followers was to build a community one person at a time.

Claire walked away from the counter toward a table by the window.

"I've worked too hard to risk alienating my followers and the brands I work with to buy follows. I'm having a hard time with people thinking I'd do such a thing." Hope walked, at a much slower pace than normal, to the table her sister had claimed.

"See, that's your problem. You want everyone to like you." Claire dropped her satchel and sat.

"Do not."

"Thou protest too much."

Hope sat and was glad she had. She definitely was overdoing it. She lifted the lid from her cup and sipped her coffee. Her sister was right. She was a people pleaser. It was in her DNA. In their mother's DNA, and their grandmother's too. Somehow, Claire hadn't inherited the gene.

"Did a bigger blogger or brand tag you in a post?"

Hope shook her head. "Not that I can find."

"Maybe it was organic. Maybe you're hitting the big time, Sis."

"Here I thought you were already a big-time food blogger." Detective Reid approached their table.

Claire groaned while Hope swung up her head. Most times she wasn't happy to see him, like her sister, but he was saving her a trip to the police department.

"Detective, good to see you. Please join us." Hope pasted on a smile to keep the mood light and friendly, despite her sister's obvious displeasure with Reid's appearance.

"Good morning, Mrs. Dixon." Reid pulled out a

chair and set his cup on the table. "I've spoken with the chief, and he filled me in on Katherine Ellis. Have you really been working with her, Miss Early?"

"Can you believe it?" Claire asked between sips of her latte and blatant dirty looks at the detective.

Reid leveled an unreadable look on Claire. He'd perfected the neutral expression, so Hope couldn't tell if he was offended or amused by her sister's behavior. Either way, she wished Claire would knock it off.

"Yes, on my first day at the magazine, she asked if I knew Lionel. With his legal problems all over the news, I didn't think it was odd. You'll look in to it, won't you?" Hope asked.

"The question I have is, will *you* be looking in to it?" Reid wrapped his tapered fingers around his cup.

"No, she won't. She's not a detective." Claire reached out and covered Hope's hand and squeezed.

Hope looked at her sister, the traitor. "Thanks for the reminder." She yanked her hand from Claire's hold and shook it. The woman had a death grip.

Reid looked at Hope over the rim of his cup. "I think where you're concerned, it's a good idea to remind you of your occupation. I appreciate you've shared this information. And I'm in contact with the detective in charge of your incident last night. I'll keep you informed when I get any updates."

"Look at this two-way street we've got going on," Hope said with a sincere smile. "I share info with you, you share info with me."

He chuckled as he stood. "Have a nice day, ladies."

He strode to the exit and Claire heaved a sigh. "I thought he'd never leave."

"I'm surprised he stayed as long as he did with you staring daggers at him."

Claire waved her hand. "Hello. Remember, he arrested me?"

"You need to move past the incident." Hope immediately drew back from the table. She probably shouldn't have said that, because her sister was now staring daggers at *her*. "Ready to go home?" she asked sheepishly.

"I am. Let's get going. I have to pick up Hannah from her friend's house and then chauffeur three girls to the movies." Claire stood and swiped up her cup.

"Remember Mom taking us to the movies?"

"I remember the time Meg went with us. Mom had to separate you two." Claire opened the door and held it for Hope. "You two always bickered. You're still bickering."

"Guess some things don't change."

Hope waved goodbye to Claire as she pulled her car out of the driveway. Now back at home, Hope's plan for the rest of the day was to ice her ankle and take two aspirins. She didn't want to be forced to lay low, but she had no choice but to admit she'd overdone it. She'd pushed her injured ankle too far.

"Looks like you're getting around." Gilbert Madison stopped at the end of Hope's driveway with his golden retriever beside him. He and his wife lived down the street in a gray Colonial. Nearing eighty, he kept fit and active, thanks to Buddy's regular walking routine, come rain or shine. Donning a baseball cap, with a cooling towel draped around his neck, he was all prepared for a stroll with Buddy. When he'd purchased the cooling towel, a set of two he got from a shopping channel, he showed Hope how it worked. He wetted the towel and snapped it, and instantly it was cold. It was like a magic trick.

She spotted Bigelow in the living room window, the spot he always went when Gilbert and Buddy passed by the house. He looked alert and eager and wistful. He wanted to come out and play with Buddy, his best friend.

"It's only twisted." She turned back to Gilbert.

"Good to hear. We're going for a walk. I'm happy to take Bigelow along with us."

"That'll be a great help."

"If it's okay with you, I'm going to take them to the dog park."

"Bigelow will love it. Let me get him leashed up. I'll bring him out the back." Hope hobbled toward the porch too fast and her ankle faltered, sending a shooting pain up her leg. She inhaled a deep breath and chided herself for not taking sound advice and staying put.

An impatient woof came from inside the house. With more caution, she climbed the porch steps, and Bigelow was a whir of energy when she opened the door. She managed to get him focused and to follow her to the mudroom. His excitement made slipping on his harness challenging. When he was all ready to go, she unlocked the door and found Gilbert waiting with Buddy. The dogs greeted each other, and Hope swore she saw them smile.

"We won't be too long. Come on, boys." Gilbert left with both dogs. He definitely had his hands full, but he loved being outside and meeting people. Hope guessed he went to the dog park more for his own enjoyment than Buddy's.

She waved goodbye and then returned inside. With Bigelow out for a little playtime, Hope searched for Princess. She found the cat seated on the arm of the sofa in the family room, striking a regal pose.

"Interested in some girl time while Bigelow is out?" Hope stroked the cat's head and held her breath, waiting for the cat's response. Princess pressed her head into Hope's hand and purred. Hope melted. It seemed the cat had two personalities—sweet and wild child. "Girl time it is."

She collapsed onto a cushion. Princess stepped off the arm of the sofa and stretched. Hope envied that long, deep stretch. When Princess was done, she butted Hope's arm. Hope melted some more and responded with pats.

Princess's purring, gentle, rhythmic vibrations, and her snuggling, lulled Hope to sleep. After another night's lost sleep and battling pain all day, the heat had gotten the better of Hope, and her eyelids closed and she rested her head back on the cushion and drifted off.

Sleep came quickly and peacefully until fragments of the past days flashed in her mind's eye. A bloodied white shirt. A body bag. Hysterical sobs amplifying, chasing Hope along a dark stretch of pavement until she reached the end and what lay before her was a plunging hole in the ground the depth of the Grand Canyon. Her heartbeat raced, her breathing shallowed, and she looked over her shoulder as a figure cloaked in black reached out its hands and cackled as it gave a hard shove, sending Hope over the edge.

Hope woke with a start, propelling her upright, jostling Princess and earning her a dirty look as the cat stood, turned, and flicked her tail at Hope before jumping off the sofa.

"Sorry," Hope muttered as she willed her heartbeat to return to normal. She leaned back and took deep breaths to help calm herself. The doorbell rang and she sighed. She tossed a look in the direction of the hall. Maybe the person would go away. Hoping for that outcome, she didn't move.

The doorbell rang again.

Hope frowned. She looked at Princess, who sat on the floor between the sofa and the coffee table. "There better not be a widow on the front porch," she said to the cat.

Princess tilted her head and yawned, signaling to Hope that if there was a widow out there, she was on her own. The doorbell rang again. Hope stood and limped to the foyer. The doorbell chimed again. Whoever it was needed to practice a little patience because she was walking as fast as she could.

Definitely not a widow standing on her welcome mat. She opened the door.

"Kitty. What are you doing here?"

The young woman's downturned mouth and dark look gave Hope a hint the visit wasn't a simple social call.

"I can't believe you went to my mother and asked about me. Was it you who told the police I'm Lionel's daughter?" Kitty's arms were crossed over her chest and her tone was disgruntled.

"No, I didn't tell the police. Did you really think no one would find out?"

"What does it matter? He could have a bunch of kids. Who cares?"

"The police care about everything. They're investigating two murders."

"I spoke with my mother. The detective wants to interview her again."

Hope shouldn't have been surprised Reid had wasted no time in contacting Miranda. She expected their next chat would be held at the police department, and probably in the same interrogation room where she and Claire had both been previously. "Come in and let's talk." Hope reached out and guided Kitty inside the house. It would be easy to be angry, but what Kitty needed at the moment was someone to listen to her.

"I can't believe my mother is a suspect."

"It seems everyone connected to Lionel has been under some level of suspicion. Your mother was present at the restaurant the night your father was killed." Hope closed the door and gestured for Kitty to walk ahead.

"Don't call him that. He was nothing more than a sperm donor." Kitty's posture was stiff, her shoulders were squared, and her footsteps were heavy. Definitely not a social call.

When they reached the kitchen, Kitty took off her leather backpack and set it down on the island while Hope filled the teakettle. "Ken was my father."

Hope nodded. "He raised you, loved you, and was there for every high or low point." Hope set the kettle on a stove burner. "Lionel was a stranger."

"Exactly. He meant nothing to me."

"What about to your mother?" Hope took out two

mugs from an upper cabinet. One was her Favorite
Aunt mug, a gift from her nephew Logan. The other
was her I'll Blog About This mug she got at a blogger
conference. She thought it was funny when she purchased it, but there wasn't anything to laugh about
now. Two people were dead and she had a very unhappy person standing in her kitchen.

"What about her? When we went through the
paperwork, we came across the divorce documents
and discovered the divorce wasn't finalized. She
thought everything was taken care of. Mom had been
a little preoccupied with her pregnancy. She told me
it was difficult."

"Your mother told me she didn't know where
Lionel was. Did you tell her when the news broke
about his arrest?"

"Yes, and I regret it now." Kitty's head hung low.

"If your mother didn't kill Lionel, she has nothing
to worry about."

"Easy for you to say. This morning, a reporter
showed up at my apartment and I've read articles
online. Once word gets out I'm Lionel Whitcomb's
biological daughter, it will turn my life upside down,
and for what reason?"

"Finding justice."

"Do you hear yourself?" Kitty threw up her hands in
the air. "I'm expected to sacrifice my privacy so Lionel
Whitcomb's killer can be found? From what I've
learned about the man, he got what he deserved."

"You don't mean that."

Kitty lowered her arms. "Yes. Yes, I do."

"You need to be careful of what you say. The police
are looking at everyone. Words matter."

"What matters is my mother!"

Hope winced. She understood the emotional roller coaster Kitty was on. Her biological father had been murdered and her mother was a suspect. But lashing out at Hope wasn't going to help the situation. Nor was Hope reacting to Kitty's outburst.

"I'd like to help you." The teakettle whistled, and Hope filled both mugs with water and dropped a tea bag in each. Tea always made things better. At least that was what Jane always said.

Kitty huffed. "Thanks, but I have friends."

"Of course you do." Hope set a carton of milk on the island and retrieved the sugar bowl and a bottle of local honey. "If you came here to yell at me for not minding my business, you're all set. You can leave." Hope stirred milk into her tea and walked to the table. Compassion wasn't working with the younger woman, so Hope needed to find another tactic.

Kitty added a hefty spoonful of sugar into her tea and a splash of milk and then followed Hope. She plopped onto a chair. She drank her tea without looking at Hope and then glanced up. "To be honest, I'm not sure why I came. I'm scared."

"I understand. Why did your mother come to Jefferson? What did she want from Lionel?"

"A divorce. She didn't want him back."

"Why not have a lawyer contact him?"

"She wanted to see him. Face-to-face. She wanted answers. To find out why he decided he didn't want to be married to her anymore."

"Closure?"

Kitty gave a half shrug. "Something like that."

"Your mom will have to answer questions from the police, and so will you."

"What if I say the wrong thing? I don't want to get my mom in trouble." Kitty's chin trembled and her eyes watered.

Hope reached out and covered Kitty's hand with hers. "If she's innocent, you don't have to worry."

"If?" Kitty cocked her head sideways. "She *is* innocent."

Hope was about to say something, but she heard the mudroom door open. Tension crept up her neck. Shoot. She'd forgotten to lock it after she took Bigelow out to Gilbert. She pulled back her hand. Her heart pounded against her chest and her palms grew sweaty. Footsteps approached.

"What is he doing here?" Kitty hissed, pushing back her chair from the table.

Chapter Seventeen

"What's she doing here?" Drew came to a halt in reaction to Kitty's outburst. He sounded confused, but Hope recognized the glimmer in his baby blues. The accidental run-in with Kitty thrilled him.

"You know him?" Kitty's eyebrows lowered and pinched together. "I don't believe this. You're both trying to railroad my mother."

"I'm not trying to railroad her. I'm a reporter. I report facts." Drew stepped farther into the kitchen. He opened the front flap of his messenger bag and pulled out a recorder.

"Like hell you are!" Kitty stood and stomped to the island. She grabbed her backpack and slung it over her shoulder.

"Would you like to make a statement on the record?" Drew switched on the device.

Hope gave him an I-can't-believe-you're-doing-this look and, as usual, he ignored her.

"Here's a fact for you. My mother is innocent. She couldn't have killed Lionel. She doesn't own a gun. But I bet he had one, and I bet his current wife used it to kill him." Kitty's face shifted from anger to frustration, and she let out a loud huff. She stormed out, and a moment later, the front door slammed shut.

Hope and Drew stared at each other, digesting the unpleasant scene that had just played out. Drew returned his recorder to his bag.

"Lionel didn't have a gun permit." Drew pointed to the kettle. "Tea?"

Hope nodded, and he draped his bag on the back of a chair and went to the stovetop. He prepared a cup of Earl Grey.

"He still could have had a gun. Has the weapon been found yet?"

"No. What was Kitty doing here?" Drew added milk to his cup and then discarded the tea bag.

"She's scared and feeling alone. Her dad died last year and now all she has is her mother. Who's now a murder suspect. And who threatened me earlier at the inn."

Drew's eyes widened and he scurried back to the table. "The inn? What were you doing there? Never mind." He waved his fingers. "Fast forward to the threatening part. Leave nothing out."

"Don't get too excited. It wasn't a threat of physical violence. She threatened to have her lawyer drag me through the mud. I believe her exact words were, and I quote 'I'll make your life a living hell,' end quote." Hope cupped her mug and took a drink.

"Why? Now, I need more details."

"Jane had called with a dire SOS. All three widows were at it again in the lobby. I got Claire to drive me over. After they broke up, I talked to Miranda. I used the opportunity to ask her about Kitty."

Drew slumped. "Hope, this is my story. You can't go around town blabbing my leads."

"I did no such thing. Besides, what's important is finding the killer, not a byline."

Drew gasped. "It's amazing you can be so cavalier about someone else's career when your own is hanging on by a thread."

Hope stiffened. "What are you talking about?"

Drew flashed an oh-come-on look.

"What?"

"I've seen those comments about your surge in followers. People don't like it when you buy followers. You have a lot of unhappy peeps."

"I didn't buy followers and I didn't blab your lead all around town."

"I'm saying it's more than *just* a byline. It's my career. But I also want to see the killer caught and brought to justice."

They drank their tea in an uncomfortable silence. In hindsight, Hope saw his point of view about her conversation with Miranda. He was also right about her followers, and she needed to figure out what had happened. Great, another mystery to solve.

"There's still pie left. Would you like a slice?" Hope asked, her way of extending an olive branch to her best friend.

Drew set down his mug. The pout on his face lessened. "Any ice cream?"

Hope nodded and went to stand, but Drew held out his hand.

"I'll get it for us. You stay where you are."

Hope eased back onto the chair while Drew went to the refrigerator.

"Sorry," she said.

"Me too. It was a kinda cheap shot. Your followers know you'd never do something so disreputable."

She traced the rim of her mug with her forefinger. "I've worked too hard to do anything to screw up my relationship with my followers."

Drew bustled in the kitchen, gathering utensils, plates, and the pie from the refrigerator. With them all set out on the island, he pulled open the freezer drawer for the ice cream. Hope had made three flavors the other night—vanilla, chocolate, and peach.

Hope craned her neck to check on Drew. He wasn't using a scoop for the ice cream. Instead, he was using a tablespoon. The scoop was in the drawer beneath the day-to-day flatware. She struggled not to say anything. After all, he was helping. With both slices topped with a generous amount of vanilla ice cream, her mouth watered. She hadn't been hungry since breakfast, but now all she could think about was diving into the large slice of pie covered with ice cream.

Drew set the ice cream container back into the freezer and then carried the plates to the table. "What are you going to do about Miranda's threat?"

She'd gotten over the whole scoop issue and lifted her fork. "There's nothing I can do. Besides, I doubt she'll pursue any legal action because she doesn't have a case." The freshness of the apples, along with the sweetness of the brown sugar and the pop of cinnamon and the creaminess of the ice cream, mingled in Hope's mouth and she was in heaven. All thoughts about Miranda, Kitty, and her followers faded as she broke off another piece of pie.

"I wonder if the truth got Lionel killed." Drew took a bite of his pie.

"The truth about Kitty or the truth about his other wives?"

"Or the truth about his business relationship with Rupert."

"Have you spoken to him?"

"No. He's not giving interviews. I wish I had a way to get inside the business. A contact. But no one is talking."

"I think I have a way. Can you get my phone for me?" Hope twisted on her chair and pointed to the coffee table. "It's over there."

Drew stood. "What are you thinking?" He dashed to retrieve the phone. "You're not planning on keeping me in the dark, are you?" He handed the phone to Hope.

"Don't be paranoid." She swiped on her phone and opened her text messages. She'd added Billie's contact information from her business card when she got home from Elaine's house. "At the reception after Lionel's funeral, I met Billie Tomlinson. She works as the executive assistant at Rupert and Lionel's company. She told me there was a lot of tension between the two men." Hope typed a text.

"What did you text her?"

"There's a position open at the publishing company. It might interest her. I asked her if she wants to meet to discuss it."

Drew nodded. "Nice." He glanced at the wall clock. "I gotta get going. I'm meeting Matt at the gym. And I'm also trying to connect with the wife of that cop from Rye Mill. Phone tag. I hate it. Let me know what happens with Billie." He stood and took his empty plate and fork to the dishwasher. "Do you need anything before I go?"

"I'm not an invalid. I can get around. Go. I'm fine."
Hope shooed him out the door and then finished her
pie in blissful peace. By the time she finished and was
taking her plate to the dishwasher, she received a text
back from Billie. A few more exchanges and they'd
agreed to meet tomorrow afternoon.

Hope hesitated before opening the dishwasher
door. Another slice of pie or not? Decisions, decisions.
She limped to the island and cut another slice of pie
and topped it with a heaping amount of ice cream,
using a scoop. She used her bruised ankle as justifica-
tion. Someone injured her and comfort food, like pie
and ice cream, was a big part of the emotional healing
process.

Yeah, she laughed after she shared her reasoning
with Princess, who remained neutral on the topic.

She'd finished cleaning up the kitchen minutes
before Bigelow returned home both hungry and tired.
After he ate, he jumped on the sofa in the family room
and dozed off. When she'd first brought him home,
she'd made a steadfast rule he'd be sleeping on one
of the three beds she'd bought him. Then the rule
became flexible to allow him to sleep on her bed at
night. And, recently, he'd been curling up on the sofa.
He looked comfortable and all he was doing was sleeping, so what harm could ignoring her own rule bring?

Hope hadn't the heart to scoot him off the sofa, so
she settled down next to him. When she'd moved into
the old farmhouse, she didn't have Bigelow. He came
later, when he found himself homeless. Now she had
a hard time remembering what life was like before she
took him in. Though she was certain it was lonely in
the big house. Having him come live with her added a
cheeriness to her days, a charming unpredictability,

thanks to his boundless energy and a major infusion of unconditional love.

A loud mewing, announcing Princess's arrival, prompted Hope to turn her head toward the doorway. The pure-white cat looked poised, but Hope's house was littered with evidence of Princess's wicked side. What on earth would she do to a Christmas tree? The thought scared the living daylights out of Hope.

Princess flicked her tail and sauntered into the room. She strutted over to Hope and rubbed her long body against her owner's leg.

From Hope's research on cat behavior, she knew it was a sign of Princess claiming Hope as her possession. Whatever the cause, she welcomed the interaction and viewed it as Princess settling into her new home.

Princess sashayed to the corner of the room and curled up in Bigelow's bed. Hope looked at her dog and then back at Princess and realized Bigelow's jumping on the sofa had started when the cat began sleeping in his bed. *Poor Bigelow.*

Hope's cell phone buzzed. She reached for the end table and grabbed the phone. The ringtone was Drew's, and she guessed he wanted to fill her in on his workout. Last month he was into Tabata workouts, and this month was all about kickboxing.

She tapped on the Speakerphone button. "How was your workout?"

"Forget about the workout. You won't believe what happened." Drew's voice had gone up in pitch, and there was noise in the background. Muffled voices and squawking radios.

"Are you at the police department? What's happened?" Her chest tightened and she braced for more bad news.

"Kitty turned herself in to the police. She's confessed to killing Lionel and Maurice."

Hope bolted upright. "What?" She looked at Bigelow, who had been jostled by her unexpected, quick movement. She reached out to pat his head and mouthed an apology while Drew kept talking.

"It's happening so fast. I will be up all night with this story. This is awesome! I'll talk to you later. Gotta go."

Hope disconnected the call and tossed her phone on the coffee table without disturbing Bigelow again. Even so, he looked at her. "Kitty confessed. Wow. It looks like Reid has closed his case."

Bigelow lowered his head on her lap.

"Unless Kitty lied to protect Miranda. Does Kitty really think her mother is capable of murder?"

Sleep had come easily last night, and for that, Hope was eternally grateful to the sleep gods. But she had no gratitude for the person calling and interrupting her slumber. She stretched out her arm and her fingers grappled for the phone on the nightstand.

Found it.

She lifted up the phone and brought it to her face. Her eye slits opened and then fully opened when she saw the time. Six! She was running late. Really late.

She swiped on the phone to take Ethan's call.

"Good morning," she mumbled, falling back to her luxurious down pillows. For the remodel of her old house, she'd maintained a tight budget, but she'd loosened the purse strings when it came to her bedding. After long days of work, either on the house or standing for hours cooking, she wanted to collapse in a cloud at night. She indulged in six hundred thread count sheets and a down featherbed her body molded into while her head rested on equally fluffy pillows.

"Hey there, sleepyhead. I wanted you to know I took care of the chickens this morning."

"You did? Are you coming inside?" Her head fell sideways, and she stared out the window. She hadn't gotten around to hanging curtains yet. In fact, her bedroom hadn't been touched, other than to change out the light fixtures. Her goal was to make the master bedroom her oasis, and for that, she needed a decent budget and time. For now, the queen-size bed, triple dresser, and wingback chair in desperate need of re-upholstering sufficed.

"No. I'm already at the office. There weren't any lights on, so I figured you forgot to set your alarm. Was I right?"

"Actually, I think I slept through it. I heard what happened last night. Kitty confessed to the murders?" Hope tapped on the Speakerphone button.

"She confessed. Beyond that, I'm not able to comment."

"She was here yesterday. She was upset with me."

"Dare I ask why?"

Bigelow stirred. His head lifted and his hooded eyes looked at Hope. He didn't seem worried about waking up late. He dropped his head back down to the comforter. Not worried at all.

"Something about making her mother look guilty. Don't you think this seems too convenient? It's obvious she confessed to protect her mother."

"I can't have this conversation with you."

"What do you mean?"

"This is an official investigation, and I can't discuss it with . . . a . . ."

"With a what? A civilian?"

"I'm sorry, Hope."

"I understand." Though her understanding came with a heavy dose of frustration. There'd always be a part of his life he couldn't discuss with her. Apprehension swept through her. At some point during her marriage to Tim, they'd stopped talking. The situation had intensified when she signed on to *The Sweet Taste of Success*. She couldn't discuss her days with him—what the challenges were, how she faired in the competition, who backstabbed who.

A coldness lodged in her belly.

When a couple stopped talking about one topic, it made it easy to stop talking about something else and then something else until one day, you realized you weren't talking at all.

If Ethan couldn't discuss his work, would the same thing happen to them as a couple eventually?

"Hope? Are you there? Did you hear me?" Ethan asked.

"What? Yeah . . . No. I'm sorry, I got distracted by Bigelow."

The dog raised his head, as if he knew she was blaming him for something he hadn't done. Great. Now she felt doubly guilty for blaming the dog for nothing and fibbing to Ethan.

"Look, I have to go. I'll call you later. Take it easy today, and please try to stay out of trouble."

"Aha . . . wait . . . what?" Before she could ask what he had said, he was gone. She'd only been half-listening because she'd been distracted by her insecurities. Had he shared a nugget of the investigation even though he couldn't officially? Or had he been talking about dinner plans? Either way, she had to figure out what to do about their situation—how they'd handle his inability to share his job with her.

Bigelow stretched out his body and then jumped off the bed. He was ready to start his day and, as the human, she should also. She tossed off the covers and stood, carefully putting weight on her injured ankle. She smiled. No shooting pains, and the swelling had gone down. She was on the mend.

Bigelow woofed.

"I know. I won't overdo it today. I just have a couple of errands to run. I need to get your food and go to the farmers market."

One of the best things about summer in New England was the farmers markets. She visited at least one every week. Her schedule had been jam-packed with work and remodeling. She hadn't had the time to plant a vegetable garden, but that was on her to-do list—some year. Until then, she'd visit markets. The bonus to her outings was that she regularly posted about them on her blog.

Bigelow woofed again and then darted out of the bedroom. His toenails clicked on the hardwood floor, and she heard him descend the staircase. It looked like someone needed to go outside ASAP. She wiggled her toes into her flip-flops, her summer slippers, and pulled on her robe. She grabbed a hair tie from the nightstand and swept up her shoulder-length dark brown hair before following Bigelow downstairs.

By the time the coffee finished brewing, Bigelow was back inside and looking for breakfast. She wanted a shower, but Bigelow's begging eyes had her scooping out his kibble. She combined the dry food with a spoonful of wet food.

Hope poured her coffee while Bigelow chowed down. She walked out of the kitchen and past the table to scan the family room for Princess. The cat liked to hide but showed herself when she was hungry. Hope had tried leaving a filled bowl of food for her, but Bigelow helped himself to the food every chance he got. A few times he'd tried in Princess's presence and she hadn't approved of his rude behavior. She'd swiped his nose with her paw. It may have felt good to Princess to put the dog in his place, but he didn't seem fazed by the assault.

The back door swung open and Claire bounded in, wearing white capri pants, a lilac-colored, short-sleeved T-shirt, and pink training shoes. Her car key dangled from her hand. "Why isn't your door locked?"

"I forgot after Bigelow came in. Coffee?"

Claire shook her head. "No. I'm on my way to the gym. Already caffeinated. Why are you still in your jammies? How's your ankle?"

"I slept late. The ankle is better. Thanks." Hope moved to the table and sat. So far, she'd experienced no discomfort and was splitting her body weight equally between both legs. Things were definitely looking up.

"I heard someone confessed to the murders." Claire walked to the table, but she didn't sit.

"Wow. That was fast."

Claire laughed. "Who needs the newspapers or news shows?"

"You're in a good mood this morning." Hope took a drink of her coffee. She'd love to go for a run but thought her usual three miles would be pushing her recovery. It was best to wait and give her ankle some more time to fully heal.

"I'm feeling good. I can't mope around forever. And my clothes were getting a little tight." Claire lowered her head. Vanity was a powerful motivator. On a scale of one to ten, gaining a few pounds was a twenty in Claire's mind. "I booked an hour with Gavin for every day until next weekend."

"You're going hardcore. Impressive."

Gavin was the most sought-after trainer at the Workout Fix, Jefferson's only fitness center. His tough-love approach yielded results. Brides-to-be and mothers-of-the-brides clamored for sessions with him. Since Claire had sold his Colonial for well over asking, he always had time for his favorite real estate agent.

"I also heard the woman who confessed works at *Cooking Now*. She's the one who's Lionel's daughter and you were talking to Reid about, right?"

Hope nodded. "Yes. In fact, she was here yesterday."

Claire's blue eyes grew wide. "What? You had the killer here in your house?"

"I'm not sure she's the killer."

"What are you talking about? She confessed. I heard she walked into the police station and told them everything."

"You heard a lot for someone who's been a hermit."

"Never mind where I get my information." Claire raised a hand in surrender. She was quiet for a moment and an uneasiness poked at Hope. What was she thinking? "You have quite a puzzle to figure out."

"What? No dire warning?"

"No. You're a big girl and can make your own decisions. If you want to entertain killers and get pushed down embankments, so be it."

"I didn't entertain a killer. She came over here to yell at me for talking to the police about Miranda. I did the right thing. I told the police what I knew. See? I'm playing it safe."

"You want a medal?"

"No. You're confusing me."

"You're being silly. I have to go or I'll be late for my session with Gavin. He doesn't like tardiness."

"Who are you and what have you done with my sister?" Hope wasn't sure why Claire opted not to lecture her and, to be honest, she wasn't sure how to handle her sister's newfound realization Hope could take care of herself.

Claire smiled. "Silly Hope." She wiggled her fingers in a wave and left the house, closing the back door behind her.

Hope dashed to the door and locked it before heading upstairs for a shower and to get ready for her day. She reached the staircase but halted when a loud screech startled her. A flash of fur followed the noise, barreling down the staircase. Hope's gaze followed the fur, and it came to a halt at the bottom of the stairs for a nanosecond and then tore off in the direction of the family room.

She heard a loud thump from the room. To think she'd been worried about high-energy Bigelow when she took him in.

He had nothing on the cat.

Chapter Eighteen

A jingling bell greeted Hope after opening the front door of the Bark Boutique. Newly opened, the shop was packed with adorable dog clothing, fun toys, food, and treats. One-stop shopping for fur moms like her. The bell also alerted the owner of her arrival.

"Hope! Good to see you." Trudy Fraser stepped out from behind the counter. Her brown eyes were warm and welcoming. A foster mom to many pets, she always wore clothing that featured a dog or cat on it. Today, it was a vest featuring a variety of dogs and was paired with a white, button-down blouse and black pants.

"Love your vest."

It seemed impossible, but Trudy's smile broadened. "Fifteen percent goes to a rescue group. I have one with cats on it too."

"I'm sure it's just as pretty. Bigelow and Princess need some food." Hope walked farther into the shop, which was divided into two sections—cats and dogs—and those sections were broken down into categories of food, apparel and leashes, toys, and health and wellness.

Trudy crammed a lot into the small square footage.

"We got a delivery of Bigelow's food this morning." Trudy turned and walked to the dog food aisle. She pulled out a ten-pound bag from the shelf.

"Here, let me." Hope leaned forward to take the bag, but Trudy swatted at her hand. "Ouch."

"I heard about your accident. I'll carry this to the counter."

"I'm doing better." She'd had the sliver of hope her incident would go unnoticed, but it made the *Gazette*, and not a little passing notice in the police blotter but rather a front-page story.

"You shouldn't be walking around." With the bag in hand, Trudy walked to the counter, and Hope followed. "I stopped at The Coffee Clique for my morning latte and everyone was buzzing about Kitty Ellis's confession." Trudy changed the subject without batting an eye. A murder confession was far more interesting than a tumble down a slope. "She works at the magazine where you've been freelancing. Do you know her?"

Hope wasn't about to get snared into the gossip chain and have any comment she made exaggerated and taken out of context. Been there, done that.

"I also need some food for Princess." Hope traveled down the cat food aisle for a few cans. Princess was addicted to salmon, so Hope grabbed four cans of the Salmon Delight entrees.

"I'm still in shock over Lionel Whitcomb's murder and poor Maurice Pomeroy. I remember when there were no murders here in town."

And so did Maretta Kingston.

Would Trudy also blame Hope for the uptick in fatal crimes in town? Not willing to find out, she steered the conversation back to feeding her cat.

"Princess loves salmon and chicken." Hope also snagged a few cans of chicken stew.

"I wonder what Whitcomb's wife will do now," Trudy said.

Which one?

With her arms full of petite cans of food—a nice variety, she thought—Hope returned to the counter. "I'm sure Elaine will survive."

"Guess you're right. She's one of *those* women, you know." Trudy scanned each can of food and dropped them into a bag with the store's logo on it. "I probably shouldn't talk out of school, but we all know what kind of person she is. I wouldn't be surprised if she was trotting around town with another man in a matter of weeks."

Trudy chuckled as she scanned the large bag of food for Bigelow.

"Why do you say that? Do you know something?" Hope reached for an individually wrapped dog cookie. She preferred to make Bigelow's treats herself, but with her jam-packed schedule, she'd been hard pressed to find time to bake.

"I shouldn't gossip."

Really?

"You may know something that could help the police with their investigation."

Trudy took the cookie and scanned it before placing it in the bag. She set down the scanner and looked torn. "I saw Elaine with a man last week. They looked pretty cozy."

"Do you know who the man was?"

"No. He was about Whitcomb's age. But more handsome and a much better dresser. With all his money, you'd think Whitcomb would have dressed better."

"Where did you see them?"

"Horseshoe Tavern. Doug and I go there at least once a month. Do you know it?"

Hope nodded. The restaurant, popular for its house brews and burgers, was a forty-five-minute drive from Jefferson, and she'd met the owner during a challenge on *The Sweet Taste of Success*.

"Elaine and the gentleman were in a deep conversation at a private table. I got the impression they didn't want to be seen."

The bell over the door jingled and a woman entered. She called out a greeting to Trudy.

"Is there anything else you need, Hope?" Trudy asked.

"No, nothing." Except maybe some more details about Elaine's dinner date. "Could I leave this here? Drew is meeting me in a few minutes and he'll carry all of this to my car." Her ankle was definitely feeling better, but she didn't think lugging around the bag of food was a good idea.

"Sure. No problem." Trudy stepped out from behind the counter and approached her next customer.

Hope left the shop. When she stepped outside, she was greeted by humidity and heat. A combo she'd be happy to pass on. But she didn't have a say in the matter, so she was glad she'd chosen to wear a white gauze dress and pull her hair into a ponytail. She'd also slipped on her favorite tan sandals and opted not to wrap her ankle with an ACE bandage. She hoped she wouldn't regret not stabilizing her ankle. She had a habit of being a bad patient.

She walked along Main Street, passing a cluster of antique shops between the Bark Boutique and The Coffee Clique. She lingered for a moment at one of the storefront windows, staring at a display of Wedgwood dessert plates. She recognized the pattern. Produced in the nineteenth century, the dishes had an unexpectedly contemporary feel with their vibrant shades of oranges and browns. The set would certainly be a nice addition to her china collection. Though the mid-four-figure price was too rich for her at the moment.

"Someday," she said wistfully.

Realizing if she stood there any longer, she'd make a rash and financially bad decision, she pulled herself away from the window and continued toward The Coffee Clique. That was when she spotted Iva Johnson. The temptation to turn and pretend she hadn't seen the bitter housekeeper was overwhelming, but they'd already made eye contact. A quick greeting and an even faster goodbye wouldn't kill her.

"Hello, Iva." Hope plastered on her best smile. She was intent on making the best of the unexpected encounter.

"See you're up and about. Recovering from your incident the other night?" Iva's voice was gravelly thanks to years of smoking, and edged with hardness.

"I'm almost fully recovered. Thank you for asking." Hope still had her smile in place.

"Well, I guess things happen when you poke around in someone else's business." Iva arched a thin, over-plucked brow.

Hope and Iva had history and none of it was good. Back then, Iva was Iva Collie, eldest daughter of an alcoholic who used his wife as a punching bag, and sometimes his kids as well. It was the least-kept secret in town. Everyone knew, but no one did anything to help. Whispers of speculation, nods of understanding, and not a single tear shed when old man Collie collapsed of a heart attack. By the time Hope was old enough to understand what was happening in the Collie household, Iva had already dropped out of school and become a teenage bride and mother. Keeping Iva's roots in mind helped Hope not take the insult personally.

"Have a nice day." Hope stepped forward. She needed to get away from Iva because there was only so much goodwill in her.

"It surprised me that woman confessed to the murders. It's all anyone is talking about at the diner. My money was on the current Mrs. Whitcomb."

Hope paused. "Why?" She was curious if Elaine had fired her. Iva's loyalty was commerce-centric. If you paid her, you had her allegiance.

"She and Mr. Whitcomb fought like . . . well, like cats and dogs."

"Marriages have their difficulties."

Iva scoffed. "Tell me about it."

"I have to get going." Hope started forward again, desperate to get to The Coffee Clique for a cinnamon roll.

"It'd gotten worse the past few weeks. And then Mrs. Whitcomb was meeting another man for dinner secretly. Their marriage was doomed. Most are anyway, right?"

"How do you know?"

"I overheard her on the phone a few times when I was at the house. She whispered, but I could still hear." Iva smiled. She hadn't gotten the memo that eavesdropping wasn't something you should be proud of.

"Do you know who the man was?" Could it be the same man Trudy had described seeing with Elaine at the Horseshoe Tavern?

"No. Never heard his name. Wait . . . come to think of it, Elaine was talking to someone the day someone killed Mr. Whitcomb. Not sure if it was the guy."

"How can you be certain she was talking to a man?"

Iva tilted her head. "You know when a woman is talking to a guy. And trust me, he wasn't a telemarketer. Not the way she was twirling her hair around her finger and keeping her voice low."

"Did you tell the police?"

Iva shook her head. "I just remembered now."

"Really?" Hope didn't bother trying to cover up her sarcasm.

"Hey, I don't need your judgment. Things have been very busy lately. My mom is sick, and I've been taking her back and forth for treatments. Maybe I should get one of those fancy planners you shared on your blog and write stuff down."

"I'm sorry to hear about your mother. How is she doing?" Hope didn't have to work hard on gathering up some compassion for Iva. Having to deal with an ill parent wasn't an easy thing to go through.

Iva lowered her eyelids. Her sparse lashes were thick with black mascara that clumped rather than volumized. "As good as can be expected. Thanks for asking."

"The conversation you overheard the day Lionel was killed—do you remember what Elaine said?"

"I do." Iva smirked. "She was meeting the person at the restaurant at six the night of the Scavenger Hunt."

"Are you sure?"

"Of course I am."

It was the meeting with a mystery man that caused Elaine to be late for the Scavenger Hunt, not wayward false lashes. She'd lied about what caused her to arrive late at the event. What else had Elaine lied about?

Suddenly, Hope craved a beer. She had to text Drew.

"Be sure to tell the police what you remembered. It's important." Hope walked away.

"Hope, wait."

Hope stopped and turned. "Did you remember something else?"

"No. It's . . . I haven't been working anywhere other than at the Whitcombs' because I've been caring for my mom, and now I think I won't be working there for much longer. So I need a job. Something. Maybe part-time."

Hope wasn't sure what Iva was looking for from her.

"You've got that big house. Maybe you need some help?"

Okay. It was now clear. Iva was asking for a job.

"I kinda need some cash quick because my car needs a repair and I use it to drive my mom to her treatments."

"I . . . I . . . don't need help with the housework. I'm sorry."

Iva's face slacked, and she broke eye contact with Hope. Her reaction tugged at Hope's heart. The woman was a walking, talking fount of bitterness and jealousy, but she was a person who was struggling and whose mother was ill.

"What would be a great help, but I'm not sure if it's something you're interested in, is taking care of my chickens. There's a bunch of chores to do, and I also need help with some yard work. It's not a lot of hours. Would you be interested?"

Iva smiled a genuinely happy smile. Hope couldn't recall the last time she'd seen Iva look happy. "Ab-solutely. We used to have chickens when I was a kid.

And a bunch of rabbits. It'll be a nice change from dusting. I can start tomorrow."

"Tomorrow?" *So soon?* "Great. Let me give you my cell number and we can confirm the time for you to start and the pay later today." Hope dug out her cell phone from her purse and entered in Iva's contact information.

"Thank you, Hope. I appreciate this." Iva turned and walked along Main Street until she disappeared into the pharmacy.

Hope stared at her phone. What had she done? Of all the people she shouldn't hire to work for her, Iva Johnson was at the top of the list, and yet Hope just had. Well, at least Iva would work outside the house, so Hope wouldn't have to worry about Iva eavesdropping or snooping.

No, what she had to worry about was breaking the news to Claire that she'd hired Iva.

Rather than continue to the coffee shop, Hope texted Drew. She told him to meet her in front of the Bark Boutique and added that it was urgent. They had a new lead.

Within minutes, she was back in front of the shop, and Drew wasted no time in loading the food for Bigelow and Princess into Hope's vehicle. For the trip to the Horseshoe Tavern, they went in his car. Pulling out of the parking space, Hope filled him in on what she'd learned from Trudy and Iva. She left out the part about hiring Iva.

She wasn't sure how that would work out. She could have Iva do the morning chores for the chickens. Those tasks didn't take up a significant amount of time in Hope's day, but having someone else do them meant she only had to close up the chicken coop at night. She also had gardens to continue prepping for fall planting and for next spring. She'd wanted to plant daffodils. She loved seeing them at the beginning of spring. And having help would free up time she could use for her blog and other freelance work.

"She could be having an affair with the unidentified man. Or he could be the killer. Maybe she hired someone to kill Lionel." Drew thought out loud as he navigated his two-door sports car along a winding back road.

"I can't see Elaine hiring a hit man." Hope's eyes flicked from Drew to the expanse of forest stretching along the quiet lane.

Splatters of red maple leaves popped from the thick patches of green. Summer was fading. A new season was on summer's doorstep, and within weeks, there would be so much change. Not only would trees take on vibrant hues of autumn, kids would return to school, the temperature would drop, and the days would shorten. A smile crept onto her lips. Evening meals of hearty stews and cozy nights of reading and snuggling with Ethan. Now, there was a change for the better.

"Earth to Hope . . ." Drew said.

She looked back to Drew, shaking off her thoughts of chilly autumn nights with Ethan and focusing back on their conversation. Maybe Drew was right. Maybe the man Elaine had met with had something to do with not only Lionel's death but also Maurice's. She shouldn't be so quick to dismiss the theory.

"It's something to consider." She leaned her head against the soft, leather seat.

"Now, let me take the lead at the restaurant. Okay?

I've interviewed hundreds of people. I know how to get people to talk to me." Drew turned into the restaurant's parking lot.

Out of his vehicle, they walked across the parking lot and entered through the main door. A smiling hostess greeted them.

"Welcome to Horseshoe Tavern. I'm Kara. Two?"

Hope and Drew nodded in unison, prompting the multipierced twentysomething to grab two menus.

"This way." The hostess, dressed all in black, led them through the main dining room, which was flanked by an exposed brick wall on one side and a view of the massive elevated bar on the other. A large wood railing with metal curlicue inserts ran the length of the bar area. Lanterns dangled from the high ceilings and the wood flooring was worn and scuffed. The dark, wood square tables were set with simple flatware and dark napkins. Six years ago, the once-stodgy, lodge-styled restaurant was transformed into a hip establishment that served craft beers and artisan meals sourced from local producers.

The hostess left Hope and Drew to peruse their menus.

Hope scanned the offerings and her stomach rumbled. She was getting hungrier by the minute.

"I love this tap list." Drew lowered his menu. "I think I'll try the Grizzly Bear Brown Ale."

Hope diverted her gaze to the list. "An American brown ale. Nice choice. It's a roasted malt with caramel and chocolatelike characters." She lowered her menu. "If I recall, they're both a medium intensity for flavor and aroma. It pairs well with meat and vegetables."

"How do you know about the beer?"

"For a challenge on *The Sweet Taste of Success.*" Hope

closed her menu. Deciding was tough, but she'd settled on the burrata salad served on Boston Bibb lettuce with tomato and pesto.

"You took the challenge seriously, didn't you? What else do you know about ales?"

"Quite a bit. I did a lot of studying to make sure I won."

"What was it?" Drew asked.

Before Hope could answer him, a tall man with flame-red hair approached their table with his arms held wide open.

"Hope Early! It's about time you came in for a meal." The man reached out for Hope and gave her a hug. "Good to see you."

"Hello, Brett. It's been a long time." She hugged him back and then untangled herself from his hold. He hadn't changed a bit. Wearing his trademark denim shirt, he looked relaxed and at ease. His deep, emerald eyes twinkled with warmth.

"Too long." He looked over to Drew and extended his hand. "Welcome. I'm Brett McGrath, the owner of the Horseshoe Tavern."

Drew shook Brett's hand. "Drew Adams."

Brett turned his attention back to Hope. "How are you doing? I heard you're a food blogger now."

"I am. *Hope at Home* is my blog. Looks like you're doing well. If you have a few minutes, please join us."

"Sure." Brett grabbed a chair from a nearby table.

Drew leaned forward and whispered, "Why didn't you tell me you knew the owner?"

"You didn't ask."

"I'm glad you've stopped in. Are you celebrating a special occasion or something?" Brett settled onto the chair.

"No, we're not. We're hoping you can help us. We have a few questions about two of your customers. Hopefully, you'll remember them both," Hope said.

"If they're regulars, I probably will. If not, I don't know. We get a lot of people in here," Brett said. "I'm curious why you're asking about my customers. What's going on, Hope?"

"I'm a reporter with the *Gazette* and I'm running down leads in the murder of Lionel Whitcomb. You heard about his death in Jefferson?" Drew asked.

"I did. Terrible news." Brett's voice lowered. Murder was definitely a conversation downer.

"His widow met someone here the night her husband was killed," Hope said.

"Are you a cop too?" Brett asked.

"No. I'm just trying to find out the truth," Hope said.

"Well, because you gave me one of our most popular desserts, I'm happy to help you. Though I know little. The man's wife was here that Friday night," Brett said with confidence.

"How can you be certain?" Drew asked.

"I've seen photos of her on the news, and she's not the type of woman you forget seeing." Brett grinned.

"I guess not," Hope mused. "Do you know the man she was with?"

Brett shook his head. "I've seen him here a few times, but I don't know his name."

A waitress approached the table. "Are you ready to order? Or is he taking your order?" she asked with a giggle, looking at Brett.

"Nope. I'm not going to infringe on your tip." He winked. "Do you know about the man who was killed in Jefferson?"

"Horrible thing." The woman frowned.

"You worked that night. His wife was here with a guy I don't know. He's a semiregular. She was the blonde with pouty red lips and made a fuss about her drink order."

It took a moment, but then realization flashed in the waitress's hazel eyes. "Right. *Her.* She wanted a cosmo. When I told her we only serve beer, she made a big fuss and settled for water because she hates beer."

"Do you know the guy she was with?" Drew asked.

"Sure. He comes in here often, but not with cosmo lady," the waitress said.

"Do you know his name?" Hope prodded.

The waitress tapped her pen on her order pad. "I can't remember. He has a funny first name. Starts with an R."

Hope and Drew looked at each other. At first the description Trudy gave Hope was pretty generic, but it fit one man with a funny first name that began with an R.

"Rupert?" Hope and Drew asked at the same time.

"Yeah! That's it." The waitress looked pleased with herself.

Brett's attention was diverted for a moment. "I need to get back to work. Enjoy your lunch. It's on the house."

"No, we couldn't," Hope protested.

"I insist. Don't be a stranger." Before he walked away, he told the waitress, "Be sure they each get the caramel toffee cake for dessert."

"Caramel toffee cake?" Drew's eyes sparkled. "I can't wait." Drew unfolded his napkin and draped it across his lap.

"Neither can I. It's one of my favorite recipes I

developed on the show." Hope gave her order, and then Drew gave his.

The waitress walked away with the promise that their entrees would be out shortly.

Hope lifted her water glass and took a drink. "I wonder why Elaine and Rupert met here."

Drew cocked his head sideways. "Oh, naïve little Hope. They're both married. This place is far from where they both live. It's clear they were, and probably still are, having an affair."

"There could be other reasons for them meeting here." Hope didn't want to jump to any conclusions. "We don't have all the facts, so we can't assume Elaine and Rupert are involved. However, it's a theory, and then it begs the question—did Lionel find out about the affair?"

Drew reached for his water glass. "If he did, we have to ask if Rupert or Elaine would have killed to keep the affair a secret."

Chapter Nineteen

Lunch at the Horseshoe Tavern was both delicious and insightful. Not only had Hope enjoyed a wonderful lunch, she'd learned three things. Elaine had lied about the night Lionel was killed. Elaine had had a secret dinner with her husband's business partner. And Brett's chef had done a fabulous job replicating her dessert recipe.

When she and Drew returned to Jefferson, they drove to her parked car, and then Drew followed her home to carry in Bigelow's food. The pup greeted them at the back door with his excited dance and wagging tail. She let him outside while Drew stored away the bag of food. He wanted to stay and continue running through theories, but he had a family obligation and reluctantly left.

With Drew gone and Bigelow back inside, she did a quick sweep looking for Princess and found her nestled on the sofa in the living room. The cat didn't seem to mind the drop cloth draped over the sofa. Hope was tempted to pat the cat's head, but she thought better of it. No need to risk waking the little terror.

Hope went to her office and dropped onto the

chair at her desk. The first order of business was checking her calendar. Being pulled in many directions lately, she needed to check where she was on all her projects. The monthly calendar gave her a quick glance at what was due over the next thirty days. There weren't any details, no running to-do lists, only short descriptions of actionable items, like "video upload sessions" or "follow-up with a brand." The calendar kept her on track so she wouldn't drop the ball on any one thing.

Her cell phone buzzed. The caller ID told her it was Billie Tomlinson.

So much for being on top of things.

"Hey, Billie. I'm on my way to the coffee shop," she lied. How on earth had she forgotten? They'd agreed to meet for coffee to discuss the position at the publishing company.

"No need to rush. I just arrived. Is everything okay?"

"Sure. I'm running a little late."

"I heard about what happened at the magazine. Glad you weren't seriously hurt. Listen, why don't I come to your house? You live close by?"

"I do. Actually, it's within walking distance of the coffee shop. And I have an upside-down strawberry cake."

The day before, she'd had enough of taking it easy and squeezed in some baking time. With a bunch of ripe strawberries begging to be baked into something, she'd set out to make her favorite upside-down cake.

"Upside-down strawberry cake? Give me your address and I'll head over now."

Hope texted Billie her address and used the few minutes she had before she arrived to prepare the refreshments. Thanks to a shift in the weather pattern, soft, warm breezes swept through, and with lower humidity, it was a lovely afternoon to sit on the porch.

She retrieved an antique pink glass pitcher from the hutch. She'd spotted the Depression-era pitcher at an antique fair last spring and had to have it. She filled it with iced tea and then plated two slices of the cake. She grabbed forks from the utensil drawer and took out two Mason jars for the iced tea. After she'd set two gingham cloth napkins on the tray, she added a biscuit for Bigelow. She whistled for him and his ears perked up.

"Come on. Company is coming over. You need to be on your best behavior."

Bigelow's big, dark eyes studied her. Was he considering taking her advice? Or would he go rogue? There was no way to predict. Bigelow's toenails clicked on the hardwood floor as he followed her out to the porch.

Running the length of the house, the porch gleamed with newly refinished wood flooring. Beside the front door was an old milk can she'd painted black to coordinate with the front door and stenciled the word *welcome* on it.

She'd added a black-and-white-checked ribbon around the neck of the can to set the cozy, welcoming tone she hoped the entire house had. All except the big, blue tarp.

She had to follow up with Liam to find out how much longer she'd have to live with the eyesore.

At the beginning of spring, she'd set out a bistro table and three chairs where she sat and drank a cup of coffee midday while Bigelow snoozed on his outdoor bed. Soft spring breezes flitted through while the chirps of birds filled the air, announcing their return for the season.

She'd added an outdoor sofa and armchair for more seating. A quilt was draped over the sofa and bright throw pillows were scattered along the cushions. She set the tray on an old wood box repurposed as a coffee table.

A car engine caught her attention. A sporty, two-door red car pulled into her driveway. When the engine stopped, Billie emerged from the car and waved.

"Beautiful home." Billie's gaze drifted to the garage and the big, blue tarp. "What happened?"

Hope sighed. How to explain that some crazy person, possibly a killer, had left a threatening message wasn't easy. She opted for something vague. "Long story. Hey, cool car."

"My husband's. He took mine for his fishing trip. It's more practical." She slung the straps of her rattan tote over her shoulder and climbed the steps. She looked less formal than she had at Lionel's funeral reception. For the Sunday afternoon, she'd tucked a white polo shirt into a green paisley skirt and slipped into white sneakers. She had added a pair of blue gemstone earrings, along with a gold wedding band and a silver-tone watch.

"I thought we'd have our cake outside." Hope led Billie to the sofa.

"And who is this handsome fella?" Billie stopped to pet Bigelow, who refrained from jumping on her. It impressed Hope. He was maturing.

"His name is Bigelow, and he's being a very good boy right now."

"He is." Billie continued to the sofa with Bigelow behind her. As she settled on a cushion, he continued to his bed and curled up. "I have a bad case of porch envy." She brushed a hand over her bangs, and her gaze traveled the length of the porch.

"It's still a work in progress." Hope reached the serving tray on the coffee table and lifted a plate.

"It looks finished. I think you're too hard on yourself." Billie accepted a plate from Hope. "This looks delicious. Definitely better than anything we could have gotten at the coffee shop."

"Thank you. I hope you enjoy the cake." Hope broke off a piece and chewed as she sat across from Billie on a deep, cushioned chair.

Billie took a bite of the cake and rolled her eyes. "You've got to be kidding me. This is scrumptious. Please tell me the recipe is on your blog."

"You read my blog?" Even though she'd been blogging for years, Hope was still surprised when someone told her they read her blog. She guessed deep down inside she'd always be that newbie blogger whose only readers were her mom and sister.

"I do. I love it." Billie took another bite and swallowed. "Tell me, what's going on with your social media? You had a surge in new followers suddenly."

Hope's insides twisted. She'd yet to figure out what had happened to her accounts because she'd been busy with the magazine and following leads in Lionel's murder.

"Oh, I'm sorry. I thought new followers is a good thing."

Hope regrouped and tried to convey an easygoing vibe. She didn't want Billie to feel uncomfortable. She apparently hadn't read the nasty comments posted.

"It's okay. I'm not sure what happened. I'm looking in to where they came from."

"There's software you can download to find out."

"You're familiar with social media?" Hope was aware of the software Billie was referring to. What she needed was a block of time to download it and sort through the data.

Billie sipped her iced tea. "I am. Tweeting, liking, and sharing isn't just for teens." She laughed as she set down the glass.

"No, it's not." Hope eased back into the chair and crossed her legs. "I'm glad you came by today."

"Me too. It was a nice ride, especially in my husband's car. I can't tell you how much I appreciate you letting me know about the job. I've applied and I'm waiting to hear about an interview. It would be great not to have to work for Mr. Donnelly any longer."

"He's a tough boss?"

Billie tilted her head sideways. "Yes and no. Lately, he's been a bear to work for. But since Mr. Whitcomb is gone, he's calmed down."

"There was that much tension between them?" If what Hope witnessed outside the real estate office the other day was any sign of how much their professional relationship had deteriorated, it was no wonder Billie had been unhappy working for them.

"Ever since Mr. Whitcomb bought the vacant commercial lot in this town."

"Why was Rupert against it?"

Billie blinked and her lips pressed together. She placed her glass on the tray and leaned forward, resting her forearms on her legs. "Mr. Donnelly doesn't confide in me. However, I heard him say he didn't want to expand into commercial properties and the whole situation with the building process here in

Jefferson was too messy for him. I believe that's why Mr. Whitcomb purchased the land through his company."

"The day Lionel was murdered, I saw him storm out of Alfred Kingston's real estate office."

"Mr. Donnelly was fuming when he got back. He marched to his office and slammed the door shut behind him. No one dared to go near him all day."

"When Rupert walked away, Lionel shouted out that Rupert owed him. Do you know what he was talking about?"

"No, I'm sorry." Billie shook her head and leaned back.

"Is there anything else that could've driven a wedge between them, other than a business deal?"

"Anything's possible. What are you thinking?"

"Could Rupert and Elaine have been having an affair?" Hope held her breath. She wasn't sure how Billie would react to the question.

Her mouth fell open.

"They were having an affair?" Hope asked.

"Mr. Donnelly and Mrs. Whitcomb? No." Billie shook her head. "I never saw any sign he was unfaithful to his wife. When he told her he was working late, he was. Why do you think they were having an affair?"

"I've been told they were together at a restaurant the night Lionel was murdered." Hope lifted her glass to her lips and sipped her iced tea.

"Huh. I would have put money on Lionel being the cheat. He often had 'late meetings' outside the office. Come to think of it . . . no . . . it can't be . . . could it?"

Hope wiggled closer to the edge of her seat. "What? What is it?"

Billie waved a hand. "I can't say. I don't want to spread gossip."

"If it can help solve the murders—and there have been two so far—you wouldn't be gossiping. You'd be helping."

Billie was silent for a moment. Hope's best guess was that she was grappling with a moral and ethical decision. It was time to help her guest decide.

"You don't want someone to get away with murder, do you?"

"No, no, of course not. If you think it can help, I'll tell you."

"I do think it can help."

"One afternoon, I wanted to try something different for lunch, Thai. I'd heard good things about a new restaurant. It was quite a drive from the office, but I'd put in extra hours and I offered to pick up lunch for my coworkers; there are three of us. When I got to the restaurant, there was a car that looked like Mr. Whitcomb's parked in the lot."

"He was at the restaurant?" Hope wanted to keep Billie moving forward with the story. She didn't want her guest to get cold feet and stop talking.

"He was inside with someone. I grabbed my order and rushed out. I made sure he didn't see me."

"Who was he with?"

"Mrs. Donnelly. They were holding hands."

Hope fell back into her seat. Lionel and Jocelyn were having an affair? Hope's mind raced with questions. The first being, why on earth would Jocelyn Donnelly have been interested in a man like Lionel Whitcomb? He was a known cheater, an alleged criminal, and a pompous blowhard. Her eyelids lowered for a nanosecond as her body went skeevy with disgust.

"Please, please, you can't let anyone know I told you that. If Mr. Donnelly finds out . . . he'll fire me for sure."

The second question was, could Elaine and Rupert have found out about their cheating spouses and met to discuss what to do? If so, they each had a motive for murder.

Question number three was whether or not the affair was over by the time of Lionel's death. Were the secret lovebirds still going hot and heavy? Another wave of disgust rippled through Hope at that thought. Or had the affair ended? If so, was it Lionel's doing?

Being dumped by a lover could be motive for murder.

"I guess it really doesn't make a difference now Someone has already confessed to the murder." Billie set her glass on the tray.

"You're right. Someone has confessed." And because of that, Hope didn't think Detective Reid would be eager to continue investigating. He had his confession. The District Attorney's office had a slam-dunk case to take to trial.

But did they have the real killer?

"I love when you share photos of him. He's so sweet. I should get going." Billie glanced at her watch and stood. "Graham Flour," she said matter-of-factly as she slung the strap of her tote over her shoulder.

"What about them?" Hope asked as she stood.

"Graham Flour. I follow them and they mentioned your blog in one of their posts. I wonder if that's why you got so many new followers."

Graham Flour had been a staple in many kitchens for decades. In fact, Hope had just purchased a twenty-pound bag on her last trip to the supermarket.

"I didn't see a tag from them. I'll have to check it out. Thank you." This was another reminder she could use a little help with her blog. Maybe having Iva take care of the chickens and lending a hand with the gardening would give her more time to focus on her blog.

Hope walked Billie down the porch steps and waved as the car backed out of the driveway. Bigelow had gotten up from his bed and joined Hope. He nudged her hand with his snout. She looked at him. Compact, with a lot of energy and love, Bigelow's tail was wagging at full force, and she knew exactly what he wanted. Road trip.

Hope and Bigelow barely made it to the farmers market before closing time. Arriving so late in the day wasn't ideal. What was left was slim pickings, but Hope was determined to find farm-fresh tomatoes. Harnessed, Bigelow walked leisurely beside Hope with no pulling or whining.

Yes, her pup was maturing.

They reached the Potter Farm stand and there was still a decent bounty of all varieties of tomatoes to choose from.

Turned out she wasn't the only one on the hunt for a good tomato. Matt was filling a bag with quirkily shaped heirloom tomatoes. They were one of Hope's favorite tomatoes. Their beauty was unique, coming in an assortment of colors, and their flavor was off the charts.

"Hi." Hope and Bigelow approached the farmer's table, and she reached for a tomato. "These green ones tend to have a light, zesty bite to them."

"Hi there. What about this yellow one?" Matt tossed a tomato he'd held up in the air and caught it.

"Milder than the red ones."

A sheen of amusement lit his caramel-colored eyes. "I guess I can't stump you when it comes to food. I'm surprised you don't have a vegetable garden." He dropped the tomato into his bag.

"I don't have the time. Maybe next year." She grabbed a few more tomatoes and approached Helena, the second half of the husband-and-wife farm team. She and the older woman exchanged greetings, and she paid for the tomatoes, which she bagged and then set into her tote. "Today Drew and I went to the Horseshoe Tavern."

"For lunch? From what I hear, they have a good menu." Matt paid for his produce and walked, with Hope and Bigelow next to him.

"They do. We did have lunch, but that's not why we went there."

"Should I ask?"

"I had reason to believe Elaine was, or still is, having an affair with Rupert Donnelly. It was confirmed they had dinner there the night Lionel was murdered."

Matt halted. "What?"

"You heard me. Your client and her dead husband's partner might be involved in Lionel's murder."

"Where do I start?" Matt dragged his hand through his dark blond hair. "First, I can't talk to you about this because Elaine is a client. Second, why on earth are you chasing down leads? Never mind. You don't have to answer that one. Have you told the police?"

"No, not yet, but I will. Elaine lied to me. She said she was late for the Scavenger Hunt because she had a problem with her false eyelashes. I believed her." An unpleasant awareness hit her like a ton of bricks. Norrie might have been right about the reason Elaine befriended her so suddenly. How could she have let it happen?

Matt's face remained stoic. He didn't give a hint of whether he knew Elaine was dining with Rupert or not. "Hope, I can't have this discussion with you."

Great. Another man who wouldn't talk to her. First Ethan, and now Matt.

"I'm not asking you to. I'm just telling you what I know and what the police will know soon. So, if Elaine lied to them, she will have some explaining to do. Though, Kitty confessed, so there probably isn't going to be any further investigation."

A little boy carrying an ice cream cone bigger than his head ran in front, cutting them off. They laughed until his mother came chasing after him, and the stern look on her face left no question he was in big trouble.

"He may need a lawyer." Hope leaned into Matt.

"Maybe I should give him my card." With his hand, Matt guided Hope around a rutted section of dirt. "Is Drew going to write about Elaine and Rupert's meal at the tavern?"

Hope shrugged. "I have no idea what he intends to do with the information. With a confession, she's in the clear, right?"

"One would expect. But I don't . . . as they say . . . count my chickens before they hatch."

"Ah, smart man." Hope approached the stand for Blueberry Acres Farm, where she intended to buy corn. The season was ending, and she wanted to get as much farm-fresh corn as she could. What she didn't eat right away, she would freeze and use in soups once the weather turned colder. Her cell phone buzzed, and she pulled it out of her bag. It was a text from Drew. Her shock must have shown because Matt quickly closed in on her.

"Is everything okay?"

"You won't believe what has happened." Hope lifted her head. "Miranda Whitcomb confessed to murdering Lionel and Maurice. What is going on?"

Matt scrubbed his hand over his face. "Looks like she's trying to protect her daughter."

"By confessing to murder? Doesn't she realize she could go to prison?" Hope asked.

"You'd be amazed at what people will do when they feel they don't have any other choice. Do you mind if I take off? I have some work to do."

"No, go ahead. I didn't mean to keep you."

Matt leaned in and gave Hope a kiss on the cheek. "I enjoyed running into you. Let's have dinner one evening soon." He pulled back and headed off to the makeshift parking lot.

With Matt gone, Hope continued shopping with Bigelow, filling her tote bag with fresh produce and vegetables. By the time she'd purchased her corn and a bag of fresh spinach, the vendors were closing their stands and preparing to leave. She headed back to her vehicle and set her tote on the back seat. She secured Bigelow to his seat belt.

Backing out of the space, her mind drifted back to the loud conversation Rupert and Lionel had had on Main Street the day Lionel died.

What was he talking about when he said Rupert owed him?

Had Lionel covered for Rupert in some way to keep him out of trouble? Did Lionel lend money to Rupert to cover up a bad investment? Or was Lionel just being a loudmouthed jerk? There was only one person who knew for sure, and she didn't think Rupert would talk to her about Lionel's comment.

She wondered if the police would be interested any longer; they now had two confessions. They'd be busy weeding through both women's statements because at least one of them was lying.

Chapter Twenty

Monday morning brought on a frenzied cleanup of Hope's desk bright and early. The haphazard pile of papers, file folders unfiled, and two empty cups on her desk left over from a late-night work session were unacceptable.

Hope Early didn't thrive on chaos. It was her kryptonite.

She finished tidying up her desk in record time and then got on the phone with her agent. She'd signed with Laurel six months ago and had already seen the benefits of their working relationship. Laurel identified the right brands for Hope to pitch to so she wouldn't waste time with brands that weren't right for her blog. She'd also negotiated a higher rate for sponsorships. More money was always a good thing. Their call went longer than she'd expected.

The call put her behind schedule, and she hated being late as much as she hated chaos. Though, one of the things that came out of their conversation was the good news that her surge in followers had indeed come from the mention of her blog on the Graham Flour website. One mystery solved.

Hope swiped up the two empty cups and hurried to the kitchen. She didn't want to be tardy for her meeting with *Cooking Now*'s editor. She grabbed her purse and patted Bigelow on her way out the back door.

Stepping outside, she took in a deep breath of refreshing air. The humidity had dropped overnight, along with the temperature. It was the quintessential drive-with-the-top-down kind of day. But she drove a responsible SUV, so the best she could do was drive with the sunroof open.

With the sunroof open and the windows lowered, a nice breeze blew through her hair, and she turned up the music for the drive. She felt like a carefree teenager again as she navigated the back roads to the magazine.

After today, she wouldn't be making any more trips to the magazine for a while, not until she landed another assignment with them. Which she hoped would be soon. The extra money from the magazine was helpful to her bottom line.

When she pulled onto the campus parking lot, she parked in the visitor section and entered the main building. The receptionist who greeted her directed her to Anna's office. Making her way through the maze of cubicles and offices, she finally arrived at the editor's office.

Anna stood and walked around her desk when Hope appeared in the doorway. About ten years older than Hope, Anna had come up the ranks of cooking magazines on both coasts before landing at *Cooking Now*. The dress code at the company was always Friday casual, and the turquoise sundress with white sandals Anna wore kept with the policy. All that was missing was a big hat and sunglasses. She gestured for Hope to enter and to have a seat at the round table in the office. At the table, Anna opened the file folder she had in her hand.

Hope wondered if it was another assignment.

"I want you to know it has been a pleasure working with you these past few days." Her cornflower-blue eyes gleamed and her rosy lips edged up at the corners.

The suspense was killing Hope. Why was she there? And when was Anna going to tell her?

"I enjoyed working here." Following Anna's lead, Hope leaned back but made sure her body language conveyed she was open to whatever opportunity Anna had for her. A quick calculation said most likely if it was a magazine feature, she'd be working on spring recipes.

"Except for the incident in the parking lot?" Anna asked.

"Well, yes. But the lights have been fixed and hopefully, something like that won't happen again." If Hope returned to the magazine for another project, she wouldn't be staying past dark again. Just to be safe.

"Nothing like that has ever happened before. And now with Kitty's confession and arrest . . . We're all in shock."

"I can imagine." Hope hadn't been sure if Anna would bring up Kitty's confession and arrest during the meeting. The situation wasn't something an employer would be happy about. "You've known her for a while. Did she ever mention Lionel Whitcomb was her father?"

"No. She said both her parents lived in Arizona. It's unbelievable. Anyway, I didn't set up this meeting to talk about Kitty Ellis."

Hope did her best to hide her disappointment. Now that the subject had come up, she wanted to talk about Kitty. To find out why she'd confessed to murders she might not have committed.

"I've appreciated the opportunity to work with *Cooking Now.*"

"May I be candid with you?"

Oh, boy. "Please, do."

"I've been watching you in the test kitchen, with the other staff members, at the tastings, and I think you've enjoyed yourself because you're back where you belong. You're a magazine editor, Hope. You were a good one, and it's still in you. I want you to work for me as an editor. With your background and experience from blogging, you'd be a remarkable resource for us."

Hope listened to Anna's description of the position, and it was a very familiar one to her.

"I'm flattered. I didn't see this coming." She laughed. It was a nervous laugh because she didn't know what to say. She'd never thought her brief assignment would lead to a job offer. A full-time job would remove some of the financial burdens weighing on her, but her blogging income was flourishing. "I don't know what to say right now."

"I understand. Think about it. But don't think for too long. This position will be filled quickly." Anna stood, signaling the meeting was over.

"I'm sure it will." Hope stood and grabbed her purse. "I'll call you soon." She walked out of the office stunned. A nine-to-five job at a magazine. Her first love. Could she go back? She passed cubicles and heard snippets of conversations between coworkers and glanced at a rack of the current issues of *Cooking Now* on her way back to the main reception area.

She pulled open the glass door and stepped outside. Anna's offer was tempting, and that scared her. She'd never thought she'd go back to editorial work. She stepped off the sidewalk and headed for her vehicle. When asked about appearing on the reality show, she liked to say she'd jumped at the chance to be on *The Sweet Taste of Success* because it sounded like fun, something out of the box, a rare moment of spontaneity in her life, but the truth was, she was burned out. Being a contestant on the show gave her an acceptable way to quit her job without having another position lined up. That was how stressed out she was back then.

The show added a whole new level of stress onto her, which she wasn't prepared for. Then there was Tim's shenanigans and the divorce. By the time she was filling out address change cards for her move back to Jefferson, she'd reached off-the-charts stress levels.

She unlocked the driver's side door and climbed into her car. She looked out the window to the sprawling, two-story building.

Being a magazine editor was her first love, but it had taken a toll on her and, unexpectedly, she had a new life path. Could she go back? Did she want to go back?

On her way back to Jefferson, Hope made a detour to her favorite consignment shop. Her last visit had yielded blue-and-white vases and a worn picture frame she planned on turning into a mirror. She pushed open the door, and the muskiness of old leather greeted her. Her nose crinkled. To her right were two well-loved leather chairs angled together for a seating area.

The shop owner waved to her as he finished up with

a customer, and she stepped farther into the shop to browse, looking for any treasures perfect for either her house or for photography props.

A silver-tone tray on top of a bureau piqued her curiosity.

She lifted it up to get a closer look.

Hefty.

There were a few scratches and a bit of tarnish. Otherwise, it seemed in good shape. It had character and a low price. Two qualities she often sought.

"Hope?"

Hope looked to the direction from which her name had come. Jocelyn Donnelly stood there holding a shopping bag. Dressed in khaki pants and an untucked, striped white shirt and spectator flats, she looked unaffected by the warm weather. Hope was certain her own makeup had melted off. She really should've left the air conditioner on in the car.

"I didn't expect to run into you."

Hope set down the tray. "Neither did I."

Jocelyn was the last person she expected to find in a consignment shop.

"Buying or selling?"

"Buying. I found the most adorable heart-shaped porcelain jewelry box for our niece." She lifted the bag. "Sometimes Zach has some fantastic merchandise."

"He does."

"I should get going. Have a great day, Hope." Jocelyn passed her and stopped when Zach, the spry, seventysomething owner, reached the front door to open it for her.

"I'll let you know when I sell those lamps for you. Should be sold in no time."

Hope followed Jocelyn outside, dodging a confused

look from Zach. "Jocelyn, wait up." Hope reached Jocelyn at the edge of the small path in front of the shop. "Have you heard two people have confessed to Lionel's murder?"

"I did. I'm sure the police will have the whole matter sorted out soon." Jocelyn turned and headed to her Mercedes.

"Possibly. I can't help but think each one confessed to protect the other."

Jocelyn looked back. Her dark hair swung as her head turned. "You think they're both innocent?"

"I don't know for sure."

"Well, then, I think it's best to leave the matter to the authorities." Jocelyn fumbled with her key fob. "I know you're trying to help Elaine, but she was his wife, and it's usually the spouse in these types of crime."

Hope approached the car. "You're right. Usually, the spouse has a strong motive. Like being cheated on."

"Elaine is flirtatious. I wouldn't put it past her to cheat on her husband."

"I'm not talking about Elaine. There's a rumor Lionel was the one cheating."

"It's a police matter. You shouldn't involve yourself."

Hope made a show of glancing at her watch. She lifted her gaze. "I'm getting a little hungry. I'm in the mood for Thai. Do you know a good restaurant?"

Jocelyn blanched. Then she yanked open the car door. Her carefully coiffed facade was showing signs of cracking. "Check your phone. I'm sure there's an app for that." She ducked into her car and closed the door.

On the surface, it appeared Hope had wasted her time, but Jocelyn's face paling when Hope asked about a Thai restaurant led her to believe Billie's observation—Jocelyn and Lionel had been involved.

Jocelyn's sedan peeled out of the parking lot, and Hope twisted around to see the car disappear down the road. Jocelyn definitely wanted to get away from Hope, and fast.

Hope was still trying to wrap her head around Jocelyn choosing to have an affair with Lionel, of all people. Surely there were far better candidates at the country club Jocelyn had to be a member of. Women like her were always country club members.

"Is there something wrong, Hope?" Zach called out from his shop's front door.

Hope dragged her gaze from the road back to the front of the shop. There was so much wrong. But nothing would get resolved there at the moment. She headed toward Zach and allowed him to usher her inside. She was there to shop.

"Small world, isn't it? You knowing Mrs. Donnelly." Zach allowed the door to close behind him.

"I've met her recently. Does she consign here often?" Hope drifted, but not too far away from Zach, and scanned a bookcase filled with knickknacks.

"Only lately. She has some nice stuff, and it sells fast. Is there anything you're interested in, or do you want to browse?"

"Browse," she replied.

"I'll leave you to it." Zach made his way to the sales counter and busied himself with paperwork while Hope skimmed the shelves unenthusiastically. What piqued her interest was Jocelyn, and where she was the night Lionel was murdered.

Hope left the consignment shop empty-handed, but she had a viable suspect for the murders. Though, with two people confessing, she doubted Reid would listen to her theories. He was on the fast track to closing his two cases.

On her drive back to Jefferson, she got a phone call from an unfamiliar number, but the area code was Massachusetts.

Hope accepted the call and said hello.

"Miss Early? You don't know me, but I'm Willa Hayes. I've just spoken with a reporter, Drew Adams."

No, Hope didn't know Willa Hayes, but she was glad the woman had called her. It looked like the game of phone tag Drew and Willa had been playing had ended.

"Great . . . I don't mean . . . I'm sorry, you caught me off guard." And unable to form a complete sentence.

"Mr. Adams gave me your number. I hope you don't mind. He asked me questions about Elaine Bass . . . wait, she has a different last name now. Whitcomb." Willa's voice was thick with a Boston accent, and she sounded apprehensive. And why wouldn't she be? She was calling a stranger about a murder.

"She does. Her fourth husband was murdered over a week ago. Someone brought it to our attention that she was a friend of yours."

"Mr. Adams asked about the relationship. I didn't understand what it had to with Elaine's husband's murder. But he explained you're dating the police chief and Elaine has befriended you."

Hope eased up on the accelerator as she approached a four-way stop. At the intersection, she stopped and looked for oncoming traffic in all directions. None was coming, so she continued through the intersection.

"Did you know Elaine before Clive's murder?"

"We went to the same hair salon and nail place. She

chatted occasionally. She really wasn't friendly and was kind of shallow, like she was always looking for an opportunity to move up the social ladder. I was a cop's wife."

It sounded like Elaine had changed little over the years. You'd think, with such a tragic event such as having your husband murdered, you'd be changed somehow. How could a life-altering event not change you? Hope hadn't gone unscathed by the losses and failures she'd endured over the years. Then again, maybe Clive's murder wasn't a tragic loss for Elaine.

Up ahead was a spot where Hope pulled off and parked while she talked to Willa. The convenience of taking calls in her car was nice. She couldn't share her focus on the road with Willa. She wanted to give Willa her full attention.

Safely situated on the side of the road, Hope continued the conversation. "But after her husband was killed, she became friendlier?"

"A day after her husband's murder, she was in the nail salon, and we both ended up leaving at the same time. She stopped and asked me to join her for coffee. She cried. I felt bad for her, so we went to the coffee shop. She said she'd kept her nail appointment because she believed if she kept her regular routine, the nightmare she was in wouldn't be real."

A lump caught in Hope's throat. She'd felt the same way when she received her divorce papers. Yes, she had been the one who contacted the lawyer first, because Tim didn't seem to think there was a problem. As far as he was concerned, the marriage worked for him. But even though she was the instigator, having those documents in her hand had broken her heart.

She remembered keeping with her regular workout routine, her blog posting, and her weekly nail appointment. Somehow, keeping the normalcy in her life would keep her from being sucked into the painful rabbit hole of hindsight and regret.

"Did she say why she chose you to confide in when you two barely knew each other?"

"She said I was always nice to her, and that she didn't have any close female friends."

Hope had heard a similar plea. "Hope, you're my only friend. I'm not sure what happened, but I realized I don't have any friends except you."

"And from then on she was leaning on you for support?" Hope asked.

"Yes."

"Did she ever ask you about the police investigation because your husband was the first officer on the scene of her husband's murder?" Hope looked out the passenger window. Up ahead, there was a pasture dotted with Jersey cows, and farther in the distance was a large red barn. This corner of the state was where she grew up, where it felt safe, and where she'd launched into the world to become the woman she was today. Never in a million years did she think she'd be talking to Willa Hayes, or that their lives would be so similar.

"Not in so many words. I mean, she never came out and asked me directly. I'm sorry, I really can't explain it. It got weird. The more she clung, the more uncomfortable I became, and the more my husband suggested I end the friendship, if that's what you want to call it. Besides, I don't think it looked good for him professionally for his wife to be involved with a murder suspect."

"Understandable."

"If you want my advice, I'd say end the relationship with Elaine. Clearly, a pattern is emerging, and I wouldn't want to be any part of it. I believe she manipulates people to get what she wants and, to be honest, I have no idea how far she'd go to get what she wants."

A crying baby wailed in the background. "I have to go. Good luck, Hope." The line went quiet while the voices screaming inside Hope's head to get away from Elaine grew louder and louder. Elaine might not be a killer, just unlucky when it came to choosing husbands, but either way, she was toxic.

Chapter Twenty-One

According to an article Hope had read weeks ago, it was hard getting toxic people out of your life. It gave steps on how to give the toxic person the heave-ho for good. Too bad Hope had paid little attention to the article.

The advice would have come in handy, because she'd just arrived at Elaine's house.

Yes, even though she'd gotten advice from Willa Hayes and her own internal warning system was throwing up red flags where Elaine was concerned, she still drove over to the Whitcomb house when Elaine called and asked her to come over. She was vague but sounded in a good mood.

Consumed with what to say to Elaine kept Hope from enjoying the walk to the double-front door of the enormous house. The striking shades of white, pink, and red of the Oriental lilies were a blur as she walked along the herringbone-patterned path. Should she mention her run-in with Jocelyn or the conversation with Willa Hayes or her visit to the Horseshoe Tavern? There was so much to talk about, yet she didn't want to discuss any of it.

What she wanted was to get the widow out of her life for good. Wrap it up. Wish her well. Be done with her.

With a fortifying inhale, she pressed the doorbell and waited. The door swung open and a perturbed Elaine appeared, dressed in a sleeveless denim jumpsuit and decked out in jewels from earlobes to toes. A diamond toe ring?

"You took long enough to get here."

Not the greeting Hope had expected. Then again, she was dealing with Elaine, so any and all expectations should be lowered.

"May I come in? Or should I go?"

"No, no, don't go." Elaine opened the door wider for Hope to enter and, after closing the door, she led her guest to the living room. "Come. We'll toast and then eat. I have food for our celebration. Wait until you see what I got for us."

The cavernous room took Hope's breath away. She couldn't even fathom the square footage or how long it took to build the floor-to-ceiling marble fireplace. Above her was a tasteful coffered ceiling and straight ahead the large windows offered a pristine view of the expansive, manicured lawn. She moved farther into the room and stopped at the sofa, placed opposite the fireplace and upholstered in a pale, golden damask fabric.

"First, we need to clear up a few things." Hope turned to face Elaine.

"Don't be a downer today. Two people have confessed to killing my Lionel. One of them has to be telling the truth, which means I'm in the clear." Elaine strutted to the champagne bucket on the coffee table and pulled out the bottle. "You need a glass of bubbly."

"What I need is for you to be straight with me."

"Straight about what?" Elaine handled the champagne bottle expertly and, a moment later, the pop of the cork was accompanied by a "woot woot" and a little shimmy action. "Time to get this party started." She poured two glasses and handed one to Hope. She raised her glass in a toasting gesture. "To freedom."

"How about to the truth? You lied about what made you late to the Scavenger Hunt. You didn't have a problem with your lashes. I can't believe I bought that excuse. You were late because you met Rupert Donnelly."

Elaine choked on the champagne. With a shaky hand, she set the glass on the table and dropped onto the sofa. "How do you know about my dinner with Rupert?"

"Did you think you could keep it a secret? Elaine, the police can find out everything. Did you tell Matt about the dinner?"

"No. I didn't. I thought if I said anything about it, everyone would assume what you're assuming."

"An affair?"

"Exactly. We weren't. I swear to God, we weren't. We met to talk about Lionel and Jocelyn."

Hope went to set her glass on the mahogany wood end table, but there wasn't a coaster. She looked around for one and then noticed Elaine had set hers on the table surface, no coaster. "Do you have coasters?"

Elaine blinked. "What? Coasters? No. Just set it down."

"You're not worried about rings? Marks?"

Elaine tilted her head sideways. "I'll buy a new end table. It's no big deal."

Hope couldn't set the glass down. Instead, she sat on the sofa, keeping the glass in her hand.

"Don't be silly." Elaine snatched the glass out of Hope's hand and set it on the coffee table next to hers. "It'll be fine. Where were we?" Elaine leaned back and crossed her legs.

"You were saying you met Rupert to talk about your spouses."

"Right. We suspected they were having an affair. We met and compared notes."

"What did you both come up with?"

Elaine lowered her eyes. "Lionel was cheating on me with *her*."

"You realize you have a strong motive to have killed your husband."

"But I didn't. Besides, two women have confessed."

"Elaine, just because they confessed doesn't mean you're in the clear. Have you talked to Matt recently?"

Elaine waved her hand. "Pfft. He called before, but I was busy taking a bubble bath. I'll talk to him later."

The doorbell rang and Elaine popped up. "Looks like there are more people coming to celebrate." She dashed out of the living room.

"Looks like you'll need coasters," Hope said.

Moments later, voices drew closer to the living room, and she was surprised to see Detective Reid, followed by several uniformed officers, enter.

"Miss Early, I didn't expect to see you here." He gave directions to the officers, who dispersed immediately.

"What's going on?" Hope rose from the sofa. "Are you searching her house?"

"Yes, they are!" Elaine waved a document in her hand. "I'm going to call my lawyer." She swiveled and stomped out.

"You have two confessions already. Why are you searching this house now?"

"I'm not at liberty to say. Miss Early, your presence is not needed here while we conduct the search."

Elaine reappeared with her cell phone in hand. "Oh, no. She's not going anywhere! I want a witness. My lawyer is on his way."

"Fine." Reid propped his hands on his hips, brushing back his dark gray blazer and revealing a glimpse of his service weapon. "But neither one of you can interfere with this search. Where is your laundry room?"

"It's off the kitchen. Why?"

"Thank you." Reid turned to an officer who appeared and then directed him to leave.

"This is disgraceful. How dare you people go through my stuff?" Elaine walked farther into the living room and stood next to Hope. "I'm so grateful you're here. Looks like our little celebration is over."

"What were you two celebrating?" Reid asked.

Elaine opened her mouth to answer, but Hope grabbed her arm. "Maybe you shouldn't say anything more until Matt gets here."

"I have nothing to hide. I didn't kill anyone." Elaine sounded defiant.

"Detective," an officer from the doorway called out. In his hand, he held an evidence bag with a gun inside.

Hope's eyes widened with shock as Elaine's confidence slipped away.

"Is that a real gun?" she whispered as she gripped Hope's arm and squeezed.

"It looks real from here."

"Is this your weapon, Mrs. Whitcomb?" Reid turned back to face both women.

"I've never seen it before," Elaine said.

"Elaine, I think you should wait until Matt gets here before you answer any more questions."

"It appears to be the same caliber used to shoot Mr. Whitcomb. Mrs. Whitcomb, do you own a compact SUV?" Reid asked.

Why was he asking about a compact SUV? Unless it was the vehicle that ran down Maurice. The tire tracks at the scene must've identified the vehicle, and maybe the one eyewitness remembered more than she thought at first.

Elaine went to say something, but Hope tugged at her.

"Wait until Matt gets here before you say anything else." Hope was sounding like a broken record. When was it going to sink into Elaine's head that she should be quiet?

Reid's lip curved upward, and he shook his head. "Haven't I warned you about interfering with my investigation?"

"I'm not interfering. I'm helping a friend." Hope held her ground, though her pulse had kicked up and beads of sweat formed on her temple. She was on shaky ground with the detective. She could easily be arrested.

"You may have a warrant, but this is still my house, and I demand to know where you found that weapon. Or rather, where you planted it." Elaine wasn't taking direction well.

Reid walked toward Elaine. "Mrs. Whitcomb, you're under the arrest for the possession of an illegal firearm. You have the right to remain silent—"

"Hope! Do something!" Elaine pleaded as Reid turned her around and handcuffed her.

"Detective, do you really need to cuff her?" Hope asked.

"Miss Early, stay out of this or I'll arrest you too." His tone was firm. "Tell her lawyer to meet us at the PD." Reid guided Elaine out of the room and disappeared with the officer who had the evidence bag.

Hope followed them, but they were already outside the door, and an officer pulled the door shut behind them.

She stood in the foyer, staring at the custom-designed oak door. Her eyes fixated on the panels of intricate carving as her mind processed what had happened. How did the police know to search the laundry room? A tip. Of course. Someone had to have told them where the gun was. Who? And why now? Why not right after Lionel was shot?

The doorbell chimed, jolting her out of her thoughts. She lunged for the door and yanked it open. Thank goodness, Matt had arrived.

"She was arrested!"

"What happened?" He breezed past Hope. Dressed in torn jeans and a graphic T-shirt, he looked like he'd been enjoying some downtime.

Hope recapped the events for Matt as she paced the foyer, from Elaine's insistence she was in the clear to her being handcuffed.

"Please tell me she said nothing." He pressed his hands together as if he was praying.

"She denied knowing about the gun. They didn't search the whole house, only the laundry room. It feels like someone tipped them off."

Matt rested his hands on his hips. "Could be. But who? No one else lives here now."

"Iva Johnson cleans the house." And Hope wouldn't put it past her to go to the police and tattle on her employer.

"I need to get to the police department. I hope Elaine has maintained her right to be silent." Matt headed to the door and Hope followed.

"You'd better get over there fast." Hope doubted Elaine would remain silent. She followed Matt outside, pulling the door shut behind her.

"So much for my day off for finishing some projects around the house." He reached into his pants pocket for his car key on his way to his vehicle parked in the driveway.

"Good thing you're in town today." Hope stopped walking and looked at Matt. Normally, his poker face shielded her from any insights of what he was thinking, but not at that moment. He looked concerned and, considering the police had found the probable murder weapon in his client's home, he should be concerned.

"If Elaine is telling the truth about the gun, how did it get into her house?"

"You don't have to worry about it." He cocked his head to the side and his mask of concern disappeared. "I mean it, Hope. She's my client. I'll worry about whether someone planted the gun to frame her. Am I clear?"

Hope nodded. "Crystal."

"Good." Matt continued to his car, while Hope stood and considered her options. She could do what he said, and everyone would be happy—him, Ethan, Reid, and Claire. Or she could do what she thought was the right thing. Besides, she didn't appreciate anyone telling her what to do.

Hope took the long way home from Elaine's house and ended up on Bennett Drive and parked in front of a shabby, ranch-style house. The front door opened, and a young man bolted out. She guessed he was Iva's son. Dressed in baggy jeans and a dark T-shirt, his brown hair was uncombed and he was holding a cigarette.

Hope drummed her fingers on the steering wheel and wondered if she'd made the right decision to stop by the Johnson home.

Iva appeared next. She shouted to her son not to stay out late. He gave a dismissive wave as he climbed into a waiting car in their driveway.

Iva watched the car back out, and that was when she noticed Hope's SUV parked on the street. Whether it was a good idea or not, there wasn't any going back for Hope. She grabbed her purse and exited her vehicle.

"What are you doing here?" Iva called out. Dressed in skinny jeans and a loose shirt, she was barefoot, and her hair was tamed into a ponytail. Deep lines creased around her eyes, and her face was haggard. She took a drag of her cigarette.

"I wanted to talk to you about your new part-time job."

Matt and the police would disapprove of her talking to a witness, but technically, Hope was there to talk to her employee. As she walked along the sidewalk, she was also bordering on the fine line between being helpful and interfering. She reached the small patch of front lawn.

"Do you have time?"

"Sure. But not too long. I have to take some food over to my mother." Iva turned and entered her house. "Sorry for the mess. My days have been hectic."

"How's your mother feeling?" Other than a few piles of papers and magazines, Hope didn't see any messiness.

"She has good days and bad days." Iva dropped to a plaid upholstered chair.

"Being a caregiver takes a lot out of a person." Hope settled on the microfiber-covered sofa. The sofa, along with the two coordinating armchairs, appeared to be new and in good condition.

"It is what it is. Now, what about the job did you want to discuss? I'm feeding the chickens and helping you with planting. Not exactly rocket science."

Iva's flippant remark had Hope bristling. "No, it's not rocket science, but it's important. Aside from providing fresh water and feeding the chickens, you'll collect eggs and look at each chicken every morning."

"Look at each chicken?" Iva rested her cigarette in the ashtray on the end table beside the chair.

"We need to make sure they're healthy. You want to see bright eyes, smooth feathers, and no indication they're becoming ill. We need to be sure they're active and alert. Then you need to be sure they have clean droppings and make sure their bedding is adequate, freshen up their nest boxes, and clean and sanitize the watering cans. In addition, there are tasks that involve sanitizing the whole coop."

"Whoa. Lot of work goes into taking care of a few chicks." Iva crossed her legs.

"Do you still want the job?"

"Sure. I'll get the hang of it."

And Hope would have to supervise closely. "I'll make up a document with all the chores and a schedule, plus a list of projects for the garden. I noticed you don't have many plantings outside."

"Nope. Too busy working. A few years ago, I had a vegetable garden. Nothing like a fresh tomato off the vine."

Hope couldn't agree more. "Great. It seems like we're all set."

"We are? You don't want to ask me about what I told the police?" Iva took a final inhale of her cigarette and then extinguished it. "People may think I'm trash, but I'm not stupid. You could've called me with the bird information. You want to know what happened at the Whitcomb house."

"First, let's be clear. I never thought of you as trash. I've found you to be a difficult person to get to know, which made it impossible for us to be friends. Second, I'm sorry people have said you were trash. They shouldn't have."

Iva remained silent for a few moments. She looked away for a beat and then looked back at Hope. "I can be difficult. I made a lot of bad choices over the years. Sometimes I blame others when I shouldn't. Maybe this new gig at your place will help me do things better."

"Maybe. You discovered the gun, didn't you?"

"Yes. I was there earlier today. I had laundry to do, nothing unusual. But when I went to get a pair of scissors from a drawer, I found the gun." Iva uncrossed her legs. "I don't know if it belonged to Mr. Whitcomb. But I knew for sure it didn't belong in the drawer. So, I called the police."

"You didn't ask Elaine about it?"

"No. If it was the murder weapon, she'd just lie and maybe kill me too. You know, two people are already dead."

It sounded like Iva had done the right thing. Hope couldn't fault her for being concerned for her own safety.

"I still have the job?" Iva asked.

"Yes, you do. As long as you follow my directions and don't smoke in the barn or in my house."

Iva's smile was genuine and lit up her face. "No problem. Thank you. You won't regret it. I promise."

Hope left Iva's home with reassurance she'd made the right decision. Now she had to tell her sister Iva would be working for her. A part of her would rather tell Detective Reid she'd questioned his witness.

Chapter Twenty-Two

Hope bounded down the stairs feeling refreshed and energized. She wasn't sure if it was because of the beautiful day that was shaping up or the fact that Claire had texted her last night asking to meet at the real estate office in the morning. She was thrilled her sister was getting back to work. Bigelow trotted after Hope, and when they arrived in the kitchen, they found Princess perched on the center island, rubbing her face with her paw.

"Oh, no, no, no. There are rules in this house that are not negotiable. There's no jumping on kitchen counters, missy." Hope swooped up the cat and set her on the floor. She then reached into a drawer and pulled out disinfectant and sanitized the whole island. "How long have you been doing this?" She looked at the cat, who yawned before strutting away.

Hope looked at Bigelow. "Do you know how long she's been doing this?"

Bigelow tilted his head sideways and gave her his best puppy-dog eyes. He wasn't snitching on the cat.

Hope put away her cleaning supplies and was ready to go out to the barn when she got a text from Drew.

Elaine out on bail last night. In seclusion per Matt.

Seclusion? Not a bad idea for Elaine.
She texted him back.

Thanks for update. Talk soon.

A woof reminded her she had been on her way outside with Bigelow. She tapped her leg and he sprinted to the back door. After she pulled the door closed behind them, she noticed Iva's beat-up old car in her driveway.

Not seeing her new employee, Hope led Bigelow to the barn, and when they reached the open barn door, she stopped because she heard Iva talking.

"Good morning, ladies. How's everything going?" Iva's voice sounded soft and kind. "I got you a special treat."

Alarm raised in Hope. What was Iva doing?

"Sweet corn. We used to give our chickens corn on the cob. You know it's good for your vision. And since you free-range, you need good eyesight."

Hope entered the barn. The hens had gathered around a galvanized pan and pecked at the ears of corn.

"Good morning."

Iva turned around, and her broad smile stopped Hope in her tracks. She couldn't recall the last time she'd seen Iva looking so happy.

"Good morning."

"They're enjoying the corn." Hope moved farther into the barn with Bigelow beside her. Up close, she noticed a shine of lipstick and a sweep of blush on Iva's oval face. The haggard look that had plagued her yesterday had diminished. "Since you're here, why don't you shadow me and get the girls outside."

"Sounds good."

For an hour, Iva worked alongside Hope and learned everything she needed to know about taking care of the chickens. She took direction well and appeared eager to do each task. By the time the hens were let out to free-range, Hope was confident her new employee would work out just fine. As long as boundaries were set and adhered to.

"They don't go far, do they?" Iva followed the birds and watched them walk around, pecking at bugs and meandering through flower beds. "The barn is big. Are you planning on getting any more animals?"

"I'd like to, but I have a lot of work to do still in the house."

"Makes sense. I should go, unless you have other work for me?"

"Not today. I have a question about what happened yesterday at Elaine's house." Hope walked with Iva toward the driveway. "When was the last time you did laundry?"

Iva stopped at the driver's side door. "Right after the funeral reception. Why?"

Hope shrugged. "Just curious. So, I'll see you tomorrow."

"Sure will." Iva walked back to her car and drove away.

Hope pulled her cell phone from her back pants pocket and texted Drew. He'd given her an update on Elaine, but what about Miranda and Kitty? Were mother and daughter still being held? Or had they been released?

Bigelow raced by her toward the mudroom. It was breakfast time, and he wanted to make sure she didn't forget. She shoved her phone back into her pocket and picked up her pace to the house. She opened the door and Bigelow zipped by her, hurrying to his placement. He wasn't very subtle.

"I know. I know." She dished out his kibble while she waited for Drew's reply. "Here you go, boy." She set down the stainless-steel bowl in front of him and then checked her phone again. A new text. But it was from Claire.

See you soon.

Claire added a smiley face.

Hope was even more excited to find out what Claire was working on, because her sister didn't do smiley faces.

Jefferson was being treated to a sneak peek of fall, thanks to a canopy of low clouds and a temperature hovering around seventy. Hope welcomed the cool weather and the opportunity to pull on a cardigan. She walked to Main Street and found Claire waiting in front of the real estate office.

"Where have you been?" Claire uncrossed her arms and began walking. In place of her usual real estate agent clothing, she wore jeans, a tank top, and her favorite jeweled flip-flops.

"I ran a little late this morning." She dashed to catch up with her sister. Where were they going? "I was training a new employee."

"It's about time you hired an assistant again."

"Not exactly an assistant. She's helping me with the chickens in the morning, and with the gardening."

"Who did you hire?" Claire asked.

"Iva Johnson."

Claire halted and gave Hope a look that should have had her running for cover. "You've got to be kidding me. Well, make sure you keep your front door locked." Claire continued walking. "I don't understand why you keep taking in strays. You can't save everyone, Hope."

"I'm not trying to save her. Did you know her mother is ill?"

"A lot of people have sad stories. You remember she stole from me?"

"You couldn't prove it. You didn't report it to the police."

"Because it was a fake diamond bracelet."

"Fake?"

"The real one is in a safe. I purchased the fake one to take on the cruise." Claire stopped again, this time in front of a storefront that had been vacant since the beginning of the summer.

"Here we are." Claire unlocked the door and entered. "Come on in."

"What's going on? I don't need a retail shop." Though maybe having a boutique wasn't a bad idea. She could sell dishes, cookware, and her cookbooks. She could hold cooking demonstrations. All the content she could produce raced through her mind.

"No. This space isn't for you. It's for me." Claire stepped farther into the empty retail space. Charmingly small, it'd been an antique shop for as long as Hope could remember. The name had changed dozens of times. Now, empty of inventory and shelving, all that remained was its warped oak floor and ancient sales counter.

"For you? What are you talking about? Are you opening your own real estate agency?"

"No. Though I am starting my own business." Claire walked to the counter. A layer of dust covered the distressed wood top. "I'm going to be a home stager. I've had requests from clients over the years, but I always had to say no because I didn't have time. Now I'm going to make the time."

"That's wonderful!"

"Kent Wilder has hired me to stage his new listing. It's an adorable little cottage. I know exactly how I'm going to stage it." Claire's face shone with excitement and her eyes were hopeful.

"Why do you need a retail shop?"

"Because I'm going to sell home accents to complement my staging business. This way, I'll have two revenue streams. I have ideas for this shop." Claire twirled and swept her arms out wide. "So many ideas!"

Words failed Hope. She couldn't recall the last time her sister had twirled. She chewed on her lower lip as everything Claire had just told her settled in. "You haven't talked about opening a shop before. I'm a little surprised."

"Well, you didn't talk about starting a blog. You just did it one weekend."

"My starting a blog was a little different." As soon as the words came out of her mouth, Claire was giving her the stink eye, challenging her comment. "I mean, it was a hobby back then. I still had a full-time job."

Claire's face tightened, and she squinted. "What are you saying exactly? Are you saying I *can't* do this? I *shouldn't* do this?"

"No, no, no. I'm saying . . . Look, starting a business is a big deal." Hope's stomach knotted. Her sister's intense glare wasn't easing up. "You know what's involved in running a business. You're incredibly talented when it comes to decorating. Your advice is priceless to your clients. You know how their homes need to look so they can sell."

"Stop buttering me up."

"Fine. While you have the knowledge of the real estate market, and the skill for decorating, what do you know about running a retail store?"

Claire's brows furrowed.

"When you're out staging a house, who'll be working here? Retail shops are open evenings and weekends."

Claire's angry face slipped away, and she looked around the empty store. Hope detected her sister hadn't thought out her plan.

"Hey, I love you. I want you to be happy, but I also want you to be smart. You can do anything you want. I believe that. Just don't rush into something. Maybe start with home staging working from your house. That way you'll keep the flexibility you had as a real estate agent."

Claire's shoulders slumped. "I'll think about everything you've said."

"Promise?"

"Pinky swear."

"The kids are at sleepovers tonight and Andy is in Michigan, right?" When her sister nodded, Hope wrapped an arm around Claire's shoulder. "Why don't we have a sleepover of our own?"

"Can we watch *Sleepless in Seattle*?"

"And we'll have popcorn and watch in our jammies. Sound good?"

Claire nodded. "I need to get going. I have to meet Kent."

Claire locked up and walked to her car, while Hope headed to the police department. She hadn't seen Ethan in what felt like forever. Their only contact had been quick calls and texts. Every day there was a new headline and arrest. He had his hands full. She hoped to convince him to take a coffee break so they could talk. Something they hadn't been doing a lot of lately.

Hope reached the police department and followed the path to the front entrance. Would she be able to get some one-on-one time with Ethan? Before she reached the door, it opened, and Miranda Whitcomb appeared, blocking the entrance.

"They've released you?" Hope sputtered, coming to a quick stop.

"It's about time. I had to spend two nights in there!" Miranda pointed to the one-story brick building behind her. Her hair was unwashed and tousled. Her eyes were bloodshot and heavy with exhaustion. "Because they considered me a flight risk. Ha! Well, let me tell you. I can't wait to get out of this awful town."

"Ms. Whitcomb, we should go," said the short man in a suit behind Miranda, who Hope guessed was her attorney.

"Are you going back to the inn?" Hope asked.

"Yes. I need a shower." Miranda brushed by Hope with the short man following. But she stopped and looked back at Hope. "I'm not sorry he's dead. Lionel was a horrible man who didn't care about his wife or child."

The short man prompted Miranda to continue walking toward the parking lot.

Hope walked to the building's front door. Inside, Ethan met her in the lobby and explained he had a few spare minutes.

"Everything okay?" He led her away from the dispatcher's station behind the partition glass.

"Yes. I was hoping you could take a break, but I'm guessing you can't."

"Sorry. It's hectic." He rubbed the back of his neck.

Hope knew his stiff neck came from sleeping on the sofa in his office. When was the last time he went home? He was in need of a good night's sleep and a shave.

"I can bring you something back," she offered.

"You already did." He lowered his mouth to hers and their lips touched. His kiss was gentle, though the heat that was kicked up in Hope was anything but gentle. It surged through her, ratcheting up her internal temperature. Remembering they were in a public place, she reluctantly pulled away, but with a satisfied smile.

"Guess I did." She laced her fingers with his.

"Look, I have to . . ."

"I know. You have to get back to work. Call me later?" She released his hand. "I ran into Miranda on my way in. Kitty's been released?"

Ethan nodded. "Yes, she was. Yesterday. We have two confessions with little evidence to back them up and the murder weapon found at Elaine's house. See why I've been here around the clock?"

"Maretta must be all over this."

As if on cue, the main entrance opened and the mayor swept in and eyeballed Ethan as her lips pinched together. "Chief, what on earth is going on? Three suspects all released? Two of them confessed? In your office, now!" She barreled through the lobby to the entry door into the inner offices. She grabbed the handle and twisted, but when the door didn't open, she turned to Ethan and scowled.

Hope leaned into Ethan. "She has to be buzzed in, right?"

"Yep." He wiggled his eyebrows. "Gotta go." He stepped away from Hope but hesitated. "Almost forgot. We're keeping the specifics of the search at Elaine's house confidential for now."

"Got it. I won't say anything."

"Thanks." Ethan continued toward Maretta, swiping his ID to open the door for her.

Hope turned to shield her laughter. It really wasn't a funny situation. But it was. She quickly exited, and outside she texted Drew. He was on his way back to the newspaper from interviewing Iva and said he'd meet her at The Coffee Clique.

The sun peeked through the clouds, and Hope didn't want to stay inside, so she ordered two coffees to go. She sat on a bench outside the store Claire had just rented and waited for Drew. Many of the businesses on Main Street had outdoor decorations, including benches and blooming flower containers. Soon mums, pumpkins, and bales of hay would replace the late summer decor.

Hope held out one cup to Drew as he approached. "Coffee alfresco. Nice change."

"I thought so." She sipped her coffee.

Drew sat and then took a long drink of his beverage. "Did you really hire Iva to work for you?"

"I did. She showed up today, and I was impressed by how well she did with the chickens."

"She didn't barbecue them?"

"Drew!"

He chuckled. "I couldn't resist. Make sure you count your chickens when they come back to the coop. Okay, now for business. Iva said Elaine hired a caterer for yesterday."

"She did? I guess Reid really did break up the party. I didn't know there was food." Hope slid down her sunglasses from the top of her head onto the bridge of her nose. Why couldn't Elaine have hired a caterer for the funeral reception? Because she had Hope, that was why. She really needed to work on saying no to people. "Wait. This means there was someone else in the house besides Iva and Elaine."

"Exactly. I'm going to check out the caterer."

"Good idea. Oh, Ethan told me they're keeping details of the search confidential for now."

"I know. I'm not mentioning it in this article. You know, if the caterer planted the gun, we may have been looking at this all wrong. Maybe the intended victim was Maurice."

Hope's mind churned with possibilities. Drew could have been on to something. The killer could have been at the restaurant to confront Maurice. Maybe the killer was lying in wait for Maurice or planned to lure him outside, but Lionel showed up and got in the way. Then, determined to finish his job, the killer returned to the restaurant and ran Maurice down.

Professional kitchens could be cutthroat. The reality shows that showcased them didn't need to work very hard at fabricating drama.

Hope and Drew finished their coffees in silence.

Hope figured Drew was also working out theories in his mind.

"What are you thinking?" He lifted his shades from his face.

She glanced at her watch. "I'm thinking I should get going. Let me know what you find out about the caterer." She stood.

"Of course." Drew leaned back. "I'm going to chill for a few minutes before going back to the office." He lowered his sunglasses to the bridge of his nose and let his head fall back.

Hope adjusted her purse strap and sipped her coffee as she walked away from the bench. On her walk home, she mentally went through a list of all the local caterers she knew and tried to remember the restaurants where Maurice worked before the Avery Bistro. Being away from town for several years, she wasn't certain of his work history. She'd check online when she got home. Had Maurice really been the target all along?

Could Lionel have been collateral damage?

Chapter Twenty-Three

"How's it going over there?" Hope looked over her shoulder as she placed the flatware in the dishwasher.

Claire stood vigilant at the microwave, watching the clock countdown. Popcorn could burn in a split second.

"Any minute." Popcorn was one of the few treats Claire allowed herself during the week, and she indulged in a gourmet brand she ordered online. While her sister preferred to make it the old-fashioned way on the stovetop, she insisted on bringing a bag of her stash.

Hope closed the dishwasher door and set the controls. "The movie's all set when we're ready." She grabbed a cleaning cloth and wiped down the island. She'd been doing it obsessively ever since she found Princess sitting on the countertop. She wanted to be irritated with the cat, but Princess had been purring and loving since the incident, making it impossible for her to stay angry at her.

The microwave beeped and Claire pulled out the bag. She carefully vented it before ripping it open to pour the popcorn into a large bowl. Hope discarded the cloth and moved to the stovetop. There was no more wonderful sight than melted sweet butter. She lifted the small pot of bubbly goodness.

"I'm glad we're having this sleepover. After the movie, I'll tell you what I have planned for the shop, and wait until you hear my marketing plan for the staging business. I think I have a new client. Bella Graham—she owns the lavender Victorian on Apple Hill Road—called me today. She's selling."

"Another client? Fabulous. Your staging business will take off, I'm certain." Hope poured the butter over the popcorn. "You may not even need the shop." With the pot empty, she set it on a trivet and then, with a spoon, tossed the popcorn, coating every kernel. She couldn't resist and popped a kernel into her mouth.

Claire pulled back from the island. "You still don't think I can make a go of a shop, do you?"

"I didn't say that. To be honest, I don't understand why you want a shop."

"I can't believe I have to explain this to you, of all people." Claire grabbed the bowl and tramped over to the sofa.

So much for a fun evening.

Hope rinsed the pot and set it to soak with soapy hot water. After wiping her hands on a towel, she joined her sister on the sofa, in the spot where Bigelow liked to curl up when he thought Hope wasn't around. For the night, she'd sent him over to the Madisons'. When she dropped him off before Claire arrived, he'd looked ecstatic as he ran off in the yard with Buddy.

"I'm sorry, but you'll have to explain. Because I can't figure it out."

Claire huffed, then leaned forward and put the bowl

on the coffee table with a thump. "I need a challenge. I've sold real estate for fifteen years and I'm bored."

"Opening a retail store is risky." Hope did a quick calculation of what her sister had to invest, and it was mind-boggling the number she came up with. Inventory, utilities, insurance, and staff, and she was sure she was missing other expenses.

"Pish." Claire waved away Hope's concern.

"Pish? Seriously?"

"I'm aware of the financial risk, and so is Andy. We're both entrepreneurs. We understand what's at stake. Besides, I have years of experience."

"Of selling houses. Not running a brick-and-mortar store. Why can't you stage houses until you've established yourself in that field and then expand?"

"Why can't you support me?" Claire stood. "I can't believe you're behaving like this. Are you worried you won't be the only successful Early sister?"

"What? Now you're being crazy. You've been very successful, more so than me over the years."

"Until I lost the mayor's race."

"Is that what this is about? Losing the race doesn't define you."

"Losing the race made me see I'm stuck. I need a change. It would be nice if my sister understood and supported me." Claire's cheeks puffed out and her neck corded. She swung around and stomped out of the room.

"I do support you!" There was no reasoning with Claire at the moment. Hope wasn't going to apologize for being concerned.

So much for movie night.

She swiped up the bowl and stood. On her way to the kitchen, the doorbell rang. She glanced at her watch and wondered who was visiting so late. On her way to the foyer, she dropped the bowl on the island, after grabbing a handful of kernels. It was nice not to have to race Bigelow to the door. Before she reached it, she popped the kernels in her mouth. She had to admit the gourmet microwave popcorn was good.

Hope opened the door and almost choked on her mouthful of popcorn. She hadn't expected to see Kitty again. Yet there she was, standing on the welcome mat.

The last time she'd come to the house, she'd stormed out, giving Hope cause to be wary of this unexpected visit.

"I apologize for showing up without calling, but I worried if I called, you'd hang up on me." Kitty glanced downward.

Hope had swallowed her popcorn. "I wouldn't have hung up on you. But I'm surprised you'd want to see me."

Kitty looked up and met Hope's gaze. Her hair hung below her shoulders, flyaways untamed and her part uneven. "I owe you an apology. I behaved poorly. And, boy, have I made a mess out of everything. Because of me, my mom was in jail." Regret flashed in Kitty's eyes.

"You're here, so you might as well come in." Hope opened the door wider and Kitty entered. "Would you like something to drink?"

"Water, please." Kitty followed Hope into the kitchen and stopped at the island while Hope retrieved a glass from an upper cabinet and turned on the faucet. "I shouldn't have confessed to killing Lionel Whitcomb to help my mother."

Hope set the glass on the island in front of Kitty. "It could have hurt the investigation into the real killer."

"You don't believe my mother is the killer either?" Kitty pulled a hair tie from her back pocket and fingered her hair, gathering it together into a ponytail. She looked more like the enthusiastic kitchen manager Hope met over a week ago. Except for her sad eyes.

"No. She confessed to protect you." Hope leaned her forearms on the island and clasped her hands. She wasn't sure how she could help Kitty, but she was willing to listen. Sometimes people just needed to be heard.

"Mom said that's also why she lied about Ken being my father. I know she loves me, but I'm having a hard time dealing with the lies."

"I'm sure you two will work it out." Just like Hope believed she and Claire would get past their little tiff.

Kitty lifted the glass and took a drink of water. "At least now we know who killed Lionel. It was Elaine."

"They arrested her on a weapon's charge, but I don't think she's guilty of the murders."

"You don't?" Kitty set the glass on the countertop. "Who else could've killed him? The gun was found in her laundry room."

"There could be another explanation." Hope's cell phone rang and she went over to the table to snatch it up. "Excuse me." She swiped on the phone. "Hey, Drew."

"I talked to the caterer. He didn't know Maurice." Drew sounded disappointed.

"Are you certain? Do you believe him?"

"He seemed to be honest, but I'll do more digging. He told me he saw a woman who wasn't Elaine or Iva come sneaking out of the house when he was closing up his van."

Jocelyn came to mind. "Could he identify the woman he saw while delivering the food?"

"No. He was in a hurry. He had another stop and was running late."

"It sounds like the caterer is a dead end. Call me when you have something." Hope ended the call and set the phone back on the table. Something niggled at her brain. Something Kitty had said.

The gun was found in her laundry room.

How did Kitty know the gun was found in the laundry room? The police hadn't shared the location of the find.

She turned around to face Kitty. She gasped.

Kitty stood solid, her eyes wild with fury, her hand gripping a chef's knife.

"What's going on, Kitty?" She glanced at the knife block on the island. There was an empty slot.

"Shut up! Step away from the table." She jabbed the knife forward. "Move!"

Hope did as she was ordered. She put more space between her and the table and, unfortunately, her phone too. Damn. She had to think fast about how to disarm Kitty and get herself and Claire out of the house alive.

"Someone saw me yesterday."

"The caterer. It seems you were careless." Hope was taking a risk by instigating, but she needed to keep Kitty engaged as she tried to devise a plan to subdue and overpower the woman. *Subdue and overpower.* This wasn't her first encounter with a killer, so she'd learned a few things that had kept her alive twice before. Now she needed to do it again.

"Damn it!" Kitty's nostrils flared as her face reddened. "You and your reporter friend had to keep

looking for answers. I get why he did. But you? I pushed
you down the embankment and you still didn't stop.
So, tell me why was it so important for you to find out
who killed a horrible person like Lionel Whitcomb?"

"If they convict the wrong person, justice isn't
served."

"Justice for Lionel? You're kidding me, right? He
used people! He discarded them when he was done.
Just like he did to my mother and to Rona." Kitty tightened her hold on the knife. Beads of sweat formed at
her temples and her face slacked.

Hope suspected killing Lionel had been a very different feeling for Kitty than standing in the kitchen
holding a knife on an innocent person. But Hope
wasn't certain she wanted to roll the dice to find out if
Kitty was indeed capable of being a cold-blooded
killer.

"When I called him to tell him who I was, he
laughed. He said he didn't have any children. He called
me a liar. He should have called me his daughter!"
Kitty stepped forward, the knife still pointing at Hope.

"You're right. He should have. He was a terrible
human being, but he didn't deserve to be murdered."
Hope backed up, slowly walking along the sofa.

"Says you. You're not the one who had to live with
being lied to and then being humiliated. But I didn't
plan on killing him. I swear. But once I did, I didn't
regret it." Kitty maneuvered like a cat, her pace slow
and precise, with her sight set on her prey.

Those last words sent a chill down Hope's spine.
"Why did you kill him?"

"All the anger and rage I felt erupted! To get him to
talk to me face-to-face, I had to lure him to the restaurant by posing as a potential investor. How pathetic.

Then I stopped him in the parking lot and told him who I was. He got angry. He yelled at me. Like I'd done something wrong. He abandoned my mother and me and I'm the one who did something wrong?"

"What *he* did was wrong."

Kitty lifted the knife. "He said he'd never acknowledge me as his child. What kind of man was he?" Kitty jabbed the knife forward. "A pathetic man who didn't care about anyone but himself."

"You're right. He didn't care about anyone. Why did you confess?"

Kitty rolled her eyes and let out a sigh. "To protect my mother."

"You believed you'd both be cleared once the murder weapon was found at Elaine's house?"

"They'd think we were just looking out for each other. It's what mothers and daughters do."

"You could have planted the gun earlier."

Kitty gave a careless shrug. "I needed to make sure I wouldn't be a suspect first. The best way to do that was to confess and then admit I lied to protect my mom. I didn't know my mom was going to confess too. She screwed up my plan."

Kitty's matter-of-fact tone chilled Hope. She was rethinking her doubtfulness of Kitty being a cold-blooded killer.

"Your plan?"

Hope stepped backward and stumbled on the end of the sofa, but she maintained her balance. She couldn't let Kitty have any more of an advantage over her.

"Your mother loves you. That's why she lied to the police and said she killed Lionel."

Kitty huffed. "She's used to lying. She lied my whole

life. There were plenty of times she could have told me the truth about my father."

"She was protecting you from Lionel. She knew how he'd treat you. She didn't want you to go through that pain. It's not too late. Nobody else needs to get hurt." Hope kept easing back slowly, and she made a slight turn, bringing Kitty perpendicular to the opening into the hall that led to the foyer. "Put down the knife and we can talk. I'll help you. I promise."

"It's too late. You're the only person who knows I killed Lionel and the chef."

"His name was Maurice. Why did you kill him?"

"He saw Lionel and me together in the parking lot. I heard you tell Drew on the phone."

Hope's mind raced as she tried to remember, and she did. If her body hadn't been so rigid, her knees would have buckled and she'd collapse.

I caused Maurice's death.

In the test kitchen, she'd stepped out to the hallway to talk to Drew. She told him what Maurice had said about the night of Lionel's murder. She'd lost the signal and couldn't tell him Maurice never saw the person with Lionel. Kitty killed him for nothing. A wave of nausea rolled through her like a tsunami.

She met Kitty's hard stare, and her fear disappeared. Anger throbbed through her and her fingers balled into fists, her fingernails cutting into her flesh. "You won't get away with this. You'll go to prison for murder."

"Ha! You really think I don't have a plan? I wasn't sure if you'd find out. But you know now. It'll look like you died in a home invasion. A shame. My statement to the police will go something like this—I came here to apologize for my rudeness the other day and

I found your body. Stabbed to death. The house a mess." Her eyes deadened as she lifted her arm to plunge the knife into Hope. She stepped forward and then her eyes bulged. She yelped before her body crumpled to the floor and pieces of blue-and-white porcelain rained down over her body.

"Nobody's gonna hurt my sister!" Claire lowered her arms and locked gazes with her sister, then tore across the room to the table and grabbed Hope's phone. She called for help.

Hope lunged for the knife. It'd been knocked out of Kitty's grip when she fell to the floor. With a shaky hand, Hope picked up the knife. Leery of approaching the woman, even though she appeared unconscious, Hope kept her distance. She doubted the vase hitting Kitty over the head had knocked her out, but hitting her head on the pumpkin-pine floor could have.

Claire hurried to her sister's side. With rasping breaths and trembling hands, she tugged her sister close to her. "The police are on their way."

"She killed Lionel and Maurice." Hope wrapped an arm around her sister's waist. "Did you hear everything?"

"No. I only came down a minute ago, and that's when I saw what was going on. How did she get in?"

"I let her in. I thought she came here to apologize, but then I realized she was the killer, and, well . . . this happened." Hope pointed to Kitty with the knife.

"Are you okay?"

Hope nodded. Her grip on the knife was unsteady, but she was okay, thanks to her sister acting quickly and stealthily.

Broken shards of porcelain were scattered around

Kitty. A twinge of sadness pricked at Hope. The vase had been the first antique she'd ever purchased. She'd saved for months to afford it. Now, it was broken into bits and pieces, but it had saved her life.

"Sorry about the vase." Claire seemed to read Hope's mind.

Hope shrugged. "Maybe I can make a mosaic."

Claire smiled. "Of course you can."

Blaring sirens approached the house. Once again, Hope's home was a crime scene. She must've set a record for the number of times the police had to respond to her house for help.

Claire pulled away from Hope. "We really should check to see if she's alive."

"Let the police do it." Hope stepped back to the island and set the knife on the countertop, all the while keeping an eye on Kitty. She wasn't experiencing an overwhelming desire to help the confessed murderer. A loud bang on the front door announced the arrival of help. Claire motioned she'd let the police in and carefully made her way around Kitty's unconscious body. She returned a moment later with a uniformed police officer, who rushed to Kitty. He confirmed she was alive and called for an ambulance.

Claire moved back to her sister and wrapped her arm around Hope's waist. "I can't believe she killed two people."

Hope shrugged. "I guess we never really know someone."

Another uniformed officer entered the kitchen and escorted them to the living room. He suggested they sit.

Hope first removed the drop cloth from the sofa and quickly bundled it up and discarded it to the side.

She sat on the middle cushion and Claire sat next to her. She stared out the window. When would the full impact of the incident hit her? An hour from now? Next week? Would it come unexpectedly? When would it hit Claire? She grasped her sister's hand and squeezed. She hated the fact that her sister had been in danger and ultimately put into the position of having to defend them.

The officer took their initial statements before exiting the room when the EMTs hurried through the front door to tend to Kitty. He reappeared to check on Hope and Claire, and both assured him they didn't need medical attention. He looked concerned but didn't push the matter and left when his radio squawked.

"I need to call Andy so he hears about this from me." Claire patted Hope's hand before she stood and exited the room to get her phone.

Hope leaned back. Now alone, her gaze fixated on the fireplace and her recent paint job. Admittedly, it wasn't the right moment for her to analyze her handiwork, but it kept her from dissolving into a puddle of tears.

She focused on the color. The cool gray tone was soothing. She looked to her trembling hands. She pressed her palms on her lap to steady them.

Time to get a grip.

She leveled her gaze back to the fireplace wall. Bare. She still hadn't decided what to hang over the mantel. A wreath? A painting? Ethan had suggested a flat-screen TV. She'd vetoed that in a heartbeat.

A *heartbeat.*

Her heartbeat was thrashing in her ears. The adrenaline rush from being threatened at knifepoint was still pumping through her.

"Hope."

Her head snapped around at the sound of her name. Ethan rushed into the room and she jumped up from the sofa. She went to run, but he was too fast. He'd pulled her into a tight hug. A whoosh of relief exhaled from his body. She'd worried him again. Once more, he'd gotten word she'd come *this close* to being his next murder victim. *This close.*

"Are you okay? Tell me you're okay."

Hope shook her head as she buried her face into Ethan's chest and inhaled his woodsy cologne. No, she wasn't okay. She'd been terrorized in her home, fearful her sister would be killed, and responsible for a friend's death.

"Kitty killed them both. Lionel and Maurice! She pulled a knife on me." She squeezed her eyes shut in an attempt to stop the replay of the confrontation, to end the nonstop loop in her mind.

"Thank God you're safe." His voice was thick with concern and his hold on her tightened. But she wanted it tighter. She needed it tighter to feel safe.

"Claire came up behind Kitty and hit her with a vase. She smashed it over Kitty's head." Tears streamed down Hope's face. The coldness in Kitty's eyes left no doubt that if Claire hadn't done what she did, she would've had to fight for her life. Kitty had wanted her dead.

She sucked in a sharp breath and her body quaked, prompting Ethan's hold to tighten. Thank goodness. She lifted her head and looked at him. "I am so glad you're here," she whispered before he dipped his head down for a kiss. Her lips parted and welcomed him. Her eyes shuttered closed as their kiss deepened, wiping away all the ugliness she'd faced. Her body calmed. Finally, she felt safe.

Someone had entered the room and cleared his throat. Ethan looked over his shoulder. "Sorry," he said, looking back at Hope.

"Go on. I understand." Hope let Ethan go and he walked out of the room with his officer.

He promised to come right back. She dropped onto the sofa and wrapped her arms around herself to stave off the coldness that filled the void left behind without Ethan's embrace.

She leaned back and stared at the fireplace again. Maybe she could work with a flat-screen TV.

"Hope, I have to ask you a few questions."

She turned her head toward the sound of Detective Reid's voice. Of course he had a few questions for her.

Chapter Twenty-Four

"What do you think?" Claire pushed open the door of the cottage on Shady Oak Lane and stepped over the threshold with her sister following behind.

A week had passed since Kitty pulled a knife on Hope and Claire came to the rescue with her protectiveness in full force with Hope's precious vase. Kitty had been arrested and charged with two murders and one attempted murder—Hope. Chills still skittered up her spine when she thought back to that night. Getting out, being among people and seeing her sister's newest handiwork helped ease the lingering anxiety over the incident.

Once inside, Hope was certain she'd been there before. Then she remembered. She'd delivered Girl Scout cookies with her mom. The homeowner had been a kind, older woman who owned a cat similar to Princess.

"It's beautiful," Hope said.

Claire had freshened up the space with white slipcovers on the upholstered furniture and added throw pillows. A short stack of hardcover books and an assortment of candles were gathered on a tray that sat on the dark-wood coffee table. The mantel above the stone fireplace had been given a breath of life by a cluster of topiaries in small pots and a familiar landscape painting hanging on the wall.

Hope had an urge to light a candle, grab a book, and sink down onto the sofa. Too bad it was another hot humid day, or else she'd love nothing more than to light a fire. She stepped farther into the living room toward the mantel.

"Isn't that the painting from Dad's study?" She pointed.

Claire nodded. "It looks perfect there, doesn't it?"

"I didn't know you had it. Where has it been?" Hope inched closer to the painting. Their dad wasn't an art collector, but he'd fallen in love with a local artist's work, and one Christmas, their mom had purchased the painting for him.

"In storage."

"Storage?" Hope spun around and propped a hand on her hip. "What storage? You've been holding out."

Claire gave a little lift of her shoulder and grinned. "I have a unit where I keep things. I guess I always knew I was going to be a home stager."

"I'm very proud of you. This place looks amazing, and Kent will sell it in no time, thanks to your work."

"Want to see the kitchen? I spruced up in there too." Claire led Hope through to the tiny kitchen and then continued through the rest of the house. Back outside, Claire locked up, and they headed for their cars.

"How did Alfred take the news you weren't going back to the agency?"

"Okay. He's excited for me, but he hates that I left the agency. I'm still keeping my license."

"Smart. Speaking of real estate, do you know what's happening with the Parson horse farm?"

"The condo deal? Not happening, at least not yet. Looks like old Hildy rules that roost." Claire laughed.

"Looks like it. What are you doing for the rest of the day?" Hope dug in her purse for her key fob.

"I have to order inventory for the shop and then get it ready for its opening. I'll be taking a day trip down to the city for merchandise. You have to come with me. Oh, and before I forget, what are you doing tomorrow?"

Hope thought for a moment. "I have a recipe to make and photograph. Why?"

"I could use help in the shop. You are, after all, the expert on all things clean. Come by with your rubber gloves and dust wipes."

"When you put it like that, how can I refuse? Call me later and we can set up a time." Hope opened the door to her vehicle.

"How's Iva working out?"

"Good so far. She cleaned out that overgrown garden by the barn. I think I'll plant a vegetable garden there next year."

"Have you had more time to work?"

"I've been more productive and I feel less stressed."

"Who would have thought Iva Johnson would mean less stress for anybody?" Claire slipped behind the wheel of her car. "See you at the shop tomorrow." She flashed a thankful smile and drove away.

Hope waved and then headed for her vehicle. She had a stop to make before heading home to film a video for her website and get ready for date night with Ethan.

* * *

"You do spoil us, dear." Jane wasted no time in taking possession of the pastry box from Hope and opening the lid. From her smile, Hope could tell her friend was pleased with the contents. Frosted brownies with sprinkles. Who wouldn't be happy with them?

Sally ambled over to the reception desk and peered over her sister-in-law's shoulder. "They look sinfully delicious."

"They are, trust me. I had to get them out of the house." Hope's recipe development process included making a recipe three times before she posted it on her blog. The upside was, by the third time, she was confident the recipe would work. The downside was, she had dozens of brownies in her house. While she could easily eat them all, she had to be a responsible adult and share, because there wasn't enough running she could do to work off the calories.

"Good morning, Hope."

Hope looked over at the staircase. "Rona, I thought you'd be gone by now."

Rona came off the last step and walked toward Hope and the Merrifields. She wore linen trousers and an eyelet top. Her hair was spiky again, and her makeup was bright.

"I'm leaving this afternoon. I had things to wrap up. Have you heard? I was interviewed by a news program, and a magazine too. I was wondering if you could give me some advice on how I can parlay my fifteen minutes of fame into something bigger, like you have."

Hope wasn't offended by the fifteen-minutes-of-fame comment. Many people considered her stint on *The Sweet Taste of Success* as nothing more than an attempt to garner attention. They didn't realize how grueling it had been to be on a constant state of alert against backstabbing, racing to finish near-impossible challenges, and to be separated from your family. She wouldn't lie and say appearing on the show hadn't impacted her new career as a full-time blogger. She definitely had cashed in on her fifteen minutes of fame. And, frankly, she wasn't ashamed of it.

"I already had my blog in place when the show ended. I'm not sure I can give you advice about what you should do next," Hope said.

"I was thinking I could write a book about my betrayal and the hurt of being lied to by the man I loved. An autobiography," Rona said.

"You'd be writing a memoir, not an autobiography, which focuses on the chronology of your life." Sally reached for the box of brownies. "Memoirs cover a specific aspect of your life, like being married to a bigamist."

Rona stared for a long moment. Hope guessed she was processing Sally's explanation.

"You know a lot about books."

Sally leveled her gaze at Rona and her lips pursed. "I'm a retired librarian. Perhaps you should visit the library to reacquaint yourself with books before you try to write one." With the box of brownies, she crossed the hall into the dining room. "I'll plate these," she said over her shoulder.

"Well, whatever, I'm sure I can find a ghostwriter. I've gotta make this sham of a marriage pay off somehow. I'll email you if I have questions, Hope. Thanks!" Rona headed to the front door and disappeared outside.

After the door closed, Jane leaned over the desk. "I didn't hear you offer to help her."

"I didn't," Hope confirmed.

"Is she gone?" Miranda appeared in the doorway of the living room. She looked more worn down than the last time Hope had seen her after she was released from the police department. Her auburn hair was pulled back into a messy ponytail, and not in a chic way. Her skin was splotchy and her dark brows were heavy. The recent events had definitely taken a toll on her.

"Yes, she is," Jane said.

"I came in from the patio, but I heard *her* voice." Miranda walked to the reception desk to join Hope and Jane. "She has some ghastly idea I'll contribute to her autobiography. She hasn't left me alone for a minute."

"Memoir," Jane corrected.

"Whatever it's called, I want no part," Miranda said.

"She's leaving today. How long are you staying?" Hope asked.

"Indefinitely. I'm moving into Kitty's apartment. I have to settle Lionel's estate, and I want to stay for Kitty. I can't believe she killed two people. Never in a million years would I have thought my baby was capable of such a thing. I've barely slept or eaten." Miranda's chin trembled as she reached into her pants pocket for a tissue. "I keep thinking about them. Especially the chef, Maurice. My heart aches for his family. Where did I go wrong?"

"You can't blame yourself for what happened." Hope was speaking from experience. After she learned Kitty had eavesdropped on her call with Drew about Maurice seeing Lionel just before his murder, she'd gone into a funk. She'd taken on all the responsibility for Maurice's murder. Luckily, as the days went on and her head cleared, she realized the person responsible for Maurice's death was Kitty.

"Ken and I should've told her the truth years ago." Miranda dabbed her eyes with the tissue. "Excuse me." She dashed around Hope and up the staircase.

"That poor woman." Jane walked out from behind the desk and linked her arm with Hope's. "It's sad what lies can do to a family, to a person." She patted Hope's hand and put on a smile. They both knew there wasn't much to smile about, but it was a lot better than crying. "Let's have a brownie."

"Good idea."

Jane and Hope headed to the dining room. "I suggest we focus on something positive and not all the sadness. We have so many wonderful things happening. I've heard Claire has staged a house for Kent and we have the parade coming up."

Hope patted Jane's hand. "You're right. We do have a lot of good things happening. I got to see the house Claire staged. She did an amazing job."

"I've been thinking it would be nice for Claire to donate her services for the holiday house tour auction." Jane let go of Hope's arm as they entered the dining room.

Sally had plated the brownies and set out three glasses of milk.

"Of course she'll donate her services to the auction," Sally said from the table. She'd already helped herself to a brownie. "Claire knows what important work the women's club does every year."

"I'll talk to her about it." Hope sat across from Sally while Jane took the seat next to her sister-in-law.

"I'm sure she'll be happy to donate." Hope bit into a brownie and savored the crunch of the sprinkles, the creaminess of the frosting, and the moistness of the cake.

They fell into a conversation that had nothing to do with murder as they enjoyed their snack. Hope also enjoyed a second brownie.

Hope's visit to the inn ran longer than she'd expected and, from the number of voice mails on her phone, she'd missed a lot of calls. Including one from the editor of *Cooking Now*. They'd been playing phone tag, and Hope wanted to tell her she'd decided about the open position. She was about to call Anna but was sidetracked by a near run-in with Maretta as Hope exited the inn.

"Everyone is looking at their phones rather than where they're walking." Maretta tilted her chin and her lips pinched. Her bright coral sheath dress with cap sleeves didn't match the sour mood she seemed to be in.

"My apologies. I'm in a hurry and trying to multitask." Hope slipped her phone back into her purse. She'd call the editor later.

"I guess it's not a big deal." Maretta's lips eased into a relaxed line and her tone lost its sharpness.

Hope wasn't sure she'd heard correctly. Maretta wasn't going to continue to reprimand her for not looking where she was going? Rather, she was being civil and understanding? Oh, no, was she ill?

"I'm actually glad we've run into each other." Maretta tucked a lock of her mousy brown hair behind her ear, revealing bow-shaped, silver-tone earrings. Since becoming mayor, she'd definitely broken out of her drab fashion rut.

"You are?" Hope was really worried about Maretta. While they weren't close, Hope had known the older woman since childhood and cared about her. How ill was Maretta? It had to be bad.

"On behalf of the town, thank you for your help in bringing to justice the killer who had terrorized our beloved Jefferson."

Maretta was now scaring Hope. "Are you feeling okay?"

Maretta's lips pinched again. "I'm perfectly well. I'm carrying out my duty as Jefferson's mayor and acknowledging your *unrequired* assistance in all this nasty business." And the sharpness in her tone returned as well.

"Thank you. I appreciate the recognition." Though it came with an admonishment, Hope was still happy to have it. And she was happy Maretta wasn't ill. Maybe there was hope for her as mayor after all.

"Now, if you'll excuse me, I have a meeting I have to get to. Running this town is a never-ending job. I assume I can count on you to volunteer for the back-to-school backpack drive?"

"Yes. I'm meeting with the committee next week. I'm baking mini-apple pies for the event." Hope planned to tie the annual event into a blog post about helping families in need of school supplies. She'd banded together a group of food bloggers last year to cross-promote their blogs to raise awareness. In the food blogging community, she'd found virtually the same type of community in which she lived. Another reason she loved her work so much.

"I'm sure they'll be a hit like your baking always is. I must get going." Maretta took off, headed for Town Hall.

Wow. A formal thank you and a compliment from Maretta. Maybe it was Hope who was dying and didn't know it. She chuckled. No, she was perfectly fine. She was just surprised by a woman she really thought couldn't surprise her.

The drive from the inn to her house would only take a few minutes if she went directly home. But she didn't. She made a last-minute decision as she pulled out of her parking space to take the long way home, past Elaine's house. Traffic was light, a cool breeze blew, and her favorite eighties station was commercial free for the afternoon.

She'd tried calling Elaine several times over the past week, but apparently, the woman was still in seclusion and not communicating with the outside world. Hope couldn't blame her. Her life had been turned upside down, and she had legal issues to deal with. Halfway to the Whitcomb house, Hope's phone rang, and she answered it through the hands-free program in her car.

"How's Long Island?"

Drew had finally gotten away for his vacation out on New York's Long Island with his college buddies.

"Freakin' amazing. You should see this house. I got lost twice. The place is so big, I think it has its own zip code."

"Impressive."

"Beyond. We're about to head out on his family's yacht. Not a boat. It's a yacht."

"La-di-da. How fancy." She laughed. "I'm glad you're enjoying yourself. You've earned it."

"Tell me about it. No deadlines, no Norrie Jennings, no murders. What's going on back home?"

"Not too much. Maretta thanked me for my assistance with the investigation."

"What the . . . Is she feeling okay?"

Hope laughed again. "Yes, she's fine. She informed me she was doing her duty as mayor by recognizing my assistance, which wasn't asked for."

"Yeah, she's okay." Drew's voice faded and came back. "Oh, on my way. Gotta go, Hope. Talk to you later."

"Bye," she said, but the line had disconnected.

Drew was gone. Off to the yacht. She tried not to be too envious. A day cruising on a yacht sounded really nice. So did her date night with Ethan. Yeah, that put a smile back on her face. He was coming over after work, which now ended at a reasonable time, thanks to the two solved murders.

The turn to Elaine's road was coming up, and she slowed down as she maneuvered her vehicle around the corner. Up ahead, she spotted the sign on the expansive lawn.

For Sale.

The sign wasn't much of a shocker. Hope didn't think Elaine would end up with much after Miranda successfully proved she and Lionel had never divorced. But still, it wasn't a pleasant thing to see.

Hope drove her car up the driveway and glimpsed Elaine standing on her front steps with a woman she didn't recognize. After Hope had parked her car, she stepped out and waved to Elaine. The woman next to Elaine said something and then disappeared inside the house.

"Hi, Hope." Elaine started toward Hope, and they met halfway.

"I've been trying to reach you. You haven't answered my calls or texts."

"You're worried about me." Elaine held her arms

wide open and embraced Hope. "I'm so fortunate to have such a good friend."

"Glad you're doing okay." Hope was overwhelmed by Elaine's fruity perfume. Her eyes watered. She wriggled free and then wiped her eyes dry with her hand.

"I've been so busy meeting with lawyers and real estate agents." Elaine turned to face her house. Her makeup was flawless and she wore one of her signature wrap dresses with shimmery, metallic, high-heeled sandals. Having her life crash down around her hadn't dampened her style.

"I'm sorry you have to sell your house."

"Me too. But don't worry, I've decided to stay in Jefferson."

Hope wasn't sure how she felt about Elaine staying in town. A part of her believed under all the makeup and cosmetic enhancements there was a kind person. Another part of her believed Elaine was a self-absorbed, social-climbing opportunist who didn't understand the concept of friendship. Talk about torn.

"I'll miss this house. It's the first one I loved." She cast a serious look on Hope. Maybe if she hadn't had Botox regularly, she would have looked more melancholy.

"If you don't mind me asking, what's happening with Lionel's estate?" Over the past few days, Hope had heard bits and pieces of speculation through various sources. It made her even more curious.

"Miranda gets it all because she was still legally married to Lionel when he died. My lawyer says I can contest, but I don't want a long, drawn-out legal battle. We settled amicably. I get half of this sale and I keep my car and all the personal items Lionel gave me." She raised her right hand and wiggled her fingers, flashing a megasize diamond cocktail ring.

"Wow. Good for you."

Elaine's head bobbed up and down. "What about you? How are you doing? Almost getting killed and all. I kind of feel I'm partly to blame because I asked you to help."

Hope's first instinct was to agree with Elaine, but the truth was, she could've easily turned Elaine down when she came to her. She had to admit that she loved a mystery and couldn't stay out of them. She had to take responsibility for her part in the situation.

"I'm doing fine. Though it was a little scary while it was happening."

"I know scary." Elaine turned and took a long look around the front lawn. "It's been a long time since I've been all on my own. Not even a housekeeper." She sighed.

Equating not having a housekeeper to having a crazed killer come at you with a knife wasn't exactly the same thing. Not wanting to undo the progress in their relationship, though, Hope bit back her response.

"I guess I'll have to find work." Elaine batted her eyelashes and placed a hand on her jutted-out hip.

"Have you ever had a job?" Hope pressed her lips together. She probably shouldn't have asked the question.

"A few. Between husbands." Elaine looked back at Hope. "You know, I think you've inspired me. I could start a fashion blog. Share my sense of style with the world. I mean, how hard can it be? I can strike a pose."

Hope glanced at her watch. She had nowhere to be other than home to write a blog post and prepare dinner, but her welfare check on Elaine had come to an end.

"I should let you get back to your real estate agent." She turned and hurried to her car.

A dreadful feeling settled in the pit of her stomach. If Elaine stayed in Jefferson and started a blog, there'd be no getting rid of her. She'd be pestering Hope nonstop for advice. If Hope got lucky, Elaine would be like most people and give up blogging after a few weeks, either because they were bored or didn't have the commitment to put in the hard work.

Seated behind the wheel of her car, she grabbed the gearshift, ready to back out of the driveway, when a knocking at her window drew her attention. She lowered the window to see what Elaine wanted now.

"Let's do lunch next week. You can tell me everything I need to know about blogging. Okay?"

"I'll call you." Hope wondered if Claire knew of a rich, eligible man who lived in another town far, far away. Maybe in another state. She'd have to ask.

Hope carried the platter of grilled-to-perfection burgers to the table. After the deadly events in town and having her life threatened by a murderer, she appreciated the normalcy of a quiet dinner at home with Ethan. It was a perfect date night.

That was until Drew and Claire crashed it.

With two extra place settings added, they gathered around the table to enjoy a simple meal of grilled burgers and homemade potato salad. She'd made the potato salad when she filmed the video earlier. The best thing about being a food blogger was that she always had food in the refrigerator for unexpected company.

Over dinner, Hope filled everyone in on Elaine's plans for the future and Drew shared his most excellent adventure on Long Island. He didn't leave out one luxurious, over-the-top detail, from lounging poolside to yachting to a last-minute helicopter flight into New York City for a private party.

"It was way too short," he said, reaching for his water glass. "But we'll get together again in the spring." His smile stretched from ear to ear.

Claire would not be outdone in the good news department. She told them how much the owner of the cottage loved her staging. She also mentioned she had a new client lined up.

"And she roped me into helping her clean the shop." Hope spooned out another helping of the potato salad as silence descended around the table and she stared at her dinner companions in confusion. "What?"

A hearty chorus of laughter broke the silence.

"You want us to believe you would turn down scrubbing and cleaning something?" Ethan asked between bouts of laughter.

Hope rolled her eyes and nodded. "Okay, okay. So I guess I didn't get roped in to anything."

"You think?" Drew's face was beet red from laughing so hard.

"Go ahead, laugh." Hope tried hard to keep a straight face, but it was pointless. She joined in, and it felt good. Really good. If it hadn't been for her sister's quick action, Hope wasn't sure if she'd be sitting there right now.

"Have you decided about the magazine?" Claire leaned into her chair after she signaled she was full by pushing away her plate and dropping her napkin on the table, leaving half her dinner uneaten.

Hope nodded. "I declined the position."

Ethan's brows drew together. "What about the attractive, steady paycheck?"

"Been there, done that. It's more important to do what I love. I've worked hard to build my blog and I don't want to give it up." What she didn't share was that the temptation was almost overwhelming, so much so she'd come very close to accepting the job.

"How did the editor take it?" Claire asked.

"She was disappointed, but we discussed a collaboration for next spring. I'm very excited about it."

"I think you made the right decision." Ethan raised his bottle of beer and smiled.

"There's more good news. Princess seems to be calming down." Hope looked around for the cat, but she wasn't in sight, while Bigelow was in view and occupied with a chew toy filled with peanut butter.

Claire looked skeptical. "She's not going to pounce anymore?"

"She's a cat, so she'll probably continue to do that. But so far, she hasn't knocked anything else off any surfaces. My Christmas ornaments might be safe."

"What's for dessert?" Ethan looked up from his empty plate. "Did I see a pie in the fridge earlier?"

Hope placed the utensils and plates in the dishwasher and closed the door. They'd finished their meal with generous slices, except for Claire, who cut her own sliver of a piece of banana cream pie. She pressed the On button before Ethan came up from behind. He spun her around into his arms. Claire had suggested a movie while they were clearing the table.

Now she and Drew were battling it out in the family room on which movie to watch.

"You got quiet. What's going on in there?" He pointed to her head.

"Not much." She glided her hands up and down Ethan's polo shirt. His chest was solid, yet comfy enough to lay her head on at night.

His hand slid down the side of her face, caressing her cheek. "You know I'm a cop and I can tell when someone isn't being honest, right?"

"We can talk about it later." She wanted to have the conversation in private.

"No. We can talk about it now. They're busy arguing." He glanced over his shoulder and then back to Hope and pulled her closer. "What's going on? Are you having second thoughts about us?"

"No, no, nothing like that. I'm scared."

"Scared about what?"

"During the murder investigation, you couldn't talk about it, which I get."

"What's the problem, then?"

"If you can't talk about one area in your life, it gets easier not to talk about another area of your life and then, before you know it, we're broken up because we're not talking."

There, she'd said it out loud. Her worry, her fear, her worst-case scenario. Breaking up.

Ethan nodded his head. "Like what happened with you and Tim."

"I know you're not him, but . . . it's so easy to stop communicating." Hope dipped her head. She was being ridiculous. She was overreacting and blowing the whole thing out of proportion, and she wouldn't blame Ethan if he turned and left to get away from her craziness.

He lifted her chin with his finger. "Look at me. There are things I can't talk about because of my job. I can't change that."

"I'm worried I'll sabotage what we have because of my fear."

"No, you won't."

"How can you be sure?"

"Because we're talking about it. As long as we keep doing this, we will be fine. Okay?"

Hope wanted to believe him. Maybe he was right. She and Tim hadn't acknowledged their lack of communication until it was too late.

"Okay." She nodded, reassured she hadn't scared him off.

"We're *not* going to make the same mistakes we made in the past. I love you, Hope."

Her breath caught. He'd said *it*.

He loved her.

"I love you too." She cupped his face in her hands and was a mere moment from a kiss when a woof drew her attention to beyond the kitchen. She lifted her gaze over Ethan's shoulder and then it narrowed.

Drew and Claire were standing with crossed arms and Bigelow was sitting in front of them. All three were watching Hope and Ethan.

Claire gave Drew a sidelong look. "Well, there you go. You wanted to watch a chick flick where they declare their love for each other at the end. Done. Now we can watch *Kill Bill*." Claire slapped Drew on the chest and walked away to the sofa, where she sank to the cushion and grabbed the remote.

Drew threw his hands up in the air and followed

Claire. "I can't believe you like *Kill Bill*. How is that even possible?"

Claire huffed. "What? You want to watch *Love Actually*?"

"What's wrong with *Love Actually*?"

"Where do I begin?" Claire shook her head as she pointed the remote control at the television.

Bigelow stood and trotted over to Hope and Ethan, wedging himself between them. Their romantic moment had passed. She dropped her forehead onto his chest and laughed.

While the evening hadn't turned out as she had planned, it was exactly what she needed.

Recipes

FROSTED BROWNIES
posted by Hope Early

When I am craving chocolate. I. Need. Brownies. These brownies. Seriously. Whipping up a batch of brownies is so gratifying. The yield on this recipe depends on how big you cut the squares. ☺

Ingredients:

For brownies
¾ cup all-purpose flour
1 teaspoon baking powder
½ teaspoon salt
½ cup unsalted butter, cut into cubes
3 ounces unsweetened chocolate, finely chopped
½ cup granulated sugar
½ cup light brown sugar
2 eggs
1 egg yolk
1 teaspoon vanilla extract
½ cup semisweet chocolate chips
Extra butter for preparing baking dish

For frosting
6 tablespoons butter, softened
2 ⅔ cups confectioners' sugar
½ cup baking cocoa
1 teaspoon vanilla extract
¼–⅓ cup whole milk

Directions for the Brownies:

Preheat oven to 350 degrees.

Butter an 8-inch square baking dish and line with parchment paper. Be sure to let excess hang over for easy removal of brownies. Butter the parchment paper and set aside.

In small bowl, combine flour, baking powder, and salt. Set aside.

Place butter and unsweetened chocolate in a double boiler. Stir occasionally until the chocolate and butter are melted and smooth.

Remove the bowl from the saucepan and whisk in the granulated and brown sugars. Next whisk in the eggs, the yolk, and the vanilla extract.

Next add in the flour mixture all at once and combine with spatula.

Fold in chocolate chips.

Pour the batter into the prepared baking dish and bake for 25 to 30 minutes, or until cake tester inserted into the center comes out with moist crumbs attached.

Cool completely, then frost and serve!

Directions for the Frosting:

In a large bowl, using either a stand or hand-held mixer, cream together butter and confectioners' sugar until light and fluffy.

Add in cocoa and vanilla and beat until combined.

Add in enough milk until the frosting achieves a smooth spreading consistency.

Spread over cooled brownies.

DOUBLE CHOCOLATE AND WALNUT MUFFINS

posted by Hope Early

It's no secret I love a good muffin, but this one is a top favorite of mine because it combines chocolate and walnuts and is dusted with powdered sugar. These are a perfect breakfast treat, a good choice for a midafternoon pick-me-up, or whenever you crave something chocolate. This recipe includes olive oil. I love baking with it, and I use a good-quality, extra-virgin olive oil.

Yield: 16 muffins

Ingredients:

2 eggs
¾ cup sugar
1 cup buttermilk
⅓ cup extra-virgin olive oil
1 teaspoon vanilla extract
2 cups flour
½ cup cocoa powder
2 teaspoons baking powder
¼ teaspoon salt
¾ cup chopped walnuts
1 cup dark chocolate chips
Powdered sugar for dusting

Directions:

Preheat oven to 350 degrees.

Line muffin pan with paper liners. Set aside.

Add eggs and sugar in a bowl and beat until creamy. Add in buttermilk, olive oil, and vanilla extract. Beat until all combined.

In a medium bowl, combine flour, cocoa powder, baking powder, and salt. Add to wet mixture and mix until combined; do not overmix the batter.

Fold in walnuts and chocolate chips.

Fill each muffin liner about ⅔ full and bake for 18 minutes or until cake tester inserted into center comes out clean.

Remove from oven and set them on a cooling rack.

When muffins are completely cooled, dust with sifted powdered sugar before serving.

ARTICHOKE AND SPINACH PASTA BAKE
posted by Hope Early

I'm a huge fan of spinach and artichoke dip, and this dish is my newest obsession. When I've served it to family and friends, there's not one morsel left. I've used regular pasta and whole-grain pasta and it's delicious either way.

Yield: 4 servings

Ingredients:
1 tablespoon extra-virgin olive oil (EVOO)
4 cloves garlic, finely chopped
1 large shallot, chopped
1 box (9-ounce) frozen artichoke hearts, thawed, halved, and patted dry*
½ cup dry white wine
4 tablespoons butter
3 tablespoons flour
2 cups milk
Salt and pepper to taste

Freshly grated nutmeg
1½ cups Gruyère cheese, shredded
1 pound penne pasta
2 boxes frozen chopped spinach, thawed and
    wrung dry in a towel
1 cup shredded Parmesan cheese

Directions:

Bring a large pot of water to a boil. Preheat oven to
375 degrees.

In a medium skillet, heat EVOO over medium to
medium-high heat. Add in garlic and shallot, cook for
2 to 3 minutes. Then add in artichokes and cook until
they are lightly brown. Deglaze the pan with wine.

In a saucepan, add butter and melt over medium
heat. Whisk in the flour and cook for 1 minute. Add
milk, whisking to combine, and season with salt and
pepper and a pinch of nutmeg. Continue to cook sauce
until thick enough to coat the back of a spoon. Adjust
seasonings and add in Gruyère cheese, stirring in a
figure-eight until all the cheese is melted into the sauce.

Salt the boiling water and cook pasta until al dente.
Drain and return to the pot. Pour in the cheese sauce,
spinach (shred it as you add it to the pasta), and artichoke mixture.

Pour out the pasta mixture into a 3-quart baking dish
and cover with Parmesan cheese.

Place baking dish on a baking sheet and set in center
of oven. Bake until the top is browned and bubbling,
about 45 minutes.

Allow to cool and set for a few minutes before serving.

*Sometimes I can't find frozen artichoke hearts, so I use
a can of artichoke hearts; just drain and dry before using.

BASIC FRITTATA
posted by Hope Early

I love this recipe for breakfast, lunch, or dinner. This recipe is good all on its own. But its versatility means it can work at any time of the day because you can add whatever you want to it. I've used up leftover potatoes and corned beef for a perfect, quick dinner. I've also used asparagus and smoked salmon for a lovely summer breakfast on the patio. Be creative!

Ingredients:

  3 tablespoons olive oil
  ½ cup onions, diced
  8 large eggs
  ½ cup milk
  ¾ teaspoon salt
  ¼ teaspoon pepper

Directions:

Preheat oven to 350 degrees.

Heat olive oil in a 10-inch, oven-safe skillet* over medium heat. Add in onions and cook until they are softened, about five minutes.

Whisk eggs, then add in milk, salt, and pepper.

Pour egg mixture into the skillet, stir, and cook until the edges start to pull away from the pan, about 5 to 7 minutes. Bake until egg is set, about 16 to 18 minutes.

*If you don't have an oven-safe skillet you can use a 2-quart baking dish.

FLOURLESS CHOCOLATE CAKE
posted by Hope Early

I'm starting to think I'm a chocoholic. Chocolate has been on my brain for weeks. I don't think it's a bad thing. There are worse things to be obsessed with. I love this recipe because there are times when I crave a deep, rich, dense chocolate something, something. This is what satisfies me when I'm in that kind of mood. This torte has never let me down.

Yield: 8 servings

Ingredients:

½ cup unsalted butter
⅔ cup bittersweet chocolate chips
¾ cup sugar
3 large eggs
½ cup cocoa powder
Powdered sugar

Directions:

Preheat oven to 350 degrees.

Grease a 9-inch springform pan and line bottom with parchment paper.

Combine butter and chocolate chips in a microwave-safe bowl. Microwave on high for 1 minute and stir. Continue in 15-second increments until mixture is melted. Stir to combine.

In a large bowl, whisk sugar and eggs together. Add melted chocolate, whisk to combine. Stir in cocoa powder and mix until smooth.

Pour chocolate mixture into the greased pan. Bake for 20 minutes or until cake tester inserted in center of cake comes out clean.

Let cake cool for 10 minutes on cooling rack and then release the side of the pan.

Serve with a sprinkle of powdered sugar.

CHOCOLATE WALNUT COOKIES
posted by Hope Early

Cookies are pure joy for me. I love baking them, I love sharing them, and I love eating them. These cookies combine chocolate, chocolate chips, and walnuts into a perfect little package. It's hard to stop at one, so don't even try!

Yield: 32 cookies

Ingredients:
>   2 cups semisweet chocolate chips
>   1¾ cup all-purpose flour
>   ¾ teaspoon baking soda
>   ½ teaspoon salt
>   1 stick butter, softened
>   ½ cup granulated sugar
>   ½ cup brown sugar, packed
>   1 large egg
>   ½ cup walnuts, chopped

Directions:

Preheat the oven to 350 degrees.

Melt ½ cup of chocolate chips in a double boiler, stirring until smooth. Cool to room temperature.

Stir together flour, baking soda, and salt in a bowl.

Beat together butter and sugars until creamy, then stir in egg and chocolate mixture, mixing until combined.

Gradually stir in flour mixture, remaining chocolate chips, and walnuts. Cover and chill for at least 1 hour.

Roll dough into balls, about 1¼-inch. Arrange them on cookie sheet, at least two inches apart. Bake until set but still soft, about 10 to 12 minutes.

Let rest on cookie sheet two minutes before transferring to cooling rack to completely cool.

Connect with

Visit us online at
KensingtonBooks.com
to read more from your favorite authors, see books
by series, view reading group guides, and more.

Join us on social media

for sneak peeks, chances to win books and prize packs,
and to share your thoughts with other readers.

facebook.com/kensingtonpublishing
twitter.com/kensingtonbooks

Tell us what you think!

To share your thoughts, submit a review,
or sign up for our eNewsletters, please visit:
KensingtonBooks.com/TellUs.